P9-AFA-453

MVFOL

The
TRINITY SIX

ALSO BY CHARLES CUMMING

A Spy by Nature

The Spanish Game

Typhoon

*The Hidden Man**

*Forthcoming from St. Martin's Press

The
TRINITY SIX

CHARLES CUMMING

St. Martin's Press ❦ New York

This is a work of fiction. All of the characters, organizations,
and events portrayed in this novel are either products of
the author's imagination or are used fictitiously.

THE TRINITY SIX. Copyright © 2011 by Charles Cumming. All rights
reserved. Printed in the United States of America. For information,
address St. Martin's Press, 175 Fifth Avenue, New York, N.Y. 10010.

Library of Congress Cataloging-in-Publication Data

Cumming, Charles, 1971–
  The Trinity Six / Charles Cumming. — 1st U.S. ed.
    p. cm.
  ISBN 978-0-312-67529-5
  1. Spies—England—Cambridge—Fiction.   2. Espionage, Soviet—
Great Britain—Fiction.   I. Title.
  PR6103.U484T75 2011
  823'.92—dc22

                                        2010040197

First published in Great Britain by HarperCollins*Publishers*

First U.S. Edition: March 2011

10 9 8 7 6 5 4 3 2 1

For my sister, Alex
for her children, Lucy, Edward, and Sophie
and to the memory of Simon Pilkington (1938–2009)

A NOTE ON "THE CAMBRIDGE FIVE"

While studying at Trinity College, Cambridge, in the 1930s, Kim Philby, Anthony Blunt, Guy Burgess, Donald Maclean, and John Cairncross were recruited by Moscow Centre as agents of the Soviet NKVD. They became known as "The Cambridge Five."

Burgess would go on to work for the BBC and for the Foreign Office. Maclean, the son of a prominent Liberal MP, also joined the Foreign Office and was Secretary at the British Embassy in Washington, D.C., between 1944 and 1948. Philby became an officer in the Secret Intelligence Service (better known as MI6). Blunt, a world authority on the paintings of Nicolas Poussin, worked for MI5 until 1945, at which point he was appointed Surveyor of the King's Pictures (and, later, the Queen's Pictures). During World War II, John Cairncross worked on Nazi code-breaking at Bletchley Park. All five men passed vast numbers of classified documents to their handlers in the NKVD.

In May 1951, Burgess and Maclean boarded a ferry in Southampton, England, and defected to the Soviet Union. Their disappearance caused an international uproar. They had been tipped off by Blunt and Philby that MI5 were about to expose them as traitors. Four years later, Philby held a press conference at which he denied being the so-called "Third Man." He was exonerated in the House of Commons by the Foreign Secretary, Harold Macmillan, and allowed to return to SIS. Seven years later, while working undercover as a journalist in Lebanon, Philby boarded a Soviet freighter in Beirut and was spirited back to Moscow. The trauma of his betrayal haunts British Intelligence to this day.

Cairncross was identified as a Soviet agent in 1952. However, his involvement in the Cambridge ring was covered up by the British government. In 1964, Blunt also signed a full confession, in return for immunity from prosecution. In 1979, Margaret Thatcher admitted to the House of Commons that Sir Anthony Blunt, one of the pillars of the British Establishment, had been a Soviet asset for more than thirty years. MI5 and SIS faced a further bout of bloodletting.

Guy Burgess died of alcoholism in Moscow in 1963. Maclean, who had been made a colonel in the KGB, died in 1983. In the same year, Blunt, who had been stripped of his knighthood, died at his home in London. Five years later, Kim Philby was granted a full state burial by the Soviet authorities. Cairncross, who had lived in Italy for most of his life, died in 1995, five years after being named as the "Fifth Man" by the Soviet defector Oleg Gordievsky.

The recruitment of the Cambridge spies is regarded as the most successful "penetration" by a foreign intelligence service in the history of espionage. In Russia, the men from Trinity College were known simply as "The Magnificent Five."

—C.C.
London 2010

You know, you should never catch a spy. Discover him and then control him, but never catch him. A spy causes far more trouble when he's caught.

—*Harold Macmillan*

The

TRINITY SIX

1

"The dead man was not a dead man. He was alive but he was not alive. That was the situation."

Calvin Somers, the nurse, stopped at the edge of the towpath and looked behind him, back along the canal. He was a slight man, as stubborn and petulant as a child. Gaddis came to a halt beside him.

"Keep talking," he said.

"It was the winter of 1992, an ordinary Monday night in February." Somers took an apple from his coat pocket and bit into it, chewing over the memories. "The patient's name was Edward Crane. It said he was seventy-six on his notes, but none of us knew what was true and what wasn't. He looked midsixties to me." They started walking again, black boots pressing through the mud. "They'd obviously worked out it was best if they admitted him at night, when there were fewer people around, when the day staff had gone off shift."

"Who's 'they'?" Gaddis asked.

"The spooks." A mallard lifted off the canal, quick wings shedding water as he turned towards the sun. "Crane was brought in on a stretcher, unconscious, just after ten on the evening of the third. I was ready for him. I'm always ready. He bypassed A and E and was put straight into a private room off the ward. The chart said he had no next of kin and wasn't to be resuscitated in the event of cardiac arrest. Nothing unusual about that. Far as anyone was concerned, this was just another old man suffering from late-stage pancreatic cancer. Hours to live, liver failure, toxic. At least, that was the story MI6 was paying us to pedal."

Somers threw the half-eaten apple at a plastic bottle floating on the canal and missed by three feet.

"Soon as I got Crane into the room, I hooked him up to some drips. Dextrose saline. A bag of amikacin that was just fluid going nowhere. Even gave him a catheter. Everything had to look kosher just in case a member of staff stuck their head round the door who wasn't supposed to."

"Did that happen? Did anybody see Crane?"

Somers scratched the side of his neck. "Nah. At about two in the morning, Meisner called for a priest. That was all part of the plan. Father Brook. He didn't suspect a thing. Just came in, administered the last rites, went home. Soon after that, Henderson showed up and did his little speech."

"What little speech?"

Somers came to a halt. He didn't make eye contact very often but did so now, assuming a patrician tone which Gaddis took to be an attempt at impersonating Henderson's cut-glass accent.

" 'From this point onwards, Edward Crane is effectively dead. I would like to thank you all for your work thus far, but a great deal remains to be done.' "

A man pushing a rusty bicycle came towards them on the towpath, ticking past in the dusk.

"We were all there," said Somers. "Waldemar, Meisner, Forman. Meisner was so nervous he looked as if he was going to throw up. Waldemar didn't speak much English and still didn't really understand what he'd got himself involved in. He was probably just thinking about the money. That's what I was doing. Twenty grand in 1992 was a lot of cash to a twenty-eight-year-old nurse. You any idea what we got paid under the Tories?"

Gaddis didn't respond. He didn't want to have a conversation about underfunded nurses. He wanted to hear the end of the story.

"Anyway, at some point Henderson took a checklist out of his coat pocket and ran through it. First, he turned to Meisner and asked him if he'd filled out the death certificate. Meisner said he had and produced a ballpoint pen from behind his ear, as if that proved it. I was told to go back down to Crane's room and wrap the body. 'No need to clean him,' Henderson said. For some reason, Waldemar—we called him Wally—thought this was funny and we all just stood there watching him laugh. Then Henderson tells him to pull himself together and gives him instructions to have a trolley waiting, to take the old man down to the ambulance. I remember Henderson didn't talk to Forman until the rest of us had gone. Don't ask me what he'd agreed with her. Probably to tag a random corpse in the mortuary, some tramp from Praed Street with no ID, no history. How else could they have got away with it? They needed a second body."

"This is useful," Gaddis told him, because he felt that he needed to say something. "This is really useful."

"Well, you get what you pay for, don't you, Professor?" Somers produced a smug grin. "What was hard is that we had other patients to attend to. It was a normal Monday night. It wasn't as if everything could just grind to a halt because MI6 were in the building. Meisner was the senior doctor, too, so he was always moving back and forth around the hospital. At one point I don't think I saw him for about an hour and a half. Wally had jobs all over the place, me as well. Added to that, I had to try to keep the other nurses out of Crane's room. Just in case they got nosey." The path narrowed beside a barge and the two men were obliged to walk in single file. "In the end, everything went like clockwork. Meisner got the certificate done, Crane was wrapped up with a small hole in the fabric he could breathe through, Wally took him down to the ambulance, and the old man was gone by six A.M., out into his new life."

"His new life," Gaddis muttered. He looked up at the darkening sky and wondered, not for the first time, if he would ever set eyes on Edward Anthony Crane. "And that's it?"

"Almost." Somers wiped his nose in the failing light. "Eight days later I was going through *The Times*. Found an obituary for an 'Edward Crane.' Wasn't very long. Tucked down the right-hand side of the page under 'Lives Remembered,' next to some French politician who'd fucked up during Suez. Crane was described as a 'resourceful career diplomat.' Born in 1916, educated at Marlborough College, then Trinity, Cambridge. Postings to Moscow, Buenos Aires, Berlin. Never married, no offspring. Died at St. Mary's Hospital, Paddington, after 'a long battle with cancer.'"

A light drizzle was beginning to fall. Gaddis passed a set of lock gates and moved in the direction of a pub. Somers pushed a hand through his hair.

"So that's what happened, Professor," he said. "Edward Crane was a dead man, but he was not a dead man. Edward Crane was alive but he was not alive. That was the situation."

The pub was packed.

Gaddis went to the bar and ordered two pints of Stella Artois, a packet of peanuts, and a double of Famous Grouse. Thanks to Somers, he was down to the loose change in his pockets and had to pay the barman with a debit card. Inside his jacket he found the torn scrap of paper on which he kept his passwords and PIN numbers and punched in the digits while the landlord made a noise through his teeth. With Somers still in the Gents', Gaddis sank the whisky as a single shot, then found a table at the back of the pub where he could watch groups of shivering smokers huddled outside and try to convince himself that he had made the right decision to quit.

"Got you a Stella," he said when Somers came up to the table. For an instant it looked as though he wasn't going to sit down, but Gaddis pushed the pint towards him and said: "Peanuts."

It was just past six o'clock. West Hyde on a Tuesday night. Suits, secretaries, suburbia. A jukebox was crooning Andy Williams. Tacked up beside a dartboard in the far corner of the room was an orange poster emblazoned with the words: CURRY NIGHT–WEDNESDAY. Gaddis took off his corduroy jacket and looped it over the arm of a neighbouring chair.

"So what happened next?"

He knew that this was the part Somers liked, playing the pivotal role, playing Deep Throat. The nurse—the *senior* nurse, as he would doubtless have insisted—produced another of his smug grins and took a thirsty pull on the pint. Something about the warmth of the pub had restored his characteristic complacency; it was as if Somers had reprimanded himself for being too open beside the canal. After all, he was in possession of information that Gaddis wanted. The professor had paid three grand for it. It was gold dust to him.

"What happened *next*?"

"That's right, Calvin. Next."

Somers leaned back in his chair. "Not much." He seemed to regret this answer and rephrased it, searching for more impact. "I watched the ambulance turn past the post office, had a quick smoke, and went back inside. Took the lift up to Crane's room, cleared it out, threw away the bags and catheter, and sent the medical notes down to Patient Records. You could probably check them if you want. Far as the hospital was concerned, a seventy-six-year-old cancer patient had come in suffering from liver failure and died during the night. The sort of thing that happened all the time. It was a new day, a new shift. Time to move on."

"And Crane?"

"What about him?"

"You never heard another word?"

Somers looked as if he had been asked an idiotic question. That was the trouble with intellectuals. So fucking stupid.

"Why would I hear another word?" He took a long draw on the pint and did something with his eyes which made Gaddis want to deck him. "Presumably he was given a new identity. Presumably he enjoyed another ten years of happy life and died peacefully in his bed. Who knows?"

Two smokers, one coming in, one going out, pushed past their table. Gaddis was obliged to move a leg out of the way.

"And you never breathed a word about it? Nobody asked you any questions? Nobody apart from Charlotte has brought up this subject for over ten years?"

"You could say that, yeah."

Gaddis sensed a lie here, but knew there was no point pursuing it. Somers was the type who shut down once you caught him in a contradiction. He said: "And did Crane talk? What kind of man was he? What did he look like?"

Somers laughed. "You don't do this very often, do you, Professor?"

It was true. Sam Gaddis didn't often meet male nurses in pubs on the outskirts of London and try to extract information about seventy-six-year-old diplomats whose deaths had been faked by men who paid out twenty grand in return for a lifetime of silence. He was divorced and forty-three. He was a senior lecturer in Russian History at University College London. His normal beat was Pushkin, Stalin, Gorbachev. Nevertheless, that remark took him to the edge of his patience and he said: "And how often do *you* do it, Calvin?" just so that Somers knew where he stood.

The reply did the trick. A little frown of panic appeared in the gap between Somers's eyes which he tried, without success, to force away. The nurse sought refuge in some peanuts and got salt on his fingers as he wrestled with the packet.

"Look," he said, "Crane didn't speak at all. Before he was admitted, they'd given him a mild anaesthetic which had rendered him unconscious. He had grey hair, shaved to look like he'd undergone chemotherapy, but his skin was too healthy for a man supposedly in his condition. He probably weighed about seventy kilos, between five foot ten and six foot. I never saw his eyes, on account of the fact they were always closed. That good enough for you?"

Gaddis didn't answer immediately. He didn't need to. He let the silence speak for him. "And Henderson?"

"What about him?"

"What kind of man was he? What did he look like? All you've told me so far is that he wore a long black overcoat and sounded like somebody doing a bad impression of David Niven."

Somers turned his head and stared at the far corner of the room.

"Charlotte never told you?"

"Told me what?"

Somers blinked rapidly and said: "Pass me that newspaper."

There was a damp, discarded copy of *The Times* lying in a trickle of beer on the next-door table. A black girl listening to a pink iPod smiled her assent when Gaddis asked if he could take it. He straightened it out and handed the newspaper across the table.

"You've heard of the Leighton Inquiry?" Somers asked.

Leighton was a judicial inquiry into an aspect of government policy relating to the war in Afghanistan. Gaddis had heard of it. He had read the op-eds, caught the reports on Channel Four News.

"Go on," he said.

Somers turned to page five. "You see this man?"

He flattened out the newspaper, spinning it through a hundred and eighty degrees. The nurse's narrow, nail-bitten finger skewered a photograph of a man ducking into a government Rover on a busy London street. The man was in late middle age and surrounded by a crush of reporters. Gaddis read the caption.

Sir John Brennan leaves Whitehall after giving evidence to the inquiry.

There was a smaller, formal Foreign Office portrait of Brennan set inside the main photograph. Gaddis looked up. Somers saw that he had made the connection.

"Henderson is *John Brennan?* Are you sure?"

"As sure as I'm sitting here looking at you." Somers drained his pint. "The man who paid me twenty grand sixteen years ago to cover everything up wasn't just any old spook. The man who called himself Douglas Henderson in 1992 is now the head of MI6."

2

I t was a long way from Daunt Books on Holland Park Avenue to that suburban September pub in West Hyde.

A month earlier, Gaddis had been launching his latest book—*Tsars,* a comparative study of Peter the Great and the current Russian president, Sergei Platov—at a bookshop in central London. His editor, the part-owner of a boutique publishing house which had paid the princely sum of £4,750 for the book, hadn't made it to the event. A lone diarist, on work experience at the *Evening Standard,* had poked her head around the door of the bookshop at six twenty-five, picked up a glass of room-temperature Sauvignon Blanc and, having established that she had more chance of finding a story on the top deck of the number 16 bus, left after ten minutes. No celebrity historian, no literary editor, nor any representative of the BBC had replied to the invitations which the PR girl insisted had gone out—"first class"—in the second week of July. A solitary notice in Saturday's *Independent* had turned up one ashen-faced matriarch who had come "all the way from Hampstead because I *so* enjoyed your book on Bulgakov," as well as a former student of Sam's named Colin who claimed that he had spent the previous year "walking around Kazakhstan reading Herman Hesse."

The rest were staff—the manager of the shop, someone to operate the till—about a dozen colleagues and students from UCL; Sam's next-door neighbour Sue, who was highly sexed and always opened the front door in her dressing gown; and his close friend, the journalist Charlotte Berg.

Did Gaddis care that the new book would most probably disappear without a trace? Yes and no. Though politically active, he was under no illusions that a single book could change attitudes to Sergei Platov. *Tsars* would be politely reviewed by the broadsheet press in London and dismissed in Moscow as Western propaganda. It had taken three years to write and would sell perhaps a thousand copies in hardback. Long ago, Gaddis had decided to write solely for the pleasure of writing: to expect greater rewards was to invite frustration. If the public enjoyed his books, he was happy; if they didn't, so be it. They had better things to be spending their hard-earned cash on. He had no desire for fame, no innate interest in making money: what mattered to him was the quality of the work. And *Tsars* was a book that he was proud of. It amounted to a sustained attack on the Platov regime, an attack which he had tried to condense, as succinctly as possible, into a 750-word op-ed in the *Guardian* which had appeared three days earlier.

Thus far, that had been the extent of the book's publicity campaign. Gaddis wasn't particularly interested in cultivating a public image. Four years earlier, for example, he had published a biography of Trotsky which had been enthusiastically talked up on Radio 4. An enterprising young television producer had invited him to screen-test for a series of programmes about "Great Revolutionary Figures." Gaddis had declined. Why? Because he felt at the time that it would mean spending too long away from his baby daughter, Min, and abandoning his students at UCL. His friends and colleagues had thought it was a missed opportunity. What was the point of being a successful academic in twenty-first-century Britain if you didn't want to appear on BBC4? Think of the tie-ins, they said. Think of the *money*. With his crooked good looks, Gaddis would have been a natural for television, but he valued his privacy too much and didn't want to sideline the career he loved for what he described as "the dubious pleasure of seeing my mug on television." There was stubbornness in the decision, certainly, but Dr. Sam Gaddis thought of himself, first and foremost, as a teacher. He believed in the unarguable notion that if a young person is lucky enough to read the right books at the right time in the company of the right teacher, it will change their life forever.

"So what do we have with Sergei Platov?" he began. The manager of Daunt was sure that no more of the thirty seats set out in the bookshop would be filled by curious passersby and had asked Gaddis to begin. "Is he saint or sinner? Is Platov guilty of war crimes in Chechnya, of personally authorizing the murder of journalists critical of his regime, or is he a statesman who has restored the might of Mother Russia, thereby rescuing his country from decadence and corruption?"

The question, as far as Gaddis was concerned, was rhetorical. Platov was a stain on the Russian character, a borderline sociopath who had, in less than ten years, destroyed the possibility of a democratic Russia. A former KGB spy, he had green-lit the murder of Russian civilians on foreign soil, held Eastern European countries to ransom over the supply of gas, and encouraged the murder of journalists and human rights activists brave enough to criticize his regime. One such journalist—Katarina Tikhonov—had been a good friend of Gaddis's. They had corresponded for over fifteen years and met whenever he visited Moscow. She had been shot in the elevator of her apartment building three years earlier. Not a single suspect had been arrested in connection with the murder, an anomaly which he had exposed in his new book.

He turned to his notes.

"History tells us that Sergei Platov is a *survivor,* from a family of survivors."

"What do you mean?" The Hampstead matriarch was sitting in the front row and already asking questions. Gaddis flattered her with a patient smile which had the useful simultaneous effect of making her feel embarrassed for interrupting.

"What I mean is that his family survived the worst excesses that twentieth-century Russia could throw at them. Platov's grandfather worked as a chef for Josef Stalin and lived to tell the tale. That in itself is a miracle. His father was one of only four soldiers from a unit of twenty-eight men who survived after they were betrayed to the Germans at Kingisepp in 1941. Sergei Spiridonovich Platov was pursued into the surrounding countryside and only avoided capture by breathing through a hollow reed while submerged in a pond. Sean Connery had the same trick in *Dr. No*."

Somebody laughed. Traffic hummed on Holland Park Avenue. Sam Gaddis was looking at a sea of nodding, attentive faces.

"Do you know about the siege of Leningrad?" he asked. He hadn't meant to start on that, not tonight, but it was a subject on which he had lectured many times at UCL and the Daunt crowd would go for it. The manager, standing near the door, was bobbing his head in a way that looked enthusiastic.

"It's the winter of 1942. Minus twenty degrees at night. Three million people in a city surrounded by German troops, a million of them women and children." The matriarch gasped. "There is so little food that people are dying at the rate of five thousand a day. Leningrad's entire supply of flour has been destroyed by German firebombs. The fires cause molten sugar to saturate the earth at the Badayev warehouses. People are so hungry that they are prepared to dig into the frozen ground to extract the sugar and sell it on the black market. The top three feet of soil sells for one hundred roubles a glass, the next three feet for fifty."

A bell and a sudden burst of traffic. The door of the bookshop opened and a young woman stepped inside: shoulder-length black hair, knee-high leather boots over denim jeans, and the sort of figure that a forty-three-year-old divorced academic who has drunk three glasses of Sauvignon Blanc notices and photographs with his eyes, even while giving a talk at his own book launch. The woman whispered something to the manager, briefly caught Sam's eye, then settled in a seat at the back.

Gaddis wished that he had brought his props. At UCL, his annual lecture on the siege of Leningrad was a must-see sellout, one of the very few events that every student in the Russian history programme felt both obliged and enthused to attend. Gaddis always began by standing behind a table on which he had placed a third of a loaf of sliced white bread, a pound of minced beef, a bowl of bran flakes, a small cup of sunflower oil, and three digestive biscuits.

"This," he tells the packed auditorium, "is all that you get to eat for the next thirty days. This is all that an adult citizen of Leningrad could claim on their ration cards in the early years of World War II. Kind of puts the January detox in perspective, doesn't it?" The lecture takes place in the early weeks of the New Year, so the joke always whips up a satisfying gale of nervous laughter. "But enjoy it while you can." Confused looks in the front row. Plate by plate, bowl by bowl, Dr. Gaddis now tips the food onto the floor until all that remains on the table in front of him are ten slices of stale white bread. "By the time the siege really starts to bite, bread is more or less the only form of sustenance you're going to get, and its nutritional value is nil. The people of Leningrad don't have access to Hovis or Mother's Pride. This bread"—he picks up a piece and tears it into tiny pieces, like a child feeding ducks—"is made mostly from sawdust, from sweepings on the floor. If you're lucky enough to have a job in a factory, you get 250 grams of it every week. How much is 250 grams?" Gaddis now picks up six slices of the bread and hands them to a student in the front row. "That's about how much it is. But if you *don't* work in a factory"—three of the slices come back—"you get only 125 grams."

"And I warn you not to be young," he continues, channelling Neil Kinnock now, a politician from yesteryear whom most of his students are too young to remember. "I warn you not to fall ill. I warn you not to grow old in the Leningrad of 1942. Because if you do"—at this point, he gets hold of the final three slices of bread, tossing them to the floor—"if you do, you'll most likely starve to death." He lets that one settle in before delivering the coup de grâce. "And don't be an academic, either. Don't be an intellectual." Another gale of nervous laughter. "Comrade Stalin doesn't like people like us. As far as he's concerned, academics and intellectuals can starve to death."

The beautiful woman in the knee-high boots was staring at him intently. At UCL, Gaddis usually picked out a volunteer at this stage and asked them to take off their shoes, which he then placed on a table at the front of the lecture hall. He liked to pull grass clippings and pieces of bark from the pockets of his jacket. Christ, if Health and Safety had allowed it, he'd have brought a dead rat and a dog in, as well. That, after all, was what the citizens of Leningrad survived on as the Germans tightened the noose: grasses and bark; leather shoes boiled down for sustenance; the flesh of vermin and dogs. Cannibalism was also rife. Children would disappear. Limbs would mysteriously be removed from corpses left to freeze in the street. The meat pies on sale in the markets of war-torn Leningrad could contain anything from horseflesh to human being.

But tonight he kept things simple. Tonight Dr. Gaddis spoke about Platov's aunt and first cousin surviving three years in a German concentration camp in the Baltics. He related how, on one occasion, Platov's mother had passed out from hunger only to wake up while she was being taken to a cemetery by men who had assumed she was dead. Towards eight o'clock, he read a short extract from the new book about Platov's early years in the KGB and, by eight fifteen, people were applauding and he was taking questions from the floor, trying to make the case that Russia was reverting to totalitarianism and all the time wondering how to persuade the girl in the knee-high boots to join his party for dinner.

In the end, he didn't need to. As the launch was beginning to thin out, she approached him at the makeshift bar and held out her hand.

"Holly Levette."

"Sam." Her hand was slim and warm and had rings all over it. She was about twenty-eight with huge blue eyes. "You were the one who was late."

A smile of what looked like genuine embarrassment. Her right cheek had a little scar on the bone which he liked. "Sorry, I was held up on the Tube. I hope I didn't interrupt anything."

They moved away from the bar.

"Not at all." He was trying to work out what she did for a living. Something in the arts, something creative. "Have we met before?"

"No, no. I just read your article in the *Guardian* and knew that you were speaking tonight. I have something that I thought you might be interested in."

They had found themselves in a small clearing in the Travel section. In his peripheral vision, Gaddis could sense somebody trying to catch his eye.

"What kind of something?"

"Well, my mother has just died."

"I'm sorry to hear that."

It didn't look as though Holly Levette needed much comforting.

"Her name was Katya Levette. Before her death she was working on a book about the history of the KGB. A lot of her information came from sources in British and Russian Intelligence. I don't want her papers to go to waste. All that hard work, all those interviews. I wondered whether you might like to have a look at her research, see if there's any value in it?"

It could have been a trap, of course. A mischievous source in MI6 or the Russian FSB looking to use a mid-level British historian for purposes of propaganda. After all, why come all the way to the bookshop? Why not just phone him at UCL or send an e-mail to his Web site? But the chances of a honeytrap were slim. If the spooks wanted a scandal, if they wanted headlines, they would have gone for Beevor or Sebag-Montefiore, for Andrew or West. Besides, Gaddis would be able to tell in five minutes if the documents were genuine. He'd spent half his life in the museums of London, Moscow, and St. Petersburg. He was a citizen of the historical archive.

"Sure, I could take a look at them. You're kind to think of me. Where are the papers?"

"At my flat in Chelsea."

And suddenly the tone of the conversation shifted. Suddenly Holly Levette was looking at Dr. Sam Gaddis in the way that mischievous female students sometimes look at attractive, fortysomething bachelor academics when they are up to no good. As if her flat in Chelsea promised more than just dust-gathering notebooks on the KGB.

"Your flat in Chelsea," Sam repeated. He caught the smell of her perfume as he drank more wine. "I should probably take your number."

She was smiling, enjoying the game, promising him something with those huge blue eyes. From the hip pocket of her slim jeans, Holly Levette produced a card which she pressed into his hand. "Why don't you ring me when you're not so busy?" she suggested. "Why don't you call and we can arrange for you to come and pick them up?"

"It's a good idea." Gaddis looked at the card. There was nothing on it except a name and a telephone number. "And you say your mother was researching the history of Soviet Intelligence?"

"The KGB, yes."

A pause. There were so many questions to ask that he could say nothing; if he started, they would never stop. A male colleague from UCL materialized beside Gaddis and stared, with abandon, deep into Holly's cleavage. Gaddis didn't bother introducing them.

"I should go," she said, touching his arm as she took a step backwards. "It was so lovely to meet you. Your talk was fantastic."

He shook her hand again, the one with all the rings. "I'll call you," he said. "And I'll definitely take you up on that offer."

"What offer?" asked the colleague.

"Oh, the best kind," replied Holly Levette. "The best kind."

3

Two days later, on a rain-drenched Saturday morning in August, Gaddis rang the number on the card and arranged to go to Chelsea to pick up the boxes. Five minutes after walking through the door of her flat on Tite Street, he was in bed with Holly Levette. He did not leave until eight o'clock the following evening, the boot of his car sagging under the weight of the boxes, his head and body aching from the sweet carnal impact of a woman who remained, even after all that they had shared, something of a stranger to him, an enigma.

Her flat had been a bomb site, a deep litter field of newspapers, books, back issues of *The New Yorker,* half-finished glasses of wine, and ashtrays overflowing with old joints and crushed cigarette packets. The kitchen had three days of washing up piled at the sink, the bedroom more rugs and more clothes strewn over more chairs than Gaddis had ever seen in his life. It reminded him of his own house which, in the years since Natasha had left him, had become a bachelor's labyrinth of paperbacks, takeaway menus, and DVD box sets. He had a Belarussian cleaning lady, but she was near-arthritic and spent most of her time chatting to him in the kitchen about life in post-Communist Minsk.

Holly's search for the KGB material had taken them downstairs, to the basement of the apartment block, where Katya Levette had filled a storage cupboard to capacity with dozens of unmarked boxes. It had taken them both more than an hour to locate the files and to carry them outside to Gaddis's car. Even then, Holly said that she could not be sure that he had taken everything with him.

"But it's a start, right?" she said. "It's something to be getting on with."

"Where did all this stuff *come* from?" he asked.

The sheer volume of material in the basement suggested that Katya Levette had either been extremely well connected in the intelligence firmament or an inveterate hoarder of useless, secondhand information. Gaddis had Googled her, but most of the articles available under her name were either book reviews or hagiographic profiles of middle-ranking business figures in the UK and United States. At no point had she been a staff writer on any recognized publication.

"Mum was friendly with a lot of Russian expats in London," Holly explained. "Oligarchs, ex-KGB. You probably know most of them."

"Not socially."

"And she had a boyfriend once upon a time. Someone in MI6. I think a lot of the stuff may have come from him."

"You mean he leaked it?"

Holly nodded and looked away. She was concealing something, but Gaddis did not feel that he knew her well enough to push for more information. There had already been hints of a fraught relationship between mother and daughter; the truth would come out in good time.

He had driven home and put the boxes—fifteen of them—on the floor of Min's bedroom, making a silent promise to get to them within a few days. And he would have called Holly again almost immediately had it not been for the grim surprise of Monday's post.

There were two letters.

The first came in an ominous brown envelope marked HM REVENUE & CUSTOMS / PRIVATE and was a demand for late payment of tax. A demand for £21,248, to be exact, which was about £21,248 more than Gaddis had in the bank. Failure to pay the sum in full by mid-October, the letter stated, would result in legal action. In the meantime, interest on the debt was accumulating at a rate of 6.5 per cent.

The second letter bore the unmistakable handwriting of his ex-wife, complete with a Spanish postmark and a stain in the left-hand corner which he put down to a wayward cup of *café con leche*.

The letter was typed.

Dear Sam

I'm sorry to have to write like this, rather than phone, but Sergio and Nick have advised me that it's best to do these things on a formal basis.

Sergio was the lawyer. Nick was the Barcelona-based boyfriend. Gaddis wasn't exactly enthusiastic about either of them.

The situation is that N and I are desperately short of money because of the restaurant and I need more help with the school fees. I know you've already been more than generous, but I can't meet my half of the payments for this term or the next. Is there any possible way you could help? Min loves the school and is already incredibly good at Catalan *and* Spanish. The last thing either of us wants is to take her out and separate her from all the friends she's made. The other school is miles away and awful, for all sorts of reasons that are too depressing to go into. (I've heard reports of bullying, of racism against an Indian child, even an accident in the playground that was covered up by staff.) You get the picture.

Will you write and let me know what you think? I'm sorry to have to ask you to help with this because we always agreed to go fifty/fifty. But I don't see that I have any choice. The figure we're talking about is in the region of €5,000. When the restaurant starts turning a profit, I *promise* to pay you back.

I hope everything is OK in London/at UCL etc. Give my love to everybody—

Hasta luego
Natasha x

Sam Gaddis wasn't the sort of man who panicked, but equally he wasn't the sort of man who had twenty-five thousand quid lying around for random tax bills and school fees. He'd already taken out two separate £20,000 loans to pay off debts accumulated by his divorce; the monthly interest repayments alone amounted to £800, on top of a £190,000 mortgage.

He took the Tube to UCL and arranged to meet his literary agent for lunch. It was the only solution. He would have to work his way out of the crisis. He would have to *write*.

They met, two days later, at a small, exorbitantly expensive restaurant on High Street Kensington where the only other clientele were bored Holland Park housewives with lovers half their age and an elderly Greek businessman who took almost an hour to eat a single bowl of risotto.

Robert Paterson, UK director of Dippel, Gordon, and Kahla, Literary Agents since 1968, had more important clients than Dr. Samuel Gaddis—soap stars, for example, who brought in 15 per cent commissions on six-figure autobiography deals—but none with whom he would rather have spent three hours in an overpriced London restaurant.

"You mentioned that you had money worries?" he said as they ordered a second bottle of wine. Paterson was three years off retirement and the sole surviving member of the generation which still believed in the dignity of the three-martini lunch. "Tax?"

"How did you know?"

"Always is, this time of year." Paterson nodded knowingly as he rounded off a veal cutlet. "Most of my clients have less idea how to manage their finances than Champion the Wonder Horse. I get three telephone calls a week from some of them. 'Where's my foreign rights deal? Where's the cash from the paperback?' I'm not a literary agent anymore. I'm a personal financial adviser."

Gaddis smiled a crooked smile. "And what financial advice would you give me?"

"Depends how much you need."

"Twenty-one grand for Her Majesty's Inland Revenue, payable last Tuesday. Four grand for Min's school fees. Likely to rise to ten or twenty in the next couple of years unless Natasha's boyfriend suddenly figures out that being the manager of a successful restaurant in Barcelona doesn't involve spending three days a week working on his off-piste skiing in the Pyrenees. They're chucking euros into the Mediterranean."

"And UCL can't help?"

Gaddis thanked the waiter, who had poured more wine into his glass. "I'm forty-three. My salary won't go much higher unless I get Chair. The mortgage alone is costing me a third of what I earn. Short of stealing first editions of *Pride and Prejudice* from the London Library, I'm not looking at raising the money any time soon."

"So you need a new deal?" Paterson dabbed the corners of his mouth with a napkin.

"I need a new deal, Bob."

"What did I get you last time?"

"South of five grand."

Paterson looked mildly embarrassed to have brokered such a meagre contract. He was a huge man, requiring a two-foot gap between his chair and the table. He folded his arms so that they were resting on the summit of his voluminous belly. A Buddha tailored by Savile Row.

"So we're talking what? Thirty thousand pounds as a signature advance?"

A small droplet of gravy had appeared at the edge of Paterson's shirt. Gaddis nodded and his agent produced a stagey sigh.

"Well, if you want that sort of money quickly, you'll have to write a strictly commercial book, almost certainly within twelve months and probably under a pseudonym, so that you have the impact of a debut writer. That's the only way I can get you a serious cheque in today's market. A historical comparison between Sergei Platov and Peter the Great, God bless you, isn't going to cut it. With the best will in the world, Sam, nobody really cares about journalists getting bumped off in Russia. Your average punter doesn't have a clue who Peter the Great is. Does he play for Liverpool? Was he knocked out in the final of *Britain's Got Talent*? Do you see the problem?"

Gaddis was nodding. He saw the problem. The trouble was, he had no aptitude for forging commercial bestsellers which he could write in twelve months. There were lectures he had given at UCL which had taken him more than a year to research and prepare. For an astonishing moment, during which Paterson was putting on a pair of half-moon spectacles and scanning the pudding menu, he reflected on the very real possibility that he would have to moonlight as a cabdriver in order to raise the cash.

Then he remembered Holly Levette.

"What about the KGB?"

"What about it?" Paterson looked up from the menu and did a comic double-take around the restaurant. "Are they *here*?"

Gaddis smiled at the joke. A small boy walked past the table and disappeared towards the downstairs bathroom. "What about a history of Soviet and Russian Intelligence?" he said. "Something with spies in it?"

"As a series of novels?"

"If you like."

Paterson peered over the spectacles, a father suddenly sceptical of a wayward son. "I don't really see you as a novelist, Sam," he said. "Fiction isn't your thing. It would take you far too long to complete a manuscript. You should be thinking along the lines of a nonfiction title which can spin off into a TV series, a documentary with you in front of the camera. If you're serious about making money, you need to start being serious about your image. No future in being a fusty old academic these days. Look at Schama. You have to multitask. I've always said you'd be a natural for television."

Gaddis hid a thought behind his glass of wine. Maybe it was time. Min was in Barcelona. He was completely broke. What did he have to lose by getting his face on television?

"Go on, then. Give me the inside take."

Paterson duly obliged. "Well, when it comes to books about Russia, Chechnya is a no-no. Nobody gives a monkey's—" He broke off to order "just a smidgen of tiramisu, just a *smidgen*" from the waiter. "Ditto Yeltsin, ditto Gorbachev, ditto His Rampaging Egoness, the late lamented Alexander Solzhenitsyn. Done to death. You've written about Platov, Chernobyl is old hat, so—yes—you might as well stick to spies. But we'd need poisoned umbrellas, secret KGB plots to knock off Reagan or Thatcher, irrefutable evidence that Lee Harvey Oswald was the lovechild of Rudolf Nureyev and Svetlana Stalin. I'm talking cover of the *Daily Mail*. I'm talking *scoop*."

The Greek businessman had finally conceded defeat at the hands of his risotto. Gaddis was at once flattered and bemused that Paterson should consider him capable of unearthing a story on that scale. He was also concerned that Holly Levette's boxes would contain nothing but secondhand, irrelevant dross from dubious sources in the Russian underworld. Right now, though, those boxes were all that he had to go on.

"I'll work on it," he said.

"Good." Paterson observed the arrival of his tiramisu with a whistle of anticipation. "Now. Is there any way I can interest you in a *coffee?*"

4

Eight hours later, Gaddis went for supper at the Hampstead house of Charlotte Berg. Berg had been his flatmate at Cambridge and his girlfriend—briefly—before he had been married. She was a former war correspondent who hid the scars of Bosnia, of Rwanda and the West Bank, beneath a veneer of bonhomie and slightly fading glamour. Over roast chicken prepared by her husband, Paul, Charlotte began to share details of her latest piece, a freelance story to be sold to the *Sunday Times* which she claimed would be the biggest political scandal of the decade.

"I'm sitting on a scoop," she said.

Gaddis reflected that it was the second time that day that he had heard the word.

"What kind of scoop?"

"Well, it wouldn't be a scoop if I told you, would it?"

This was a game they played. Charlotte and Sam were rivals, in the way that close friends often keep a quiet, competitive eye on one another. The rivalry was professional, it was intellectual, and it was almost never taken too seriously.

"What do you remember about Melita Norwood?" she asked.

Sam looked over at Paul, who was concentratedly mopping up gravy with a hunk of French bread. Norwood was the so-called "Granny Spy," exposed in 1999, who had passed British nuclear secrets to the Soviet Union during the 1940s and '50s.

"I remember that she was swept under the carpet. Spied for Stalin, sped up his nuclear programme by about five years, but was allowed to die peacefully in her bed by a British government who didn't want the negative publicity of trying an eighty-year-old woman for treason. Why?"

Charlotte pushed her plate to one side. She was a gestural, free-spirited woman of vast appetites: for cigarettes, for drink, for information. Paul was the only man she had ever been with who had been able to tolerate her many contradictions. "Fuck Melita Norwood," she said suddenly, grabbing Sam's glass of wine by mistake and swallowing most of it.

"If you say so."

"What about Roger Hollis?" she asked quickly.

"What about him?"

"Do you think he was a traitor?"

Sir Roger Hollis was a grey area in the history of British Intelligence. In 1981, the journalist Chapman Pincher had published a bestselling book, *Their Trade Is Treachery,* in which it was alleged that Hollis, a former head of MI5, had been a KGB spy. Gaddis had read the book as a teenager. He remembered the bright red cover with the shadow of a sickle falling across it; his father asking to borrow it on a seaside holiday in Sussex.

"To be honest, I haven't thought about Hollis for a long time," he said. "Pincher's allegations were never proved. Is that what you're working on? Is that the scoop? Is there some kind of connection between Hollis and Norwood? She was associated with a KGB spy code-named HUNT who was never identified. Was HUNT Hollis?"

Charlotte laughed. She was enjoying tapping into Gaddis's reserves of expertise.

"Fuck Hollis," she said with the same abrasive glee with which she had dismissed Norwood. Gaddis was bemused.

"Why do you keep saying that?"

"Because they were small potatoes. Bit-part players. *Minnows* compared to what I've stumbled on."

"Which is . . . ?" Paul asked.

Charlotte finished off what must have been her ninth or tenth glass of wine. "What if I told you there was a sixth Cambridge spy who had never been unmasked? A contemporary of Burgess and Maclean, of Blunt, Philby, and Cairncross, who is still alive today?"

At first, Gaddis couldn't untangle precisely what Charlotte was telling him. He, too, had drunk at least a bottle of Côtes du Rhône. Hollis a Cambridge spy? Norwood a sixth member of the Ring of Five? Surely she wasn't working on a crackpot theory like that? But he was a guest in her house, enjoying her hospitality, so he kept his doubts to himself.

"I'd tell you that you were sitting on a fortune."

"This isn't about *money*, Sam." There was no admonishment in Charlotte's tone, just the bluntness for which she was renowned. "This is about *history*. I'm talking about a legendary KGB spy, codenamed ATTILA, who matriculated at Trinity College, Cambridge, in the 1930s. A man every bit as dangerous and as influential as Maclean and Philby. A mole at the heart of Britain's political and intelligence infrastructure whose treason has been deliberately covered up by the British government for more than fifty years."

"Jesus." Gaddis tried to hide his scepticism. It surely wasn't plausible that a sixth member of the Trinity ring had escaped detection. Every spook and academic and journalist with the slightest interest in the secret world had been hunting the sixth man for decades. Any Soviet defector, at any point after 1945, could have blown ATTILA's cover at the drop of a hat. At the very least, Cairncross or Blunt would have given him up at the time of their exposure.

"Where are you getting your information?" he asked. "Why was there no mention of ATTILA in Mitrokhin?"

Vasili Mitrokhin was a major in the KGB who passed detailed accounts of Russian intelligence operations to MI6 after the collapse of the Soviet Union. The documents were published in the UK in 1992.

"Everybody thinks the entire history of Soviet espionage was contained in Mitrokhin." Charlotte lit a cigarette and looked utterly content. "But there was a *ton* of stuff he didn't get his hands on. Including this."

Paul put his knife and fork together. Charlotte's husband was a tall, patient man, impassive to the point of diffidence. A successful City financier—hence the seven-figure, five-bedroom house in Hampstead—he loved Charlotte not least because she allowed him to blend into the background, to maintain the privacy he had worked so hard to protect. He was so inscrutable that Sam could never work out whether Paul viewed him as a threat to their marriage or as a valued friend. It was almost a surprise when he joined the fray, saying: "Come on, who's your source?"

Charlotte leaned forward into an effectively conspiratorial cloud of cigarette smoke and looked at both men in turn. Her husband was the only person she could entirely trust with the information. Gaddis was a loyal friend, of course, a man of tact and discretion, but he also possessed a streak of mischievousness which made sharing a secret like this extremely risky.

"Stays between these four walls, okay?" she said, so that Gaddis was aware of what it meant to her. He felt a sudden thrust of envy, because she seemed so convinced of her prize.

"Of course. Four walls. Won't breathe a word."

"Can I tell Polly?" Paul muttered, placing his hand on Charlotte's back as he stood to clear the plates. Polly was their arthritic black Labrador and, in the absence of any children, their most cherished companion.

"This is serious," she said. "I'm sworn to secrecy. But it's so mind-boggling I can't keep my mouth shut."

Gaddis felt a historian's excitement at the prospect of what Charlotte had uncovered. The sixth man. Was it really *possible*? It was like finding Lucan. "Go on," he said.

"Let me start at the beginning." Charlotte filled another glass of wine. Paul caught Sam's eye and frowned imperceptibly. She was a functioning alcoholic: a bottle of wine at lunch, two at dinner; gins at six; a couple of tumblers of Laphroaig last thing at night. None of it ever seemed to affect her behaviour beyond a certain decibel increase in the volume of her voice. But the booze was undoubtedly beating her: it was putting years on, adding weight, black-bagging her eyes. "About a month ago I received a letter from a man called Thomas Neame. He claims to be the confidant of a British diplomat who spent his entire career, from World War II to the mid-1980s, working as a spy for the KGB. I made some basic enquiries, discovered that Thomas was kosher, and went to meet him."

"Went where?" Paul was oblivious to the comings and goings of his wife's career. Often she would disappear for weeks on end, pursuing a story in Iraq, in California, in Moscow.

"That's secret number one," Charlotte replied. "I can't tell even *you* where Thomas Neame lives."

"Trust is such a wonderful thing between husband and wife," Gaddis muttered. "How old is this guy?"

"Ninety-one." Charlotte gulped more wine. Her skin had darkened under the low lights of the kitchen, her mouth now ruby red with lipstick and wine. "But ninety-one going on seventy-five. You wouldn't fancy taking him on in an arm wrestle. Very tough and fit, sort of war-generation Scot who can smoke forty a day and still pop to the top of Ben Nevis before breakfast."

"Unlike someone else I know," said Paul pointedly, looking at the cigarette in his wife's hand. Charlotte's years of reporting overseas had weakened, rather than strengthened, what had once been an iron constitution. Both Paul and Gaddis worried about this but could no more have curtailed her lifestyle than they could have biked to the moon.

"And how does Neame know that his friend was a spy?" Gaddis asked. "How come it hasn't leaked out before?"

His phone rang before Charlotte had a chance to respond. Gaddis plucked it from the pocket of his jacket and looked at the display. It was a text from Holly Levette.

NIGHTCAP . . . ?

He was possessed by two contradictory impulses: to polish off his wine as quickly as possible and to grab a taxi south to Tite Street; or to come clean to Charlotte about his quest for a headline-grabbing story of his own.

"Do you know this woman?" he said, holding up the phone, as if there were a photograph of Holly on the screen. "Holly Levette?"

"Rings a bell."

"Mother's name was Katya. She was working on a history of the KGB when—"

"Katya Levette!" Charlotte reacted with mock horror. She shook her head and said: "Commonly regarded as the world's worst hack."

"How so?"

She waved a hand in front of her face. "Not worth going into. Our paths crossed once or twice. She was constantly telling me how wonderful I was, but clearly looking for a quid pro quo. I think her daughter sent me an e-mail after she died, saying how much Katya had admired something I'd written about Chechnya. Then offered me a load of old junk from her research papers."

"A load of old junk," Gaddis repeated, with a thump of despair.

"Well, not junk." Charlotte looked sheepish. "Actually, I palmed her off on you. Told her to give them to a proper historian."

"Gee, thanks."

"And now she's been in touch?"

Gaddis nodded. "She didn't mention that I was getting them secondhand. She told me how much she'd admired my *Guardian* article about Sergei Platov."

Paul smothered a laugh. "Flattery will get you everywhere."

Gaddis poured himself a glass of wine. Skirting around the dirty weekend in Chelsea, he explained that Holly had come to Daunt Books and offered him the KGB material on a plate.

"A beautiful girl turns up like that, willing to hand over several hundred documents about Soviet Intelligence, you don't exactly turn a blind eye. How was I to know Katya was a fruitcake?"

"Oh, she's beautiful, is she?" Charlotte asked, animated by the opportunity to tease him. "You never said."

"Holly is *very* beautiful."

"And she came to the launch? How come I didn't meet her?"

"Probably because you'd told her to get stuffed," Paul replied.

Charlotte laughed and picked at a chunk of candle wax on the table. "And now this girl is texting you at half past ten at night. Is there something you're not telling the group, Dr. Gaddis? Does Miss Levette need a bedtime story?"

Gaddis took a Camel from her open packet. "You're lucky," he said, deliberately changing the subject. "Right now I'd sell my grandchildren for your Cambridge story." He lit the cigarette from the candle. Paul grimaced and waved a hand in front of his face, saying: "Christ, not you as well."

"The sixth man? Why?"

"Financial problems." Gaddis made a gesture with upturned hands. "Nothing new."

There was a strange kind of shame in being broke at forty-three. How had it come to this? He took the cigarette smoke deep into his lungs and exhaled at the ceiling.

Charlotte frowned. "Alimony? Is the fragrant Natasha turning out to be not quite as fragrant as we thought?"

Paul poured water into a French press of coffee and kept his counsel.

"Tax bill. School fees. Debts," Gaddis replied. "I need to raise about twenty-five grand. Had lunch with my agent today. He says the only hope I have of working my way out of the situation is to write a hack job about Soviet Intelligence. Doesn't even have to be under my own name. So a sixth Cambridge spy is the perfect story. In fact, I'll steal it off you. Bury you under the floorboards to get my hands on it."

Charlotte looked genuinely concerned. "You don't have to *steal* it," she said. "Why don't you cowrite a book with me? We can even use some of Katya's magic files." Paul grinned. "Seriously. I'll break the Cambridge story as an exclusive, but after that someone will want a book. You'd be *perfect*. I don't have the patience to sit down and compose two hundred thousand words about a piece I've already written. I'll want to move on to the next thing. But you could put ATTILA in context. You could add all the juice and flavour. Nobody knows more about Russia than you do."

Gaddis declined outright. It would feel wrong to be piggybacking on Charlotte's triumph. She was drunk and the booze was making promises she might not, in the cold light of morning, be willing to keep. Yet she persisted.

"Sleep on it," she said. "Christ, sleep on it while you're sleeping with Holly Levette." Paul plunged the coffee. "I'd *love* to work with you. It would be an honour. And it sounds as though it will get you out of a nasty situation."

Gaddis slotted his mobile phone back in his jacket pocket and took Charlotte's hand. "It's an idea," he said. "No more than that. You're incredibly kind. But let's talk more in the morning."

"No. Let's talk *now*." She wouldn't let pride and British etiquette stand in the way of a good idea. Polly, her buckled legs seized by arthritis, came hobbling into the kitchen and lay at her feet. Charlotte leaned over and fed a piece of bread into her mouth, saying: "Do *you* think it's a good idea, Pol?" in a voice for a child. "*I* think it's a good idea."

"Okay, okay." Gaddis's hands were again raised, this time in mock surrender. "I'll think about it."

Charlotte looked relieved. "Well, thank God for that. Talk about looking a gift horse in the mouth." She stood and found three cups for the coffee.

"And you say ATTILA is presumed dead?" It was a first, conscious signal of Gaddis's desire to explore things further.

"Yes. But this Neame guy is slippery. Says he hasn't seen Crane for over ten years. I'm not sure I believe that."

"Crane? That's his name?"

"Edward Anthony Crane. Wrote everything down in a document which Neame claims to have partially destroyed. Says the document also contained a revelation that would 'rock London and Moscow to their foundations.'"

"You mean over and above the fact that our government has covered up the existence of a sixth Cambridge spy?"

"Over and above even that, yes."

Gaddis was staring at her, staring at Paul, trying to work out if Charlotte was being duped. It was too good to be true and, at the same time, impossible to ignore. "And he hasn't said what this scandal involved?"

Charlotte shook her head. "No. Not yet. But Thomas was Crane's confessor. His best friend. He knows everything. And he's willing to spill his guts before he pops his clogs."

"Not to mix metaphors," Paul muttered.

"They would both be about the same age," Charlotte continued. "Ninety, ninety-one. Contemporaries at Cambridge. What do you think are the chances of both of them still being alive?"

"Slim," Gaddis replied.

5

Alexander Grek had been watching the Berg residence for five hours. He had witnessed Paul returning from work with two bulging Waitrose carrier bags at 18:45. While smoking a cigarette at 19:12, he had seen Charlotte at the first-floor window, recently emerged from a bath or shower, closing a set of curtains after securing a towel around her chest. Just after eight o'clock, an unidentified white male—early forties, dishevelled hair, carrying two bottles of red wine—had entered the property. Grek assumed that the man was coming for supper.

The unidentified male left the building at 23:21. He was approximately six feet tall, about eighty kilos, wearing a corduroy jacket with a leather satchel slung over his shoulder. The man shook Paul Berg's hand in the doorway of the house. He then embraced and kissed Berg's wife, Charlotte. Grek had a long-lens camera on the passenger seat of his car, but was unable to take a photograph of the man's face because he walked backwards from the front door, moving towards the street while continuing to converse with his hosts. Having reached the pavement, the subject walked in the direction of Hampstead High Street, away from Grek's vehicle.

Grek decided to stretch his legs. He followed the subject the length of Pilgrim's Lane and observed him hailing a cab outside a branch of Waterstone's bookshop. The taxi headed south. Grek lit a cigarette and walked back towards his vehicle. Halfway along the street, clamping the cigarette between his lips, he urinated at the base of a chestnut tree concealed from the street by a tarpaulin-covered Dumpster.

Murders, he had long ago concluded, broke down into three distinct categories. They could be political, they could be military, and they could have a moral characteristic. Alexander Grek did not concern himself with conventional morality. His work was either military or political, and usually defensive. Tonight's plan, for example, had the laudable goal of preventing graver consequences for his government. Grek was not an assassin in the formal sense. He could not be hired. As a young man, he had been trained by his country's domestic intelligence service—commonly known as the FSB—and, following his retirement in 1996, had run a small, highly successful security company with offices in London and St. Petersburg. In such circumstances, a man learns a great deal about the business of death. Yet Grek considered himself, first and foremost, a political animal. The ATTILA investigation was a threat to the state. That threat must therefore be removed. He was simply responding to his patriotic duty.

Setting down a half-empty bottle of mineral water, he pulled a woollen hat low over his head, exited the vehicle, and walked across the street. Pilgrim's Lane was deserted. Grek moved towards the eastern side of the house and picked the simple lock on the wooden gate which led into the garden. He had oiled the hinges the previous night so that the gate opened without a sound. He was now in a narrow channel in which were kept a bicycle, some garden tools, and several rusted cans of paint. He looked up at the house to ensure that no lights were on in the upper floors. He then walked across the garden.

During the day, Charlotte Berg worked in a converted shed at the southern end of the property. She used a laptop computer which, at night, was kept inside the house. The shed contained a cheap colour printer, an outdated telephone and fax machine, some filing cabinets, a battered wooden chair, and one or two photographs of sentimental value. To Paul, she would argue that it was better to keep the shed unlocked rather than to fit a padlock, which might convey the impression to any potential burglar that the office contained something worth stealing. Grek opened the shed, stepped inside, and closed the door behind him.

Sodium fluoracetate is a fine white powder, derived from pesticide. Odourless and inexpensive, it is commonly used as a poison to control the spread of rats in sewers. Grek had 10mg, in liquid form, in a vial which he now removed from his jacket pocket. The tiny surveillance camera, fitted in a light above Berg's desk, had shown a small bottle of Evian, half finished, beside the printer. Grek picked it up, poured the colourless liquid into the water, and sealed the cap. Sufficient moonlight was coming into the room that he was able to remove the camera without the need for a torch. He also withdrew a listening device from the underside of Berg's desk. He placed both items, and their tangle of wires, in the pockets of his jacket. When he had finished, Grek studied the paperwork on the desk. A telephone bill. An invoice for some painting and decorating. A copy of the second volume of *The Mitrokhin Archive*. Nothing which seemed to refer directly to ATTILA.

A noise outside. Something within three or four metres of the shed. Grek dropped to his knees. He heard the noise a second time and recognized it as an animal, possibly a fox. The Berg's dog, Polly, had no access to the garden at night and would presumably be asleep indoors.

Grek stood up slowly. He opened the door of the shed and walked back along the garden. He checked the street as he emerged from the shadows of the house and crossed Pilgrim's Lane when he was sure that he was not being observed. He unlocked the car, emptied his pockets on the passenger seat, and pulled out in the direction of Hampstead High Street.

6

addis was in his study at UCL when he received the call. The number had come up as "Unknown."

"Sam? It's Paul."

"You sound terrible. Is everything all right?"

"It's about Charlotte." His voice was strangely apologetic. Even at this wretched hour, he somehow managed to maintain a sense of decorum. "I'm sorry to have to be the one who tells you. She had a heart attack this morning. She's gone."

Gaddis had had three such telephone conversations in the course of his life. When he was sixteen, his older brother had been killed in a car crash in South America. At Cambridge, a close friend had hanged himself on the eve of finals. And, just before his fortieth birthday, he had learned that Katarina Tikhonov had been assassinated at her apartment in Moscow, the victim of a contract killing tacitly approved by Sergei Platov. He remembered each conversation, each occasion, very clearly, and his distinct reactions to them. He found himself saying: "What? A heart attack?" because he needed words with which to douse the nausea of shock.

Paul replied simply: "Yes," then, almost immediately, because this was just one of a dozen call he would have to make: "Nothing more to be said now."

"Yes, of course. I'm so sorry, Paul."

"I'm sorry for you, too."

Gaddis went to the floor in a slow crouch, with the strange and vivid sensation of his bones expanding, his skin stretching, as if his body wanted to escape itself. The news did not at first seem coherent, but then generated a grim logic. Charlotte drank too much. Charlotte smoked too much. Charlotte's heart had given out. He stood and leaned on his desk. He was concerned that a student or colleague might knock on the door of the office and walk in. He locked it from the inside and, needing fresh air, opened the window, struggling with the latch until it opened suddenly, the noise of building works bursting into the tiny, cramped room. And Sam was ashamed of himself, because within minutes of absorbing what Paul had told him, he was thinking about Edward Crane. With Charlotte gone, it would no longer be possible to cowrite the book. He would have to find another source of income, another way of paying off his debts. He felt utterly bereft.

Charlotte had apparently gone to her office in the morning, typed a few e-mails, read *The Times* online. At some point, probably between ten and eleven o'clock, she had come back into the house to make some toast, bringing the wastepaper basket from the office. Paul had found her on the floor of the kitchen, Polly whimpering at her side, the toast popped. No autopsy had been carried out. The doctors and coroner had both agreed that Charlotte had suffered a massive heart attack as a result of a genetic coronary weakness allied with an unhealthy lifestyle.

In the ensuing days, Gaddis helped Paul to arrange the funeral. He wrote a eulogy, at the family's request, and drew up the Order of Service, which he arranged to have printed at a small shop in Belsize Park. It helped to have practical tasks to occupy his mind, to lift his constant sense of despair. He felt that he was a support to Paul, who had withdrawn into an almost impenetrable privacy. Day and night, Sam's mind shuttled back and forth across more than two decades of memories: the first years of his friendship with Charlotte at Cambridge; their brief love affair; then the span of Sam's eight-year marriage to Natasha, and the long-running tension between the two women.

Sam reflected that there was now nobody in his life—certainly no woman—with whom he had a comparable friendship. Over the previous ten years his group of friends had thinned out, either sidetracked by the demands of small children, or living with partners with whom he felt no real affinity. It was part of the journey into middle age. Charlotte had been one of the few long-term friends who had survived this period and who remained as a link to his past.

The funeral took place eight days after her death, with a wake at the house in Hampstead. By then, time had partly numbed Sam's sense of grief and he was capable of putting on a front of charm and fortitude, acting almost as a host in the absence of Paul, who spent most of the afternoon upstairs in his room.

"I just can't face them, you know?" he said, and Gaddis realized that there was nothing he could do to comfort him. Sometimes people are just better left to grieve. Polly was with him, as well as a dozen photographs of Charlotte, strewn across the bed. "Are you all right?" he asked Gaddis. "Are you surviving down there?"

"We're surviving," Gaddis said, and reassured him with his eyes. "Everything's fine."

By six o'clock, only half a dozen people remained. Colleagues who had known Charlotte from her days on *The Times* had long since returned to their offices, filing copy on deadline for a morning edition which would not wait. Acquaintances from every nook and cranny of her life had paid their respects and dispersed into the late afternoon. When Paul came back downstairs, only a few members of the close family remained.

Gaddis had briefly given up smoking in the early part of the year, but was at it again, twenty a day since her death. Life, as Charlotte had proved, was indisputably too short. He smiled as he thought of that, lighting a Camel at the bottom of the garden and realizing that he was alone for the first time in almost twelve hours. A couple of caterers—a teenage boy and girl, both dressed in black—were clearing glasses from windowsills at the front of the house. Polly was watching them, stretched out on the grass, scratching behind her ear with a bent, arthritic paw.

In the fading light of the early evening Gaddis opened the door of

Charlotte's office and stood in the room where his friend had been working on the morning of her death. The shed was as she had left it. Her laptop was on the desk, some documents had spooled out of the printer, a copy of *The Mitrokhin Archive* was open on the floor. Sam sat at the desk. He was snooping, no question, pretending to himself and to anyone who might walk in that he was convening with Charlotte's spirit. But the reality was tawdry. He was looking for Edward Crane.

He picked up the document from the printer. It was an article about John Updike from *The New York Review of Books*. He looked down at the floor. What was he hoping for? Photographs? CD-ROMs? He flicked through an address book on the desk, even thought about switching on her mobile phone. His breathing was sharper and he was looking out of the window of the shed, checking to make sure that he would not be disturbed as he opened the first few pages of her diary. He looked at the days leading up to her death, saw only "Dinner: S" scrawled on the night that he had come for supper. The last night that he had seen her alive.

"What are you doing?"

Paul was at the door, staring at him in disbelief.

Gaddis snapped the diary shut and placed it on the desk.

"Just trying to get close to her," he muttered. "Just trying to make sense of everything."

"In her *diary*?"

Sam stood up. "I don't know why I did that." He guessed that Paul knew. "I just ended up in here. I don't know what the hell I'm doing."

"I don't either."

They looked at one another. Paul was so tired, so strung out, that he simply shook his head and stepped ahead of Sam, trying to reclaim his wife's office as his own by rearranging the items on her desk. "Let's go inside," he said. "Let's go back to the house."

When they got there, it was as if the incident had been forgotten, but it sat heavily with Sam, who felt the shame of an otherwise decent man who has inexplicably let himself down. Why had he allowed himself to behave in such a way? It was Paul, oddly, who broke the impasse between them, phoning Sam two days later and inviting him to dinner at the house. No sooner was he inside the door than Sam was apologizing for what had happened. Paul waved away the incident and invited him into the kitchen, where a homemade lasagne—prepared by a worried neighbour—was baking in the oven. He poured two glasses of red wine and sat at the table.

"I've been thinking a lot about your eulogy," he said. "One particular section."

This made Gaddis uneasy. He had been honest about Charlotte's shortcomings in his speech, her ruthlessness in the early years of her career, her habit of abandoning friends who did not live up to expectations. Paul had asked for a printed copy and might easily have taken offence.

"Which section?" he asked.

Gaddis saw that Paul was holding the eulogy in his hand. He began to read aloud: "In our lives, if we are lucky, we occasionally meet exceptional people. Sometimes, if we are even luckier, those people become our friends." Paul stopped and cleared his throat before continuing. "Charlotte was not just one of the most exceptional people that I have ever met, she was also my most treasured friend. I envied her and I admired her. I thought that she was reckless but I also thought that she was brave. Dostoyevsky wrote: 'If you want to be respected by others, the great thing is to respect yourself. Only by self-respect will you compel others to respect you.' I cannot think of another person to whom this applies more than Charlotte Berg. And so death continues to take the best people first."

Gaddis put his hand on Paul's shoulder.

"You were absolutely right about that. I just wanted to tell you that what you said has been a great support to me."

"I'm glad."

"And I thought about what you were doing in her office. I tried to imagine what Charlotte would have made of it." Gaddis began to respond but Paul interrupted him. "I think she would have done the same thing. Or, at least, I think she would have understood why you were there. You wanted to go into her office to see where she had been that morning, to get close to her, as you said at the time. You found yourself reminded of Edward Crane, you became distracted by the possibility of looking at her research. It was a long day. You were tired."

"I was snooping," Gaddis replied bluntly. He was touched that Paul had tried to find a way of forgiving him, but didn't want to be let off the hook. "I was saying good-bye to the Cambridge book. I knew it was over and I was feeling sorry for myself."

"What do you mean you knew it was over? Why?"

The reply to the question seemed so obvious that Gaddis did not bother making it. Paul went to the oven and checked the lasagne. He seemed more at ease than he had been two days earlier; his privacy had been restored. He had the luxury of being alone with his grief. Turning, he said: "Why don't you keep going? Why don't you take a look at Charlotte's research and try to work it up into a book?"

Gaddis could think of nothing to say. Paul saw his confused reaction and tried to convince him.

"I don't want her efforts to go to waste. She'd agreed to write a book with you. She would have wanted you to continue."

"Paul, I'm not an investigative journalist, I'm an archives man."

"What's the difference? You interview people, don't you? You can follow a trail from A to B. You know how to use a telephone, the Internet, a public library? How hard can it be?"

Gaddis was taking a packet of cigarettes from his jacket but it was just a reflex and he quickly replaced them, fearful of seeming tactless.

"Go ahead and smoke."

"I'm fine. I'm going to quit."

"Listen"—Paul switched off the oven, took out the food—"I won't take no for an answer. Next time you have a free afternoon, come up to the house. Have a look through Charlotte's research and see what you make of it. If you think she was on to something, if you think you can track down this Cambridge spy, write the book and put Charlotte's name alongside yours." He made an uncharacteristically extravagant gesture with his hand. "You have my blessing, Doctor. Go forth."

7

As it turned out, Gaddis didn't need much persuading. A letter had arrived from his accountant flagging up the outstanding tax bill. At the weekend, he had sat through a telephone conversation with Natasha, who was worried that Min would have to drop out of school altogether if the fees weren't paid by Christmas. Needing to secure an advance as quickly as possible, he had no choice but to set to work on the Cambridge book and to put together a proposal for Paterson.

Paul had left a set of keys at a newsagent in Hampstead. Gaddis let himself into the house late on Monday morning. He made a cup of coffee in the kitchen, found Charlotte's laptop, and walked out to the garden. He went to the shed, closing the door behind him. There was a cobweb in the apex of the roof and he felt that he could still catch the faint smell of Charlotte's perfume, a thing which unsettled him. A pen mark was scrawled down one wall, torn newspaper cuttings and postcards pinned to a mottled corkboard which looked as if it had succumbed to a bout of woodworm.

Sitting down, his arms braced on the desk in front of him, he experienced an acute sense of trespass and wondered if he should just stand up and walk away from the whole thing. Was he honouring Charlotte's memory or just making a fast buck?

A bit of both, he admitted to himself. A bit of both.

He opened the laptop and powered it up, pushing the plug into a socket in the wall. He did the same with her mobile phone, realizing at once that there would be text messages and voicemails from friends and colleagues who had not yet learned of Charlotte's death. Sure enough, the phone beeped repeatedly as it powered up, three texts from people whose names he did not recognize. He took down the numbers on a scrap of newspaper and knew that, before the day was out, he would have to phone them and tell them that Charlotte Berg had passed away.

There were so many files, so many folders and photographs on the computer's desktop that Sam was at first overwhelmed. Where to begin? He thought of his own computer at UCL, of the thousands of e-mails and essays, research notes and photographs which, if accessed, would build up to an almost total picture of his personal and professional life. How does a person begin to pick his way through that?

He double-clicked all of the documents on her desktop, one by one, moving across the field of files, none of which appeared to relate to the Cambridge investigation. To simplify things, he ran a hard drive search for "Edward Crane" and "Thomas Neame," but the results were meaningless. He tried "Philby," "Blunt," "Maclean," "Burgess," and "Cairncross," but again drew a blank. There was clearly no first draft of Charlotte's story, no interview transcripts, no notes. It was as if they had been wiped away.

Towards midday, Gaddis became so frustrated that he sent Paul a text message with the question: DID C USE A SECOND COMPUTER? to which Paul replied: NOT TO MY KNOWLEDGE. None of her e-mails related to work on the story. Searches for "Cambridge," "Neame," and "Crane" within Outlook also proved useless. He concluded that Charlotte must have been carrying around most of the research in her head.

Towards two o'clock, Gaddis found a small, alphabetized box of files, designed as a portable case, in the far corner of the office. He opened it and began to go through her private papers: bank statements; details of her pension plan; letters from accountants. All of it would have to be given to Paul, who had been left with the task of completing probate. Another box contained cuttings from newspaper and magazine articles which Charlotte had written, dating back to the early 1990s, a gone-away world of Clinton and Lewinsky, of Rwanda and Timothy McVeigh.

At last he discovered something which he was sure would start him on the path to Thomas Neame: a Sony digital recorder lodged in the inside pocket of a coat which Charlotte had left hanging behind the door of her office. Gaddis switched it on, but found only an old interview about Afghanistan. It was as if the Cambridge investigation had never taken place. Had she made a deliberate decision to write nothing down? What else could explain the complete absence of a paper trail?

By three o'clock, Gaddis was hungry and stir-crazy. He took out an entire drawer from her desk and carried it into the kitchen, where he microwaved a supermarket chili con carne and ate it while picking through the contents. The drawer was awash in gas bills, half-finished strips of ibuprofen, chequebooks, and rubber bands. Chaos. He was reminded of Holly's flat and sent her a text message to which she did not respond.

Finally, while mopping up the dregs of the chili with a hunk of stale bread, he found an envelope of expenses receipts, dated within two months of Charlotte's death. Gaddis pushed the plate to one side and poured the receipts, perhaps thirty or forty of them, onto the table. He might as well have been looking at grains of rice. How was a till receipt from WH Smith going to lead him to Edward Crane? He said to himself, in an audible whisper: "You're an idiot," and put the receipts back in the envelope. Then he found a beer in Paul's fridge, drank it from the bottle, and contemplated the possibility of going into the garden for a smoke. He had given up cigarettes twenty-four hours earlier. Was one more packet going to give him lung cancer? Would five quid break the bank? No.

He drained the beer, took Paul's house keys from the kitchen table, and headed towards the front door. He would buy a packet of Camels, his usual brand, on Hampstead High Street and, when they were finished, quit for good. No point in spending a torturous day in

Charlotte's house without the backup of tobacco. It was counterproductive.

As he was opening the front door, jingling a lighter against the loose change in his pocket, a gust of wind shot into the house, sending junk mail scattering down the corridor. Gaddis spotted one of Charlotte's handbags on a hook behind the door. He closed the door, took the bag down, and freed the brass catch. Her wallet was inside, bulging with credit cards and cash. He took the billfold out and held it in his hand. Of all the objects which had belonged to Charlotte that he had touched that day, this was the one to trigger his grief. A hoop of sadness came up through his body and he had to stop for a moment to compose himself. There was £120 in cash in the wallet, as well as a press ID card and several more receipts. He wondered if the credit cards had been cancelled. Should he do that himself and save Paul the trouble? Visible behind a plastic cover, perhaps so that Charlotte could press the purse against a ticket machine without the need to take it out, was an Oyster card. Thanks to the common room ravings of a colleague at UCL who was obsessed, to the point of paranoia, by the "surveillance society," Gaddis knew that it was possible to go to any Tube station in London and to see a computer listing for the last ten journeys undertaken by Oyster. That gave him a plan. If he could discover where Charlotte had travelled in the last few days of her life, he might be able to match that information to details on her phone bills or expenses receipts. This would at least provide him with the possibility of a link to Thomas Neame.

At Hampstead station he queued behind a backpacking German tourist and placed the Oyster on a reader at the ticket machine. What he saw intrigued him. The same five journeys, there and back, over a period of fifteen days, from Finchley Road station, which was a fifteen-minute walk from Charlotte's house, to Rickmansworth, in the suburbs of northwest London. He found a Tube map and traced the simple journey north on the Metropolitan line. It would have taken about forty minutes. For some reason, this small triumph of amateur detection was enough to persuade him not to buy the cigarettes, and Gaddis returned to the house with a renewed sense of purpose.

He took the receipts from the envelope a second time, pouring them onto the kitchen table: WH Smith's, Daunt Books, Transport for London. Some writing caught his eye: scrawled on the back of two receipts which were from the same pub in Chorleywood, Charlotte had written: *Lunch C Somers.* The dates matched the days on which she had travelled north from Finchley. Gaddis knew that Chorleywood and Rickmansworth were no more than a couple of miles apart. He went back outside and returned to the computer, running a search for the name "Somers." Nothing came up. Just the same black hole of false leads and dead ends which had wiped out his morning.

Perhaps she had made telephone calls to a landline in the Rickmansworth area? Gaddis typed "Dialling code for Rickmansworth" into Google and wrote down the number: 01923. The same prefix was listed for Chorleywood. He then checked the results against an itemized phone bill which he had discovered while drinking a cup of coffee at her desk almost five hours earlier. Sure enough, in the three weeks of her journeys from Finchley, Charlotte had made half a dozen calls to the same 01923 number. Gaddis took his own phone from the pocket of his coat and dialled it.

A woman answered, bored to the point of despair.

"Mount Vernon Hospital."

Gaddis said, "Hello?" because he was unsure precisely what she had said and wanted it repeated.

"*Yes,*" she said, sounding impatient. "Mount Vernon Hospital."

He scribbled the name down. "Please. Yes. I'm looking for a patient of yours. Thomas Neame. Would it be possible to speak to him?"

The line went dead. Gaddis assumed that he was being connected to a separate part of the hospital. If Neame answered, what the hell was he going to say? He hadn't thought things through. He couldn't even be sure that the old man would know what had happened to Charlotte. He would have to tell him about her heart attack and then somehow explain his interest in Edward Crane.

"Sir?" It was the receptionist again. Her tone was fractionally less hostile. "We don't have a patient of that name here."

There didn't seem to be any future in asking to check the spelling of "Neame." Nor could he enquire about Somers. The receptionist might smell a rat. Instead Gaddis thanked her, hung up, and called Paul at work.

"Do you have a relative who works at the Mount Vernon Hospital in Rickmansworth?"

"Come again?"

"Rickmansworth. Chorleywood. Hertfordshire suburbs."

"Never been there in my life."

"What about Charlotte? Could she have had a relative up there or a friend that she was visiting?"

"Not to my knowledge."

Somers was obviously the key. But was he a patient at the hospital or a member of staff? Gaddis redialled Mount Vernon using the phone in the house and was put through to a different receptionist.

"Could I speak to Doctor Somers, please?"

"*Doctor* Somers?"

It was the wrong call. Somers was a patient, a porter, a nurse.

"Sorry . . ."

"You mean Calvin?"

The Christian name was a lucky break. "Yes."

"Calvin's not a doctor."

"Of course not. Did I say that? I wasn't concentr—"

"He's a senior nurse in Michael Sobel." Gaddis scrawled down *Michael Sobel*. "He's not due back on shift until the morning. Is there anything else? Would you like to leave a message for him?"

"No, no message."

Gaddis replaced the receiver. He pulled up Google on Charlotte's computer. Michael Sobel was the name of a new cancer treatment centre at the Mount Vernon. He would go there in the morning. If he could find Somers on shift, he might be able to find out why Charlotte Berg kept taking him out to lunch in the days leading up to her death. That information, at the very least, would take him a step closer to Edward Crane.

8

The Mount Vernon Hospital was only half an hour by car from Gaddis's house in west London, but he took the Tube in order to re-create, largely for sentimental reasons, the journey on the Metropolitan line which Charlotte had taken from Finchley Road to Rickmansworth in the last week of her life.

These were the suburbs of his childhood, red-brick, post-war houses of indistinct character with gardens just large enough to play a game of swingball or French cricket. He remembered his racquet-wielding father launching a tennis ball into near-orbit one hot summer afternoon, a yellow dot disappearing towards the sun. The train passed through Harrow, Pinner, Northwood Hills, the indifferent streets and parks of outer London, starved of sunlight. The hospital itself, far from being the gleaming twenty-first-century new-build of Gaddis's imagination, was a vaguely sinister, neo-Gothic mansion with a gabled roof and views across the Hertfordshire countryside. It looked like the sort of place that a soldier might have gone to recuperate in the aftermath of World War II; he could picture starchy nurses attending to men in wheelchairs, veterans and their visitors spread out across the spacious lawn like guests at a garden party.

Gaddis had taken a taxi from Rickmansworth station and was deposited at the hospital's main reception, located in a modern building a few hundred metres east of the mansion. He followed the signs to the Michael Sobel Centre and drifted around the ground floor until a female doctor, no older than most of his students, saw that Gaddis was lost, offered him an accommodating smile, and asked if she could "help in any way."

"I'm looking for one of the nurses here. Calvin." He had assumed that the use of Somers's Christian name might generate an effect of familiarity. "Is he around?"

The doctor was wearing a stethoscope around her neck, like a gesture to Central Casting. She took a good long look at his shoes. Gaddis never gave much thought to his appearance and wondered what it was that people thought they could discern from analysing a stranger's footwear. Today, he was wearing a pair of scuffed desert boots. In the eyes of a pretty twenty-five-year-old doctor, was that a good or a bad thing?

"Calvin? Sure," she said, her face suddenly opening up to him. It was as if he had passed some unspecified test. "I've seen him around this morning. He has an office on the second floor, just beyond Pathology. Do you know it?"

"It's my first time," Gaddis replied. He was not a natural liar and there seemed no point in misleading her. The doctor duly gave him directions, all the while touching her stethoscope. Two minutes later, Gaddis was standing at the door of Somers's office, knocking on chipped paint.

"Enter."

The voice was reedy and slightly strangulated. Gaddis put an age and appearance to it before he had even turned the handle. Sure enough, Calvin Somers was midforties, slightly built, with the stubborn, defensive features of a man who has spent the bulk of his life wrestling a corrosive insecurity. He was wearing a pale green nurse's uniform and there was gel in his thinning black hair. Sam Gaddis had good instincts about people and he disliked Calvin Somers on sight.

"Mr. Somers?"

"Who wants to know?"

It was a smartarse line from a second-rate American cop show. Gaddis almost laughed.

"I was a friend of Charlotte Berg's," he said. "My name is Sam Gaddis. I'm an academic. I wondered if you might have time for a quick chat?"

He had closed the door behind him as he asked the question and Somers looked grateful for the privacy. The mention of Charlotte's name had caught him off guard; there was perhaps some shameful or calculating element to their relationship which he was keen to obscure.

"*Was?*" Somers had noted the use of the past tense. He pulled himself up in his chair but did not stand to shake Gaddis's hand, as if by doing so he might undermine an idea he possessed of his own innate authority. Gaddis noticed that his right hand was spinning a ballpoint pen nervously around the surface of his desk.

"I'm afraid I have some bad news," he said.

"And what's that?"

The manner was artificially confident, even supercilious. Gaddis watched Somers's face carefully.

"Charlotte had a heart attack. Suddenly. Last week. I think you may have been one of the last people to see her alive."

"She *what?*"

The reaction was one of annoyance, rather than shock. Somers was looking at Gaddis in the way that you might look at a person who has just fired you.

"She's dead," Gaddis felt obliged to repeat, though he was angered by the callous response. "And she was a friend of mine."

Somers stood up in the narrow office, walked past Gaddis, and double-checked that the door was properly closed. A man with a secret. He carried with him a strange, mingled smell of cheap aftershave and hospital disinfectant.

"And you've come to give me the three grand, have you?"

It was a completely unexpected remark. Why was Charlotte in debt to this prick by £3,000? Gaddis frowned and said: "What's that?" as he took a small, disbelieving step backwards.

"I said have you brought the three grand?" Somers sat at the edge of his desk. "You say you were a friend of hers, she obviously told you about our arrangement or you wouldn't be here. Were you working on the story together?"

"What story?" It was an instinctive tactic, a means of protecting his scoop, but Gaddis saw that it was the wrong move. Somers shot him a withering glance that developed into a smile which bared surprisingly polished teeth.

"Probably best if you don't play the innocent," he sneered. Two sheets of paper slid off the desk beside him, undermining the remark's dramatic impact. Somers was obliged to stoop down and pick them up as they floated to the ground.

"Nobody's playing the innocent, Calvin. I'm just trying to ascertain who you are and what your relationship was with my friend. If it helps, I can tell you that I'm a senior lecturer in Russian History at UCL. In other words, I am not a journalist. I'm just an interested party. I am not a threat to you."

"Who said anything about a threat?"

Somers was back in his chair again, swivelling, trying to regain control. Gaddis saw now that this embittered, hostile man had probably felt threatened for most of his adult life; men like Calvin Somers could not afford to display a moment's self-doubt. The room had grown hot, central heating pumping out of a radiator beneath a locked window. Gaddis removed his jacket and hooked it on the door.

"Let's start again," he said. He was used to awkward conversations in cramped rooms. Students complaining. Students crying. Every week at UCL brought a fresh crisis to his office: illness, bereavement, poverty. Students and colleagues alike came to Sam Gaddis with their problems.

"Why did Charlotte owe you money?" he asked. He set his voice low, trying to offload any inference from the question. "Why hadn't she paid you?"

A laugh. Not from the belly but from the throat. Somers shook his head.

"I'll tell you what, Professor. Cough up the money and I'll talk to you. Get me three thousand quid in the next six hours and I'll tell you what your friend Charlotte was paying me to tell her. If not, then can I politely ask you to get the fuck out of my office? I'm not sure I appreciate strangers coming to my place of work and—"

"Fine." Gaddis took the sting out of the attack by raising his hand in a gesture of conciliation. It was a moment of considerable self-control on his part, because he would rather have grabbed Somers by the narrow lapels of his cheap polyester nurse's uniform and flung him against the radiator. He would prefer to have coaxed even the smallest gesture of respect for Charlotte out of this shiftless parasite, but he needed to keep Calvin Somers onside. The nurse was the link to Neame. Without him, there was no Edward Crane. "I'll get the money," he said, with no idea how he would find £3,000 before sunset.

"You will?" Somers seemed almost to wilt at the prospect of it.

"Sure. I won't be able to get more than a thousand out on my cards today, but if you'll accept a cheque as a guarantee of good faith, I'm sure we can come to some kind of an arrangement."

Somers looked shocked, but Gaddis could see that a promise of immediate payment had done the trick. The nurse was ready to spill his guts.

"I get off shift later this afternoon," he said. His earlier antagonism had entirely evaporated. "Do you know Batchworth Lake?"

Gaddis said that he did not.

"It's in a stretch of parkland. Runs beside the Grand Union Canal. Follow signs to the Three Rivers District Council and you'll find it." Gaddis was astonished by how rapidly Somers was making arrangements for delivery of the cash. "Meet me in the car park there at five o'clock. If you've got the money, I'll talk. Agreed?"

"Agreed," said Gaddis, though the deal had been struck so quickly that he wondered if he was being played. Why hadn't Charlotte paid this man? Was the information he possessed even worthwhile? Somers could have accomplices, engaged in a simple con. It was quite possible that Gaddis would now go back to Rickmansworth, withdraw a large sum of money from his bank accounts, hand it to Calvin Somers, and be told only that the Earth was round and that there were seven days in the week.

"What guarantees do I have that you have the kind of information I'm looking for?"

Somers paused. He picked up the pen and began tapping it on the desk. Somebody walked past the office, whistling the theme tune to *EastEnders*.

"Oh, I've got the information you're looking for," he said. "You see, I know about St. Mary's Paddington. I know what that nice MI6 did to Mr. Edward Crane."

9

Curry Night—Wednesday.

Gaddis was staring at the poster tacked up on the wall of the pub in West Hyde. The jukebox had shifted to a song he didn't recognize, an antimelodic squawk run through software and drum machines. Somers had gone to the Gents' again, his second visit inside half an hour. Was he nervous, or had the peanuts disagreed with him? Gaddis didn't much care either way.

Seven hours earlier, in a trance of determination to find out what Somers knew, he had called for a taxi and driven from Mount Vernon Hospital to a supermarket three miles up the road. At a cash machine he had withdrawn £1,000 on three separate cards, maxing out his current account, putting £400 on his already debt-ridden Visa bill, and, to his shame, making up the difference with £100 from an account set up in Min's name which contained christening money given to her by her godparents. That had been an absolute low point and he promised himself that he would put £500 back in the account as soon as he received the signature advance on the book.

As arranged, Somers had been waiting for him in the car park.

Gaddis had handed over the cash, along with a post-dated cheque for £2,000. He had then accompanied Somers on their damp, enlightening walk along the banks of the Grand Union Canal.

This is what he now knew. That in February 1992, Sir John Brennan, currently the head of the Secret Intelligence Service, had bribed four people to fake the death of Edward Anthony Crane, a former Foreign Office diplomat prominent enough to earn an obituary—albeit one that had been faked—in *The Times*. Crane was now almost certainly living under an assumed name in some FCO variant of the Witness Protection Programme, his whereabouts known only to Brennan and certain privileged members of MI6.

"So who do you think he was?" he asked Somers. "Why do you think it was necessary to kill him?"

"Search me."

Gaddis had put the questions as a means of discovering what, if anything, Somers had subsequently discovered about Crane's identity.

"You never looked into it? You never saw Brennan again?"

"Haven't we been over this?" Somers picked up his pint and drained it. In the bathroom, he had swept his hair back with the assistance of a little water; the collar of his shirt had become soft and wet as a result. "Like I said, all I know is that MI6 was prepared to fake someone's death. So I conclude from this that the person involved must have been important, right? You see, I've been a nurse for over fifteen years, Professor. I've met a lot of other nurses. And when we get together, at the Christmas party, say, or a leaving do, it's surprising how rarely we talk about being asked to pretend that someone's dead. It's not a daily occurrence. It's not something we're trained for. In fact, the departure of Edward Crane from planet Earth is probably the only time in the long and distinguished history of the National Health Service that something like that has happened."

"Drink?" Far from annoying him, the speech had reassured Gaddis that Somers knew nothing about Crane's link to the Cambridge spies.

"What?"

"I said, do you want another drink, Calvin? My round."

Somers looked at his watch. The strap was worn, the freckled wrist slim and pale.

"Nah. I've got to go." Gaddis stared at him, deadening his lively eyes. It was a trick he sometimes employed on particularly recalcitrant students and it had the desired effect. Somers looked immediately sheepish and said: "Unless, of course, you're not satisfied that you've got your money's worth."

Gaddis moved very slightly to one side. "One more question."

"And what's that?"

Two more smokers moved past the table and disappeared outside. A cold blast of wind ran through the open door.

"How were you first introduced to Charlotte? How did you find her?"

"Oh, that's easy."

"What do you mean 'easy'?"

"Bloke called Neame put her on to me."

"And would you have any idea how I can find him?"

10

It looked as though Thomas Neame did not want to be found.

He wasn't in the phone book. He couldn't be traced online. Charlotte had told Gaddis nothing about his life, even less about his whereabouts. All he knew was that Neame was Crane's oldest friend—his "confessor," to use Charlotte's description—and was willing to reveal everything about Crane's work for the KGB. He was "ninety-one going on seventy-five" and still in robust good health. How had Charlotte put it? "Very tough and fit, sort of war-generation Scot who can smoke forty a day and still pop to the top of Ben Nevis before breakfast."

Why had she mentioned Ben Nevis? Was there a clue in that? Did Neame live in Scotland? Gaddis was lying in bed one night when that thought came to him, but it moved on as quickly as a car passing outside in the street. After all, what was he going to do about it? Take the sleeper to Fort William and start knocking on doors? It would be another wild goose chase.

Over a period of several days he went through the files that had been given to him by Holly Levette, but found no mention of Neame's name. He felt, as each fruitless search led to the next, as though he was standing in a long queue that had not moved for hours. Gaddis had no contacts in the police, no friend in the Inland Revenue, and certainly no money to spend on a professional investigator who might be able to dig around in Neame's past. He did not even know where Neame had been to school. Always in the back of his mind was the humiliating thought that he had handed Calvin Somers £3,000 for what was effectively no more than a dinner party anecdote.

It helped that Gaddis wasn't melancholy or defeatist by nature. Four days after meeting Somers in the pub, he decided to abandon the search for Neame and to concentrate instead directly on Edward Crane. He would, in effect, be looking for a man who no longer existed, yet that prospect did not unsettle him. Historians specialize in the dead. Sam Gaddis had spent his entire career bringing people he had never met, faces he had never seen, names he had read about only in the pages of books, vividly to life. He was a specialist in reconstruction. He knew how to piece together the fragments of a stranger's existence, to work through an archive, to pan the stream of history to reveal a nugget of priceless information.

First off, he made a visit to the British Library's newspaper archive in Colindale, retrieving Crane's faked obituary and making a copy of it from a 1992 microfilm of *The Times*. There was no photograph accompanying the piece, but the text matched the broad facts that Somers had given him beside the canal: that Crane had been educated at Marlborough and Trinity College; that the Foreign Office, over a twenty-year period, had posted him to Russia, Argentina, and Germany; that he had never married or produced any children. Further biographical information was thin on the ground, but Gaddis was certain that some of it would later prove useful. The obituary stated that Crane had been sent to Greece in 1938 and had spent several years in Italy after the war. It transpired that his mother had been a society beauty, twice married, whose first husband—Crane's father—was a middle-ranking civil servant in India who was later briefly imprisoned for embezzlement. In Argentina, in the 1960s, Crane had been seconded to a British diplomat whom the obituarist—perhaps with a flourish of poetic licence—suspected of having an affair with Eva Peron. Having retired from the Foreign Office, Crane had sat on the board of several leading corporations, including a well-known British oil company and a German investment bank with an office in Berlin.

Two days later, Gaddis drove the short journey from his house in Shepherd's Bush, via Chiswick, to the National Archives, a complex of buildings in Kew which stores official government records. At the enquiries desk he made a formal request for Crane's war record and ran Crane's name through the computerized database. The search produced more than five hundred results, most of them relating to Edward Cranes born in the eighteenth or nineteenth centuries. Gaddis tried "Thomas" and "Tommy" and "Tom Neame" but found only the Medal Card of a Thomas Neame who had been a private in the Welsh Regiment and Army Service Corps between 1914 and 1920. The wrong generation. Another dead end.

Finally, he got lucky. A National Archives assistant directed Gaddis to the Foreign Office Lists, which comprised several shelves of well-thumbed hardback volumes in burgundy leather containing basic biographical information about employees of the Foreign Office. He picked up the volume marked "1947" and began searching the Statement of Services for the surname "Crane." What he saw almost brought him to his feet with relief. Here, at last, was concrete proof of ATTILA's existence.

CRANE, EDWARD ANTHONY

Born 10 December 1916. Educated at Marlborough College, and Trinity Hall, Cambridge. Granted a Certificate as 3rd Secretary in the Foreign Office, 11 October 1937, and appointed to the Foreign Office, 17 October 1937. Transferred to Athens, 21 August 1938. Transferred to the Foreign Office, 5 June 1940. Promoted to be 2nd Secretary, 15 November 1942. Transferred to Paris, 2 November 1944. Promoted to be an Acting 1st Secretary, 15 December 1944.

He went back to the shelves and drew out the List for 1965, which was the last available volume before the Foreign Office records were computerized. By then, Crane had served all over the world but, as the obituary confirmed, had never been promoted to ambassador. Why?

Did it have something to do with the fact that Crane had never married? Was he homosexual, and therefore—back in those days—regarded as unreliable? Or had the government, in the wake of Burgess and Maclean, developed suspicions about Crane's links to Soviet Russia?

Charlotte had told Gaddis that Crane had been known to the Ring of Five, so he picked up the volume for 1953. When he found what he was looking for, he experienced that particular buzz to which he had been addicted for more than twenty years: the thrill of history coming alive at his fingertips.

BURGESS, GUY FRANCIS DE MONCY
Born 16 April 1911. Educated at Eton College, and Trinity Hall, Cambridge. Granted a Certificate for Branch B of the Foreign Service 1 October 1947 and appointed with effect from 1 January 1947 to be an Officer, Grade 4. Transferred to Washington as 2nd Secretary, 7 August 1950. Suspended from duty, 1 June 1951. Appointment terminated 1 June 1952, with effect from 1 June 1951.

Donald Maclean was included in the same volume:

MACLEAN, DONALD DUART
Born 25 May 1913. Educated at Gresham's School, Holt, and Trinity Hall, Cambridge. M. 1940, Melinda Marling. Granted a Certificate as 3rd Secretary in the Foreign Office or Diplomatic Service, 11 October 1935, and appointed to the Foreign Office, 15 October 1935. Transferred to Paris, 24 September 1938. Transferred to the Foreign Office, 18 June 1940.

This last detail caught Gaddis's eye. Crane had also been posted back to London in June 1940. Had he worked alongside Maclean? Were the two men friends?

The entry continued:

Promoted to be a 2nd Secretary, 15 October 1940. Transferred to Washington, 2 May 1944. Promoted to be an Acting 1st Secretary, 27 December 1944. Promoted to be a Foreign Service Officer, Grade 6, 25 October 1948, and appointed Counsellor at Cairo, 7 November

1948. Transferred to the Foreign Office and appointed Head of American dept., 6 November 1950. Suspended from duty, 1 June 1951. Appointment terminated 1 June 1952, with effect from 1 June 1951.

The same phrases. "Appointment terminated." "Suspended from duty." 1951 had marked Burgess and Maclean's flight from England. Two of Her Majesty's brightest stars escaping to Moscow aboard a cross-Channel ferry on a cold spring morning, tipped off—by their fellow traitors, Kim Philby and Anthony Blunt—that MI5 had exposed them as agents of the KGB.

Gaddis now looked for Philby's name, under *P* in the Statement of Services. Nothing. He picked up the Foreign Office List from 1942 and drew the same blank. Gaddis checked the volume for 1960. Again, no mention of Philby. Why had he not been included in the list of Foreign Office employees? Did MI6 officers enjoy anonymity? Gaddis began to go through every volume of the List, from 1940 to 1959, finding no reference to Philby at any stage. Instead, he stumbled upon an anomaly: Edward Crane's listings disappeared between 1946 and 1952, the period in which *The Times* obituary had placed him in Italy. Had he joined MI6 during this period? Or had Crane taken an extended postwar sabbatical? There were so many questions; too many, if Gaddis was honest with himself. To research a story on this scale, to do justice to Charlotte's book, would take years, not months. There were historians who had dedicated their lives to the search for the sixth man; none of them had been successful. If only he could track down a surviving employee of the Foreign Office who might have known Crane. Surely there was a colleague who had sat on the same delegation or attended a conference at which Crane had been present?

Towards midday he walked downstairs, ate a tasteless cheese sandwich at the National Archives café, and took a seat at a public Internet terminal. He had one more line of enquiry: a colleague at UCL had tipped him off that senior diplomats often deposited their papers and private correspondence in the archive at Churchill College, Cambridge. Gaddis might find a cross-reference between Crane and, say, a retired British ambassador to Argentina, or a 1st Secretary in Berlin. Seagulls were clacking outside as he typed "Churchill College, Cambridge" into Google. He pulled up the Janus Webserver at Cambridge and typed "Edward Crane" into the search bar. Three catalogue entries came up, none of which made specific reference to Crane. When he typed in "Thomas Neame," the server returned no results at all.

It was hugely frustrating. He went out to the car park, found an old packet of Camels in the glove box of his car, and abandoned his latest attempt to quit. The cigarette did little to ease his mood and he drove back to Shepherd's Bush under light autumnal rain. It was as if all mention of Crane and Neame had been deliberately and methodically erased from the historical record. Why else was it proving so difficult to track them down? He had never known such slow progress on the early stages of a project. Locked in heavy traffic on the M4, Gaddis made a decision to take a flight to Moscow and to approach Crane from the Russian side. If ATTILA was a prized KGB asset, as Charlotte had claimed, somewhere in the vaults of Soviet Intelligence there would be a file on Edward Crane. Whether or not, in the wake of *Tsars,* he would be granted access to the files by the Russian authorities was a different matter altogether.

11

Ordinarily, the activities of an anonymous London academic conducting research at the National Archives in Kew would not have been drawn to the attention of the head of the Secret Intelligence Service. But Edward Crane was no ordinary spy. When Gaddis had made a formal request for his war record, an automated alert had been sent from Kew to Sir John Brennan's private office at MI6 headquarters. When Gaddis had then typed "Edward Crane" and, minutes later, "Thomas Neame" into Google on a public computer, a second automated message had flashed up at Vauxhall Cross. Within an hour, Brennan's secretary was placing a report on his desk.

PERSONAL FOR C / GOV86ALERT / 11-1545-09
Samuel Gaddis, Doctor of Russian History at UCL School of Slavonic and East European Studies (SSEES), made a formal request this morning at NA/KEW for the war record of Edward Anthony Crane.

Alert shows that a member of the public, also thought to be Gaddis, later conducted separate, related Google searches on a public computer at NA/KEW for "Edward Crane" and "Thomas Neame."

By the end of the day, Sir John Brennan had discovered, via a third automated message, that Gaddis had also run Crane and Neame through the Janus server at Churchill College, Cambridge. Who had tipped him off? Less than half a dozen people on the planet knew about the ATTILA coverup. What had happened to make one of them start talking?

He found Neame's number in his desk and dialled his private room at the nursing home in Winchester. It had been six months since Brennan had last given any thought to Edward Crane, and years since he had used the Henderson alias. For all he knew, Thomas Neame was dead.

The number rang nine times. Brennan was about to hang up when the old man picked up, his voice dry and cracked as he said: "Two double one seven."

"Mr. Neame? This is Douglas Henderson. I'm calling you from London."

"Good Lord! Douglas. How long has it been?"

The accent was as clear and precise as the wireless announcers of Neame's youth.

"I'm very well, Tom. And you? How are you keeping?"

"Oh, can't complain at my age. So, so. To what do I owe the pleasure?"

"Business, I'm afraid."

"It always is, isn't it?"

Brennan heard the note change in Neame's voice, the charm going out of it. "Have you been talking to anyone, Tom?" he asked. "Had any visitors to your room? Been roaming around the Internet?"

Neame feigned ignorance. "The *what?*" He was ninety-one years old and could comfortably pass for a Luddite, but Brennan recalled very well how much he liked to play the fool.

"The Internet, Tom. I'm sure you've heard of it. Tim Berners-Lee. The World Wide Web. Bringing us all closer together. Pulling us all further apart."

"Oh, the *Internet.* Yes. What about it?"

"Let me be frank." Brennan was looking out at the grey Thames, pleasure boats sliding towards another winter. "Have you been in contact recently with anybody in relation to our friend Mr. Crane?"

A prolonged silence. Brennan couldn't tell if Neame was offended by the question or merely struggling to put together a reply. At one point it sounded as though he might have fallen asleep.

The old man eventually spoke. "Eddie? Good God, no. Haven't thought about him for twenty years."

"It hasn't been that long," Brennan replied quickly. "An academic by the name of Samuel Gaddis has been asking questions. About you. About him. Running around Kew, requesting war records, that sort of thing."

"About bloody time."

Brennan was stopped short. "What does that mean?"

"It means exactly what you think it means. It means that it was only a matter of time before somebody started scratching around. You chaps couldn't keep a secret like that forever."

"We've done a pretty good job of keeping it secret for the past fifty years."

When Neame did not respond, Brennan decided to take a risk. "So, are you helping him scratch around? Are you throwing light on Eddie's past for some reason? I'm sorry, but it's my duty to ask." He was surprised that he had landed the accusation so directly.

"Don't be bloody ridiculous. Every part of my body aches. I need help getting into the bath. If I walk down the corridor, a nurse has to hold my hand. I can barely remember my own name." The words sounded heartfelt, but when it came to Thomas Neame, Brennan didn't know what to believe. "You know I've always taken a vow of silence about Eddie. If anybody came knocking on my door, I'd know what to do. And if this Gaddis chap, by some miracle, manages to associate me with him, believe me, I have ways and means of putting him off the scent."

That, at least, was true. "Well, that's good to hear."

"Was that all, Douglas?"

"That was all."

"Good. Then I will thank you to leave me in peace."

Brennan was, both by nature and by the definition of his chosen trade, a resourceful man, clear-sighted and unflappable. He would not allow the abruptness of Neame's mood to unsettle him. Three floors below there was an open-plan office awash with thumb-twiddling spooks: fast-stream *wünderkinds* eagerly awaiting their first postings overseas, as well as older hands whose idealism had long ago been broken by one too many stints in the godforsaken outposts of a vanished empire. As he replaced the receiver, he realized that he would need an attractive woman. There was no way around this, no denying the implications of gender, no means of avoiding the ancient human truth that bachelor academics are as vulnerable to attractive women as they are to a pay raise. Brennan already knew that Gaddis was divorced. He also knew—from a cursory glance at his Internet and telephone traffic—that he had recently been seeing a woman named Holly Levette, who was almost half his age. Given a choice between spending an evening with a charming, intelligent man, and a charming, intelligent woman, Dr. Samuel Gaddis was almost certainly going to opt for the latter.

One name sprang to mind immediately. Having spent two years as a graduate student at LSE prior to joining the Service, Tanya Acocella could speak the language of academia. She was fluent in Russian and had proved a vital, imaginative member of SIS Station in Tehran, playing a crucial role in the recent defection of a senior figure in the Iranian military. Since returning to London, Tanya had become engaged to her long-term boyfriend, much to the frustration of several fast-stream alpha males, and was scheduled to take a four-month sabbatical after her wedding in the summer. Matching her wits with an intellectual of Gaddis's calibre would be just the sort of challenge she would relish.

He put a call down to her desk. Three minutes later, Acocella was in the mirrored lift to the fifth floor. It was a measure of her self-confidence that she felt no need to check her appearance in the panelled glass.

"Tanya, do come in. Have a seat."

They exchanged pleasantries for no more than a few seconds; an officer of Acocella's calibre did not need to be put at her ease.

"I want you to put CHESAPEAKE to one side for a few weeks." CHESAPEAKE was an operation against a Russian diplomat in Washington whom SIS were sizing up for recruitment. Tanya was running the London end in conjunction with a junior colleague. "I've found something else to exercise your talents."

She nodded. "Of course."

Brennan stood up and paced in the direction of a bookshelf. He was aware that staff members who came into his office were often on their best behaviour. It was one of the drawbacks of his position: an excess of polite rigidity. Still, he stopped short of offering her a drink. A little hierarchical posturing never hurt anybody.

"Long ago," he began, "I learned that spying isn't about strengths in human nature—ideological conviction, duty, loyalty to one's country. Spying is about weaknesses—the lust for money, for status, for sex. This is the guilty secret of our secret trade."

Tanya felt that she was expected to agree with this thesis, so she said: "Right," and stared at Brennan's tie. He had a reputation in the Office for pompous longueurs.

"I'd like you to find out everything you can about a man named Samuel Gaddis. He's a doctor of Russian History at UCL, Department of Slavonic and East European Studies. Get close to him, befriend him, earn his trust. Gaddis has been digging around in a Cold War secret that the Office is rather keen to suppress."

"What sort of secret?"

There were other questions she wanted to ask. How close? Befriend in what way? Is Dr. Gaddis married? But she knew the nature of such operations. She would not be asked, nor would she be expected to do anything that would compromise her relationship with her fiancé.

"Long ago, the Service took into its employment a gentleman by the name of Edward Crane, who subsequently operated in various different guises." Brennan, now standing beside the bookshelf, drew a finger along the spine of a volume by Sir Winston Churchill. He did not attempt to keep an edge of the sensational from what he was about to say. "Crane was a graduate of Trinity College Cambridge in the 1930s." He looked into Tanya's eyes and waited for the penny to drop. "He was known to Messrs. Blunt and Philby, Messrs. Burgess and Maclean. He was an associate of John Cairncross. Do you follow?"

Tanya felt a lurch of shock which quickly warped into a feeling of profound satisfaction. How many people knew what she had just been told? The identity of the sixth man was the most carefully guarded secret of the Cold War.

"Crane's operational code name was ATTILA. He's managed to remain anonymous, largely because we've managed to keep people off his scent and largely because there was no record of ATTILA's activities in Mitrokhin." Tanya had a sense, even as Brennan was talking to her, that he was holding back a vital piece of information. "The finger was pointed at Victor Rothschild, the finger was pointed at Tom Driberg. Christ, at one point they even suspected Roger bloody Hollis. But nobody has ever identified Crane. Until now." Brennan pivoted away towards a broad, sunless window in the north corner of the office. "Doctor Gaddis is on the trail of a gentleman by the name of Thomas Neame, a ninety-one-year-old currently resident at a nursing home near Winchester. Neame, for reasons that I am not yet in a position to divulge, knows more or less all there is to know about Crane's work for the Russians. I've put some basic information in this file." He passed a slim manila envelope to Acocella, which she secured in her lap. "It goes without saying that this is a sealed operation. You will report solely and directly to me. I have given you the name of an officer at GCHQ Cheltenham who will assist you with any communications information you may require." Both of them took a beat to absorb the euphemism. "I don't have the manpower to spare on surveillance, so you'll be operating alone unless there are exceptional circumstances. Any questions?"

Tanya was experienced enough to send that one back over the net. It was better to say: "I think perhaps I should read the file first, sir," so that Brennan could be assured of her professionalism.

"Good." He seemed pleased. "Have a look at it, come up with a plan of attack."

She stood up, the file under her arm. "There was just one thing, sir."

Brennan was planning to open the door for her, but stopped mid-carpet. "Yes?"

"What did you mean when you referred to status, to sex, to the lust for money? Are you implying that these are particular weaknesses in the Gaddis character?"

Brennan reached for the door handle. "Well, who knows?" he said. "That will be for you to find out."

12

Some things are so obvious that they can embarrass you with their simplicity.

Gaddis had been working at home over the weekend—preparing a lecture for the new term at UCL, fixing a leaking pipe in his leaking bathroom—when he needed to boot up an old laptop in his office in order to find an e-mail sent to him by a colleague several years earlier. As he was scrolling through the cluttered inbox, he saw a cluster of e-mails sent to him by Charlotte from a Hotmail address that Paul had known nothing about: bergotte965@hotmail.com. Charlotte had set up the account during a difficult period in her marriage in order to communicate privately with three of her closest friends, Gaddis among them. It was a eureka moment, a solution that had been staring him in the face. More than a week had passed since Gaddis had spent the fruitless day in Hampstead searching through Charlotte's office. It had never occurred to him that she might have used Hotmail to communicate with Thomas Neame.

He needed a password, of course, but that was easy. Gaddis simply had to type Charlotte's mother's maiden name into a security check, give her date of birth, and the details were forwarded instantly to her Outlook inbox. Gaddis could access this via Webmail and within five minutes was staring at the messages.

It was like a sequence of lights illuminating a darkened highway. Before his eyes was a list of every main player in the St. Mary's cover-up. There were e-mails from Benedict Meisner, messages with the subject heading "Lucy Forman," as well as frequent exchanges with Calvin Somers. Gaddis had surely stumbled upon the key which would unlock the door of Charlotte's research. It was all here, everything he would need to find Neame.

He began with the Meisner correspondence, but quickly realized that it was a legal and factual dead end. Now working as a homeopathic doctor in Berlin, Meisner denied ever having met Calvin Somers or playing any role in faking the death of Edward Crane.

> As I have repeatedly pointed out to you, any suggestion that I was involved in gross professional misconduct of the sort you describe is as absurd as it is defamatory. Should you continue to pursue this matter, I would have no hesitation in instructing my lawyers to instigate proceedings against you, and against any newspaper or publication which chooses to publish these bizarre allegations.

Gaddis turned to the message with the subject heading "Lucy Forman." The e-mail was from Forman's sister. It transpired that Forman had died in a car accident in December 2001. In a second e-mail, the sister confirmed that Forman had indeed been working in London in February 1992, the winter of Crane's supposed death.

As Gaddis was finishing Charlotte's correspondence with Somers—most of which related to arrangements for various meetings in West Hyde and Chorleywood—he noticed a new message in the Hotmail inbox, addressed to bergotte965@hotmail.com from "Tom Gandalf" with the subject heading "Wednesday." It could have been spam, but he clicked it.

> tomgandalf@hushmail.com has sent you a secure e-mail using Hushmail. To read it please visit the following Web page. . . .

A Weblink was listed below. For a moment, Gaddis was concerned that it would download a virus into his computer. But the coincidence of the Christian name "Tom," added to the clandestine nature of the message, convinced him that the e-mail had originated with Neame. He clicked the link and was taken to the Web site for an e-mail encryption service.

Your message has been protected using a question and answer which was created by the sender. You must correctly answer this question, word for word, to retrieve your message. You will be limited to five incorrect responses.

Question: Who was in the photograph that I showed you at our last meeting?

Gaddis typed "Crane," then "Edward Crane" into the response box, but his guesses were rejected. What had Neame shown Charlotte? A photograph of Sir John Brennan? A picture of Maclean or Philby? Christ, for all he knew, it could have been a shot of the Loch Ness Monster swimming to Fort William and clambering up Ben Nevis before breakfast. Without an answer to the question, he was no closer to Neame, no closer to Crane. All of his initial enthusiasm over the Hotmail account had evaporated inside an hour: Forman was dead, Somers had spilled his guts, and Meisner would doubtless slam the door in his face if he hopped on a plane to Berlin.

It was square one again. Gaddis Redux. Charlotte had been carrying around the entire story in her head. He looked at his desk, where he had scribbled down the cost of a cheap flight to Sheremetyevo on the back of a bank statement. His only hope now was a miracle in Moscow.

13

Miracles come in many different guises. This one came late on Sunday night, while Holly Levette was cooking supper at her flat in Tite Street. Gaddis was lying back on the sofa, reading the papers and drinking a glass of red wine. Holly's laptop was open on a low table in front of him and he called out to her in the kitchen.

"Mind if I check my e-mails?"

"Be my guest."

Glass of wine in hand, Gaddis logged into his UCL account and clicked through his messages. There was one from Natasha in Spain, another from a colleague in Washington, and a round robin from a distant relative in Virginia trying to persuade friends and family to buy the paperback of his latest book. Gaddis checked the spam folder—"Be a Master of the Universe with a Huge Broadsword in Your Pants"—and within the mass of junk offering him tertiary education courses and Viagra, he spotted a message that he could scarcely believe:

tomgandalf@hushmail.com has sent you a secure e-mail using Hush-mail. To read it please visit the following Web page. . . .

The same Weblink that he had seen on Charlotte's Hotmail account was listed below. Gaddis looked up at the kitchen door, expecting Holly to walk into the room with two steaming bowls of spaghetti. He clicked the link and was again taken to the Hushmail Web site:

Your message has been protected using a question and answer which was created by the sender. You must correctly answer this question, word for word, to retrieve your message. You will be limited to five incorrect responses.

Question: Who was the doctor at St. Mary's Hospital, Paddington, in 1992?

Gaddis quickly typed in the answer.

Benedict Meisner

It was wrong. He had only four responses left.

He tried "Ben Meisner" and swore when the answer was again rejected. Third time lucky, gulping wine, Gaddis typed in "Dr. Benedict Meisner," whispering, "Come on, come on," under his breath as he hit Return.

Like the click of a lock on a safe, the door swinging open, he was taken to a private message:

Dear Dr. Gaddis

I knew Eddie Crane very well. Indeed, he was my closest friend for more than fifty years. For reasons that will become obvious to you, this is not the sort of information that I tend to make public.

If you would like to contact me, I suggest that you present yourself at the branch of Waterstone's bookshop in Winchester High Street at 11 A.M. on Monday. If this is inconvenient for you, do *not* reply to this e-mail directly. Instead, please send a *blank* e-mail with the subject heading "Book" to the following address:

parrot1684@gmail.com

If you are able to make the journey to Winchester, please carry a

copy of the *International Herald Tribune* with you and, having entered
the bookshop, make your way upstairs. This is so that I might more easily
recognize you. Eddie taught me a trick or two about tradecraft.

    Sincerely,

    Thomas Neame

Gaddis was flabbergasted. How did Neame know that he was investigating Crane's death? Holly called out, "Food's ready!" and her voice made him lurch half out of his seat in surprise. He quickly scanned the text a second time. He was aware that he should probably remove evidence of the correspondence from her computer, yet Gaddis had no idea how to clear the history quickly from an Internet browser.

He heard the strike of a match in the kitchen. Holly was lighting candles. Unsure of what to do, he simply signed out of his e-mail account and shut off the computer. Holly put her head round the door just as he was closing the lid.

"I was planning to eat the spaghetti *tonight,*" she said.

"Sure." Gaddis stood up. He had a head full of questions and an empty glass in his hand. "What do you know about Winchester?"

14

Winchester was just as Holly had described: a well-scrubbed, moneyed cathedral city an hour south of London with a clogged-up one-way system and memorials, seemingly at every corner, of Alfred the Great.

Gaddis arrived an hour early. He had not slept well and left Holly's flat at eight o'clock for fear of being stuck in traffic or, worse, of his superannuated Volkswagen Golf breaking down on the M3. He bought a copy of the *Herald Tribune* on the Fulham Road, knowing that it would be difficult to find one at any newsagent in Winchester, and drove, too fast, with a takeaway cappuccino wedged between his legs and *Blonde on Blonde* on the CD player. In Winchester he ate a breakfast of scrambled eggs at a faux-French café in the centre of town, having established that Waterstone's was not yet open. He had the latest issue of *Private Eye* and a photocopied *Prospect* article about Moscow to read, but found that he could concentrate on neither. The *Herald Tribune* lay untouched in a leather satchel at his feet. His waitress, a bottle-blond Hungarian, was pretty and bored, stopping to chat to him in fractured English about a course she was taking in design and technology. Gaddis was grateful for the distraction.

At half past ten, the morning moving with a tectonic slowness, he made his way to the entrance of the bookshop, drifting about on the ground floor with no discernible purpose other than to look up at every customer who walked through the entrance, hoping to see a ninety-one-year-old man. By force of habit, he searched for traces of his own work and found a single hardback copy of *Tsars,* nestled alphabetically in the History section. Ordinarily, Gaddis would have introduced himself to a member of staff and offered to sign it, but it seemed important to maintain a degree of anonymity.

At five to eleven, he walked upstairs. To his surprise, the first floor was not a large, open-plan area, comparable in scale to the ground floor, but instead a small, brightly lit room, no larger than the open-plan kitchen in his house, enclosed on all sides by shelves of travel guides and self-help manuals. There was one other customer present, a dreadlocked, tie-dyed girl of perhaps eighteen or nineteen who was working her way through a copy of *South-East Asia on a Shoestring.* Cross-legged on the floor, she looked up at Gaddis when he appeared at the top of the stairs, her mouth forming an acknowledging smile. Gaddis nodded back and took his copy of the *Herald Tribune* out of the satchel, preparing to make the signal. He tucked it under his arm, making sure that the banner was visible; the act of doing this felt both awkward and embarrassing and he drew a book at random from the shelves in front of him in an effort to make his behaviour appear less self-conscious.

It was a copy of *Men Are from Mars, Women Are from Venus.* Gaddis felt the dreadlocked girl staring at him as he tried to pin the newspaper under his left elbow while at the same time flicking backwards through the pages. A minute passed. Two. His arm began to ache and his face was flushed with an involuntary embarrassment. What would Neame make of him for reading such a book? He put it back on the shelf and transferred the newspaper to his right hand, feeling as though he was standing in the middle of some vast stage, overlooked by a crowd of thousands. Would Neame approach him in the presence of the girl? Would he make himself known with a nod of the head and expect Gaddis to follow? It was like performing in a play that he had never rehearsed.

At precisely eleven o'clock, a second customer, a shaven-headed man in his midtwenties, appeared at the top of the stairs. What excitement Gaddis had felt at the sound of his approach quickly dissipated. He was wearing torn denim jeans, white Adidas trainers, and a blue Chelsea football shirt with the name LAMPARD printed across the back. Hardly likely to be an associate of Neame's. Without making eye contact, the man moved past Gaddis and headed straight for a stack of cut-price paperbacks at the far end of the room. Gaddis felt that he should still be seen to be browsing and picked up a second book from the Self-Help section, again pinning the *Herald Tribune* under his elbow. This one was called *Who Moved My Cheese? An Amazing Way to Deal with Change in Your Work and in Your Life* and Gaddis quickly replaced it with another Day-Glo paperback, this one entitled *The Last Self-Help Book You'll Ever Need,* which at least brought a smile to his face.

What had happened to Neame? He looked back at the staircase but could see only promotional posters, a swaying light, and a beige carpet worn by years of use. Five long minutes later, the dreadlocked girl finally stood up from the floor, put her guide to Asia back on the shelf, and went downstairs. Lampard was now his only companion.

Things happened quickly. As soon as the woman had gone, Lampard turned and walked directly towards Gaddis. Gaddis prepared to move to one side to allow the man to pass, but saw, to his consternation, that he was taking a piece of paper from his back pocket and attempting to pass it to him.

"You dropped this, mate," he muttered, in a thick Cockney accent. Gaddis took the paper in a state of bewildered euphoria. Before he had a chance to respond, Lampard was halfway down the stairs, leaving only a cloud of BO behind him and a memory of his pale, undernourished face.

Gaddis unfolded the piece of paper. There was a short message, handwritten in a spidery scrawl:

GO TO THE CATHEDRAL. TURN RIGHT OUT OF WATERSTONE'S, LEFT INTO SOUTHGATE STREET. AT THE EXCHANGE PUB TURN LEFT INTO ST. CLEMENT STREET. LEFT AGAIN AT BLINKERS. TURN RIGHT INTO THE HIGH STREET. GO AS FAR AS THE MEMORIAL AND TURN RIGHT AGAIN.

AT THE PASTIE SHOP, DRINK AN ESPRESSO AT CAFÉ MONDE. DO
NOT SIT IN THE WINDOW OR AT ANY OF THE OUTSIDE TABLES. WHEN
YOU LEAVE, TAKE THE AVENUE TO THE CATHEDRAL. SIT ON THE
RIGHT-HAND SIDE OF THE NAVE, HALFWAY UP.

Gaddis read the instructions a second time. He had seen enough
spy movies to realize that Neame wanted to ensure that he was not
followed from Waterstone's to the cathedral. Lampard was obviously
a hired hand, a facilitator. An old man of ninety-one would not be
capable of carrying out countersurveillance of any kind; nor would
he wish to expose himself in public without first being able to ascertain that Gaddis was bona fide. All of this seemed logical and straightforward, yet he felt a strange sense of unease, akin to a fear of the
law, as he made his way to the exit, turning right into the pedestrianized high street. On Southgate Street, he checked the message a second
time, unfolding it in a manner that he felt was certain to draw attention. He tried to make a mental note of its contents, but was forced to
check them again at Blinkers, which turned out to be a small hair-
dressing boutique on a narrow road where sparrows hopped on the
pavement and a young mother was pushing a pram. As he emerged
from St. Clement Street, Gaddis saw the entrance to Waterstone's a
few metres away and realized, with a dumb embarrassment, that Lampard's directions had taken him in a simple clockwise loop.

He continued to walk downhill, as instructed, wondering how
many eyes were watching him. He saw a narrow stone monument,
about four metres high, on the right-hand side of the street. There was
a shop selling pasties beside it and he concluded that this was the
memorial mentioned in the note. Outside the pastie shop—a drifting
smell of mince and curry powder—Gaddis found himself in a low,
narrow alley which opened into a smaller, still pedestrianized street.
The glass-fronted Café Monde was clearly visible a few metres to
his left. He had no need for coffee—he'd drunk four cups in as many
hours—but ordered an espresso all the same and took a seat at the
back of the café, wondering how long he should take to drink it. He felt
restless and pushed around, but was prepared to honour the tradecraft
of Lampard's note because it would surely guarantee a meeting with
Neame.

After a minute of waiting, he drank the espresso, paid for it, and went outside. He had glimpsed the cathedral on his way into the café and now walked through the gates of a small park bisected by a tree-lined avenue, making his way towards the southern façade. Clumps of teenagers—French exchange students, anoraked Americans—were milling around outside, buffeted by an unruly wind. Gaddis was drawn into a short queue and paid five pounds to enter the cathedral. Whispers echoed off the vast vaulted ceiling as he walked between several rows of wooden chairs and took a seat on the right-hand side of the nave. He put his satchel on the ground, set his phone to mute, and looked around for Neame. There was an old, free-standing radiator next to his seat and he tapped his fingers against the scuffed iron as he waited. It was almost half past eleven.

He had been seated for no more than a minute when he heard a noise behind him, the sound of a walking stick clicking briskly on stone. Gaddis turned to see an elderly man in a tweed suit moving towards him along the nave, his eyes catching a source of light as he looked up to greet him. The man was so close to Charlotte's description of Thomas Neame as to remove all doubt about his identity. Gaddis began to stand, as a gesture of respect, but the old man made a brisk, sweeping movement with the base of the walking stick which had the effect of pushing him back into his seat.

Neame shuffled along the row and settled beside Gaddis. He did so without apparent physical discomfort but was slightly breathless as he sat down. He did not offer to shake Gaddis's hand, nor did he look him in the eye. Instead, he stared directly ahead, as if preparing to pray.

"You're not one of these Marxist academics, are you?"

Gaddis caught the ghost of a smile in Neame's stately profile.

"Born and bred," he replied.

"What a pity." The old man moved a hand in front of his face, distracted by something in his field of vision. His back was stooped, the skin on his face and neck dark and loose, but he looked remarkably robust for a man of ninety-one. "Sorry about all the scurrying around," he said. The voice was imperially upper-class. "As you can probably understand, I need to be very careful who I'm seen to be talking to."

"Of course, Mr. Neame."

"Call me Tom."

Neame laid the walking stick across the three seats adjacent to his own. Gaddis looked at his hands. He was moving them constantly, as if squeezing a small exercise ball in the palm to strengthen the wrists. The near-transparent skin across his knuckles was as taut as parchment.

"I don't think I was followed here," Gaddis said. "Your colleague's instructions were very clear."

Neame frowned. "My *what?*" He had not yet turned to face him.

"Your friend from the bookshop. Your colleague, Lampard. The one wearing a Chelsea shirt."

Neame generated a small but infinitely condescending silence before responding.

"I see," he said. Now he turned, slowly, like a statue with a cricked neck, and Gaddis saw concern within the folds and lines of the old man's face. It was as if he was worried that he had overestimated Gaddis's intelligence. "My friend's name is Peter," he said.

"Is he a relative of yours? A grandson?"

Gaddis had no idea why he had asked the question; he wasn't particularly interested in the answer.

"He is not." Somebody, somewhere, was dragging a steel trolley across a stone floor in the cathedral, the sound of the wheels squealing in the echo chamber of the nave. "You followed his instructions as requested."

Gaddis couldn't work out if Neame wanted an answer. He decided to change the subject.

"As you can imagine, I have a lot of questions I'd like to ask."

"And I you," Neame replied. He turned to face the distant altar. There was already a tension between them, a fractiousness which Gaddis had not anticipated. He felt the gap in their respective ages as a chasm which he would struggle to cross, almost as if he was a small boy again in the presence of his grandfather. Neame was still exercising his hands, the counter to an apparent arthritis. "How did you come to hear about Eddie?" he asked.

"From Charlotte. She was one of my closest friends."

Neame cleared a block in his throat. "Yes. I would like to express how sorry I was to hear about her death." The words sounded sincere. "A lovely girl. Very bright."

"Thank you. Yes, she was." Gaddis took advantage of the improving atmosphere between them to discover more about their relationship. "She said that she met you on several occasions."

This was confirmed with no more than an abrupt nod. Neame then looked down at the satchel and asked if Gaddis was recording their conversation.

"Not unless you'd like me to."

"I would not like you to." Again the response was quick and clipped; Neame clearly wanted to leave no doubt as to who was in charge. He winced as a sharp pain appeared to jag across his hunched shoulders, then quickly suppressed his discomfort with an almost imperceptible shake of the head. Gaddis recognized the familiar, uncomplaining stoicism of the war generation. His own grandfather had possessed it, his grandmother also. No fuss. No complaints. Survivors. "Charlotte visited me on three occasions," Neame continued. "I am resident at a nursing home not far from here. The Meredith. Twice we met at country pubs for a chat about Eddie, and once in my room. In fact, that occasion was rather amusing. She had to pretend to be my granddaughter." Gaddis thought of Charlotte engaged in the subterfuge and found himself smiling. It was the sort of ruse she would have enjoyed. "I must say that I was shocked when I heard that she had died."

"We all were."

"Do you suspect an element of foul play?"

Both the implication of the question and the calm, matter-of-fact way in which Neame had posed it took Gaddis by surprise. "Not at all," he said. "Do you?"

Neame sighed deeply in a way that Gaddis thought of as overly theatrical.

"Well, I wouldn't know, would I? But now you're the man on the scene. You're the chap tracking the story. And I suppose you want me to tell you all about Eddie."

"You approached *me*," Gaddis replied, because he was becoming slightly irritated by Neame's manner. "You were the one who wrote the e-mails. You were the one who sent Peter. I have absolutely no idea how you knew that I was taking over from Charlotte. I can only assume that she told you we were planning to write a book together."

"That is correct." Gaddis did not suspect that Neame was lying. The metal trolley was again being dragged across a distant stone floor, the metal scream of wheels further adding to the combative atmosphere between them. "I'm assuming that you know about St. Mary's?"

"I know about St. Mary's."

Here at last was an area of the story with which Gaddis was familiar. The old man turned to face him again, a smell of lavender in the air. His teeth were faded to yellow-grey, his blue eyes as clear and as deep as stained glass.

"Then you'll know that Eddie's death was a put-up job. You'll know that the Office cooked the whole thing up to protect him."

"Protect him from what?"

"Or from whom?" Neame reached out to touch the handle of his walking stick. The answer to the question appeared to be as much of a mystery to him as it was to Gaddis. "All I know is that Eddie wanted to say good-bye. He told me what was about to happen. I knew that this would probably be the last time that I ever saw him."

"And was it?"

Neame produced another of his deep, regretful sighs. "Oh, he's probably dead by now. Most of us are by the time you get to my age."

Gaddis acknowledged the remark with a half smile but felt the familiar sting of disappointment. A dead Cambridge spy wasn't as valuable to him as a Cambridge spy who was alive and well. More out of frustration than common sense, he decided to test the limits of Neame's knowledge.

"So you don't know for sure that Edward Crane has died?"

Neame leaned back very slightly, tilting his head upwards and gazing at the distant ceiling. It became clear, after a few seconds, that he had no intention of responding to the question. Gaddis tried a different tack.

"You'd known him since childhood?"

"Since Trinity. That hardly qualifies as childhood. I will say this, though. Eddie sent me a document about a year after the St. Mary's operation. A sort of shortened autobiography, if you will. Highlights from the life of a master spy."

This revived Gaddis. Here, at last, was something concrete. He felt a rush of satisfaction, a feeling of the pieces at last coming together. Charlotte had mentioned the document, but he did not want to betray to Neame too much of what he knew.

"Jesus," he said, momentarily forgetting that he was sitting in the body of a thirteenth-century cathedral. Neame grinned.

"This is a place of Christian worship, Doctor Gaddis. Do mind your language."

"Point taken." It was their first shared joke and Gaddis again tried to take quick advantage of Neame's lighter mood. "So what happened to this document? Do you still have it? Have you attempted to get it published?"

"*Published!*"

"What's so ridiculous about that?"

Neame coughed and again appeared to be seized by a short, intense pain in his chest. "Don't be absurd. Eddie would have had a fit."

"Why is that?"

"Because he was a creature of habit. That habit was privacy. He gave me his memoirs on the tacit understanding that I would not disseminate them."

"Do you really believe that?"

Neame looked as though nobody had questioned his judgement for forty years. Gaddis tried a different approach.

"By writing down an account of his life and by sending it to you, wasn't Crane subconsciously hoping that his story would see the light of day?"

"*Subconsciously?*" Neame made the word sound utterly absurd.

"I take it from your reaction that you're not a Freudian."

A thread of spittle appeared on the old man's lower lip which he was forced to wipe away with a folded white handkerchief. The effort appeared both to annoy and to embarrass him; here were the small humiliations of old age. Replacing the handkerchief in the pocket of his tweed trousers, he turned to face the altar.

"Look, I have arranged to meet you here today because I have made a decision to set the record straight about Eddie Crane, whom I believe was a hero to our country."

"A hero." Gaddis repeated the word without inflection.

"That is correct. And not the modern sort of hero, either. These days a young man can dip his toe in Afghanistan and be given a VC. It's a nonsense. I mean the proper sort of heroism, the hero who risks not just life and limb, but *reputation*." Neame coughed with the effort of driving home his point. "But I want to be able to tell the story in my own way and in my own time. I cannot simply betray Eddie's confidence by releasing his manuscript to the highest bidder. I want to be able to control the flow of information. I want to be dealing with somebody that I can trust."

Gaddis wanted to say: "You can trust me," but thought better of it. He knew that he was slowly earning Neame's respect, moment by moment, but did not want to jeopardize that with an incautious remark.

"The manuscript came to me with some information about Eddie's new circumstances. There was also a set of instructions." Just as he had felt beside the canal, Gaddis longed to be writing notes, but he was obliged to commit everything to memory. "Eddie told me that he was living quietly in Scotland under a new identity, protected by his former masters in the Foreign Office. He was not, he said, in particularly good health and did not expect to see me again. *'These are some private recollections of an unusual life,'* he wrote. *'I have set them down for my own personal satisfaction.'* That sort of thing. I have no idea if he made other copies. I very much doubt that he did. As I said, Eddie was in the privacy business. But I believe in *history*, Doctor Gaddis. I think Eddie knew that about me. And I believe the world has a right to know what this man did for his country."

"For *Russia?*"

Neame suppressed a knowing smile and his eyes caught the light again. It was remarkable to see so much life, so many thoughts and ideas, pulsing through a man now in his tenth decade.

"Not for Russia, Doctor Gaddis. For *England*."

"I don't understand."

"Oh, it will all become clear," he said, settling a featherlight hand on Gaddis's knee. There was something startling about the sudden intimacy. "Why don't we begin by walking the cat back?"

15

"Walking the cat back?"

"An old spying term, isn't it?" Neame could see that Gaddis was confused. "Tracing a man's steps. Taking a jig-saw apart so that you can put it back together."

He wiped his nose a second time on the carefully folded handkerchief. "Perhaps it's best if we go back to the winter of 1933."

"Whatever is easiest for you."

Neame leaned back in his chair, preparing to begin. But his balance was off. Gaddis had to reach out to steady him and felt the rough tweed of Neame's suit as it stretched tight against the hunch of his back. When, finally, Neame was comfortable, he folded his arms across his chest and glanced briefly towards the aisle.

"How much do you know about Eddie's time at Cambridge? How much have you been able to discover?"

"Very little."

Neame pursed his lips. He was perhaps wondering where to begin.

"Eddie and I went up at the same time," he said. "Met on the first day. Both of us eighteen, both of us from fairly similar backgrounds."

"What kind of backgrounds?"

Neame's response was quick. "Like yours, I should imagine, Doctor. Aspirational middle class. What difference does it make?"

Gaddis was about to point out that it was Neame, and not he, who had raised the issue of class, but thought better of it. Best just to ignore his little slights and quips; they were evidence of the old man's frustration at his ailing health, not criticisms to be taken seriously.

"Could you tell me anything else about Crane's family?" he asked. Behind him, towards the main entrance, a group of perhaps twenty tourists were gathered in a loose group, listening intently to a guide. "How did you first come to be introduced to him?"

"Oh, that's quite straightforward." Neame's tone implied that Gaddis was the only man in Winchester Cathedral who did not know the story. "We were both inveterate lovers of crossword puzzles. I came across Eddie and a copy of the *London Illustrated News* one evening in the junior common room. He was stuck on a rather ingenious clue. I helped him with it. Would you like to hear what it was?"

Gaddis reckoned Neame was going to tell him anyway, so he nodded.

" 'Are set back for a number of years.' "

"How many letters?"

"Three."

Gaddis had a knack for crosswords and solved the clue in the time it took Neame to check the time on his wristwatch.

"Era."

"Very good, Doctor, very good." Neame sounded impressed, but a restlessness in his hands betrayed his irritation. It was as if the speed of Gaddis's mind was a threat to his intellectual superiority. "Well, after that introduction, the two of us became firm friends. Eddie's father had been killed in the war, as had mine. There were rumours, never confirmed, that the senior Mr. Crane had taken his own life. You might like to look into that, chat up a military historian or two. See what they make of it."

"I'll do that," Gaddis told him.

"Eddie's mother, Susan, then remarried, a man whom Eddie detested." Neame's mouth had tightened, but folds of skin hung loose beneath his chin. "His name escapes me, for some reason. I never met him. Scoundrel, by all accounts."

"Rather like Philby's father."

Gaddis hadn't meant to draw other members of the Cambridge Ring into the conversation so quickly, but was pleased by the impact of his observation. Neame was nodding in agreement.

"Precisely. Both absolute monsters. Kim's father was an epic charlatan. Converted to Islam, if you can believe it, even took the name Abdullah and married a Saudi slave girl. Rumour has it he worked as a spy for the Saudi monarchy."

"I've heard that," Gaddis said. *"Cherchez le père."*

Neame understood the implications of the remark and again nodded his agreement.

"Indeed. Every member of the Trinity cell, to a greater or lesser extent, had complicated, in some cases nonexistent, relationships with their fathers. Guy's died when he was very young, ditto Anthony's. Maclean was the same. What would they call Sir Donald nowadays? 'An absentee father?'" Neame gave the phrase the same withering tone of dismissal that he had reserved for the word "subconsciously." "Strict Presbyterian, too. More interested in furthering his political career than he was in looking out for the welfare of his own son. In my experience, men are all, to a greater or lesser extent, at war with their fathers. Would you agree, Doctor?"

Gaddis wasn't one for sharing family confidences, so he proffered a joke instead.

"You're a Freudian after all, Tom."

Neame did not react. It struck Gaddis that he was as covetous of his moods as a small child.

"Tell me about Cambridge at that time," he asked, skidding over the awkwardness. "What were your impressions of the place?"

The question appeared to lift the old man's spirits, because he turned to face him and smiled through his clear blue eyes.

"Well, of course there has been a good deal of nonsense spoken about that period. If certain 'experts' are to be believed, we spent our entire time at Cambridge eating cucumber sandwiches, punting along the Cam and singing 'Jerusalem' in chapel. Believe me, times were a lot tougher than that. Of course, there were any number of highly privileged undergraduates from wealthy backgrounds in situ, but it wasn't all *Brideshead Revisited* and picnics on the lawn."

"Of course." Gaddis was wondering why Neame felt the need to set the record straight.

"But one thing is certainly true. Oxford and Cambridge in the prewar years were both absolutely riddled with Communists. Any self-respecting young man—or woman, for that matter—with even the vaguest sense of social justice was profoundly sceptical about the direction Western capitalism was taking. This wasn't too long after the Great Depression, don't forget. Unemployment was running at three million. Throw into the mix the lovely Adolf and you had a climate of apprehension unmatched by anything since."

"Go on," said Gaddis. "The lovely Adolf" was a phrase he might steal for a lecture.

"Well, it's quite simple." Neame touched the perfect Windsor knot on his wool tie. There was a small stain on the fabric halfway down. "All of us became rather enamoured of the Russian experiment. Some more enamoured than others."

"You're talking about Eddie?"

"Eddie, certainly. But everyone in my circle of acquaintance was touched by an interest in Marx. To be a Communist in 1933 was as unremarkable as taking mustard with roast beef. We were everywhere. You couldn't move for people who wanted to buck the system."

"People like Burgess and Maclean? People like Philby and Blunt?"

Neame shot him a sideways glance and Gaddis was concerned that he would now digress into yet more petty power games. Two tourists had appeared at the end of their row of seats wearing tracksuit trousers and bulging money belts, thousand-euro Nikons trained at the ceiling. They were speaking loudly to each other in German and Neame waited until they had moved along the aisle before continuing.

"Of course," he said. "Guy and Anthony were particularly visible in the Party. Donald was a great protestor. Always manning the barricades, always first in the queue when there was an opportunity for dissent."

"But not Crane?"

Neame paused, seemingly concerned to render as accurate an account of his friend's behaviour during this period as was possible at a distance of over seventy years.

"Eddie was more subtle," he said finally. "Eddie kept his head down."

"What do you mean?"

"He was known to Blunt, certainly, because he was a student in one of Anthony's French classes, but he wasn't active. He didn't come into the orbit of Maurice Dobb, for example, who was the don responsible for pushing Guy in the direction of the Party. He never officially joined the Communists, either."

This astonished Gaddis, not least because membership would have been a prerequisite of working for the NKVD, the arm of Soviet foreign intelligence in operation in the UK at the time.

"You look surprised, Doctor."

Again, a pain appeared to jag across Neame's back, cutting the end off the question. The old man bent slowly forward, wincing.

"Are you all right?" Gaddis was obliged to make sure that Neame was comfortable, yet he was loath to give him an opportunity to bring the interview to an end. It had taken an eternity to reach this point. They might never meet again. He had to try to extract as much information as possible.

"I am fine," Neame reassured him, making a determined gesture with his hand. Gaddis noticed that he was once again squeezing it into a fist, fighting off the arthritis. "Look, I tried on many occasions to persuade Eddie to join the Party. Many of us did."

"But without success?"

"Without success." Neame's voice had softened, almost into regret, but suddenly he was energized again, seized by the urge to defend Crane and to put his argument across more forcefully.

"I concluded, largely in retrospect, that there was more than one way to skin a cat. One does not have to be a member of the Labour Party in order to vote for a Labour candidate. One can hold right-wing views in England without subscribing to the *Daily Mail*. Do you follow?"

"I follow."

"Eddie was a subtle animal. He wasn't much for making an exhibition of himself. He played what you might call a long game. Now, did he do that because he didn't want anything on his record that might jeopardize any future involvement in public service, or did he do that because he was a rather shy young man and, at that tender age, perhaps lacking in the sort of self-confidence which distinguished his more celebrated colleagues in the cell?"

"What do you think?"

Neame weighed up his answer, and took his time about it. Almost half a minute passed before he responded.

"I think a fairly hefty dose of the latter. To my mind, Eddie had no real ambition to join the Foreign Office, no heart set on a career in government. Bear in mind that he was only eighteen and just out of school. He wasn't like Kim, who made a great song and dance about everything. Heavens, as I recall, Kim signed up for CUSS thirty seconds after landing in Cambridge."

"CUSS?"

"The Cambridge University Socialist Society. He was so over-the-top the Soviets wondered if he might have been a plant."

"And Burgess?"

The mention of his name had a strange, almost melancholy effect on Neame, who looked into his lap and brought his hands together, gently knitting the fingers. In the distance, a young girl laughed.

"Guy is certainly central to all this," he said quietly. "He had a huge impact on everybody, not just Eddie. In fact, Eddie writes at length about him in the memoirs. I myself have certainly thought back many times to the conversations I enjoyed with Guy."

The memoirs. How could Gaddis get hold of them? It seemed a cruel twist of fate that Neame should be sitting on a document which would not only validate ATTILA but radically enhance the quality and historical importance of his own book. There was something of the narcissist in Neame; he was eager to play up his own role in the affair but also keen to taunt Gaddis with his proximity to Crane's autobiography. Increasingly, it appeared that there would be a drip-feed of information, possibly over many weeks, and nothing Gaddis could do to control it.

"So you were involved in the political scene yourself?" he asked. "You were studying French as well? You were socializing with Eddie?"

Neame halted the flow of questions with a pained sigh and Gaddis realized that he had moved too fast. He had to learn to allow the story to emerge at its own pace. Neame would continue to manipulate him, certainly, but if Gaddis was patient, he would eventually be rewarded with a complete picture of Crane's time at Cambridge.

"Eddie and Guy were the two I was closest to, certainly at Trinity," he said. "I eventually lost touch with Burgess during the war, although of course one kept up with his exploits. The interesting thing was that he and Eddie were in many ways polar opposites. Where Eddie was self-contained, disciplined, very much a realist, Guy was perpetually drunk, always wearing filthy clothes, living on high ideals. But a marvellous talker. Such control of the language, you know?"

"I've heard," Gaddis said. Something regretful in the tone of Neame's recollections caused him to wonder if he and Burgess had been lovers. The old man's next remark did nothing to lessen this suspicion.

"Guy was also, of course, a famous philanderer. What Kim was to the girls, Guy was to the boys. And not just pretty little Cambridge undergraduates. He liked rough trade: truck drivers, workingmen. Couldn't get enough of that sort of thing."

"Do you think he was involved with Eddie?"

Gaddis might as well have asked if Neame himself was gay.

"What on earth do you mean?"

"Was Eddie homosexual? He had no children. He never married. I wondered if he was ever romantically involved with Blunt or Burgess?" He longed to add: "Or you, Tom?" but lacked the courage.

"How on earth am I supposed to know?" Neame seemed more embarrassed than angry, as if Gaddis had crossed some threshold of decency.

"There's a theory in one of the Blunt biographies that Blunt's sexuality may have had an influence on his preparedness to betray his country. Homosexuality was illegal in Britain in the 1930s. Therefore any homosexual was, by definition, regarded as a criminal outsider by the state."

Neame straightened the fabric of his trousers and stared into his lap. "That seems a bit far-fetched to me." He tried to divert Gaddis with an anecdote. "Eddie and I arrived in Guy's third year. Both of us immediately fell under his spell. It was Guy, for example, who organized the waiter's strike. Do you know about that?"

"No." Gaddis was lying, but he wanted to hear Neame's version of events.

"Quite straightforward, really. At that time, many of the staff who worked behind the scenes at Trinity weren't paid a salary during the holidays. Guy believed, with some justification, that this was outrageous and, with Eddie's assistance, persuaded them to down tools."

"How did they do that?"

Neame looked annoyed to have been interrupted.

"Because Guy and Eddie were both, in their different ways, absolutely marvellous with people. Guy could tell you that the sun wasn't going to come up tomorrow morning and you'd believe him. Eddie was the same. There were any number of reluctant souls among the waiters and kitchen staff, but he convinced them not only that it would be in their best interests to strike, but that they would also be in no danger of losing their jobs. He had no guarantee of this, of course, but that was the calibre of the man. If Eddie told you something, you believed him. The whole saga was a rare example of him sticking his head above the parapet. Very few people really knew how central Eddie had been to orchestrating the whole thing."

"So who knew the full truth? Burgess? Blunt?"

"Blunt certainly. He and Guy were inseparable and, as far as I know, on the lookout for recruits all the time. No doubt they tipped off their NKVD controller that Eddie was cut from the right cloth."

"That's all it took? Surely membership of the Party was a prerequisite for the Russians?"

"If you say so."

Gaddis pushed again.

"Does Eddie write about his recruitment in the document? Does he shed any light on that?"

It was better to refer to the memoirs simply as a document; Gaddis didn't want to give Neame the impression that he was sitting on material of incalculable value to his investigation.

"Well, you see, that's where it gets interesting. The Soviets did a very clever thing, which was probably the reason Eddie was able to survive undetected for as long as he did." Another party of tourists, this time Japanese, shuffled past the pew. "A gentleman by the name of Arnold Deutsch was tipped off about Eddie by Guy. Have you heard of Deutsch?"

Gaddis had certainly heard of him. Deutsch—known by the code name "OTTO"—had been responsible for the recruitment of the Ring of Five.

"Yes, of course."

"Well, Deutsch recruited Eddie, but without telling Burgess or Blunt."

"I don't understand."

"Moscow was worried that the network was already too big. They had Kim, they had Anthony, Guy, Donald, and John. All it would take was for one of them to crack and the Brits would be able to dismantle the entire cell. So Eddie was set up on his own. In due course, Cairncross became what they call 'conscious' that Crane was an asset, but none of the others, not even Guy, had a clue what was going on. Eddie was given the code name ATTILA. Deutsch told Burgess that he had no interest in working for the Party and that was that. Everybody moved on."

Gaddis reached out and ran his hand along the wrought-iron radiator beside his chair. He was trying to work out the implications of what Neame had revealed, trying to walk the cat back.

"That makes sense," he muttered, but Neame interrupted him.

"As things turned out, the Soviets had actually done MI5 a favour."

"How's that?"

The old man appeared to amuse himself with a private thought. It was clear that he enjoyed toying with Gaddis's appetite for information. "Well, that's another part of the story," he replied softly. "I'd be jumping ahead if I told you."

"Jump away."

Neame smiled. "Oxford first."

"Oxford?"

"Didn't you know, Doctor?" Neame turned in his seat, first to the left, then to the right, reassuring himself that they were not being observed. Gaddis could feel another secret coming. "The Russians sent Eddie to Oxford."

16

Calvin Somers left the Michael Sobel Centre via the staff entrance just after six o'clock and walked in pale evening sunlight towards Batchworth Heath. On autumn nights he preferred to take one of the narrow, overgrown paths through the woods and to cross a network of open fields towards the outskirts of Harefield, where he lived in a one-bedroom flat in the centre of town. It was mid-September and there would be only a few more opportunities to walk to work before the clocks went back and the nights closed in and he was obliged to take his car. Beneath a thick Land's End fleece, he was still wearing his pale green nurse's uniform because he liked to wash when he returned home, rather than to use the showers in the more impersonal surroundings of the Mount Vernon Hospital.

A thirty-four-year-old cancer patient had died on the ward three hours earlier, but Somers wasn't thinking about him, wasn't thinking about the patient's grieving relatives or the student doctor who had cried when she glimpsed the mother collapsing in tears in the car park just after lunch. He was thinking about the box of Wolf Blass Chardonnay he was going to finish that night and the range of microwaveable ready-meals stacked in his fridge. What did he feel like for dinner? A curry? Fish pie? Nowadays—and he would happily admit this to anyone who asked, even to colleagues who felt quite differently about things—the deaths on the ward just seemed to blend into one another. You forgot who was who, who had suffered from what, which family member went with which patient. Maybe he was just sick of the job. Maybe Calvin Somers was finally sick of the sick.

He was about to cross the main road towards the Heath when he heard a noise behind him in the northwest car park and turned to find a man stepping out of a dark blue C-Class Mercedes with blacked-out windows. For a brief moment, Somers considered breaking into a run, because panic had surged inside his chest like an electric charge. But to run was a stupid idea. You didn't run from a man like Alexander Grek. Grek could find you. Grek knew where you lived. The best thing, Somers decided, would be to do what he always did when it came to moments of uncertainty. He would become confrontational.

"Are you following me?"

"Mr. Somers?"

"You know who I am. Why are you here? Why have you come to my place of work? I thought our business was concluded. You assured me that our business was conclu—"

Grek interrupted him. "Please stop walking, Mr. Somers." He had a deep voice, almost baritone in texture, with a certain music in it, a certain appalling charm. He was wearing a dark grey suit and a crisp white shirt with button-down collars and a navy tie.

"I wonder if I might join you on your walk?" he said. Grek spoke a precise, formal English, but it was a coat of varnish on an utter ruthlessness. "You are walking home, are you not? This is the route that you always take?"

Somers felt the panic again, the charge in his chest, and knew that he had been rumbled. Why else had Grek come for him? They must have found out about the academic and Charlotte Berg. Why had he been so greedy? The FSB had paid him twenty grand for the Crane story, for the tale of Douglas Henderson and St. Mary's Hospital. There had been one condition to that transaction: that he never again speak to anyone about Edward Anthony Crane. But since then he'd been paid twice for the same information; he just hadn't been able to help himself. And now Alexander Grek had come to find out why.

"You've been following me," he said, but his voice betrayed him, stuttering twice on the word "following."

"No, no," Grek replied, smiling like an old friend. "We just have two more questions that we would like you to answer." He held up his fingers, splayed like a V for Victory. "Two."

Somers unzipped the fleece. He was suddenly very hot.

"Why don't we walk as we talk?" the Russian suggested, and Somers agreed, not least because he did not want to be seen with Grek by other members of staff. They turned towards the main road, crossed it and joined a narrow, overgrown path into the woods. They were obliged to walk in single file and Somers moved quickly, desperate to reach the open ground of a field. Grek was no more than three metres behind him at any point, but barely made a sound as his five-hundred-dollar loafers caressed the damp path.

"So what was it you wanted?" Somers asked, carrying the fleece now because the vest beneath his uniform was soaked with sweat.

Grek came to a halt. They were still on the path, bent trees and summer grasses hemming them in on all sides. Somers had to stop and turn around, pale sunlight filtering through the branches.

"I wanted to ask you about Waldemar."

At first, Somers didn't understand what Grek was asking, because the Russian had pronounced the name of the Polish janitor at St. Mary's with a Slavic expertise that stripped "Waldemar" of recognizable consonants. Then he put two and two together and decided to stall.

"Waldemar? The *porter*? What about him?"

"We cannot find him." From his relaxed tone of voice, Grek might have been reporting on the status of nothing more significant than a lost watch. "We have had difficulty in tracking this man down."

Somers laughed. "I thought you were meant to be Russian Intelligence? Doesn't say much for your capabilities, does it? Doesn't say much for your, er, *intelligence*?" It was a mistake, of course, to sound glib, to taunt a man like Grek, but Somers couldn't help himself. He was always like this when the cards were stacked against him: cocky and sarcastic, fighting fire with fire.

"Perhaps," Grek said, and Somers couldn't work out what he was referring to. Perhaps what? He experienced a renewed desire to get off the path, because he felt that Grek, at any moment, might throw a punch at him. Calvin Somers had a profound fear of physical violence and knew that he would not be able to defend himself if the Russian attacked. He turned and saw the edge of a field no more than fifty metres away. If only they could keep walking.

"So you do not know where we can find this Waldemar?" Grek continued. "You have had no contact with him in the intervening period?"

"In the *what?*" Somers was laughing again, choosing to mock Grek's choice of phrase.

"You heard me, Calvin."

To hear his Christian name spoken in such a context was nauseating. To control his fear, Somers turned and began to walk towards the field, praying that Grek would follow him. He did not.

"What about Benedict Meisner?" the Russian called after him and Somers was again obliged to stop, to turn around, and to walk back along the path. It felt as if he were heading into a spider's web.

"What about him?" His voice quickened as he added: "Can we move along, please? I'm keen to get home. Can we start walking towards my—"

"You will remain here while we speak." Grek gestured in the direction of the car park. "I do not want to move far from my vehicle. Where is Meisner, please?"

Somers spluttered another laugh and wondered why Grek was asking him questions about colleagues he hadn't seen for more than ten years. How was he supposed to answer? He wasn't friends with Meisner, he wasn't friends with Waldemar, never had been. The Crane deception was all that they had in common.

"Look, I don't have a fucking clue," he said, and regretted swearing, because the temperature dropped in Grek's eyes.

"I see." They were narrow eyes, a very pale brown, and within them Somers could see the extent of his own betrayal. "This is interesting. Nor have we had any success in locating Mr. Crane himself."

Somers felt as though he was being swung from point to point, as if the Russian had no real interest in the answers to the questions he was asking, only in generating a sense of unease. Was that a standard spy tactic? Why did Grek even suspect that Crane was still alive?

"Why do you keep telling me how bad you are at your job?" he said. "I don't get it. I don't walk around telling people when I've made a mistake on the ward. All you've seemed interested in talking about for the last ten minutes is what a fuck-up you're making of your investigation."

Grek did something now that was commonplace, and yet utterly unsettling. He spat on the ground. The Russian then reached into the inside pocket of his jacket and took out a cigarette, not from a packet, but from a pristine silver case. He placed the cigarette in his mouth, rolled a Zippo lighter across his thigh, and held Somers's gaze as he brought the flame to his lips. He was no longer a suit-wearing officer in the Russian FSB with a chauffeur-driven car and five-hundred-dollar loafers; you could see in his movements, in the stillness of his eyes, the remnants of the St. Petersburg thug that he had once been.

"A cigarette case," Somers said, his throat narrow and dry. The words were barely audible. "Don't see those very often."

Grek closed the Zippo. Click.

"No, you do not." Then, as calmly as slipping a knife into Somers's ribs, he said: "Have you spoken to anybody else about Edward Crane, Calvin? Anybody apart from Charlotte Berg?"

Somers lost a breath as he realized what Grek had said. The Russians knew about Charlotte. If that was the case, Christ, they probably knew about the academic. For the second time in a matter of minutes he thought that his legs were going to go. He cursed his own stupidity, his cowardice.

"What?" he said, trying to buy time. "Who's Charlotte Berg?"

Grek exhaled a lungful of smoke which held in a neat column above the path before it was parted by a gust of wind. "Please," he said. "We are both men of the world, Mr. Somers. Do not waste my time."

"Have you been bugging my telephone? Have you been hacking into my computer? How do you know about Charlotte?"

This was a confession, of course, and if Grek had possessed any lingering doubts about the nature of Somers's betrayal, they were now finally dispelled.

"This is England," he replied, gesturing at the countryside. He was smiling. "We do not have jurisdiction to bug telephones." A fly settled on Grek's arm, but he ignored it. "My colleagues have seen transcripts of your e-mail correspondence with Miss Berg. These were in strict violation of our agreement."

"And you're in strict violation of my human fucking rights getting your 'contacts' to bug my computer. How dare you?"

Somers was surprised by the ferocity of his response, even taking a step towards Grek in an attempt to impose himself. But neither his words nor his actions had any visible impact at all.

"Please calm down," he was told, as the Russian took another drag on the cigarette. "Tell us who else you have been talking to."

Us? Who else was here? Somers had never felt more isolated in his life, but Grek was talking as if their conversation was being monitored by a dozen members of the FSB. "What do you mean 'us'? Look, I haven't been speaking to anybody, okay? Charlotte got the story off her own back. She came to me because somebody had told her I was working at St. Mary's that night. Maybe that person was *you*."

"This is unlikely." Grek was looking at his cigarette, turning it in his fingers, speaking calmly. Somers knew that he had tried a feeble tactic and wished that Grek would just come out and call him a liar to his face. He couldn't bear the faux politeness, the sense of fair play. He heard a dog barking in the distance and hoped that somebody—a walker, a jogger—would come past and interrupt what was happening.

"Why is it unlikely?" he asked, moving away from Grek and again heading towards the field. Still the Russian did not follow him and, once again, Somers was obliged to turn and to walk back along the path.

"You must stop your act," Grek told him. "It deteriorates you in my eyes. I have come today to warn you that if you speak again to any member of the media or to any individual in any capacity whatsoever about Edward Crane, there will be grave consequences in terms of our arrangement." Grek saw that Somers was about to speak but raised his hand to silence him. "Enough," he said, screwing the cigarette into the path with the toe of his shoe. "Next time, the gentlemen who visit you will be considerably less polite than I am. Next time, for example, they may ask you to return the twenty thousand pounds which we paid for your silence. Your *silence,* Calvin. Do I make myself understood?"

"You do," said Somers. All of his bravado had fallen away in the intense relief of knowing that he was forgiven and would soon be free to return home. "Of course you do."

"Good."

"And can I just say that I didn't mean to cause any trouble—"

But Alexander Grek had already turned and was walking back towards his Mercedes, leaving Calvin Somers talking to the space where he had been standing, a space which now buzzed with insects in a backlit haze of seeds and pollen. The nurse felt a bubble of relief rise in his stomach and almost jogged to the edge of the field, sweat on his vest cooling in the evening air so that he was obliged to put on the fleece to keep warm.

The field was a great expanse of dusty, harvestable corn which opened up his mood and gave him the time and the confidence to think more clearly. He was free. He had been caught, but the Russians had given him a second chance. He walked along the perimeter of the field, emboldened by this thought, and was very soon imagining the glass of Wolf Blass Chardonnay he was going to pour himself, perhaps even the packet of cigarettes—ten, not twenty—that he would buy at the garage near his flat. He craved a cigarette. Something to batten down the last of his nerves.

Ten minutes earlier, the two FSB officers who had driven to the Mount Vernon Hospital with Alexander Grek had waited until their boss was out of sight before locking the Mercedes and crossing the main road. The first man, whose name was Karl Stieleke, had walked three hundred metres west before entering the woods and circling back towards the path where Grek and Somers had been talking. The second man, whose name was Nicolai Doronin, had walked in an easterly direction from the car park until he had found himself at the end of a dusty farm track which circled the heath. Stieleke had waited beneath a chestnut tree, listening to Grek's interrogation. He now tracked Calvin Somers in the last of the evening light as the nurse walked along the edge of the cornfield, heading towards his home in Harefield.

Somers became aware that he was being followed when he reached the perimeter of a large wood, about half a mile from the hospital. It was necessary to go through the wood in order to reach his house; there was no shortcut, no other way around. He turned and saw a man in his late twenties wearing a pair of jeans and a polo shirt. The man was not accompanied by a dog, nor did he look like the type to be taking a walk in the countryside on a late summer evening. He was almost certain that the man was Russian.

So Calvin Somers panicked. He knew that there was a gate into the woods, and a path, but it was at least a hundred metres away, so he tried to climb over the fence which ran around the wood and caught his fleece on a stretch of barbed wire in the process. As it tore, he swore under his breath, looking back to check if he was still being followed. The Russian had disappeared. Somers was standing in dense undergrowth, with no way of hiding nor of reaching any of the paths in the wood without cutting and scratching himself on a wall of thorns and bushes. He was, in effect, trapped. So, with an odd sense of embarrassment, he decided to climb back over the fence and to return to the field. It would be safer out in the open, he told himself. Somebody might walk past and see him.

That person was Nicolai Doronin. Guided by Stieleke on a mobile phone, Doronin had jogged around the northern edge of the cornfield and completed a pincer movement by circling back towards the woods into which Somers had just disappeared. Somers saw him as he clambered back over the fence, gingerly holding his fleece, and almost waved in relief. This man looked more local: he was shaven-headed and wearing a shell-suit and a pair of expensive-looking trainers. Somewhere, in the depths of the field, he probably had a bullmastiff or a Doberman busily chasing rabbits.

Then Somers looked to his right. The Russian was suddenly beside him, and springing at him like a cat. Somers was on the ground before he realized that the second man, the shell-suit, was also there, close in against the fence, and he felt an awful, irretrievable shame as he let them go about their business. In a sense, he had been ex-pecting this and still believed, in some vague, hopeful way, that it would just be a beating, just a lesson from the FSB, a few kicks to the stomach, a blow to the head, maybe a black eye at work for a couple of weeks.

After a minute or so, however, Calvin Somers knew that it wasn't going to end. He felt a warmth in his body which was more than sweat and realized that something wasn't right in his stomach. One of the men had used a blade on him. He started to beg them to stop and hated himself for pleading, but it was all that he could do. It was all that he had ever done. Were they going through his pockets? Was one of them going through his bag? It seemed as though only one of the men was left now and that he was the one who had done all the damage. Was that right? Somers couldn't focus. The blood in his gut was turning cold and he wondered about the woods. If he could just get into the woods again, maybe back onto the path. If he could get away, all this would stop happening.

But it would never stop. Somers knew that he wasn't ever going to stand up again. Had they meant to go this far? Had they meant to kill him?

He shouldn't have talked to Charlotte Berg. He knew that now, just as he knew that he was never going to make it back home. And he passed in and out of consciousness with the sorry realization that she, too, had been murdered by these men. Why hadn't he realized that Charlotte Berg hadn't died of a heart attack?

He wondered if her friend knew, the academic. What was his name? For some reason, Somers couldn't remember. He wondered if he should get a message to him, to somehow let him know that his friend had been killed. Somers tried to reach for his phone but found that it had disappeared.

Sam Gaddis. That was it. Gaddis. He should try to call him. He should try to get in touch. Somebody needed to let this guy know that the things he was getting himself involved in were going to get him killed.

17

There was a seven-mile traffic jam on the M3 out of Winchester, which gave Gaddis all the time he needed to digest what Neame had told him about Eddie Crane's year at Oxford. If true, it was an astonishing story.

In the summer of his graduation from Cambridge, Crane had been instructed by his NKVD handler, Arnold Deutsch, to apply for a postgraduate position at Oxford. Moscow's requirements were simple: Crane was to spend a year talent-spotting Communists whom he felt had the potential to work as agents for the Soviet Union. In other words, he was to perform the same job that Burgess had done, to such great effect, in the earlier part of the decade at Trinity.

Crane's controller at Oxford was a man named Theodore Maly, an undercover Soviet intelligence officer. Maly had already succeeded in recruiting Arthur Wynn, a former student at Trinity, to the Soviet cause. According to Neame, ATTILA and Wynn had succeeded in penetrating Oxford's left-wing community and had effectively green-lit a ring of at least seven spies which, it transpired, had been every bit as successful as their counterparts at Cambridge. For Gaddis, this wasn't just a major development in the Crane story; it was a huge scoop in its own right. An Oxford Ring had always been one of the great conspiracy theories of the Cold War. He now had evidence that such a ring had existed.

Yet that wasn't the end of it. What Neame had told him about the identity of one of the members of the Oxford Ring was little short of astonishing. Crane's memoirs apparently contained a cryptic reference to a Modern History undergraduate from Yorkshire named James who had been talent-spotted by ATTILA and subsequently recruited as an agent by the Soviets in 1938. Russian Intelligence had given James the code name AGINCOURT. In the memoirs, Crane had revealed that AGINCOURT had gone on to hold "one of the highest offices in the land." Gaddis was convinced that this was the revelation that Charlotte had referred to at dinner in Hampstead three weeks earlier: a secret which would "rock London and Moscow to their foundations." Neame had insisted that he did not know AGINCOURT's identity, but Gaddis felt certain that, with enough time, he would be able to put the clues together and, at the very least, draw up a short list of suspects.

There were three days until his next scheduled meeting with Neame. Gaddis used the time to find out what was already in the public domain about Arthur Wynn. He also turned his attention to Oxford in the prewar years. In his memoirs, *Spycatcher,* the former MI5 officer Peter Wright had raised the possibility of an Oxford Ring, identifying the academic Jennifer Hart, the politician Bernard Floud and his brother, Peter, as suspected members. According to Neame, all three names appeared in Crane's memoirs as active Soviet agents.

What intrigued Gaddis was that several suspects in the Oxford Ring had died in suspicious circumstances; one had even taken her life shortly after being interrogated by MI5. This had prompted the Security Service to suspend its investigations and to cover up the existence of the Oxford Ring for fear of a public scandal. But was Peter Wright's version of events true, or a clever attempt to create a smokescreen not only for ATTILA and Wynn, but also for AGINCOURT?

That night, Gaddis went to the Donmar Warehouse theatre with Holly to watch a new play written by a friend with whom she had been at university.

"You look bored," she said at the interval. "You look distracted."

She was right. He couldn't concentrate on the production. He wanted to walk out, to take Holly to dinner and tell her about Neame and Lampard, about "James" and the Oxford spy ring. But it was impossible; he could not involve her. If he was honest with himself, he still did not know why Holly had approached Charlotte with her mother's research papers. Had it just been a coincidence, or had Katya Levette in some way been involved in the Crane conspiracy? His mind was scrambled with possibilities.

The barman at the Donmar was a friend of Holly's, an out-of-work actor called Piers whose girlfriend was performing in the play. Afterwards, the four of them went for dinner in Covent Garden and Gaddis found that he enjoyed their company, that Piers, in particular, was easygoing and likeable. But a part of him was floating through the meal, killing time until he was able to get home and attack the books once again. He persuaded Holly to spend the night at his house but left her asleep in his bed while he went to his office and trawled the Internet looking for information about AGINCOURT. All he was able to dig up was an old conspiracy theory about the former British Prime Minister, Harold Wilson, working for the Soviet Union. Had Neame sent him on a wild goose chase?

On Thursday morning he set off for Winchester, following the instructions that Neame had given him when they left the cathedral. He was to return to Waterstone's and to wait for Peter on the first floor. This time, they had joked, there would be no need to carry a copy of the *Herald Tribune*.

Peter duly appeared at 11 A.M. wearing a red Manchester United shirt with ROONEY emblazoned across the back. They were alone in the room and Gaddis laughed when he saw the shirt, Peter grinning back and handing him a small box and a piece of paper on which he had written a set of instructions.

"GPS," he said. "It's already switched on. Just press the green button and do what it tells you. Your friend is waiting in the pub."

Gaddis opened the box and found a small TomTom loosely wrapped in bubble plastic. The written instructions explained that he was to take the route preprogrammed into the GPS, a journey which would eventually lead to a village outside Winchester. Peter would be following Gaddis's car at a discreet distance to ensure that he was not being tailed. If, at any point, he suspected that Gaddis was under surveillance, he would text the word "LONDON" to his mobile phone, thereby aborting the meeting.

The plan seemed straightforward and, by now, Gaddis was familiar enough with the eccentric customs of the secret world to be neither surprised nor concerned by it. He returned to his car, put the TomTom on the passenger seat, switched on the engine, and pressed Go.

"At the end of the road, turn left."

He was startled to hear the voice of Sean Connery, preprogrammed into the software. Another of Peter's private jokes; Gaddis was beginning to like him. Pulling out into shuffling late-morning traffic, he was soon being slung around the narrow lanes and B-roads of southern Hampshire by an actor doing his very best impression of Commander James Bond. Peter had programmed the GPS with a series of turns and loops which often brought Gaddis back to a roundabout or junction that he had passed five or ten minutes earlier. The purpose of this was clear: any vehicle attempting to follow him would quickly be exposed. Gaddis kept an eye on his rearview mirror, certain that Peter was driving a red Toyota. It would appear, six or seven cars back, on dual carriageways and at sets of traffic lights, and Gaddis found himself slowing down at regular intervals to allow him the chance to catch up.

When he had been on the road for almost half an hour, a text message came through on Gaddis's phone. He reached for it and saw with a feeling of dread that the message had come from a "Withheld" number. To his relief, though, Peter was simply instructing him to switch off the phone, doubtless to prevent it being tracked to the pub. Within five minutes, the GPS had brought him into the car park of a mock-Tudor pub in the village of Easton, just a few miles north of Winchester.

Neame was already seated in the corner of the dining room, far enough from neighbouring tables that their conversation would not be overheard. He was wearing the same tweed suit, the same wool tie, and the same polished brown brogues that he had sported at their first meeting. It was almost as if he had walked directly from Winchester and had been waiting in the pub ever since. There was a pint of what looked like real ale in front of him and he appeared to be in jovial spirits.

"Ah. The good doctor."

Neame rose to his feet.

"Is this your local, Tom?"

The old man's hand was soft and damp as Gaddis shook it. His walking stick was resting in the crook of the wall behind his chair and he still carried about him the same smell of lavender which had drifted between the rows of Winchester Cathedral.

"There's a tunnel from the nursing home. Certain residents refer to it as the Great Escape. How's Peter?"

Gaddis considered mentioning the Rooney shirt, but thought better of it.

"I didn't know he was such a joker," he replied instead. "Sent me here with Sean Connery as a tour guide."

"I'm not sure I follow you."

Gaddis privately conceded that it was an unhelpful way to have started the interview and spent the next three minutes trying to explain that actors' voices could be downloaded onto GPS via the Internet. Neame looked utterly baffled. The "good doctor" might as well have been speaking in Swahili.

"I really don't understand all this newfangled technology," he said. "Peter's the one who keeps himself up to date. I'm very lucky to have him."

"Where did you find him?" Gaddis asked, because it wasn't every day that a ninety-one-year-old resident of an old people's home had an expert in countersurveillance at his beck and call.

"State secret," Neame replied, tapping the side of his nose. His mood was relaxed and amenable. He looked well rested, not a day older than seventy-five. "Let's just say that Eddie introduced us shortly before he went into hiding."

There was something too convenient in this answer, but Gaddis was certainly not going to accuse Neame of lying. It was perfectly possible that the two men were still in regular contact and that Crane was using Neame as a willing go-between, drip-feeding information as and when it suited him. Equally, Crane could have hired Peter from the private sector to give his old friend an extra layer of protection.

"Talking of newfangled technology," Gaddis said, "would you mind if I took your photograph?"

Neame hesitated. "In principle, no, but it must only be for the book. You mustn't show the picture to anybody before publication. That's absolutely vital for my security."

"I understand," Gaddis replied with a smile.

It was a cynical move, not least because he planned to take the picture with nothing more sophisticated than the camera on his mobile phone. No lights, no makeup, just a shot of Crane's best friend drinking a pint in an English pub. He was rather touched as the old man steadied himself, adjusted his jacket, and flattened down his hair, then held a steady gaze as Gaddis lined up the shot.

"Don't say cheese."

The photograph looked perfectly good, but Gaddis took a couple more for luck. Every meeting with Neame could be his last; he might never have the same opportunity again.

"Can we talk a little more about Oxford?" he said, when he had put the phone away. He had ordered a pint of lager from the bar and had a list of questions to get through before Neame grew tired.

"Of course."

"I'm still interested in the identity of AGINCOURT."

"Aren't we all."

"In *Spycatcher*, Peter Wright suggests that—"

Neame did not even allow him to complete the sentence.

"For goodness' sake, Sam. Please don't take anything that man says seriously. Wright was an absolute charlatan. Eddie couldn't stand him. Always playing people off against one another. Obsessed by money, obsessed by petty vengeance. If the government had handled Peter with even a modicum of common sense, he would have evaporated into anonymity."

"So you knew Wright as well?"

Neame looked confused. "Did *I* know him?"

"It's just that you called him 'Peter.' As if you were on first-name terms."

Neame frowned, dismissing the theory with a slow shake of the head. "You're mistaken."

Was he? Always with Neame there was the feeling that he was holding something back, dissembling, protecting Crane from exposure. He wondered if they had worked together at SIS. "So where does that leave us?"

"Us?"

"I mean, how can I find out more about the Oxford Ring?"

"Well, there's very little about it in Eddie's memoirs. I've told you all I can remember."

The bluntness of this reply tested Gaddis's goodwill.

"Mind if I check that?"

Neame smiled. "Patience," he said, and Gaddis felt the irritation rise still further. It was so hard to be anything other than compliant and reasonable with a man of such advanced years, but he longed to be freed from the shackles of respect for the elderly.

"Patient for what?"

"I really have absolutely no idea about AGINCOURT. Eddie said he climbed fairly high in the Labour Party in the sixties and seventies. But that was all a long time ago."

"The Labour Party?"

Neame looked up. Beneath his eyes were patches of discoloured skin, years marked on the face as black stains. "Labour, yes."

"It's just that you didn't mention that in the cathedral."

"And?"

"It's helpful, that's all."

"Well, he was hardly likely to be a Tory, was he? We're talking about a working-class Yorkshireman, a Communist."

Suddenly, some of the energy seemed to go out of Neame, like the fading grandeur of a once great house, and he was left looking breathless and tired. As if to confound this impression, he reached down to the floor and, with considerable effort, lifted a flimsy plastic carrier bag up onto the table.

"I wanted to give you something," he said, stifling a cough.

"Are you all right, Tom?"

"I'm all right." Neame's half smile was almost paternal in its affection. Gaddis looked down at the bag and realized, with an excitement close to euphoria, what it contained.

"Is that what I think it is?"

He was convinced it was the memoirs: there was something in the looseness of the plastic, the weightlessness of it as Neame had lifted the bag to the table. When he again glanced down, he could see the stapled corner of what looked like a manuscript. There was not much of it, just a few pages, but it was surely at least a part of the prize he craved.

"Call this an act of faith," Neame said, encouraging Gaddis to open the bag. "It's also evidence of my faltering memory. I'm afraid I have proved quite incapable of memorizing the details of ATTILA's behaviour during the war."

"His behaviour during the war." Gaddis repeated the phrase without inflection, because he now had the stapled manuscript in his hands and was focused solely on what it contained. To his disappointment, he saw that it was merely three pages of hastily scrawled notes, written on fresh sheets of A4. The handwriting was identical to that on the notes which Peter had handed to him in Waterstone's. In other words, Edward Crane hadn't been anywhere near it. "What is this?"

"A brief summary of what Eddie admits to having passed to the Soviets." Neame was looking beyond him, at the bar. "The extent of his treachery."

Gaddis didn't understand. Crane had continued working for MI6 until the 1980s. He had betrayed his country for the better part of fifty years. How could these three flimsy pages constitute the full extent of his treachery? He was suddenly sick of questions and dead ends, sick of being mislead. He didn't care if Neame was feeling unwell. He wanted answers.

"Tom, I thought this was—"

"I know what you thought it was." Neame was again touching the knot on his wool tie, as if doing so would somehow preserve the dignity of their discussion. "I'm not ready to give you that yet. But have a look at what there is. It should still be of considerable interest to you."

Gaddis felt like an errant child being set a task by a particularly exacting father. He saw a word which he recognized as "Bletchley" and read what Neame had scribbled underneath:

E works briefly at Bletchley in 42
First-hand access to ULTRA/ in tandem with the Carelian
Armour-piercing shells + Tiger tanks (Kurskaia Douga)

"I'm having trouble understanding this," Gaddis told him, flicking to the next page. Here, Neame appeared to have copied out verbatim a passage from the memoirs.

That winter, with Cairncross's assistance, we were able to save the lives of thousands of Soviet soldiers on the eastern Front. This was the period of the Citadel offensive. Thanks to the code-breakers, I was able to pass detailed information about Nazi troop movements to MANN, allowing the Soviet commanders to move their men out of harm's way in good time.

MANN, Gaddis knew, was the NKVD cryptonym for Theodore Maly.

Of course, John and I did not know that our efforts were having any impact at all, but that did not lessen our sense that the work we were doing was of profound importance to the cause.

"Which cause?" Gaddis muttered to himself, still coming to terms with what he was seeing. Was this an extract from the memoirs? Why would Neame bother to have copied it out? What value was there in playing such a game?

Neame saw his confusion but gestured at him to continue reading.

During the same period, the Carelian was also able to obtain a list of Luftwaffe squadrons operating in the Kursk area. He became ill, so it fell to me to pass on that information to his handler. I believe that, as a result, fifteen Nazi aerodromes were bombed and 500 planes destroyed. A marvellous coup for which both John and I received The Order of the Red Banner.

"Christ, is that true? Cairncross and Crane were both decorated?"
Neame nodded. "If that's what it says."
Gaddis went back to the first page. He pointed to the note: "Armour-piercing shells + Tiger tanks" and asked Neame to elaborate.
"Elaborate?" The old man tapped a finger against a dried crust of skin, just beneath the hairline. "I believe 'The Carelian' was one of

the names by which John Cairncross was known to the Russians, yes?"

Gaddis nodded.

"Well, Eddie recalls that the Soviets were able to develop armour-piercing shells capable of destroying Nazi Tiger tanks at the battle of . . ." He did not appear to know how to pronounce "Kurskaia Douga," so Gaddis did it for him. "Precisely. Again, he credits ULTRA for the intelligence which allowed for this."

"I see."

Gaddis went to the final page, where Neame had written more notes.

1939. Appointed to Soviet counter-espionage at MI5. Gives names of potential Soviet defectors to MANN. Diplomats subsequently withdrawn to Moscow.

Full knowledge of counter-espionage activities in London and beyond. Ditto extent of MI5 infiltration of Communist Party.

Tell Dr. SG about diplomatic bags.

1943. Guy and E in Casablanca at clandestine talks between Churchill and Roosevelt.

Passed plans for the Allied landing in Sicily and the invasion of the Italian peninsula to MANN.

"It says here you're supposed to tell me something about diplomatic bags."

Neame was sipping his pint. A couple of men had walked into the pub. One of them appeared to know the landlady. Above the noise of their conversation, Neame said: "What was that?"

Gaddis leaned forward, pointing at the back page of the manuscript.

"Something about diplomatic bags, Tom."

"Search me."

Why had the energy gone out of him again, just at the point when he needed Neame to be at his most alert? Was he playacting, or was age really defeating him?

"Can I get you something to eat?"

"That would be very kind."

Perhaps that was all that it would take. Some soup, some bread to revive his spirits. It took ten minutes for the food to arrive, a period which Neame spent talking about the staff at the nursing home. He was bored, he told Gaddis, bored "out of my tiny mind." That explains your parabolic mood swings, Gaddis thought, and bought himself another pint of lager. When the soup came, Neame took two spoonfuls of it and set the bowl to one side.

"Did I tell you what happened to Eddie after the war?"

It was instantaneous. He was revived once again. In the space of a few seconds, Neame appeared to have regained his mental and physical acuity. Gaddis was reminded of an actor stepping back into character; it was unnerving to watch. He may have forgotten all about the manuscript, all about the diplomatic bags, preferring to talk about Crane's experiences after the war, but as far as Gaddis was concerned, that was fine. Let the old man tell his story in his own way and in his own time. Just as long as he tells it.

"You didn't mention that, no."

"Do you know what, Sam?"

"What?"

Neame leaned forward, almost slipping on the patched elbows of his tweed jacket. "I think Eddie may have experienced what might nowadays be called a nervous breakdown."

"Really?"

Now it was Gaddis's turn to come forward in his chair. He felt as though he was involved in a piece of high theatre. Once or twice, in the dead of night, he had considered the possibility that Thomas Neame was nothing but a fraud, a mischievous, elderly con man spinning tall tales about a man called Eddie Crane who had never existed. That thought was not far away at this moment.

"The truth is, we lost touch with one another." Neame looked depressed. "Eddie went to Italy in '47 and the next few years are a blank. We didn't see one another, we didn't write. I even wondered if he had been killed."

Gaddis nodded. Where was this going? What part of the story was he attempting to spin? Two elderly ladies sat down at the next-door table and popped their napkins.

"I think there was a boyfriend," Neame added, a remark which took Gaddis completely by surprise. "In fact, I'm sure that there was a boyfriend." So Crane's sexuality was no longer a delicate subject? In the cathedral, Neame had baulked at any mention of a male lover, yet here he was, happily outing Crane at the first opportunity. Perhaps he had decided that he could trust Gaddis with even the most delicate details of his friend's story. That was now the best-case scenario. "What we do know is that Guy and Donald defected, yes? A ferry to France in '51 and the Cambridge Ring gradually exposed."

Gaddis nodded. He could feel his nerves quicken again at the hands of this master manipulator. Neame instinctively reached beside him for his walking stick, but his hand was shaking, like a man fumbling in the dark.

"There's a background to all this," he said. "To the breakdown. If you ask me, Eddie had never properly come to terms with the Pact."

"The Hitler-Stalin Pact?" Gaddis looked down at the bowl of soup, which was giving off a vapour of curry powder. He wished that the landlady would take it away. "Seems odd that you would think that. The Pact was in '39, more than ten years earlier."

"Yes, yes." Neame appeared to be aware of the contradiction. Crane, after all, had continued working for the Soviets long after Stalin had allied himself to Nazi Germany. "The others, you see—Guy, Anthony, Kim, Donald, John—all of them had been reconciled to the treaty. But Eddie never found the justification for it. It completely shook his faith in the Soviet system. He wasn't programmatic, he wasn't intellectual in the way that, say, Guy and Anthony were. He didn't see a deal with Hitler as a necessary evil. He saw it as opportunistic, as a complete rebuttal of Marx."

"He wasn't alone in feeling that way."

"No." Neame seized on this, meeting Gaddis's eye, like a traveller who has at last found a sympathetic ear. "Eddie came deeply to regret his association with the Soviets. He was proud of some of the things that he had achieved, some of the things that we have touched on today"—he indicated the papers on the table in front of them, and suddenly the purpose of the notes made sense to Gaddis—"but he saw the direction Stalin was taking and realized that he had backed the wrong horse."

"So why did he keep going?" Gaddis asked. "Why did he carry on working for the Russians throughout his career?"

"He didn't."

"Excuse me?"

"Eddie was a double, Sam. That's what I've been wanting to tell you. ATTILA was the greatest postwar coup in the history of the SIS and only a few men on the face of this Earth know about it. Eddie Crane spent thirty years convincing Moscow he was working for the KGB, but in all that time, he was secretly working for us. Isn't that marvellous? It was an epic of disinformation. That's why I want the world to know his story."

18

Tanya Acocella had never laid eyes on Sam Gaddis, but she felt as though she knew him intimately.

She knew, for example, that he owed the Inland Revenue more than £20,000 and was in debt to the tune of £33,459 on two separate £20,000 bank loans secured against the value of his house. Gaddis had also submitted an application for a further loan of £20,000 which had recently been approved by Nat West.

She knew, having obtained a copy of his divorce settlement, that his marriage had broken up because his wife, Natasha, had begun an affair with a failed restaurateur named Nick Miller three weeks before Gaddis himself had started seeing one of his Ph.D. students at UCL. He was paying his ex-wife monthly alimony of €2,000 via a standing order with Banco de Andalucia, and had mortgage payments amounting to around £900 per month.

Tanya knew that Sam Gaddis downloaded Herbie Hancock albums on iTunes; that he bought most of his clothes in Zara and Massimo Dutti; that he ate takeaway Lebanese at least two nights a week and rented old Howard Hawks movies from a store in Brook Green. She had read his book on Sergei Platov and was three-quarters of the way through the biography of Mikhail Bulgakov. She knew that he played squash in Ladbroke Grove every Wednesday morning and football under floodlights on Sunday evenings at six. He was popular with the students she had spoken to at UCL and widely admired by his colleagues. He had six points on his driving licence for two counts of speeding and hadn't paid the BBC licence fee for seven years. He had attended A&E at Charing Cross Hospital, Hammersmith, with a dislocated jaw and a broken nose as a result of a fight on 5 October 1997. For a brief period, around the time of his divorce, he had been prescribed temazepam for insomnia. He was otherwise in perfect health and had never seen a shrink. Tanya had ordered intercepts on Gaddis's mail and had seen the postcards which he wrote to his five-year-old daughter, Min, in Barcelona. He was, by all accounts, a loving and dutiful father.

What else did she know about Sam Gaddis? That his current girlfriend, Holly Levette, was an out-of-work actress who spent a lot of time alone and was prone to bouts of melancholy which she kept hidden from Gaddis because she was increasingly serious about their relationship (an e-mail to a friend had revealed as much). That he drank, on average, a case of wine and a bottle of whisky every month (a quick glance at his online account with Majestic had confirmed this). But it was Gaddis's more recent Internet traffic which was of most interest to the Secret Intelligence Service. A URL history obtained from a source at AOL was alarming in its scope and intensity. It was this file which Tanya was taking to Sir John Brennan. Everything else, at this stage, was just background.

"There's a lot of interest in Edward Crane," she said, settling into the same chair in Brennan's office at Vauxhall Cross which she had occupied at their first meeting. "A lot of interest in Crane and a lot of interest in Thomas Neame."

Brennan looked out at the greying Thames. "I thought we'd already established that."

Tanya betrayed no irritation at the slight.

"It looks as though Doctor Gaddis was put on to the story by a journalist named Charlotte Berg. The late Charlotte Berg, as a matter of fact."

Brennan kept his eyes on the river. "Late?"

"She died suddenly a few weeks ago."

"How suddenly?" He had turned to face her now, sensing something.

"Heart attack. She was forty-five."

"History of that sort of thing in the family?"

"I don't know, sir. I can look into it."

"Do that."

Tanya returned to her notes. "From e-mail traffic, it looks as though Gaddis is going to put together a book proposal which his literary agent will then sell to the highest bidder. Newspaper serialization a certainty. There's also been a lot of research activity on an old KGB cryptonym, AGINCOURT."

This seemed to relieve Brennan, who snorted in satisfaction.

"AGINCOURT? He's not chasing that wild goose, is he? Well, long may it continue. If that's all Doctor Gaddis has got to work on, we're in the clear." He let out a deep sigh. "Christ, I thought the Russians were on to him. Anything seedy in his cookies?"

Tanya adjusted her skirt. She wasn't sure what Brennan had implied by Russian involvement. "Nothing, sir. He's been seeing a young woman, Holly Levette, for the past few weeks. The relationship appears to be becoming quite serious." She might have added that Gaddis and Holly exchanged up to fifteen text messages every day, some of them very funny, almost all of them climbing a scale from the flirtatious to the highly erotic. At times, reading them, she had felt like a parent snooping on a pair of lovestruck teenagers. "He has substantial debts, but most of those have accrued from his divorce and from late tax payments. There's quite a lot of alcohol being put away, but no substance abuse, no point of weakness in that area."

"Yet," said Brennan pointedly.

Tanya removed a single strand of hair from the sleeve of her jacket. She was a skilful judge of character and had a sure sense that Sam Gaddis was one of the good guys. Brennan was never going to control him with something as crass as blackmail.

"You mentioned that Mr. Neame was resident at a nursing home in Winchester," she said. Brennan was tapping something into a computer.

"Yes."

"Well, it's just that Gaddis drove there last week."

He looked up. "You followed him?"

"I'm afraid there wasn't the opportunity, sir."

"But you think he went to see Neame?"

Tanya set the file to one side. "I assume so, yes. I haven't been able to trace any e-mail or telephone communications between the two of them."

"Fuck it." Brennan spat the words into his keyboard. "What the hell is Tom up to?"

Tanya felt that the question was rhetorical and did not offer a response. She had run a trace on Neame through the SIS mainframe and drawn a blank. This, in itself, had struck her as strange, even obstructive, but she felt that to raise the subject with Brennan would only irritate him further.

"You say that Gaddis has been looking into AGINCOURT?" he said.

"Yes, sir."

The Chief smiled. He had regained his composure. He knew Thomas Neame. He knew the way his mind worked.

"Then we may not need to worry." He turned to the window, putting both hands against the glass. "You keep going with Gaddis," he said. "Press on. I think Tom may be trying to put him off the scent."

19

So Crane was never the sixth Cambridge spy?"

Gaddis could feel the whole book crumbling around him, weeks of false leads culminating in a final dead end at a mock-Tudor pub in Hampshire.

"Come again?"

"You spent our last meeting telling me that Crane was recruited at Trinity by Arnold Deutsch, that he was a close friend of Guy Burgess, that he ran a ring of NKVD spies out of Oxford in the late 1930s. You're now telling me that he was a double agent for MI6. Which was he?"

"Both."

Gaddis put his elbows on the table, his head in his hands, and stared across at Neame, on the edge of losing his temper. He was going to have to think of another way of paying Min's school fees, another way of paying the tax. He would have to write a book about oligarchs, pitch a bloody documentary about Abramovich to the BBC. Neame's testimony was about as reliable as Peter Wright's.

"What do you mean 'both,' Tom?"

It was the first time that Gaddis had raised his voice against him.

Neame placed his walking stick against the wall and finished his pint with a gingerly sip. The bowl of soup had at last been carried away by the landlady.

"After the war, Eddie suffered a crisis of conscience." Neame was speaking slowly, crisply, but without a hint of ill-feeling; it was as if he understood Gaddis's frustration and wanted him to feel reassured. "He bitterly regretted his association with the Soviets. With the exception of some of the ULTRA intelligence, he felt that he should not have passed Allied information to Moscow. He could see the direction that Stalin had taken and didn't like it. So, as soon as Guy and Donald had disappeared in '51, he turned himself in."

Gaddis felt a faint pulse of hope, life coming back to a dead circuit.

"Eddie had a close friend in MI5, a man by the name of Dick White. I'm sure you've heard of him. Director B, counterespionage. Went on to become Director-General of the Security Service, then Chief of the SIS. He was the golden boy of the postwar generation in British intelligence and therefore precisely the right man for Eddie to approach with his plan."

A window cleaner had appeared at the far side of the lounge, working on the exterior of the pub. He was in his late twenties and had a pair of iPod headphones plugged into repeatedly pierced ears. Neame saw him and gestured to the landlady, who approached him with the deference of a lady-in-waiting attending to the needs of an ailing monarch.

"Yes, love. What can I do for you?"

She put a hand on Neame's shoulder and Gaddis was afforded a glimpse of his life at the nursing home: the humiliation of being treated as a child by carers flushed with good intentions.

"Your window cleaner," Neame asked. "Is he local by any chance?"

The landlady looked back across the room as the man swiped a set of French doors with a chamois leather.

"Who? Danny?"

"Danny, yes. Has he worked for you before?"

Gaddis could see what Neame was doing. He wanted to check the window cleaner's credentials. Was he bona fide or MI5 surveillance?

"Yes, love. Lives just down the road. Been looking after us for years. You need someone to clean your windows?"

Neame smiled gratefully. "Well, if you can recommend him, that would be enormously kind." It was an utterly convincing performance. "Could you fetch his number?"

"Of course, love."

And the landlady walked off, leaving Neame assured that their table was not being bugged.

"As I was saying," he continued. There was no acknowledgement of the exchange which had just taken place: not a sideways glance, not even a knowing smile. "White was an old friend of Eddie's from the war. Eddie went to him and told him what he had done. It was a private conversation which took place at the Reform Club. It constituted a full confession."

"Full to what extent?"

"Everything he had ever done. Every name, every agent, every Soviet controller. He gave them Wynn, he gave them Maly, he gave them Cairncross."

"I thought Cairncross confessed in '51?"

"That's what the history books would have you believe. He did, but only after Eddie exposed him."

"And Blunt? Philby?"

"Sadly not. Because ATTILA had been ring-fenced by the NKVD at Trinity, in isolation from the Ring of Five, Eddie had no idea that Kim was working for Moscow. He thought Anthony was an art scholar, for God's sake. We all did. He only knew for certain about Guy, and of course it was too late to alert London about Burgess and Maclean. They were already drinking vodka in Derjinsky Square. No, Eddie's real area of expertise was Oxford."

"So he gave White the names in the ring? He gave them the Floud brothers, Jennifer Hart? That's why it was rounded up?"

"Speculation," Neame muttered, taking a stern gaze back to the window cleaner. Gaddis heard the squeak of cloth on glass. "But he named Leo Long, Victor Rothschild, James Klugmann, and Michael Straight as possible troublemakers. Some names were cleared, others were not. By then, Straight was back in the United States living the life of a responsible citizen. Ten years later, he was to make a similar confession of his own to the American government which led to the exposure of Blunt."

"And White went for this? He didn't just want to string him up?"

"A number of factors were in play, Sam. White was very fond of Eddie and could understand why he had fallen for Communism. A lot of us did. It was a heady time. In many ways, the decision to aid Mother Russia was a noble one, taken in good faith. Dick was also able to distinguish between the different personalities involved. Donald, for example, had a very deep and profound hatred of America. Later, White would come to recognize that Kim was a sociopath. Anthony, it transpired, was also utterly self-serving. Now you wouldn't necessarily have said that about Guy or Cairncross. Along with Eddie, they were the ones who were steadfastly ideological, who spied out of conviction rather than from some misguided sense of their own importance. White also knew that Edward Crane was a brilliant intelligence officer. Furthermore, the country couldn't afford another spy scandal. Had Eddie been exposed following the defection of Burgess and Maclean, there is every possibility that the government would have fallen. So it was in everyone's best interests to keep ATTILA under wraps and, yes, this was a golden opportunity to strike back at Moscow. Never underestimate the extent to which SIS and the Russians loathe one another. It's a blood feud."

"You're missing something out."

"What's that?"

Gaddis took his jacket off and secured it over the back of his chair.

"Why didn't Crane tell White about AGINCOURT?"

"Who's to say that he didn't?"

Neame's reply was lazy; there was a hole in the logic.

"Because if he did, then AGINCOURT's identity would have been revealed and we would now know all about him. But you've told me that Crane talent-spotted somebody who went on to become a senior figure in the Labour Party in the 1960s and '70s. Who was he? Harold Wilson?"

"That would be a sensation," Neame replied, as if the idea had never occurred to him.

Gaddis laughed at his sheer nerve. "A Soviet defector called Anatoly Golitsin named Wilson as a KGB agent in 1963. Did you know that?"

Neame nodded. It was the first time that Gaddis had seen him looking unsure of himself.

"Wilson's first name was James," Gaddis continued. "He was born in Yorkshire. According to *Spycatcher*, MI5 were convinced he was a spy."

"Then go ahead and run the story." Neame's hands were in the air, eyes exaggeratedly wide at the prospect.

"Oh, come on. You know what I need from you, Tom. Does Eddie name Wilson or doesn't he?"

"I have told you, I have no idea. Everything I've related to you is based on a single conversation which took place over ten years ago and on a document which Eddie asked me to destroy. My specific area of expertise is ATTILA. All I know for certain is that Edward Crane was used by MI5 and MI6 in a variety of different ways between 1951 and the late 1980s, spreading disinformation to Moscow, that sort of thing. He found out what the Soviets wanted to know, gave London an idea of the enemy's knowledge gaps. Everything flowed from there."

"Everything flowed from there," Gaddis repeated witheringly. He was tired of evasions, tired of false leads. He was certain that AGIN-COURT was a red herring and that Neame was just stringing him along for his own personal amusement. The story was too old; the conspiracy theory about Wilson had been flogged to death in the 1980s. He put that theory to Neame now, because it felt as though his pride was at stake.

"Here's what I think, Tom. I reckon AGINCOURT was Harold Wilson and there's nothing new on him in Eddie's memoirs. I reckon Wilson danced with the Russians at Oxford but never took his clothes off. In other words, you brought him up just to make your own story look more convincing and didn't think I'd bother checking it out. On that basis, less than half of what you've told me is probably true. Was Crane the sixth man? Was Crane a double agent? Was Thomas Neame his best friend or does Thomas Neame just like playing games with nosey historians to make his lunchtimes more exciting?"

Neame was staring at him, his face absolutely motionless. Gaddis suddenly saw the man as he would have looked at thirty, at forty, eyes blazing with indignation. It may have been the first time in a generation that anybody had summoned the nerve to question Neame's integrity.

"You don't trust me," he said. It was more of a statement than a question.

"I don't trust you," Gaddis replied plainly.

There was a prolonged silence. It was strange, but Gaddis felt a sense of relief. He had cleared the air, he had spoken his mind. If Neame now stood up from the table, shook his hand, and walked off into the sunset, he would not be unduly disappointed. It was impossible to write a book of this kind based on the testimony of an unreliable witness; far better to bring things to an end rather than risk his reputation on a story with so many loose ends.

"Mea culpa," Neame announced suddenly. His expression had changed to one of benevolent contrition and he was holding two shaking hands above the table as an indication of his seriousness. Gaddis could see deep lines scarred into the palms. "You're right," he said. "I went too far, old chap. I shouldn't have been so heavy on AGINCOURT. I confess that I became intrigued by the references in Eddie's memoirs. He did indeed tap Wilson up at Oxford, but states categorically that he was never a Soviet agent. I just wanted the whole thing double-checked by an expert. Wilson has since been investigated until the cows come home and nobody has ever been able to lay a finger on him." Gaddis said nothing. He was enjoying the sight of Neame coming clean. "I also wanted to test your limits. I wanted to see how much you would swallow. If I had managed to convince you that Wilson was a Soviet asset without your obtaining any corroborating evidence, who knows what others might have been able to persuade you of, further along the road? I need a man I can *rely* on, Sam. I need a man who isn't going to get excited at the first mention of the NKVD. What I have told you is just the beginning. In a sense, you have passed a test. I congratulate you."

Gaddis was dumbfounded. He summoned a look which he hoped would be suitably contemptuous and closed up the space between them.

"Look, this isn't a game, Tom. I'm not doing this for laughs. I don't want to waste my time fucking about with GPS and window cleaners and encrypted e-mails just to polish your ego. I'm here because I'm convinced that Edward Crane was the sixth Cambridge spy and that you're the key to finding him. But I won't stay here a minute longer if I think I'm being manipulated. I won't risk my reputation on an old man who thinks it's funny to have academics chasing their tails. So you either convince me that these so-called memoirs exist, prove to me that Edward Crane was the sixth man, or call up Peter and ask him to drive you home. Because our business is done."

"Oh, I very much doubt that," Neame replied, with a sting of malice, and Gaddis heard the voice of a man who had lived his life outwitting others, who had always been one step ahead of the pack. He stared into the old man's fixed blue eyes and suddenly, like a bone-deep shudder, felt that Thomas Neame and Edward Crane were the same man. Was this *possible*? He reeled at the thought of it, heat flooding his neck. The idea had caught him completely off guard and he tried to compose himself by remaining steadfast in the face of Neame's reply.

"Try me," he said.

Neame grabbed a shallow breath and the pain which had repeatedly jagged across his shoulders in the cathedral suddenly did so again. He winced as he brought a hand up onto his shoulder, clutching the thick tweed of his jacket and rubbing the bone. Gaddis instinctively stood up out of his seat and leaned forward, placing a hand on Neame's arm. Who was he touching? Neame or Edward Crane?

"Are you all right?"

Neame was looking down at the table, weighing up his options. Gaddis felt that he could read his thoughts. *Should I continue with this man, or find another outlet for my story?* But suddenly he spoke.

"Dick White ordered a full internal vetting of Eddie that was specifically designed to clear him of any suspicious links to Communism."

Neame had clearly convinced himself that the only way to persuade Gaddis of his legitimacy was to keep talking.

"It helped that Eddie had never joined the Party," he said. "His year at Oxford was also carefully recalibrated. Furthermore, there was nothing in the files about his friendship with Burgess at Trinity."

Gaddis felt that he had no choice but to play along.

"But it was still a miracle that he managed to survive undetected for so long—on *both* sides of the Iron Curtain. The Yanks must have smelled a rat. And surely any number of Soviet defectors down the years would have known about ATTILA. Golitsin, for starters."

Neame enjoyed that one.

"Of *course* they did. But it didn't *matter*. Golitsin told the Americans about Crane and the Yanks came to us—flustered, to say the least. We put them in the picture about ATTILA's double life and Eddie's name was then erased from the Golitsin transcripts. Exactly the same procedure when Gordievsky came over. 'Oh, you know about Crane? Keep it hush-hush.' It was straightforward."

"Came to us." "Came to *us*." Why would Neame put himself at the centre of that process?

"But Golitsin came over in '61," Gaddis replied. "Eddie kept going for another twenty-five years. Didn't the Soviets smell a rat when, one by one, their agents in the West started being exposed? Lonsdale? Vassell? Blake? Didn't they think it was a little fortuitous that ATTILA was still out there, alive and well and working for Mother Russia?"

Neame remained impassive.

"My dear boy, I think you'd be better off directing these sorts of questions at a member of the KGB. I have no idea *what* they were thinking. I should imagine the Soviets had thousands of agents all over the world. Just because one or two of them were exposed in Europe doesn't mean they were going to doubt a source who had been working for them since before the war."

"Then why has Crane's story never come out? If the Russians still think ATTILA was one of theirs, they'd love to have rubbed London's nose in it by now."

"Ah." Neame seemed pleased that Gaddis had joined the dots. "My own particular theory is that Moscow discovered ATTILA was a double agent shortly after the collapse of the Soviet Union."

"As late as '91? What makes you say that?"

"Think about it, Sam. Think about the date."

It took a few seconds for Gaddis to make the connection.

"St. Mary's. MI6 faked Eddie's death in early 1992."

"Precisely. Because they were worried that the KGB was going to come after him."

"Eddie told you that?"

"Of *course* Eddie told me that. When your best friend informs you that MI6 are planning to fake his death, you tend to ask why. Eddie said that ATTILA had been blown in Moscow and that anybody associated with him was being systematically bumped off."

Gaddis acknowledged the logic of this, but found a flaw in what Neame was saying.

"Okay, but by the same token, why haven't the British told their end of the story? As you said, ATTILA was one of the great intelligence coups of the Cold War. Why didn't London take the opportunity to humiliate Moscow?"

"Because of the war years. Edward Crane had been a Soviet agent. You don't go making that sort of thing public, especially after the Blunt fiasco. Besides, this was a new era in Anglo-Russian relations. Why rock the boat? SIS likes to keep its secrets. It's in the spying game, not the PR business. What Eddie always wanted to know was who blew his cover. How did the Russians eventually find out?"

Gaddis thought for a moment that Neame expected him to know the answer, but saw that he was going to continue speaking.

"This was as far as I came with your friend, Miss Berg," he said. He caught Gaddis's eye and appeared to be genuinely troubled by her loss. "She was trying to find out the answer to that question when she died."

"And did she?"

"She was your friend, Sam. You tell me."

There was a long silence. Gaddis felt that Neame was still holding something back.

"Tom?"

"Yes?"

"You look like you want to tell me something. Is it about Charlotte?"

Neame looked up at the bar then down to his shaking, mottled hands. The whites of his eyes were glassy, free-floating, as if he was struggling to focus. "There is a woman in Moscow by the name of Ludmilla Tretiak. She is the widow of ATTILA's third and final KGB handler, Fyodor Tretiak. I had suggested to Charlotte that she try to find her."

"And did she?"

Neame looked back at the bar. "I have no idea. Ludmilla was a lead that Eddie had wanted to follow before he was forced underground. All I did was to warn Charlotte about her."

"Why?"

"Tretiak was murdered in St. Petersburg in 1992."

"The same year that Eddie met his maker at St. Mary's."

"Precisely. That always struck me as too much of a coincidence. If Ludmilla suspects that her husband was killed by the KGB, she might want to talk to somebody about it. Which means that there are bound to be people watching her. Even now." Neame cautioned Gaddis with a resigned smile. "If you seek her out, Sam, take the appropriate precautions. That's all I'm saying. Make sure she isn't observed talking to any nosey historians."

20

addis was certain that he had seen Ludmilla Tretiak's name in Charlotte's files. Back in London, he called Paul, went round to the house in Hampstead, and rummaged through her office. Sure enough, after searching for less than fifteen minutes, he found a listing for Tretiak under *T* in one of her Moleskine notebooks, complete with an address and telephone number in Moscow. Later that evening, Paul remembered that Charlotte had been booked on a flight to Russia six days after her heart attack and called Gaddis to tell him. In her diary for that date, she had written the initials *FT/LT* and *SU581,* which turned out to be an Aeroflot flight number. Gaddis was convinced that the two women had arranged to meet, although there was no trace of an e-mail correspondence between them on any of Charlotte's accounts.

It took him forty-eight hours to arrange a flight and emergency visa to Moscow via his usual travel agents in Pembridge Square; the publication of *Tsars* had clearly made no impact on Gaddis's status at the Russian Embassy. He arrived at Sheremetyevo late on a Monday evening, endured the traditional chaos at passport control, and found his suitcase in a corner of the baggage area fifty metres from Aeroflot's advertised carousel. Gaddis had arranged for Victor, the driver that he always used in Moscow, to pick him up outside the airport, and they shunted along a five-lane highway in permanent gridlock towards the Sovietsky Hotel, assaulted by smells of cigarettes and diesel.

The following morning, after breakfasting on an omelette and two cups of metallic black coffee, he took the Metro three stops from Dinamo to Voykovskaya, emerging two blocks from Ludmilla Tretiak's apartment. Whenever he was in the centre of Moscow, Gaddis felt that he had a memory for almost every building and street that he passed. But Voykovskaya was beyond the Garden Ring, a grey and sunless neighbourhood that he knew only by name. Tretiak's apartment turned out to be on the ninth floor of a typical panel-built, twenty-storey, post-Soviet tower finished in three shades of beige. It was on a busy street characterized by erratically parked cars and kiosks selling pirated DVDs and cheap makeup. To ensure that Tretiak was in the city, Gaddis had called her number from a phone box in Shepherd's Bush, pretending to be a telesales assistant offering cheap rates on wireless broadband. She had politely informed him that she did not use a computer and wished him a good day.

Residents were coming in and out of the building all the time and Gaddis was able to enter without pressing the buzzer. He had decided to make his approach at lunchtime, when Tretiak was most likely to be at home, and had written a short note in Russian which he now passed under her door in a sealed envelope.

Esteemed Ludmilla Tretiak,

Please excuse this method of contacting you. I am an historian from University College in London. I was also a friend of Charlotte Berg. I am aware of what happened to your husband in St. Petersburg in 1992. For reasons that I am sure you will appreciate, I do not wish to put your safety at risk by telephoning you or even by introducing myself to you in person at your home.

I have information about the events leading to your husband's death. If you would like to discuss this matter further, I will be sitting in the branch of Coffee House opposite this building for the rest of the day. I am wearing a blue shirt and will have a copy of *The Moscow Times* on the table in front of me. Alternatively, if you would prefer to contact me by e-mail, I have left an address at the bottom of this page.

With my respect,
Dr. Samuel Gaddis

When he had pushed the envelope inside the apartment, Gaddis rang the bell twice, in quick succession, then took the lift back down to the ground floor. He wondered if he had sounded the right tone in the letter. Tretiak had been courteous and polite over the phone, but he could not be sure of her age and had perhaps pitched the letter too formally. Would she be prepared to risk a meeting with a man she neither knew nor could possibly trust? She might pass the letter directly into the hands of the FSB, with potentially disastrous consequences. But it was a risk that he had to take.

As it transpired, he had no need to be concerned. Twenty minutes after he had sat down towards the back of the Coffee House, Ludmilla Tretiak walked in, appeared to recognize Gaddis immediately, and came towards his table. She was younger than he had imagined, perhaps no more than forty, and looked almost amused as she shook his outstretched hand and removed a bottle-green overcoat secured around her waist by a narrow leather belt.

"I wish you good health," he said in Russian. "You are kind to come."

"How could I not? I was intrigued by your letter, Dr. Gaddis."

She was dressed in designer jeans and a dark red blouse which fitted her pale, slender frame so precisely it might almost have been tailored. Gaddis was reminded of a certain type of married woman in the wealthier avenues of Kensington and Notting Hill, preserved in the dignity of early middle age, manicured and undernourished. He wondered if Ludmilla had remarried, and searched her hands for a ring which wasn't there. Had she had children with Tretiak? They would be teenagers by now, schooled in Moscow.

"I apologize for all the subterfuge," he said. He used the word "uhlovka" for "subterfuge" and Tretiak's calm eyes flared for a split second as she acknowledged his proficiency in Russian.

"You must have been warned about me," she replied.

Was this the same woman that he had spoken to from the phone box in London? Her voice was very faint, but oddly playful. He tried to recall her end of the conversation, how she had pitched it, but his memory failed him.

"I think you were supposed to meet Charlotte in Moscow last month," he said.

"That is correct. I never heard from her again." Ludmilla took off a pair of leather gloves and set them on the table. Her fingers were witch-thin and bitten. "You said in your letter that you *were* a friend of hers. I hope that she is all right."

"I'm afraid I have to tell you that Charlotte died suddenly."

Ludmilla reacted in a way that reminded Gaddis of Holly's indifference towards her late mother's death. "I am sorry for your loss," she replied, without inflection.

He craved a cigarette, but had made yet another private pact to quit. The Aeroflot flight had started it: smoking was banned on board, of course, but the upholstery of his seat had been so marinated in nicotine that he had considered lighting up in the toilet at 35,000 feet.

"Did Charlotte mention why she wanted to talk to you?"

"Of course." A waitress wearing a beige shirt and a long brown skirt approached them. Tretiak ordered a cup of tea with lemon. Gaddis was increasingly unnerved by her almost glacial sense of calm. "She told me that she was a reporter who knew about the circumstances leading to my husband's death. In fact, she adopted almost exactly the same phrase that you used in your letter. 'I know what happened to your husband in 1992.' Nothing more, nothing less. Only this."

Gaddis could see that he was expected to reply, to explain himself, but he was confused by Tretiak's manner, which was at once confident and yet oddly disconnected.

"Perhaps I should explain why I am here," he suggested.

"Perhaps you should."

She suddenly smiled with a jarring, false rictus. Had she popped a pill before leaving her apartment? Sunk a couple of shots of vodka? Something had taken the edge off her anxiety and calmed her nerves. It was like talking to a doll.

"I'm an academic in the Department of Eastern European and

Slavonic Studies at UCL. Charlotte and I were friends. She was investigating a story relating to an NKVD operation in the United Kingdom before World War II which involved a graduate of Cambridge University named Edward Crane. When Charlotte died, I took on the story myself, with the idea of writing a book about it. My primary source of information is a man named Thomas Neame, a British citizen resident in England. It was Mr. Neame who gave me your name."

"I have never heard of this man." Tretiak's tea arrived in a tall glass and she stirred three packets of sugar into it, the tiny granules funnelling around the spoon. Gaddis watched them dissolve, hypnotized, and wondered how much he could risk revealing about ATTILA.

"In the twilight of his career, Edward Crane was living in Berlin. Your husband was his final KGB handler."

Tretiak produced a look which suggested an almost complete indifference to her husband's career.

"I was not privy to Fyodor's work," she replied. "We were married when I was very young. My husband was a rising star in the Komitet Gosudarstvennoy Bezopasnosti." This was the formal, unabbreviated name for the KGB. "He was forty-seven when he died. I was just twenty-six. We had a small baby, my son, Alexey. We were left alone, to fend for ourselves. Everything is fine."

A faultline ran through her features, like a crack in the makeup of her personality. The effect of whatever medication she had taken had briefly shut down. Tretiak struggled to resume her customary air of intelligent hauteur and took a straight-backed sip of tea.

"Would you have met any of your husband's informants?" Gaddis asked. He heard his own voice and felt like the worst kind of snoop. This woman was evidently unstable; he was no better than a tabloid hack door-stepping a grieving widow.

"Of course not. Are you suggesting that agents would come to our apartment in Dresden? That I would cook for them while Fyodor talked business in the living room?"

"Dresden? Why Dresden?"

"Because that is where we lived, Doctor Gaddis." She was looking at him in the way that an aunt looks at a nephew of whom she is not particularly fond. "That is where we kept our apartment."

Gaddis was puzzled. He could only assume that Fyodor Tretiak had made trips from Dresden to Berlin whenever he had been required to meet Crane. It was a distance of—what?—a couple of hundred kilometres. He looked up to find that Tretiak's widow was still staring at him and felt as if he was on the losing side of the conversation. Unless he could extract something useful in the next few minutes, he was facing the prospect of a wasted trip to Moscow.

"Look," he said, trying to summon as much charm as he could muster. "I know from my limited understanding of intelligence work that wives can play a useful role in providing cover for their husbands. There was a famous example of an MI6 officer in Moscow whose wife passed information to a KGB colonel. He eventually defected to the West."

"Oh?" Tretiak's voice was like the song of a distant bird. "Who was that?" She had no interest in the answer.

"Never mind." Gaddis steeled himself. "Can I ask, please, how did your husband die?"

Tretiak looked to one side, numbly surprised that this stranger from England had suddenly crossed a line into an area of her past which was still raw and private. Gaddis saw this and apologized for being crass.

"It is all right," she said. "If I was not prepared to talk about this, I would not have come downstairs. I knew from your note that this would be the subject of our conversation. As I have already told you, I was intrigued."

This seemed hopeful. Gaddis encouraged her to tell the story.

"It is quite simple. He was walking home one night to our apartment in St. Petersburg when he was shot by three men."

"Three? Were they ever identified? Were they brought to trial?"

She gave a resigned smile. She was resigned to everything. "Of course not. These men were gangsters. Mafia, you call them. It was simply an act of vengeance against a senior figure in the KGB."

According to Neame, Tretiak had been murdered by the KGB, yet his widow had the story the other way around. Gaddis suspected that she had been hoodwinked. In all probability, the KGB had simply hired a trio of St. Petersburg thugs to do their dirty work for them. It was the most plausible thesis: the links between Russian Intelligence and Russian organized crime were murky, to say the least.

"Vengeance for what?" he asked.

"How would I know?" Tretiak shrugged and stared outside at the traffic. "As I have told you, I was not privy to the secret nature of my husband's work."

Gaddis looked down at his lukewarm tea and drank it, just to give himself something to do with his hands. Tretiak was gazing out of the window, like a teenage girl bored by her date.

"It's interesting," he said. "My understanding of what happened to your husband is quite different."

"Go on," she said.

Gaddis lowered his voice beneath the clatter and chat of the café. There was music playing on a broken stereo; it sounded as though the speakers were fizzing. "Look, I know that it's hard for you. I know that you have no reason to trust me—"

"Doctor Gaddis—"

He spoke over her interruption.

"But this is what I know. The source your husband was running had been working for Russian Intelligence for almost fifty years. His KGB cryptonym was ATTILA. He was the greatest Western asset on the books at Moscow Centre for decades—but he was a double agent."

Tretiak's mouth parted very slowly, strands of saliva appearing between her lips like a thin glue.

"How do you know this?"

"I'm afraid I can't tell you that."

"You cannot tell me who has levelled this accusation?"

"Mrs. Tretiak, what I am suggesting to you today is that the KGB wanted to cover up the existence of ATTILA. They wanted to save themselves the embarrassment of being deceived by the British Secret Intelligence Service. So they killed anybody who had anything to do with him. They murdered your husband to silence him."

"What was Crane's position in Berlin?" she asked. Lines had appeared in the light foundation around her eyes, further cracks in the mask. Gaddis recalled a detail from the obituary in *The Times*.

"He was on the board of a German investment bank which had offices in Berlin."

She swore under her breath. For the first time, Gaddis caught a vapour of alcohol, sharp and full.

"Why do you swear?" he asked.

"Why do I *swear*?" She laughed so loudly that several customers turned to look at them. "It's just that only recently I was told never to speak about this affair."

Gaddis wasn't sure that he had heard her correctly. Then why had she responded so freely to his letter? Why had she come down to the café?

"What do you mean?"

"It was only last month, shortly after Berg had been in contact with me." Tretiak said "Berg" as if she had no energy for the full name. "I received a visit from a government official."

Gaddis felt a threat in his gut, tugging at him like the grinding traffic outside.

"What does that mean? Somebody from Belyi Dom came to see you?"

Belyi Dom was the Russian translation of "White House," the seat of government in Moscow. Tretiak nodded. She looked weary, almost bored. She might have been talking about a visit from a postman or a plumber. "This man told me that he was under instructions from Sergei Platov himself."

"*Platov?*" Gaddis couldn't believe what he was hearing. "I don't follow, Mrs. Tretiak. What would the president want with you? What did this man say?"

"I was instructed not to talk to your friend."

Gaddis had the strange sensation of staring through her, into a dimension of secrets and obfuscations that he would never penetrate. He was about to ask how the Kremlin knew that Tretiak was planning to talk to Charlotte when he realized the answer to his own question: they had seen her e-mails. Christ, Charlotte had probably been bugged as well. That was why he had been unable to find any evidence of the Crane investigation on her computers; FSB technicians had wiped them clean. He watched Tretiak across the table, tiny and broken and shrugging her shoulders like a petulant schoolgirl. He wanted to shake her, to snap her out of her medicated reverie. A drizzle of rain appeared on the windows of the Coffee House as she managed a weak, consoling smile. Gaddis pressed her for more information, but she remained vague and indifferent to details.

"The official told me that I should not talk to anyone about Edward Crane. That if I was approached by any individual from the United Kingdom or America wishing to speak to me about an agent code-named ATTILA, I was to inform them as a matter of urgency."

Gaddis pushed back from the table, an instinct for self-preservation. He did not feel that Tretiak had lured him into a trap—she was too stoned for that—but Moscow was now a threat to him, a city closing in. He looked around the café. Any one of the office workers, the students, the kissing couple in the corner, could be surveillance operatives.

"You shouldn't have agreed to meet me," he said. "It's not safe for you. You could get in a lot of trouble over this. You need to sort yourself out."

"Perhaps," she replied.

"You must destroy the letter that I wrote to you."

"Take it," she said, instantly producing the note from the pocket of her jeans.

"And don't speak to anyone about this, okay? It's for your safety as well as mine. Think of your son, Mrs. Tretiak. Our conversation didn't happen. Do you understand?"

She nodded dumbly. Gaddis surprised himself by gripping her by the arms. They were so thin he felt that he could have snapped them with a flick of his wrists.

"Ludmilla. Focus." He looked into her eyes and saw that she must once have been transfixingly beautiful. All that was gone now. The waitress, changing a CD behind the counter, looked across as he released her. "Forget about our conversation. Forget what I have told you. About Edward Crane, about ATTILA, about your husband's murder. It's for your own safety, okay? Be smart. This situation is far more dangerous than I imagined."

21

Dresden didn't make sense until Gaddis was somewhere over the North Sea drinking a Bloody Mary on the Aeroflot back to London. In 1985, as a fledgling spy, Sergei Platov had been posted to Dresden by the First Chief Directorate of the KGB. He would have worked alongside Tretiak. He would almost certainly have known that ATTILA was operating out of Berlin.

Gaddis spent most of the journey trying to untangle the implications of this. Why was the Russian president personally interfering in the ATTILA cover-up more than fifteen years after leaving the KGB? Had Charlotte uncovered a scandal with the potential to obliterate Platov's career and reputation? She hadn't mentioned anything about that at dinner; the threat from ATTILA, as she saw it, was to the British, not the Russian government. Perhaps Platov, as a loyal KGB man, was simply keen to uphold the reputation of his former employers by ensuring that the Crane story never came to light.

There was a darker possibility, of course; that Charlotte had died not from natural causes, not from a heart attack brought on by too many cigarettes and too much booze, but that she had been murdered by Platov's cronies to ensure her silence. Trapped between a sprawling, restless teenager on the aisle, and an overweight Estonian business-man sleeping fitfully in the window seat, Gaddis picked at a freeze-dried stroganoff and a stale bread roll, his mouth dry, his appetite lost to the sickening thought that Charlotte might have become the latest victim of the Russian government's near-psychotic determina-tion to silence journalists, at home and abroad, who failed to toe the party line. His only cause to doubt this theory was his own continued well-being. Ludmilla Tretiak was also alive and well, albeit pickled in vodka and tranquilizers. Who else had Charlotte spoken to? Thomas Neame. But the old man was still going strong in Winchester. And Calvin Somers, as far as he knew, was still doing his shifts at the Mount Vernon Hospital.

Five hours later, Gaddis returned home to find that he had been contacted by a researcher at the National Archives in Kew. A woman named Josephine Warner had left a sprightly message on his landline informing him that she had dug up a copy of Edward Crane's will. It was the last thing that Gaddis had been expecting—he had forgotten even lodging the request—but it helped to give some direction to his thoughts and he drove down to Kew the following morning, plan-ning to continue to Winchester if he could get Peter to answer his phone. He needed to see Neame. Tom was still the only contact he could think of who might have information about Tretiak's career in Dresden.

On the first floor of the archive building he asked a member of staff to point out Josephine Warner and was directed towards the enquiries desk. There were two women seated next to each other on red plastic chairs. Gaddis knew one of them on sight, an Afro-Caribbean woman called Dora who had helped him with his enquiries several times before. The second woman was new. She was in her late twenties, with black hair cut to shoulder length and a face whose beauty revealed itself only slowly as he walked towards her; in the stillness of her dark eyes, in the lucidity of her pale skin.

"Josephine Warner?"

"Yes?"

"I'm Sam Gaddis. You left a message on my phone yesterday."

"Oh, right." She stood up immediately, as if sprung from her seat, and turned towards the bank of cabinets behind her. Gaddis nodded as Dora gave him a smile of recognition and Warner opened a drawer, fingers flicking rapidly through a file of documents. "Here it is," she said, almost to herself, picking out a manila envelope and handing it to Gaddis.

"It's very kind of you," he said. "Thanks for digging it out. It could be very useful."

"Pleasure."

He would happily have spoken to her for longer, but Josephine Warner was already looking beyond him, inviting the next customer with her eyes. Gaddis took the envelope to a reading table on the far side of the room, removed the will, and began to read.

The contents were relatively straightforward. Crane had left the bulk of his estate to a nephew, Charles Crane, now sixty-seven and resident in Greece. Gaddis wrote down the address in Athens. Substantial donations had been made to Cancer Research UK and to the SIS Widow's Fund. The will had been executed by Thomas Neame, to whom Crane had left "the contents of my library" and witnessed by a "Mrs. Audrey Slight" and a "Mr. Richard Kenner." Addresses were given for both and Gaddis wrote them down. He had no recollection of Neame mentioning that he had acted as executor on Crane's will, nor that he had been left any books, but he was at least now reassured that the two men were separate individuals.

At about eleven o'clock, two hours behind Athens, Gaddis went downstairs and called international directory enquiries from a phone box in the foyer. The operator found Charles Crane's number within a couple of minutes and Gaddis called it from his mobile. A man answered in Greek.

"*Embros?*"

The voice sounded slightly dotty, with a laboured Greek accent. Gaddis had an image of an ageing Englishman, sunburned and decked out in linen, reading Gibbon on the steps of the Parthenon.

"Charles Crane?"

"Speaking."

"My name is Sam Gaddis. I'm an academic in London, at UCL. I'm sorry to bother you out of the blue. I'm researching a book on the history of the Foreign Office and wondered if I might be able to ask you some questions about your late uncle, Edward Crane."

"Good Lord, Eddie." It sounded as though the nephew who had benefited so handsomely from the generosity of his late uncle had not given a moment's thought to him since 1992. "Yes, of course. What would you like to know?"

Gaddis told him what he knew of Crane's career in the Diplomatic Service, sticking firmly to the template of *The Times* obituary and avoiding any mention of Cambridge, SIS, or the NKVD. To draw him out further, he flattered Crane by telling him that his late uncle had played a vital, yet unheralded role in the winning of the Cold War.

"Really? Is that so? Yes, well I suppose Eddie was quite a character."

Gaddis now began to wish that he had been sitting somewhere more comfortable, because Crane embarked on a series of rambling, near-nonsensical anecdotes about his uncle's "mysterious life." It transpired that the two men had met "only a handful of times" and that Charles had been "stunned, absolutely stunned" to be the main beneficiary of his will.

"He never married, of course," he said, the spectre of a black sheep hovering over the good name of the Crane family. "*Entre nous,* I think he was batting for the other side. Dormant, perhaps, but certainly a feature of his youth, if you know what I'm driving at."

Gaddis found himself saying that, yes, he knew exactly what Charles Crane was driving at.

"Retired rather late. No children to look after, you see. Not like the rest of us. Nothing to occupy his time except the Foreign Office."

It was clear that Crane did not even know that his uncle had worked for SIS. As far as he was concerned, he had just been a middle-ranking diplomat with "one or two postings overseas."

"Does the name Audrey Slight mean anything to you?"

"Afraid not, Mr. Gaddis."

"She was one of the two witnesses on your uncle's will."

The name finally rang a bell. "Oh, *Audrey*. She was Eddie's housekeeper for yonks." Crane sounded like a contestant on a game show who discovers the answer to a question fractionally late. "I think she died a few years ago. Getting on a bit. Thomas Neame was my main point of contact for the estate."

"You didn't speak to Richard Kenner?"

"Who?"

"The other witness."

"No. But if memory serves, Kenner was also Foreign Office. A colleague of Eddie's. Might be worth looking him up."

Most probably another wild goose chase. Kenner would almost certainly be dead, or erased from the official records to protect AT-TILA's anonymity. Gaddis asked Crane about his dealings with Neame but learned nothing that he did not already know; simply that the old man was "highly intelligent," "irascible," and "occasionally bloody rude."

"So you met him?"

"Only once. Lawyer's office in London. I spoke to him on the telephone a number of times as we ironed out the flat in Bloomsbury, the house here in Athens. The estate was rather substantial."

This, at least, was new information, although Gaddis was still desperately short of facts about Crane's postwar career. Then it occurred to him that he did not have a photograph of Crane and took a chance that a nephew might at least have an old family Polaroid lying around in an attic.

"I was wondering," he said. "Would you have a picture of your uncle? Anything at all? I've had trouble tracking one down. When a man dies without children, with no siblings or close relatives, there are very few people who keep hold of such things."

Crane was immediately sympathetic to Gaddis's predicament. "Of course," he said. "I'm sure I can dig one up for you from somewhere. There's bound to be one lurking around. I'll get on to it."

"That would be very kind."

Gaddis gave an address at UCL to which Crane could send the photograph and then hung up. As he did so, he wondered if he should have invited himself out to Greece. If Crane was living in his late uncle's property, there might be files or boxes lurking in a basement which could be of use to the ATTILA investigation. Instead, he put the mobile back in his pocket, walked to the ground-floor café, and ordered a cup of tea.

22

addis bumped into Josephine Warner in the car park. She was unlocking a black Renault and putting a Waitrose carrier bag on the backseat. She might not have seen him if Gaddis hadn't waved and shouted "Hi!" across a line of parked cars. He was halfway through a cigarette, having abandoned yet another attempt to quit, and stubbed it out on the ground.

"Hello. Doctor Gaddis, isn't it?"

"It is," he said. He came towards her, looking at his watch. "You already going home?"

He privately hoped that she was. Peter still wasn't answering his phone and he had given up on going to Winchester. He was at a loose end, feeling restless, and might invite her out to lunch.

"Not home," she said. "Just popping to Richmond to pick up a colleague. I'm the new kid on the block, so they've got me running errands."

She looked at him, a quiet appraisal, and Gaddis was certain that he detected the faintest trace of an invitation in her eyes. Then he thought of Holly and wondered why the hell he was succumbing to a car park flirtation with an archivist from Kew. No good was ever going to come of it.

"Thanks again for the will," he said, taking a step back.

"Was it useful?" Instinctively, she had moved forwards, following him. A wind kicked up, sharp and autumnal. Warner held loose strands of hair away from her face as she said: "I read your Bulgakov biography. Are you writing a new book?"

This took him by surprise. She had appeared indifferent earlier in the morning, showing no indication that she even knew who he was. "You did? Why? Were you stuck for something to read on the Trans-Siberian? Killing time in prison?"

She smiled and said that she had loved the book and Gaddis felt the awful, shallow thrill of a woman's flattery. If he was honest with himself, within moments of seeing her at the reception desk he had wanted to pursue her, just as he and Natasha had pursued other lovers during their marriage. Why had they done it? Their behaviour had fractured the relationship irreparably. And yet he would happily go through the very same process again with this woman whom he did not know, jeopardizing something promising with Holly. Perhaps the distraction of an affair would take his mind off Crane and Neame. In which case—walk away. The book was far more important. But he found that he wanted to keep talking to her, to see where the conversation led them.

"A boyfriend put me on to *The Master and Margarita* at Oxford," she said, stepping beyond the Renault so that they were now no more than a metre apart. "In fact I think he plagiarized most of your book for his dissertation."

"There's a good Russian department at Oxford," Gaddis said, noting the cool, gliding reference to a past lover. "I haven't seen you here before."

"I just started. Part-time. Finished my Ph.D. in June."

"And you couldn't stand being away from archives and librarians?"

"Something like that."

What followed, in the next few minutes, was an exchange as commonplace as it was predictable. Gaddis said that he was heading back to Shepherd's Bush and Josephine Warner, seizing on this, happened to mention that she lived "just around the corner" in Chiswick.

Gaddis then found a way of suggesting that they should get together for a drink one night and Warner enthusiastically agreed, supplying another inviting gaze as she offered her mobile number in exchange for his. It was a first dance, a step on the road to the possibility of seduction, with both parties playing their roles to practised perfection.

Gaddis gave it forty-eight hours before telephoning to arrange to meet for a drink. Josephine sounded pleased to hear from him and encouraged the idea of meeting up for dinner. He suggested a restaurant in Brackenbury Village and, three nights later, they were ensconced at a candlelit table, working their way through a bottle of Givry. He was surprised by the candour of their conversation, almost from its first moments.

"Let's just say that my love life is complicated," Josephine told him, before they had even ordered their food, and Gaddis had felt obliged to reveal that he, too, had been "seeing someone for the last month or so." It was obvious to both parties that they were sizing each other up. Gaddis was not one of those people who believed that a platonic friendship between a man and a woman was impossible, but he was also realistic enough to know that he and Josephine hadn't agreed to meet solely for the pleasure of discussing historical archives. She was continuously and discreetly flirtatious all night and he returned the compliment, trying as best he could to ease her towards a second date. As the meal progressed, he began to think that she was almost too good to be true: quick-witted, funny and sharp, and able to talk engagingly on seemingly any subject, from cricket to Tolstoy, from *Seinfeld* to Graham Greene. She was also astonishingly beautiful, but without an apparent trace of vanity or self-regard. Every now and again, as if sensing his attraction, Josephine found a way of reminding Gaddis that there was a more-or-less permanent boyfriend lurking in the background of her life, but these reminders served only to convince him that she was looking for a way out of the relationship.

"He's asked me to marry him twice," she said, spinning spaghetti on her fork.

"And you keep saying no?"

"I keep asking him to give me more time."

She asked him why his own marriage had ended, which was a subject Gaddis had avoided with Holly for a considerable time, but there was something in Josephine's open, trusting spirit which encouraged him towards full disclosure.

"Neither of us was suited to it," he said. "Marriage put bars around us, restrictions which we weren't prepared to respect."

"You were unfaithful?"

"We were both unfaithful," he said, and was grateful when Josephine turned her attention to Min.

"And you said that your daughter lives in Barcelona?"

"Yes. With her mother. And a boyfriend that I do my best to . . ."

"Torture?"

Gaddis smiled. "Tolerate."

"But it's complicated?"

"Past a certain point, everything becomes complicated, don't you think?"

They ordered a second bottle of wine and Gaddis talked of his frustration at missing out on Min's formative years. He said that he tried to go to Spain "at least once a month," but that it was difficult for Min herself to come to London because she was still too young to fly unaccompanied by an adult. He revealed that, from time to time, he would discover one of her toys stuck behind the sofa, or a single pink sock hidden at the bottom of a laundry basket. He might have added that there had been nights when he had found himself curled up on Min's bed in the house, sobbing into her pillow, but that was a revelation for a fifth or sixth date; there was no point in entirely dismantling the image he was trying to project of a robust and civilized man.

Pudding came and finally they talked about his research at Kew. It was, out of necessity, the only point in the evening when Gaddis lied outright, claiming that he was preparing a lecture on the activities of the NKVD during World War II. The truth about Edward Crane was a secret that he could share only with himself; it certainly could not be trusted to Josephine Warner. He mentioned the possibility that his research might take him to Berlin.

"There's a contact there who I'd like to talk to."

"Somebody who was working for the Russians during the war?"

"Yes."

Josephine straightened the napkin in her lap.

"My sister lives in Berlin."

"Really?"

"Yes. Moved there two years ago. I still haven't been to visit."

Looking up from his plate, with a mixture of surprise and delight, Gaddis realized that Josephine was presenting him with the opportunity to invite her to Germany.

"Maybe I should look her up when I go over," he suggested.

"She's trouble," Josephine replied, and Gaddis was sure that he caught a flash of jealousy in her eyes.

However, this proved to be the high tide of their flirtatious rapport. By eleven o'clock, Gaddis had paid the bill and they had walked north towards Goldhawk Road, where Josephine's behaviour changed markedly. Within seconds she had flagged down a cab, aware perhaps that they were both a little drunk, both attracted to each other and, in different circumstances, might easily have succumbed to a late-night pavement clinch.

"I had fun tonight," she said, ducking into the backseat after kissing Gaddis cursorily on the cheek.

"I enjoyed it, too," Gaddis replied, surprised by how quickly Josephine had cut off the romantic possibilities of the evening. He concluded that she was returning to the "complicated" love life that she had referred to at the beginning of dinner.

"Got to be up at five," she explained, and waved briefly through the rear window of the cab as it pulled away towards Chiswick. Gaddis had known dates like this before and wondered if he would see her again. She had promised to "dig up" a photograph of Edward Crane at Kew, but they had crossed a professional and personal boundary tonight and he suspected that she would pass the job to a colleague, to avoid any unnecessary complications. Perhaps he was being unduly pessimistic, but there had been something in Josephine's manner as they walked away from the restaurant which had seemed to shut down any possibility of a relationship. Throughout the meal, she had been unquestionably seductive, raising oblique prospects of further meetings—movies, lunches, even Berlin—but that playfulness had disappeared once he had paid the bill. It was a pity, because he liked her. Walking home through a crisscross of dimly lit residential streets, he realized that it had been a long time since a woman had crept under his skin like Josephine Warner.

23

Two days later, Gaddis was sifting through his mail at the start of the new term at UCL when he turned up an A4-sized manila envelope with a Greek postmark.

Inside, he found a handwritten note on monogrammed paper from Charles Crane.

What a wonderful surprise to speak to you on the telephone yesterday. I've managed to track down a couple of photographs of Uncle Eddie. One taken during the war and another at my mother's house in Berkshire in the late 1970s (possibly '80 or even '81). If memory serves, Eddie had just retired from the Foreign Office and was about to take up a position on the Board of Deutsche Bank in West Berlin.

When you're finished with them, could I ask that you send them back to the address above? I would be most grateful.

Gaddis pulled out the photographs, his hand snagging on the envelope in his enthusiasm to see them. At last he was going to set eyes on Edward Crane.

The picture from the war was a formal black-and-white portrait of a soldier in full uniform. It was mounted on a frayed square of greying cardboard and signed and dated "1942" in near-illegible blue ink. Crane was in his early thirties, with brooding, saturnine features and thick black hair which had been carefully combed, parted to one side, and run through with oil. It was not the face that Gaddis had been expecting; in his imagination, Crane had been a less physically imposing figure, slim and cunning, perhaps even a touch effete. This Crane was a bruiser, tough and thick-set. It was difficult to imagine that the man in the photograph had possessed the subtlety to hoodwink intelligence services on both sides of the Iron Curtain for more than fifty years. And why the soldier's uniform? At the time the photograph was taken, Crane would most probably have been working in counterespionage at MI5, passing the names of potential Soviet defectors to Theodore Maly. Gaddis concluded that Crane had perhaps worn a soldier's uniform while assisting Cairncross at Bletchley.

The second photograph was a close-up Polaroid taken in a hazy, sun-filled English garden. The hair was still carefully tended, but thinner now and white as chalk. Gaddis was reminded of pictures of the older W. H. Auden because Crane's face was craggy and tanned, loose about the neck. Calvin Somers had described his skin as looking "too healthy" for a man suffering from pancreatic cancer, but perhaps he had been referring to the colour and texture of Crane's face, rather than to his apparent youthfulness. The nose, he noted, was flushed, either with wine or sunburn—Gaddis couldn't tell—and the smile was broad and energetic; this time you could see the charm of the master spy. Gaddis felt relieved, because this second image conformed far more closely to his mental picture of Crane. Furthermore, it put to rest any lingering doubts he might have possessed that Crane and Neame were the same person. It was not difficult, for example, to imagine the man in the photograph as an avuncular figure passing himself off as a patrician banker in Berlin; at the same time, Crane's face had a bohemian quality, the eyes betraying a wild streak bordering on the eccentric. Gaddis could only guess at the secrets stacked up behind those eyes, five decades of bluff and counter-bluff, culminating in the mysteries of Dresden.

He was not to know that Charles Crane did not exist. The man Gaddis had spoken to on the telephone was one Alistair Chapman, a colleague of Sir John Brennan's from an era in which the Chief of the Secret Intelligence Service had been a mid-level officer operating in Cold War Vienna. Chapman had agreed to allow SIS to divert an Athens phone number to his London home and to masquerade as Crane's nephew as a favour to Brennan. The Chief had been delighted with his performance.

"Thank you, Alistair," he had said, speaking to Chapman that evening. "I doubt that in the long history of the Secret Intelligence Service we have ever employed a more distinguished backstop."

The photographs that Charles Crane had supposedly posted to Gaddis were, in fact, pictures of a former SIS officer named Anthony Kitto, who had died in 1983. Brennan had simply dug them up from an archive and placed them in the envelope. Gaddis, of course, was none the wiser, and even made a mental note to write Crane a letter of thanks as he turned to his other post.

There was a letter from a colleague in America, a postcard of Gaudí's Sagrada Família signed by Min and, at the bottom of the pile, a bank statement from Barclays. He was in the habit of throwing away correspondence from the myriad organizations to which he owed money, but on this occasion he glanced at the statement and was surprised to see that his balance was healthier than he had imagined. Over a month after he had handed Calvin Somers a cheque for £2,000, the money had still not been cashed. The cheque had been postdated, but at least two weeks had passed in which Somers could have presented it to his bank.

Gaddis was confronted by a dilemma. He could cross his fingers and hope that Somers had forgotten about the cheque, but it was hopeless to think that a man as grasping and as manipulative as that would simply forget he was sitting on two grand. More likely Somers had lost the cheque and would come asking for a replacement in three or four weeks' time. The last thing Gaddis needed was somebody asking him for two grand in the run-up to Christmas. By then, any cheque he wrote would almost certainly bounce. He ran through the address book in his mobile phone, found the number of the Mount Vernon Hospital, and called Somers's office.

The call was diverted to the main switchboard. Gaddis was fairly sure that the woman who answered was the same bored, impatient receptionist who had brushed him off in September.

"Could you put me through to Calvin Somers, please? I'm having difficulty getting him on his direct line."

There was an audible intake of breath. It was definitely the same woman; she sounded irritated even by this modest request.

"Can I ask who's calling, please?"

"Sam Gaddis. It's a personal call."

"Could you hold?"

Before Gaddis had a chance to say "Of course," the line went dead and he was left holding the receiver, wondering if the connection had been lost. Then, just as he was on the point of hanging up and re-dialling, a man picked up, coughing to clear his throat.

"Mr. Gaddis?"

"Yes."

"You're looking for Calvin?"

"That's right."

Gaddis heard the awful hollow pause which precedes bad news.

"Could I ask what your relationship was with him?"

"I'm not sure that I understand the question." Gaddis instinctively knew that something was wrong, and regretted sounding obstructive. "Calvin was helping me with some research on an academic thesis. I'm a lecturer at UCL. Is everything all right?"

"I am very sorry to tell you that Calvin has been involved in a terrible incident. He was mugged on his way home from work. Attacked, you might say. I'm surprised you didn't see the reports in the newspapers. The police are treating it as murder."

24

Gaddis was standing in the same room in which he had learned of Charlotte's death, but his reaction on this occasion was quite different. He hung up the phone, turned towards the shelves of books which lined one side of his cramped office, and experienced a sensation of pure fear. For a long time he was almost motionless, his stalled brain trying to deny the inescapable logic of what he had been told. If Calvin Somers had been murdered, Charlotte had most probably been killed by the same assailants. That meant that his own life was in danger and that Neame and Ludmilla Tretiak were also threatened. Gaddis found that he began to think about himself in the third person, as an entity separate and distinct from his own familiar, protected existence; it was some kind of brain trick, an atavistic impulse to deny the truth of his predicament. But the truth was inescapable. Whoever had killed Somers would now surely direct their attention towards him.

He continued to stare blankly at the bookshelves, his eyes jumping from spine to spine. Should he go to the police? Could he claim that Charlotte had been murdered? Who would believe him? There had been no evidence of foul play at the house in Hampstead. Charlotte had a weak heart and an unhealthy lifestyle; that was it. Besides, she had been cremated; it was too late to carry out an autopsy. Gaddis did not know why Somers had been killed or who had perpetrated the act. His best guess was Russian Intelligence, but why murder a man simply for knowing that Edward Crane's death had been faked by MI6? The British themselves might be involved, but would they kill one of their own citizens simply for breaking the terms of the Official Secrets Act? It didn't seem likely.

He tried to clear his mind. He tried to be logical. Fact: the Russian espiocracy was systematically eradicating anybody with links to AT-TILA. But if that was the case, why had the embassy in London given him a tourist visa ten days earlier, no questions asked, allowing him to pass unchecked through Sheremetyevo? This small thought offered Gaddis a brief moment of solace until he realized that there was every chance the FSB could have deliberately allowed him to fly into Russia in order to follow him around Moscow and to isolate his contacts. If that was the case, he would have led them straight to Ludmilla. Turning from the bookshelves, he opened the window of his office, inhaled a lungful of dank London air, and stared up at a black, pre-rain sky. It felt as though he had no moves left; the conspiracy was too large, the main players either dead or far beyond his reach. Who could he talk to who might be able to shed light on what was happening?

Neame.

Gaddis grabbed his jacket and bag, locked his office, and took the Tube to Waterloo. He called Peter from a phone box near the ticket hall but the number still wasn't picking up. A Winchester train, scheduled for 11:39, was sitting on Platform 6, adjacent to a Guildford service which departed five minutes later. With what he hoped would be a successful tactic for shaking off any surveillance, Gaddis walked onto the Guildford train, sat on a fold-down chair beside the automatic doors, then moved quickly across the platform at 11:38 to join the Winchester service. He was not able to determine whether or not he had been followed, but the train moved off within thirty seconds and he sat back in his seat with the dawning realization that his life was about to take on a quality of evasion and trickery for which he was far from prepared.

An hour later he was trying Peter again from a phone box outside Winchester station. This time, he picked up. The sound of his voice felt like the first piece of good fortune Gaddis had experienced in weeks.

"Peter? It's Sam. I need to see our friend. *Now*."

"I'll call you back."

The line went dead. Gaddis was left standing in a phone booth which stank of piss and unwashed men. He opened the door to allow fresh air to funnel inside from the road and as he waited, leaning his body against the worn, age-frosted glass, he realized that he was no longer pursuing Crane for the money. This wasn't about alimony anymore, or tax bills or school fees. It was purely a question of survival; without the book in the public domain, he was a dead man.

The phone rang. Gaddis grabbed at the receiver before the first ring had even finished.

"Sam?"

"Yes?"

"It's not going to be possible today. Afraid the old man's not feeling too good. Head cold."

Ordinarily, Gaddis would have been polite enough to offer his sympathy, but not this time. Instead he forced the point, raising his voice to impress upon Peter the importance of setting up the meeting.

"I don't really give a shit if he's feeling unwell. When he hears what I have to tell him, believe me, he'll be relieved he's only got a cold."

"It's more than that, I'm afraid." Peter was calmly changing his story. "Running a temperature, as well. Confined to his bed at the home."

"And where is the home?"

"I'm afraid I can't tell you that."

"Can you tell me this, then? Can you tell me why Calvin Somers has been murdered?"

"Calvin who?"

"Never mind." There was no point entering into an argument with Neame's gatekeeper, no matter how much satisfaction it might have given Gaddis to vent his anger. Instead, he asked if he had a pen.

"I do."

"Then write this down. Tell Tom that Calvin Somers has been

killed." He spelled out the name. "Charlotte Berg was also murdered. The way things are going, Tom could be next."

"Jesus." It was the first time that Gaddis had sensed Peter losing his cool. "You're not leading these people to us, are you, Sam?"

Gaddis ignored the question. "There's more," he said. "Ludmilla Tretiak"—again, he had to spell out the name—"has been personally instructed by Sergei Platov never to discuss ATTILA. Tretiak is almost certainly under FSB surveillance. There's a link with Crane's time in Dresden, but I'm not sure what it is. Ask Tom if he can find anything in the memoirs about Crane's activities in East Germany in the late 1980s. Charlotte's computer hard drives were deliberately wiped. Somebody knew that she was on to Crane. Tell him all of this."

"It sounds like something you should be telling him in person," Peter replied, and for a moment Gaddis thought that he had breached his defences sufficiently for a meeting to be arranged. But he was to be disappointed. "I just don't think Tom's going to be up to this for the next couple of days. Any chance you could be down here at the weekend?"

"I'm going to Berlin at the weekend," Gaddis replied. He had made the decision on the train and would rack up the cost on a credit card. Benedict Meisner was now his sole remaining chance of a breakthrough. "Monday?"

"Monday," Peter confirmed. "You get to the cathedral by eleven, I promise we'll be there."

25

Now Gaddis had to gamble.

Was there a chance that Russian Intelligence might have linked him to Calvin? Was he next in the line of fire? If Moscow had been listening to Somers's telephone calls, bugging his office at the Mount Vernon, or analysing his e-mail traffic, then the answer was almost certainly yes. If his own Internet activity had been under any kind of scrutiny, either by the FSB or GCHQ, the myriad searches he had performed for information about Edward Crane would almost certainly have been flagged up and reacted upon.

There was less reason to believe that British or Russian Intelligence could have tied him to Charlotte's investigation. True, they had discussed the Cambridge book at supper in Hampstead, but they had not spoken about it on the telephone nor exchanged any e-mails after that night. It was the same with Ludmilla Tretiak: Gaddis had been careful to leave no e-mail or telephone footprint prior to his visit. Unless the FSB had deliberately lured him to Moscow in order to track his movements, his meeting with Tretiak should have passed unnoticed.

Other factors seemed to be working in his favour. Somers had been killed more than two weeks earlier. Charlotte had been dead for over a month. If the Russians were going to come for him, they would surely have come already. As long as he remained vigilant, as long as he avoided making any further references to Crane or ATTILA on his computers or phones, he would surely be safe. But was it dumb to go home? Christ, was Min in danger in Barcelona? That thought, more than the threat to his own safety, left Gaddis with a feeling of complete powerlessness. Yet what could he do? If they wanted to get to Min or Natasha, they could do so at a moment's notice. If they wanted to silence him, they could strike at any time. It would make no difference if he moved into a hotel, slept at Holly's apartment, or emigrated to Karachi. Sooner or later, the FSB would track him down. Besides, he didn't want to be driven out of his home by a bunch of gangsters; that was cowardice, pure and simple. He would rather stay and confront them; to give in was another kind of suicide. He would never be able to go back to his old life while the men who had killed Charlotte and Somers were still at large. What would Min make of him if he did that? What would she think of a father who had run?

Several hours passed before Gaddis allowed himself to think that he was perhaps overreacting. There was, after all, every possibility that Charlotte had died of natural causes. As for Somers, people were knifed in London all the time. Who was to say that Calvin hadn't just been the wrong man in the wrong place at the wrong time? True, the coincidence of their sudden deaths, so recent and so close together, was unsettling, but Gaddis had no proof of foul play beyond a hunch that the Russian government was bumping off anybody associated with ATTILA.

What happened next restored his faith still further. While booking a flight to Berlin at an Internet café on Uxbridge Road, Gaddis saw, to his consternation, that Ludmilla Tretiak had made contact on the e-mail address which he had given to her in Moscow.

The message had gone into his spam folder, perhaps because it was written in Russian.

Dear Dr. Gaddis

    I am sending you this message from a friend's computer using her e-mail address so I hope that it will not be discovered. I enjoyed talking to you when we met. I feel that I must thank you for bringing to my attention new information concerning my husband's death.

I am in a position now to be able to help you further. You may already know that the MI6 Head of Station in Berlin while my husband was working in East Germany was Robert Wilkinson. Fyodor also knew him by the alias Dominic Ulvert. I do not know what use you will be able to make of this information, if any. But you asked me who else in Berlin might have known Mr. Edward Crane and it seems likely to me that this man would have been in contact with the most senior officer from British Intelligence working in Berlin at that time.

This is all that I can think of at present which may be of assistance to you. But I could see in Moscow how dedicated you were to solving this mystery and your enthusiasm touched me.

It could have been a trap, of course, an attempt by the FSB to lure him into a meeting with a nonexistent former SIS officer. Yet the slightly breathless, dreamy tone of the e-mail sounded like Tretiak, and offered hope that she remained unharmed.

He looked again at the screen. Finding a loose scrap of paper in his trouser pocket, Gaddis scribbled down the names "Robert Wilkinson" and "Dominic Ulvert" and tried to remember if he had seen them before, either in Charlotte's files or in the boxes which Holly had given to him. He couldn't recall. He knew that there was a risk in trusting Tretiak and that his natural optimism was both a strength and a weakness at times like this, but there was no way he could ignore what she had told him. The information was crying out to be investigated. At the very least, he could ask Josephine Warner to run the names through the Foreign Office archives. Where was the harm in that?

Gaddis rang her an hour later from a payphone on Uxbridge Road.

"Josephine?"

"Sam! I was just thinking about you."

"Good thoughts, I hope," he said. "How are things down at Kew?"

They briefly exchanged pleasantries but Gaddis wasn't in the mood for small talk. He was keen to secure Josephine's help in tracking down the information.

"Do you think you could do me a favour?"

"Of course."

"Next time you're at work, could you see if there's anything in the records about a Foreign Office diplomat named Robert Wilkinson? If that doesn't work, try Dominic Ulvert. Anything you can get on them at all. Letters, minutes from meetings in which they were involved, conferences they may have attended. Anything."

It was only the second time that they had spoken since their dinner in Brackenbury Village and Gaddis was aware that his manner was direct and businesslike. It surprised him when Josephine suggested getting together a second time.

"I can have a look," she replied. "In fact, why don't we have another supper? This one on me. I can bring copies of any documents I find."

"That would be incredibly kind."

And suddenly Gaddis's memories were no longer of Josephine's strange, withdrawn behaviour on the Goldhawk Road, but of her face across the candlelit table at dinner, promising something with her eyes.

"I'm afraid I'm busy this weekend," she said. "Next week would be easier if you're around."

"Why? What are you doing this weekend?"

"Well, thanks to you, I finally got my act together."

"Thanks to *me?*"

"You made me feel so guilty about not visiting my sister, I invited myself to stay. I'm leaving for Berlin tomorrow."

He reflected on the serendipity of the coincidence. "That's extraordinary. I just booked a flight to Berlin this afternoon. We'll be there at the same time."

"You're *kidding?*" Josephine sounded genuinely excited at the prospect; perhaps her "complicated" boyfriend had not been invited along for the trip. "Then let's meet up. Let's do something at the weekend."

"I'd love that."

Gaddis told her where he would be staying—"a Novotel near the Tiergarten"—and they made a tentative plan to have dinner on Saturday evening.

He couldn't believe his luck.

26

Forty minutes earlier, Tanya Acocella had been passed a note informing her that Dr. Sam Gaddis—now known by the cryptonym POLARBEAR because, as Brennan had observed, "he'll soon be extinct"—had visited an Internet café on the Uxbridge Road and purchased an easyJet flight to Berlin. He was due to leave London Luton at 8:35 on Friday morning, returning two days later. The fare had been charged to Gaddis's MasterCard and he had booked two nights at a Novotel at Tiergarten as part of a package deal with the airline. Tanya had wondered why Gaddis was using a public computer, rather than the PC at his house in Shepherd's Bush, and concluded that he was at last becoming aware of the surveillance threats posed by his interest in ATTILA.

As the sun was coming down on what had been a crystal-clear day in London, she called Sir John Brennan.

"Do the names Robert Wilkinson and Dominic Ulvert mean anything to you in the context of ATTILA?"

Brennan had just come off the Vauxhall Cross squash court and was boiling with sweat. He asked Tanya to repeat the names and, when she did, swore so loudly that his voice could be heard by a cleaning lady in the women's changing rooms.

"Where the fuck is Gaddis getting his information?" he snapped. "Meet me in the courtyard. Half an hour."

While Brennan showered and changed back into a grey suit, Tanya ran a trace on Wilkinson and Ulvert, encountering the same wall of obstruction and restricted access which had characterized her earlier searches for Crane and Neame. Somebody, somewhere, was trying to prevent her from doing her job. It was the first thing that she mentioned to Brennan in the courtyard. He had closed the access door back into the building so that they were alone in an area normally populated by smokers. Nobody would disturb the Chief in such a situation.

"Forgive me for saying this, sir, but I believe there are some things you haven't told me about ATTILA."

Brennan peered down at Tanya's legs. He had pulled a muscle in his arm playing squash.

"Perhaps there are things you aren't telling *me*," he replied, turning around. He didn't feel that it was appropriate for Acocella to be criticizing his methods. "Last time we spoke, you told me that Gaddis was investigating Harold-bloody-Wilson. Now, for some reason, he's stumbled on Robert Wilkinson."

"As you said, sir, AGINCOURT was a wild goose chase."

"Fair enough, fair enough." Brennan's mood now changed abruptly. He had known, as he put on his suit, that he would have to come clean about certain aspects of the ATTILA cover-up. Tanya could hardly be expected to perform effectively with one hand tied behind her back. "I should perhaps have been more candid from the start."

Tanya was surprised that Brennan should capitulate so readily.

"Bob Wilkinson was Head of Station in Berlin when the Wall came down. He'd been operating in East Germany for the best part of a decade. Ulvert was one of his pseudonyms. In 1992, the FSB tried to assassinate him in London. The attempt failed, but he consequently emigrated to New Zealand, to get as far away from his old life as possible."

"Why did the FSB want him dead?"

"Because of his relationship with ATTILA." Tanya searched Brennan's face as she listened, still sensing that he was holding something back. "The Russians were embarrassed that they had been duped for so long, so they set about bumping off anybody who had been associated with Crane."

"*Anybody?* Doesn't that constitute quite a large number of people? Crane was operational for almost fifty years."

Brennan took her point but could not, for reasons which he hoped she would never be aware, express himself more candidly.

"The victims tended to be senior figures who had been directly involved with Crane in the 1980s," he said, fudging it. "A KGB officer named Fyodor Tretiak, for example, had been ATTILA's handler in East Germany from '84 onwards. Tretiak was assassinated while walking back to his apartment in St. Petersburg in 1992. Bob Wilkinson had a bomb attached to his car in Fulham and only survived because he checked his vehicles religiously as a hangover from Northern Ireland. Left shortly afterwards for Auckland, under rather a cloud, if I'm honest. Hasn't spoken to anybody in the Service for over ten years and not likely to."

"What sort of cloud?"

Brennan mumbled his answer, to the extent that it was almost carried off on the wind. Tanya had to take a step towards him and wondered why he was still being so obtuse. She looked down and saw that one of his immaculate brogues was scuffed, as if somebody had scrubbed the toe with a wire brush.

"Bob felt that we hadn't done enough to protect him." Brennan seemed genuinely contrite as he recalled the incident. "He felt that the measures extended to ensure the safety of Edward Crane might also have been extended to him."

"What kind of measures?"

A smile briefly flickered on Brennan's face as he recalled the heyday of Douglas Henderson. "I arranged for Eddie to die of natural causes."

It had always been Tanya's deepest fear that she had signed up for an organization which would stoop to murder as easily as it stooped to deceit. But she had misinterpreted what Brennan was telling her. He allayed her fears with a gesture of apology.

"No, no. There's no need to be alarmed." Tanya nodded, but she had seldom felt more uncomfortable in the five years that she had been working for SIS. "Eddie was already in his midseventies. As you say, he'd given decades of loyal service. He deserved a peaceful retirement, so I had him brought into a hospital in Paddington, crossed a few palms with enough silver and, lo and behold, he died of pancreatic cancer in February 1992."

"Did one of the palms you crossed go by the name of Meisner?"

Brennan hesitated for a fraction of a second.

"Meisner, yes." Tanya was studying him intently. What was he holding back? "He was the senior doctor on duty the night Crane was brought into the hospital. How did you find out about him?"

"Gaddis mentioned his name on one of the surveillance tapes." It was strange, but at this moment she felt a greater loyalty towards Gaddis than she did towards her own side. Tanya knew that she was being lied to, and it irritated her intensely. "He's obviously going to Berlin to meet him."

"You might try to keep an eye on him there," Brennan suggested.

"It's already organized." Tanya enjoyed the look of surprise on Brennan's face. "I'm flying out tomorrow. There'll be a surveillance team in place."

It was a coup, no question. Brennan nodded approvingly. Tanya saw this and seized the opportunity to push for more information.

"So what about Crane?" she asked.

"What about him?"

"Where is he now? Where did he go to? What happened to him after the hospital?"

Brennan looked back towards the door. It was the question to which everybody wanted an answer.

"Eddie lives near Winchester," he replied, knowing that it was only a matter of time before Tanya discovered the truth for herself. "I'm sorry that I wasn't able to tell you before. After Paddington, we gave him a new identity. You'll find him at the Meredith Nursing Home in Headbourne Worthy. He now goes by the name of Thomas Neame."

27

Gaddis had realized that there was no point in door-stepping Benedict Meisner. He recalled the e-mail Meisner had written to Charlotte threatening legal action if she continued to allege that he had been involved in faking the death of Edward Crane. If Gaddis showed up in Berlin making the same accusation, Meisner would most likely slam the door in his face or, worse, call the police.

So he needed a more subtle plan of attack. He found a listing for Meisner's surgery online and called the number from a public phone at UCL. The receptionist spoke perfect English and Gaddis asked if it would be possible to make an appointment for Friday afternoon.

"Of course, sir. But we have only limited opportunities tomorrow. I can offer you a consultation with the doctor at four o'clock. Is this suiting you?"

Gaddis took the appointment, gave the number of his hotel in Berlin, and wondered what he was going to use as a cover story. *I'm having trouble sleeping, Doc. Do you have a cure for paranoia?* The next morning, he set his alarm for five, drove up the M1, parked his Volkswagen in an offsite car park three miles from Luton Airport, and caught the

8:35 easyJet to Berlin Schönefeld. A two-euro ticket on the 171 bus from the airport took him, at snail's pace, through a grid of bright, well-tended suburbs peopled by German geriatrics. The bus, which stopped perhaps thirty or forty times en route, eventually came to a halt in Hermannplatz, where Gaddis caught the U-Bahn to Tiergarten. The Novotel was just across the street from the underground station, an upmarket executive hotel with a polished-stone lobby, trilingual receptionists, and businessmen killing time between meetings in a low-lit bar. Ordinarily, Gaddis would have searched out a more idiosyncratic place to stay—a twelve-room, family-run hotel, a place with some character and charm—but on this occasion he was grateful for the soullessness of the Novotel, for his starched third-floor room and his flat-screen plasma TV showing films-on-demand and CNN. It made him feel reassuringly anonymous.

He had a couple of hours to kill until his appointment with Meisner and decided to go for a walk, winding along the quiet, narrow paths of the Tiergarten, then alongside the traffic on the Strasse des 17 Juni, past the Siegessäule and the memorial to Bismarck, then east in a plumb line to the Brandenburg Gate. Though he knew that there was no possibility he would ever be able to shake off whatever surveillance was thrown at him by the British or the Russians, Gaddis had made an effort to ascertain if he had been followed from London. At Luton, for example, he had made a mental note of his fellow passengers as they waited in the departure lounge, then scanned the 171 bus for matching faces, trying to work out if someone was tracking him into Berlin. At the Novotel, before embarking on his walk, he had left through the main entrance, loitered in the car park for ten seconds, then turned on his heels and returned to the lobby, in an effort to flush out a tail. Though he realized that these were amateur tricks, culled from movies and thrillers, at no point did he sense that he was being followed. Increasingly, in fact, as the hours and days went by, Gaddis began to believe that his interest in ATTILA had gone completely unnoticed.

All of which was a credit to the SIS watcher who had sat five rows behind him on the easyJet, then followed the 171 bus to Hermannplatz in a hired Audi A4 which had been waiting for him at the airport. "Ralph," who was in his midthirties and usually operated for MI5 in London, had also taken a room at the Novotel and now tailed POLARBEAR on foot as Gaddis made his way towards the Brandenburg Gate. Two hundred metres behind him, on a rented bicycle, Ralph was being backed up by a second pavement artist, known as "Katie," who had flown out to Berlin with Tanya Acocella twenty-four hours earlier. The third member of the surveillance team, known as "Des," was holding back in the Audi on Hofjägerallee, awaiting further instructions from Tanya. Tanya herself was installed in an SIS-rented apartment half a mile from the British Embassy on Wilhelmstrasse. She knew that POLARBEAR planned to meet Meisner, but did not yet know where the encounter would take place, nor for what time it had been scheduled.

Gaddis hadn't been to Berlin since 1983, when he had been a student on a school trip peering over the Berlin Wall at East German border guards who stared back through war-issue binoculars, trying to put a gloss on their boredom. The span of time put Gaddis in a contemplative mood, and for five long minutes he stood directly beneath the Brandenburg Gate, reflecting on how the city had changed in the past quarter of a century and pressing the palms of his hands against the stonework in a moment of sentimental contemplation which sent Ralph into paroxysms.

"He's doing something weird underneath the Gate," he told Tanya, speaking into a mobile phone. "Looks like he's stretching his back. It might be a signal."

"Hold your position," Tanya replied. "Let's see who shows up."

But nobody showed up. POLARBEAR eventually walked towards the Reichstag, seemed to be put off by the length of the queue taking tourists inside to gape at Norman Foster's dome, then retraced his steps and spent fifteen minutes on the south side of the Brandenburg Gate, strolling around the Holocaust Memorial.

"Don't lose him in there," Tanya warned Ralph, because she knew that the memorial was a five-acre maze of granite blocks, some as high as fifteen feet, into which Gaddis could quickly disappear. She was now sure that he was using amateur tradecraft—hence his little platform jig at Waterloo station—and it was certainly not beyond his capabilities to have arranged to meet Meisner in the centre of the memorial, where they could not possibly be overheard.

Meanwhile, Katie had ridden her bike to the corner of Ebert and Hannah-Arendt Strasses, at the southwestern edge of the memorial, working on the assumption that POLARBEAR would eventually come out and make his way south towards Checkpoint Charlie.

"I reckon he's just doing the tourist thing," she said, a view with which Tanya and Ralph concurred when POLARBEAR's head was observed poking out from a granite block twenty feet from the street. Moments later, Gaddis had emerged onto Hannah-Arendt, lit a cigarette, and walked east on to Friedrichstrasse, where he stood beside a postbox, looking around for a cab.

"He's obviously waiting for a taxi," Ralph duly announced, and Tanya ordered the Audi to within two hundred metres of his position while Ralph looked around for a cab of his own.

"This is it," she said. "Don't lose him."

They didn't. The Audi got there in three minutes and tailed PO-LARBEAR all the way to Prenzlauerberg, a fashionable quarter of former East Berlin where the city's bohemian elite bought their vinyl records and drank their lattes. Ralph found a taxi two minutes after Gaddis but was called off after being reassured by Des that the "situation is very much under what I like to call control." At 15:46 Gaddis was observed paying the driver of the cab and stepping out on to Schön-hauser Allee.

"He's a block from Meisner's office," Tanya declared, looking down at a map of Berlin. She had visited the location at nine o'clock the previous evening. "Let's see if we can get his phone to work."

POLARBEAR's mobile was her only potential problem. Two days earlier, when Gaddis had left it unattended in his office at UCL, an SIS technician had succeeded in installing a piece of software which turned the phone into a remotely activated microphone. The bug had worked once, successfully, when Ralph had tested it from a car parked outside Gaddis's house, but things were always more complicated in an overseas location. Meisner's surgery was also on the third floor; getting a clear signal down to the Audi would take a mixture of luck and finesse.

Out on the street, Gaddis had found the entrance. A plaque outside announced:

BENEDICT MEISNER

AKUPUNKTUR
HOMÖOPATHIE
WIRBELSÄULEN UND GELENKTHERAPIE

It was a mystery. How did a trained medical doctor end up prac-
tising acupuncture and homeopathy in Berlin? Had Meisner been
struck off? Gaddis looked at his watch and realized that he had ten
minutes to kill before his appointment. It was enough time in which to
call Josephine Warner.

"He's taking out his phone," Des announced.

Josephine answered the call with an enthusiasm appropriate to
the circumstances.

"Sam! Are you here?"

"*Ja,*" Gaddis replied in cod-German, immediately regretting the
joke. "How's your sister?"

She lowered her voice to a conspiratorial whisper. "Annoying the
shit out of me. I've realized why I never come to visit."

Gaddis smiled. "Then I can persuade you to abandon her for dinner tomorrow night?"

"You definitely can." Josephine was already flirting with him
and—who knows?—perhaps even toying with the prospect of a post-
dinner nightcap on the third floor of the Tiergarten Novotel.

"I know a place," Gaddis told her, because he had researched decent Berlin restaurants on the Internet and booked a table for two—
just in case—at Café Jacques in Neukölln.

Before long, they had fixed a time and a place and Gaddis had
hung up, ringing the bell of Meisner's surgery. Des duly activated the
bug in POLARBEAR's mobile and, within moments, Tanya Acocella
was listening to Gaddis as he introduced himself to the receptionist.

"*Güten tag,*" he said. "I apologize. I don't speak German."

"This is all right, sir."

"I have an appointment with Doctor Meisner at four o'clock."

To Tanya's relief, the take quality was first class; she was listening
through a set of headphones and it was as if the conversation were
taking place in the next room. She heard the receptionist asking

Gaddis to fill out a form—"just some of your personal and medical information please"—then the sigh of Gaddis slumping into an armchair, a brief crash on the bug as he reached for a pen in the inside pocket of his jacket, and a rustle of paper as he filled out the form.

Three minutes later, a telephone rang in the waiting room. The receptionist picked it up and Gaddis was invited "please to go through now" to Meisner's surgery. He offered to return the medical form but was told to keep it with him and to "please to show it to the doctor when you arrive." Tanya tried to picture Gaddis ducking through the connecting door and shaking Meisner's hand. She was wondering what the hell he was planning to say to him.

"So! We are both doctors!"

Meisner had a thick German accent and sounded chirpy and easygoing.

"That's right." Gaddis's voice was flatter, more nervous. "Different areas of expertise, though. I don't tend to save lives on a daily basis."

She liked that, the flattery. Gaddis was softening him up.

"Oh, I don't save lives anymore, Doctor. I simply relieve the pain. And what is your area of expertise?"

"I'm an academic, at University College, London."

"Ah! UCL! Sit down, please, sit down."

Another cushioned slump as Gaddis settled into a chair. Tanya heard him explain that he was a lecturer in Russian History in the Department of Slavonic and Eastern European Studies. Meisner kept saying "Ja, ja," and appeared to be enormously interested in everything Gaddis was saying.

"Really? Is that right? How fascinating. I myself lived in London some time ago."

"You did? Whereabouts?"

"In the Hampstead area. I worked at St. Mary's Hospital in Paddington for a number of years. Do you know it?"

"I know it."

This, of course, was POLARBEAR's opportunity and Tanya wondered if he would take it. Typically, in a conversation of this type, it was better to show one's hand earlier, rather than to build up an implicit trust which was then shattered by the truth.

"In fact, that's sort of the reason why I've come today."

He was going for it. Tanya heard Meisner say: "I am sorry, I don't quite understand," and felt her stomach kick. She pressed the headphones closer to her ears.

"I'm afraid I'm here under false pretences, Doctor."

"False pretences—"

Meisner sounded confused, defensive.

Gaddis pressed on. "I don't have an underlying medical condition. I'm not looking for treatment of any kind. I wanted to talk to you about your time at St. Mary's. I knew that you wouldn't see me if I told you who I was or why I was coming here today."

Tanya tried to imagine Meisner's reaction. He wore tortoiseshell glasses over lively, expressive eyes, and his broad, tanned face was genial and unassuming. There was a long silence. Somebody sniffed. She could hear a tapping sound and assumed that Meisner was rapping his fingers on the surface of his desk.

"You were in communication with a friend of mine," Gaddis began.

"Charlotte Berg," Meisner replied immediately. All of his bedside bonhomie had evaporated. "I must ask you to leave immediately." Tanya heard the noise of a chair scraping back on a hard floor. Meisner was getting to his feet.

Gaddis said: "Please, just hear me out. I have come here to warn you. My visit is for your own safety."

"Doctor Gaddis, please do not let me lose my temper. Do you wish me to call the police? I can either ask you to leave in a civilized fashion or I will have no hesitation—"

"Charlotte Berg is dead." POLARBEAR had held his nerve. "She was most probably killed by Russian Intelligence."

The ensuing silence was so pronounced that Tanya wondered if the microphone had failed. She was about to call Des when Meisner responded:

"And why is this of any concern to me?"

"You remember Calvin Somers?"

"As I told Miss Berg, I have no recollection of an individual of that name and, if you insist on making allegations of this kind, I will have no hesitation to pursue libel actions against you in a court of law."

"Somers is also dead." Gaddis's reply contained just the right level of threat. "He was murdered, again most probably by Russian Intelligence."

She heard Meisner sniff, then a hole of silence. Gaddis spoke into the void.

"I don't need to tell you that this only leaves you and the porter still alive."

"The porter?"

"Waldemar. Lucy Forman died in a car accident in 2001." This piece of information pushed Meisner back into his chair. Tanya knew that Waldemar had died in Krakow in 1999. "I don't know if the crash was an accident or if it was engineered. All I'm saying is that you need to watch your back."

"That is not what you are saying, Doctor."

Gaddis conceded the point. "You're right. I need your assistance as well. There are things you may know which could help to keep both of us alive."

Another silence. Tanya scratched an itch at the end of her nose.

"Do you still retain any links to Douglas Henderson?" Gaddis's tone of voice had become more conciliatory. "Are you aware that his real name is Sir John Brennan and that he is now the Chief of the British Secret Intelligence Service?"

Careful, Sam, thought Tanya. *Don't be giving away too many of our secrets.*

"I did not know this," Meisner replied. His throat was dry and it sounded as though he took a sip of water.

"The man whose death you orchestrated was called Edward Crane. He was a double agent for MI6. The Russians wanted him dead, so Brennan made them think that he had died of cancer."

"I had always wanted to know the answer to this question," Meisner replied quietly.

Gaddis pushed for more. "Do you remember anything at all about Crane? Did MI6 give you any indication what would happen to him? Were you ever asked to perform similar duties for British Intelligence at any point since?"

"Of course not."

"What about ATTILA? Did anybody ever mention that name to you? Has anybody, apart from Charlotte Berg, ever spoken to you about what happened in 1992?"

"You are the first person I have ever spoken to about it."

Without seeing his eyes, Tanya could not tell if Meisner was lying, but the answer sounded truthful enough.

"Then why do you think Somers was killed? Why do you think the Russians murdered Charlotte?"

Meisner emitted a strange, choked laugh. "Doctor Gaddis, it sounds to me as though these are questions to which you yourself should know the answer. I have nothing more. I have done nothing wrong. I was paid by MI6 to keep my mouth closed. I have *kept* my mouth closed. I signed your Official Secrets Act, just as once upon a time I signed a Hippocratic Oath. These things *mean* something to me. My reputation is important. If Benedict Meisner puts his name to something, if he makes a promise of any kind, then he keeps it. This is not a very modern concept, I grant you, but it is nevertheless essential to my own philosophy."

There was another silence. The headphones had formed what felt like a pressure seal around Tanya's ears and she briefly pulled them apart, feeling the sweat on her temples.

"What about Thomas Neame?" Gaddis asked. "Does that name mean anything to you?"

It was almost as if Tanya could see Meisner shaking his head. "I have never heard this name. Who is he, please?"

She swore lightly under her breath and thought back to the Vauxhall Cross courtyard. Sooner or later, she had told Brennan, Gaddis is going to find out that Neame is the sixth man. *Exactly,* the Chief had said. *And when he does, that's precisely the point at which we step in.* She had been furious at his deception, humiliated that her boss should have tasked her with tracking Gaddis's movements without first supplying what was surely the most vital piece of information associated with the operation. *Need to know, I'm afraid,* he had told her, trying to soften the blow with one of his toadying smiles. *Only a handful of people in the world know what happened to Edward Crane. Now you're one of them.*

Gaddis was doing something in his seat. Tanya could hear what sounded like a scratching of cloth and wondered if he was taking off his jacket. But then the take quality became even clearer and she realized that POLARBEAR had removed the mobile phone.

"I have a photograph of him," he was saying. Tanya put two and two together as Gaddis began to click through the images in the phone's gallery. "Have you seen this man before?"

She waited. There was nothing she could do to prevent what was about to happen. She heard Meisner lift out of his chair and then the noise of the phone being passed across the desk. The sound Meisner made when he saw the photograph of Neame in the pub was just what she had expected: a breath of disbelief.

"But this is the man," he told Gaddis. "This is the man who was admitted to the hospital. The person in this photograph is not your Thomas Neame. The person in the photograph is Edward Crane."

28

It was only a small consolation to Gaddis that he had briefly suspected Neame and Crane of being the same man. Otherwise, he felt wretched and embarrassed, duped by a master liar. There was no memoir, he reflected. There was no memoir because Thomas Neame *was* the story. All that time, he had been talking to the sixth man but had been too dumb and too greedy to see it. The sensation was not dissimilar to the hollow feeling of being betrayed by a friend, or manipulated by a jealous colleague; he was humiliated, but he was also intensely angry. All his life, Gaddis had wanted to think the best of people, to take them at face value and to trust that human decency would win through. Of course, it was naïve to think this way, to believe that the world had his best interests at heart. He should have seen what Crane was up to. Here was a man, like Philby, who had lived his entire adult life as an elaborate masquerade. Crane did not so much possess a personality as a series of masks; as each mask was removed, it was replaced by another. Neame was simply the latest in a long line of parallel lives, a role played as much for Crane's personal amusement as for the practical purpose of disguising his real identity. In his youth, Crane had pretended to the British government that he was a loyal and dedicated servant of the Crown, yet all the while he had been passing secrets to the NKVD. He had then coolly switched allegiances, having long since convinced Moscow that his heart belonged to Mother Russia. The two positions were mirrors of each other, reflections of the same ideology. Edward Crane had no country. Edward Crane had only himself.

Looked at from this perspective, it made absolute sense to Gaddis that Crane should have chosen to tell the ATTILA story through a shell personality; it would have been contrary to his nature to expose his true self. A spy needed the protection of a cover story, a pseudonym. Besides, Crane would have enjoyed the intellectual challenge of duping Gaddis; doubtless he had derived enormous satisfaction from gulling a so-called leading academic. At what point had he been planning to come clean? Would he have gone to his grave as Thomas Neame, holding on to this last, elusive secret? Almost certainly. Why break the habit of a lifetime?

"POLARBEAR looks well fucked off," said Des, following Gaddis on foot from Meisner's surgery. Meisner had agreed to meet him at a café near his apartment in Kreuzberg at eight o'clock. "Whoever the fuck this Edward Crane is has put our boy in a very bad mood indeed."

Two hundred metres away, Nicolai Doronin was also watching Meisner's surgery, though he paid scant attention to Gaddis as he came out onto the street at half past four, incorrectly assuming that the six-foot man with a corduroy jacket and leather satchel was a resident of one of the luxury apartments on the fourth or fifth floors. Nor did Doronin notice Des getting out of a blue-black Audi A4 on the corner of Schönhauser Allee in order to tail Gaddis to the U-Bahn at Eberswalder Strasse. Doronin's interest lay solely in Benedict Meisner. He had been watching the doctor for forty-eight hours. He had established that he lived alone, had learned his daily routine, calculated his approximate physical strength, pondered his likely resistance to violent assault. On balance, Doronin felt that it would be wisest to pursue a similar strategy to that which had succeeded with Charlotte Berg. Just as Alexander Grek had broken into her office, he would access Meisner's apartment, add 10mg of sodium fluoracetate to the bottle of water which Meisner kept by his bed, and return to London on the next scheduled flight from Tegel.

Doronin had not expected to carry out the plan until the following day, but having tailed Meisner back to his apartment on Reichenberger Strasse he had waited outside for an hour, only to see the doctor emerge at ten to eight wearing a fresh set of clothes and carrying a copy of *Der Spiegel*. It was obvious that he was going out for dinner. Sure enough, Doronin followed Meisner the length of Liegnitzer Strasse to his favourite café, which was a few hundred metres away on the corner of Paul-Lincke-Ufer. Meisner took an outdoor table, scanned the menu, and ordered a glass of beer. This presented Doronin with a window of opportunity. He was keen to return to London so that he could spend at least some of the weekend with his young son. If he could pull off the Meisner operation tonight, he could be back at his flat in Kensington by lunchtime the next day.

So Doronin missed seeing the six-foot man with the corduroy jacket and the leather satchel getting out of a cab on Liegnitzer Strasse. Less than three minutes after he had turned and walked back in the direction of Meisner's apartment, Sam Gaddis had pulled up, spotted Meisner, and sat down at his table.

British Intelligence, on the other hand, were ahead of the game. Knowing that Meisner and Gaddis had arranged to meet at the café, Katie and Ralph had positioned themselves on the terrace, ordered two enormous bowls of onion soup, occasionally held hands for cover, and waited for POLARBEAR to show up. Tanya was sitting outside Meisner's apartment, at the opposite end of the street, texting them from the front seat of the Audi. To her fury, POLARBEAR had left his mobile at the Novotel, which meant that audio coverage of his conversation with Meisner would now be impossible.

The café was popular with local families. Even at eight o'clock in the evening, young mothers were breast-feeding their children in the cool autumnal air, fresh-faced fathers bouncing toddlers on their knees. But service was slow. Gaddis had been sitting with Meisner for five minutes before the ageing hippie waitress deigned to show up and take his order for a cup of coffee.

"You want a *coffee?*" asked an incredulous Meisner. "At this time of night?"

Gaddis explained that it had been a long day—"I was up at five"— and turned his attention to the menu. The café offered the sort of food he loathed: right-on stews, bean soups, tofu salads sprinkled with snow peas and pine nuts. He would have killed for a rib-eye steak.

"What the hell's a bio-bratwurst?" he asked, but the doctor merely stared at him blankly through his tortoiseshell glasses. He had the distracted look of a man coming to terms with the indiscretions of his past. Gaddis scanned the food on the neighbouring tables. Surely there was something worth eating? Beside him, two undernourished Scandinavians were picking gingerly at an arugula salad. A string of lights was suspended over their table, hung between two chestnut trees. In the other direction, a young couple—British, by the look of their clothes—were holding hands and finishing off two large bowls of onion soup.

Gaddis froze.

He had seen the woman before: that afternoon, on the southern edge of the Holocaust Memorial, leaning on a bicycle and staring past him in the direction of the Reichstag. He had noticed her because she had been wearing a yellow overcoat identical to one that Holly had worn on a date to the cinema. He looked at the woman's chair. Sure enough, the same coat was draped around the back of her seat.

Was he under surveillance? Gaddis's coffee arrived and he was grateful for the distraction because it meant that he could fix his attention on the waitress. There was a small macaroon resting on the saucer and he swallowed it in an attempt to keep his behaviour natural.

"Damn," Meisner said.

"What?"

"I forget my cigarettes." The doctor was checking his pockets, patting the inside of his jacket. "Would you mind waiting here while I go back to my apartment? It is just around the corner, just a few minutes away."

Was this part of the surveillance operation, part of some pre-arranged plan? Was Meisner working in tandem with the British? Gaddis was about to offer him one of his own cigarettes when he realized that Meisner's suggestion had presented him with the opportunity to leave the café.

"Can I be honest?" he said.

Meisner frowned. "Excuse me?"

"Would you mind if we ate dinner somewhere else?"

"Are you cold or something? They have blankets inside."

"No. It's not the cold. I'd just rather we finished our drinks, fetched your cigarettes, and went somewhere else to eat."

Meisner suddenly saw what Gaddis was driving at. His face seemed to draw back onto its bones. When he lowered his voice, it was tight with nerves.

"You think there is a possibility that—"

Gaddis interrupted him. "Yes," he said. "I think there is that distinct possibility."

They stood up immediately. Gaddis drained his coffee in a single gulp, secured a ten-euro note under a sugar bowl, and led Meisner off the terrace. They were fifty metres up Liegnitzer when he turned and saw the man who had been sitting with the woman in the yellow overcoat crossing the street behind them. He was speaking into a mobile phone.

"I think POLARBEAR just made us," Ralph was telling Tanya. He was embarrassed, spitting with rage. "*Fuck* it. He's coming towards you. Looks like they're heading to Meisner's apartment."

"We will go into my home and think what to do," Meisner was muttering. Gaddis was concerned by how quickly his companion's mood had deteriorated into outright panic. "Why did you bring these people to me? Everything was fine in Berlin until Doctor Sam Gaddis shows up."

Gaddis turned again but could not see anybody following them. A part of him wanted to walk back to the café and to confront the couple at their table. Who were they? Who had sent them? He was certain that nobody had followed him from Schönefeld, but it would have been all too easy to trace his movements via his credit cards, or even by locking on to the signal emitted by his mobile phone. Yet he had accidentally left that at the Novotel. How had they found him?

At the north end of Liegnitzer, Meisner turned left into Reichenberger Strasse, a broad residential street, now in semidarkness. At one point, Tanya was no more than fifteen feet away from them, concealed in the gloom of her parked Audi. She saw Meisner reach for his keys as Gaddis followed him into the building. They both looked tense. There had not been time to install audio/visual in Meisner's apartment, so she knew that whatever took place between them, whatever they discussed, would remain secret.

The building was a restored nineteenth-century apartment block with two flats on each level. Halfway up the stairs they passed a teen-age Goth wearing torn denim jeans and a black leather jacket. She ignored Meisner and kept her head bowed as she walked past Gaddis, clomping down to the lobby. On the second floor, Meisner placed his key in the lock, opened the door of his apartment, and stepped inside.

Something caused him to pause on the threshold and Gaddis bunched up behind him as they walked in. He looked up. A gun had appeared from behind the door, levelled at the left side of Meisner's head. In the same instant, a shot was fired, a shot almost without noise, which sent a spume of brain tissue thumping into a gilt mirror on the right-hand side of the passage. Instinctively, Gaddis put all of his weight against the door and forced it open. Meisner had slumped to the ground beneath him. He felt someone blocking the door on the other side and pushed harder. A man swore in Russian and Gaddis saw the gun fall out into the corridor.

He should have run. That would have been the smart thing to do. He should have closed the door and sprinted downstairs. But Meis-ner's body was blocking the way. Instead, terrified that the Russian would pick up the gun, Gaddis went forward into the apartment and scrambled across a polished wooden floor. He could sense Meisner's assailant behind him, already clambering to his feet, but he had time to reach the gun and to turn, levelling the barrel at the man's body. The Russian came towards him and Gaddis fired.

The bullet hit Nicolai Doronin on the right side of the chest, just below the shoulder blade. There was a gasp of pain as he slumped to the ground, staring wildly at Gaddis. His finger still on the trigger, Gaddis fired again, this time out of panic. The second shot seemed to go through the man's neck and there was a sharp crack, as if a wall or a door jamb had been hit. Gaddis had not fired a pistol since he was seventeen years old, shooting at targets in a field in Scotland, and he was bewildered by the power, by the simplicity of what he had done. He glanced down at the barrel and saw that a silencer had been fitted.

That was why there had been no noise. All he could hear was the sound of his own breathing, as fast as if he had sprinted up the stairs. He looked back towards the door. There was blood on the walls, blood in the passage. Meisner wasn't moving. The Russian was moaning and turning away from him, bunched up in a foetal crouch near the wall.

He should have stayed. He realized that later. But in that moment, in the aftermath of what he had seen and done, Gaddis wanted to be out of the building, as far from the apartment as possible. He moved towards Meisner and saw, to his horror, that the entire left side of his head had been completely removed. He was looking into a man's brain and it was no more than a few shards of tissue and bloodied hair and he was almost sick on the floor. He did not look at the Russian. He knew that he did not have the courage to shoot him again or to check if he was still alive. Had he killed a man tonight? He should have rung the police. He should have alerted a neighbour. But instead Gaddis sprinted, almost flew, in three-step leaps down the stairs of the apartment building and out onto the road.

Tanya jerked forward in the Audi when she saw him coming out. She instantly knew that something was wrong. It was as if a wind had blasted Gaddis into the street. She saw him begin to jog along Reichenberger, apparently without direction or purpose. She switched on the engine, reversed into the street, and followed him in a first-gear crawl.

Gaddis became aware of the Audi when he was about three hundred metres from Meisner's apartment. It could only be the Russians, he thought, the accomplices of the man he had just shot. They were following him down the street and they meant to finish the job. His mind was scrambled. He was sick with fear, sick with guilt at what he had done. He wished that he had kept the gun that had felled the Russian, but realized that he had dropped it onto Meisner's body as he stared at his wounds. He looked back. The Audi was fifty metres away. Why was it coming so slowly? Why were they not intent on killing him? He stopped and turned, suddenly overcome by a desire to confront them. There were two members of the public walking on the pavement on the opposite side of the street. Would they dare to kill him in the presence of so many witnesses?

"Sam!"

It was a woman's voice, a scream in the night. It made no sense that somebody should know his name. Gaddis veered into the road.

The car came to an immediate halt. Gaddis was standing in front of it, the headlights blinding him. As he adjusted his gaze, squinting and shielding his eyes from the glare, he saw, to his utter consternation, that Josephine Warner was at the wheel.

"Get in," Tanya said.

29

"What happened, Sam? Tell me."

Gaddis was staring at her, pressed back into the front seat as Tanya accelerated along Reichenberger.

"Why are you here? What's going on?"

"I am not who you think I am," she said. "Tell me what happened." She turned to look at him. "You have blood on your jacket. Where's Meisner?"

"Meisner is dead." He knew that she was MI6. It was obvious to him now: the deception at Kew; the dinner; the coincidence of her trip to Berlin. He wished that he had kept running. "Meisner was shot. I just killed a man. What the fuck is happening? Why are you here?"

"My name is Tanya Acocella. I'm an officer with the Secret Intelligence Service. We've been following you because of your investigation into Edward Crane. I'm sorry, it was necessary for me to pretend to be somebody else. Please try to stay focused. What do you mean, you just killed a man?"

It was almost a relief to hear her confession. At least he knew, finally, what he was up against. Then Gaddis told her what had happened and, as he did so, heard the truth of his own life and career, annihilated by what he had done. "Somebody was in the apartment," he said. "A Russian. Maybe the same man who killed Charlotte. Maybe the same man who killed Calvin. You know who these people are. You know what I'm talking about?"

"I know what you're talking about." Tanya's eyes were fixed on the road.

"We went back to get cigarettes." Gaddis wanted to be inside the car and outside the car. He wanted to be protected by this woman and yet he wanted to be as far from her as possible. "A man was inside the front door. He must have been waiting for Meisner. We must have surprised him. I don't know what he was doing there. He shot him as soon as he walked in."

"Are you carrying a gun?"

Tanya was making a fast left-hand turn through a green light on a deserted roundabout. She could not understand how POLARBEAR had got out alive.

"Of course I'm not carrying a fucking gun. I forced the door and it fell out of his hand. He can't have been expecting two people. It fell in front of me. I picked it up because there was nothing else I could do. I just turned and shot. I think I may have killed him."

"Jesus, Sam."

He didn't like the fact that she used his name so easily. He had been duped by Crane and now he had been duped by Josephine Warner, a woman that—Christ!—he had hoped to sweet-talk into bed twenty-four hours later.

"Look," she said, turning to face him, "do you understand what has happened to you?"

Gaddis moved in his seat, aware that he was soaked in sweat. He looked at his jacket and saw spots of blood sprayed across the sleeve. He felt as though he was locked down, trapped, and experienced a vivid need to wrench the wheel from Tanya's hands and to send the car piling into a newsstand at the side of the road.

"I should go to the police," he said, trying to remain calm. "I need you to stop the car."

"I'm afraid I can't do that." Wipers swept dirt from the windscreen. "If you go to the police, Crane will be exposed. We can't allow that to happen. The German authorities would very quickly start to piece things together. Whoever you killed tonight was almost certainly working for the Platov government. I need to get you out of Berlin and back to London."

Gaddis looked again at his sleeve, streetlights pulsing on the blood.

"How am I supposed to get out of Berlin?" he said. "There are fingerprints on the gun. I passed a girl on the stairs as we came in. I was seen at the café with Meisner. The police will have a description of me in less than twenty-four hours. The only thing I can do is tell them the truth of what happened. Why I was meeting Meisner, why I was in Berlin, why the Russians wanted him dead."

"You cannot do that."

He was bewildered and yet he knew why she was obstructing him. It was an MI6 cover-up. Nobody could know about Crane, about AT-TILA, about Dresden.

"Why?" he said. "Tell me why? What is so fucking important about a twenty-year-old secret that people have to die in order to stop it coming out? I saw a man's brains tonight. I saw Meisner's head completely blown away."

"We are simply trying to protect the relationship between London and Moscow," Tanya replied feebly. She knew that she was retreating into platitudes and could hear the disgust in Gaddis's voice.

"What? What does that *mean*, Josephi—" He began to use her cover name and felt a fool. "What relationship between London and Moscow? There *isn't* a relationship between London and Moscow. You *loathe* each other."

Tanya tried again, although she knew that what Gaddis had said was close to the truth. "The German press can't get hold of this story, nor can they know about your involvement with Crane."

Gaddis shook his head.

"What happened in Dresden?" he said.

"What?"

"Dresden. Something happened in Dresden. On ATTILA's watch, in the twilight of his career. Something involving Platov and Robert Wilkinson. Tell me what it was."

"Sam, I have no idea what you're talking about." This was the truth. She thought of Brennan and wondered if Gaddis had stumbled on the very secret which the Chief himself was surely trying to conceal from her. "We need to concentrate on *you* at the moment. We need to get you out of Berlin. There'll be all the time in the world to hear your concerns when we are back in London."

"My concerns," he repeated witheringly. Tanya's mobile rang and he gazed out of the window as she picked up.

"Yes?" Gaddis could hear a male voice speaking on the line and assumed that it was the man who had been watching him at the café. "No, I've got him," she said. "Something happened. Yes. Everything's fine. I can't speak now. Get everyone back to the flat. I'll contact you there."

"Friend of yours?" he asked when she had hung up.

"Friend of mine," she replied.

"Tell him I liked his girlfriend's coat."

Tanya ran an amber light. "Look. What can you remember? Was there any CCTV in the apartment building? Did you see a camera?"

"I wasn't looking. We were just going upstairs for cigarettes. We left the café to get away from your friends."

"But you say you passed a girl on the stairs?"

"A Goth. Yes."

Tanya was piecing things together, trying to find a way of saving him. He was oddly grateful for the effort. "And the receptionist saw your face at the surgery today."

"Oh, great," he exclaimed. "You were there as well?"

"We were there."

She did not have the heart to tell him about the bug in his phone. The Audi was skirting the edge of a park. In a floodlit cage, men were playing five-a-side football under floodlights. Gaddis watched them and thought of Sunday nights in London. Another world.

"What about Berlin?" Tanya asked. She pulled the car into a quiet residential street and switched off the engine. "Who knew you were coming to meet Meisner?"

"Just you," he replied. "Just Josephine Warner."

She ran a hand through her hair, pushing away the slight. "What about Holly?"

"What about her?" Gaddis could glimpse another nail being landed in the coffin of his humiliation. "Is she one of yours too?"

"Holly has nothing to do with us."

"Then why did she give me the files on the KGB?"

"What files?"

"Never mind."

The street was deserted. He could smell Tanya's perfume, the same scent that had drifted towards him at Kew. He was still drawn to her and he hated that about himself.

"Don't worry about the gun," she said suddenly, and again he had the feeling of being removed from himself, of looking at Sam Gaddis in the third person. "There'll be fingerprints, but to the best of my knowledge, you don't have anything on record. Is that the case?"

Of course. They knew all about him. They had combed through his past. MI6 would know about the divorce, about Min, about his work at UCL. Everything he had said and done for weeks had been analysed by Tanya Acocella.

"That is the case," he said quietly.

There was nothing else to do but to go back to the Novotel. Tanya explained that one of the members of the surveillance team had taken a room on the third floor. By now, Gaddis was so numb to surprise that he merely nodded, his mind fixed on an image of Meisner's brain which he could not erase.

"We need to get rid of your jacket," she said, and Gaddis gave it to her without objection, then watched as she stepped out of the car and dropped it in a nearby bin. It was an old jacket, a cherished gift from his late father, but he felt no dismay; she might as well have been throwing away a newspaper. Tanya then made a call to Des and instructed him to buy two tickets to London on the first available flight out of Berlin. Twenty minutes later, he had rung back, telling her they were booked on a British Midland out of Berlin Tegel at 8 A.M.

"My car's at Luton," Gaddis said.

"Somebody will pick it up for you."

They drove back towards Tiergarten station, along the banks of the Landwehrkanal, the oblivious city slipping by. Tanya felt desperately sorry for him, wondering what must be going through his mind and regretting that it had been necessary to involve this decent man in a world that had now all but destroyed him.

"I want you to promise me something," she said when she had parked at the hotel. They had been driving in silence for ten minutes.

"What's that?"

"You can't go to the police. Do you understand that, Sam?"

Gaddis did not reply.

"If you turn yourself in, we can't help you. The Russians will know who you are. You will face months, even years of legal problems in Berlin, and eventually Platov's people will find you. Allow us to strike a deal with the Germans."

He nodded, but she could not be sure if he had agreed.

"We can protect you in England," she said. She needed to be absolutely certain of his cooperation. "We can make arrangements with the German authorities. Your involvement in what happened this evening need never come to light."

"You can't possibly make a guarantee of that kind."

Tanya reached for his hand and squeezed it. The gesture surprised both of them.

"Let me at least try to convince you that I can. Stay in your room tonight. Leave with me in the morning. When we're back in London, I promise you that everything will become easier."

"Easier," he said, wiped out by shock. He was hungry and craved a cigarette, but realized that he had left his packet in the inside pocket of a jacket which was now in a bin on the other side of Berlin.

They went into the hotel. Tanya walked beside him and, as they came into the lobby, put her arm around his back, whispering to him.

"We are lovers," she said. "You are happy."

It was enough of a trick to take them past any snooping eyes at reception. Gaddis looked at her as they reached the lifts.

"You think of everything," he said, but she knew from his eyes that he despised her.

In the room, he took four miniature bottles of whisky from the minibar, filled a glass, and drank them as a shot. He then went into the bathroom and sat under the shower for almost half an hour. All the while, Tanya waited in the room. She called Brennan in London, explained what had happened, then watched German television for reports on the shootings in Kreuzberg. At eleven o'clock, a news channel went live to Reichenburger Strasse and she recognized the door of Meisner's apartment building, now with police tape slung across the entrance. There were shots of bewildered neighbours—old women in nightgowns, young Turkish men in jeans and T-shirts—gazing up at the windows on the second floor.

"Turn it off," Gaddis told her.

She sat with him, but they barely spoke. She had ordered sandwiches from room service but Gaddis left his food untouched. At around half past two, sedated by hunger and whisky, he finally fell into a light sleep, waking an hour later to find Tanya staring at him from an armchair across the room. She wasn't concerned for his welfare, he reflected. She was simply making sure he didn't make a run for it.

"What was true and what wasn't?" he said. His voice was low and cracked.

"I don't understand the question."

"Was there a sixth man or wasn't there?"

"There was a sixth man."

Gaddis felt a pulse of satisfaction.

"And the details? Did Crane really work with Cairncross at Bletchley? Did he run a ring of NKVD spies out of Oxford?"

Tanya shook her head. "I really don't know," she said.

He turned onto his side. "What about the switch? What about Dick White? Did Crane become a double agent or did he dupe you for another thirty years?"

"That seems very unlikely," she said, sounding almost dismissive, but he wanted to educate her. It occurred to him that she was young enough to be one of his students.

"Philby went to White," he said. "Did you know that? In '63. They were on to him, so he made a marginal confession. Told them he'd been a Soviet spy but insisted that his betrayal had been confined to the war years. Everything after that, he said, had been for Queen and Country." Tanya was looking at him intently. "And they believed him. They let him go. Philby was such an accomplished liar that the finest minds in MI5 and MI6 fell for his line of bullshit. Less than a week later he was on a ship to Moscow. Maybe Crane pulled the same trick."

"I don't think so," she said, though this was no more than a hunch.

"Why do you think people are being killed, Tanya?" He had found a new belligerence, and took a bite from the stale club sandwich. "Why haven't the British shouted from the rooftops about Crane? Do you ever think about that? Why is Sergei Platov ordering the assassination of anybody linked to ATTILA?"

"Sam, I keep telling you, I don't know." She realized now why she liked and admired him. At twenty-five, steered by ambition, Tanya Acocella had abandoned a promising career in academia for the lure of the secret world. Gaddis represented both her past and her alternative future: a life of free enquiry, of scholarship. "There are elements to this operation which are so secret even I haven't been made privy to them. Nobody on my team even knows who Crane is. As far as they're concerned, this is just another job. My task was to find out what you knew. I wasn't privy to your conversations in Winchester. All I know is that, under the terms of the Secrets Act, Crane was under oath never to discuss his career. That was the quid pro quo for setting him up as Neame. But obviously he's got to the point where he wants to tell somebody about ATTILA, about what he's done, because he's ninety-one and doesn't like the idea of going to his grave without people realizing what a bloody hero he is. So he told your friend, and now your friend is dead. He told her about Calvin Somers, and now Somers is dead as well. It may not be what you want to hear right now, but it's only by extreme good fortune that you are still alive."

Gaddis laughed. "And do I have you to credit for that, Tanya? Should I be writing MI6 a thank-you letter?"

She shook her head in frustration and looked at him as if he was being unnecessarily confrontational.

"Who's Peter?" he asked her.

"Special Branch," she replied, because she wanted to be as honest as the circumstances would allow.

Of course, Gaddis thought. Not a private-sector spook hired by Crane to protect Neame, but a first line of defence for the most illustrious spy in the history of MI6. "And he was happy to cooperate in Crane's decision to go public? Why didn't he come running and tell you lot what was going on?"

"Divided loyalties, I suppose. You know as well as anybody that Edward Crane can be a very persuasive man." It was a mean-spirited remark, but Gaddis accepted it without objection. "Perhaps he offered to cut Peter in on the profits. Perhaps Peter came to believe that ATTILA's story deserved to be told. Who knows?"

He lay back on the pillow. His head throbbed and he asked Tanya to pass him the water. He drank from the bottle, setting it on the bedside table. It was strange, but she was beautiful to him again. He remembered their conversation at dinner, the way that she had looked at him, and felt a fool for having believed in her.

"We need to talk about the morning," she said. "In a few hours we'll be checking out. The airport is one place they might be looking for you."

"Why's that?"

"You say the person that you shot was Russian. The police may assume he was working with an accomplice. They'll be looking for a third man, for the person who left the crime scene. That somebody would probably try to leave Berlin as soon as possible."

"Then why are we going?" he asked.

"Because they won't suspect us."

"Us?"

"We'll be together. We'll be arm in arm."

He sat up and hit the master switch on the panel of lights beside the bed. The room blazed. "There's no way I'm doing that."

"It's the best option, believe me. The simplest strategy. Just a couple coming back from a romantic break in Berlin. A lone man would draw more attention. You'll just have to trust me, Sam. It's the only way."

30

They left the hotel at six. Further news had emerged about the shootings at Reichenberger Strasse. According to German television, Meisner's assailant was still alive and had been taken into intensive care, where he was in a stable condition. This was scant consolation to Gaddis and did nothing to lift his mood of despair. He may no longer have been responsible for taking a man's life, but the horror that he had witnessed at Meisner's apartment was still as vivid and as shocking to him as the mutilation of a child.

"We need to be careful," Tanya told him as Des drove them out to the airport. "If you see someone you know at any point, either in the terminal or on the plane, and if you can't avoid them, act normally." She seemed oblivious to Gaddis's state of mind, thinking only of the security of the operation. "If you feel the need to explain who I am, introduce me as your girlfriend. My name is Josephine. We've been staying in Berlin since Tuesday."

Gaddis shook his head and gazed out of the window in disbelief.

"Sam, this is important." She turned in her seat to face him. "You need to concentrate. You need to pull yourself together. I know that you have misgivings about me. But we need to get this thing done. It's the only way for you to get home with no questions asked."

"Have we enjoyed ourselves?" he asked. A tone of macabre humour coloured the question. "Has it been fun spending time together? Do you think our relationship might lead to something more serious?"

Des glanced across and caught Tanya's eye.

"This isn't helpful, Sam." Tanya had barely slept. She was dressed in a smart blue suit and had the organizing, nervous energy of a woman with a lot on her mind. As soon as they landed in London, she was under orders to head directly to Vauxhall Cross for an emergency meeting with Brennan, who was "incensed" that she had broken cover. "As I said last night, posing as a couple is the most sensible strategy."

"Of course." Gaddis made no attempt to disguise the contempt in his voice. "Your complicated love life."

They checked in at seven. In the security area, Gaddis was obliged to remove his boots and a leather belt from his jeans, but was glad to have something to occupy his hands as he queued in front of the scanner; it was the standing around, the waiting, which made him despondent and anxious. For the next fifteen minutes they loitered in a bookshop, flicking through paperbacks and guides to Berlin. Tanya occasionally attempted to engage Gaddis in polite conversation, but he knew that it was solely for cover and his replies were monosyllables of indifference. Forty minutes before they were due to take off, they made their way in silence along a series of strip-lit corridors to passport control.

"I'll do the talking," Tanya said, settling into the queue, but when the time came to approach the booth, their respective passports barely merited a glance from the customs official. At this early hour, they were simply waved through with a stifled yawn.

Gaddis slept most of the way back but the brief rest did nothing to lighten his mood. Landing in London, the wretchedness of Friday's events settled on him again. He thought continually of Charlotte and of the obliterated skull of Benedict Meisner. There was a driver waiting for them in Arrivals, another Des wearing a pair of jeans and a nylon anorak, holding a sign which said JOSEPHINE WARNER in bold, handwritten capital letters. Gaddis saw it and felt a lurch of anger: the double life was all around him. He longed to be free of it, to be in Barcelona with Min or away in Paris with Holly, to go back to the life he had known before Charlotte's death.

"You're going to go home," Tanya told him when they had made their way to the car park at Gatwick and settled in the backseat of a bottle-green Vauxhall Astra. "There's no need to come with us, no reason to fear for your safety. As far as we are aware, nobody else has been looking at your Internet traffic, nobody else has been listening to your phone calls. The man in the apartment was obviously waiting for Meisner. He was the next link in the chain after Charlotte and Somers. For some reason, the Russians don't know about you. You should feel very grateful for that."

"Well, I guess that's one advantage of having MI6 snooping around in your dustbins," Gaddis replied. It was a damp, featureless morning in England, no blue in the sky. "They can at least reassure you that they're the only organization committing a flagrant breach of your privacy."

Tanya had grown accustomed to his fractious moods. She was sympathetic to them, but knew that she had a duty to toe the party line.

"Look, Sam, I'm trying to tell you that this has worked out very well for you. You can go back to your life. You can live normally. It will be like none of it ever happened."

As soon as the words were out of her mouth, she realized the mistake. Gaddis turned on her.

"I think Charlotte being murdered *happened*, Tanya."

"I know. That's not what I meant, I'm sorry—"

"Calvin Somers's death *happened*."

She reached to touch his arm. "Sam—"

"Last night, an innocent man lost his life because sixteen years ago he was dumb enough to go into business with MI6. Benedict Meisner's assassination *happened*. How am I supposed to forget that? In what way can I go back to a 'normal life'?"

Tanya tried a different approach. "What I'm telling you is that you *have* to forget about it." She was under no illusions that things were going to be easy. "Just as you have to forget about the book. That's the deal we're making. That's the only choice you've got."

Gaddis knew that there was no point in arguing with her. She was on her way to see the great and the good of MI6, men with sufficient influence to have his involvement in the shooting erased from the record. That was their speciality, after all—the rewriting of history. Tanya had promised that MI6 would "strike a deal with the Germans." In return, all Gaddis had to do was stop digging around Edward Crane.

"ATTILA is over," she said. "Crane will be moved from Winchester. Peter is going to lose his job. You won't see either of them ever again."

They were crawling around the M25, boxed in by lorries and bored men in vans. Gaddis thought of Peter pulling him around the Hampshire countryside with a Sean Connery GPS for company and felt a sting of guilt that he would now be out of a job. "What if Crane tries to contact me?" he asked. He hadn't thought through the question; he had merely wanted to provoke a reaction in Tanya. But the thought gave him a glimpse of an idea. Had MI6 seen the hush-mails? Might he still be able to communicate with Crane via an encrypted message?

"Crane won't try to contact you," Tanya replied, but there was no conviction in her voice.

"How can you be sure?" Gaddis was beginning to believe that he could save the book. It was extraordinary to him, but in spite of everything that had happened, he was determined to finish what he had started. "You think a man like that isn't capable of deceiving MI6?"

"I think Edward Crane is capable of anything."

"Precisely." He looked out of the window. He needed to give the impression that his interest in ATTILA was over, to lie with the same finesse that Tanya had shown in deceiving him. "Anyway, you have nothing to worry about. I understand my situation. If he calls, I'll ignore him. I'd rather wash my hands of the whole thing."

"You would?"

"Sure. What am I going to do, run the risk of getting shot by the

FSB?" Tanya acknowledged the inevitability of Russian involvement with a brisk nod. "I understand the terms of our deal."

He looked at her face, tiredness beginning to colour her eyes. It was strange, but it felt wrong to be deceiving her. The events in Berlin had forged a strange kind of bond between them.

"I'll go back to UCL," he said. "The book won't get written. With any luck this will be the last time we ever see one another."

31

They dropped him at his house in Shepherd's Bush and Gaddis found it just as he had left it a little more than a day earlier.

But, of course, it was no longer the same house. It was now a house with tapped phones, a house with bugged rooms, a house with a computer that spoke to faceless geeks at Vauxhall Cross and GCHQ. He opened the curtains in the sitting room and looked out at the cars parked on the street. There was a van directly opposite his front door, a van with blacked-out windows.

This is my future, he thought. *This is the price of consorting with Edward Crane.*

In an act of petty defiance, he walked outside, banged on the panelling of the van, said: "Make mine with two sugars," then went down to Uxbridge Road, entered a phone box, and dialled Peter's number. The connection was dead. No message or sound. Just a void at the other end of the line. Hungry and strung out, he took a Tube to UCL, dealt with his post and e-mails, then bought a new jacket at a store on Great Marlborough Street from a teenage shop assistant who popped bubbles of gum as she ran his credit card through the till.

He needed cash. He needed a new mobile phone. He needed to

find a way of living his life which would restore some degree of privacy to his punctured existence. Nowadays everything left a trail: there would be number plate recognition on his car; alerts on his Oyster card; triggers every time he used a bank account. Gaddis would have to assume, at least in the first few weeks of his arrangement with Tanya, that MI6 would continue to watch him, to ensure that he did not break his word. His calls, his e-mails, his movements around London would all be monitored by an army of watchers whom he would never sense, never identify, never see.

He took out £900 from an ATM on Shaftesbury Avenue, the daily limit on his three accounts now that Nat West had wired him the proceeds of yet another £20,000 personal loan. He bought a monthly Travelcard. He paid cash in a shop on Tottenham Court Road for a Nokia mobile, registering a new SIM with the address of a flat in Kensal Rise which had been his temporary home following the split with Natasha. He planned to alternate between the phones, reserving the new number for any conversations or text messages relating to Crane. He would not give it out to any of his friends—not even to Natasha or Holly—for fear that their own phones were compromised.

Holly. He wanted the opportunity to check her story, to ask her why she had handed over her mother's files. Was it, as she had insisted at the time, because Katya Levette had admired Charlotte's reporting, or had there been another, more sinister motive? He simply did not believe Tanya's claim that Holly was an innocent party.

He called her from the lobby of a vast Gothic hotel on Southampton Row. She was free for dinner, which again aroused his suspicion. Why would a beautiful twenty-eight-year-old actress not be doing something on a Saturday night? Why was Holly Levette always available to see him, even at short notice? It was as if she had been deliberately planted into his life as another pair of eyes, another layer of surveillance to add to Josephine Warner and the spooks of Berlin.

She showed up at his house at half past eight. Gaddis had spent the early part of the evening carrying the KGB boxes downstairs and piling them at one end of his open-plan kitchen. Holly was wearing a pair of cork-soled platform shoes, a vintage dress from the 1940s, and, to judge by the strap of her bra, a set of extremely expensive underwear. She did a double-take when she saw the files blocking the door to Gaddis's garden and looked at him as if he had gone mad.

"Spring cleaning?"

"Research," he said. "They're the boxes you gave me. Your mother's files."

Her reaction only fed his growing sense of suspicion. Her hands went up to her face, closed together as if in prayer, and she let out a stagey gasp of relief.

"Thank God you've reminded me. I've had six of the bloody things clogging up my car for the last two weeks. Do you want them?"

It seemed an uncanny coincidence. "There are *more* files?"

"It's never-ending. We missed about a dozen boxes in the basement when you came over the first time. Next time you stay, will you take them?"

He scanned her face for the lie. Why would she have waited more than a month to offload more information from her mother's archive? Why now? Had Tanya spoken to her since they had landed at Gatwick? It felt like a plan to test the seriousness of his promise to jettison Crane.

"I'll help you carry them in," he said.

Holly was parked fifty metres from Gaddis's front door. The van across the street had disappeared. She unlocked the boot of her car and passed him the first of six small shoe boxes, piling four of them on top of one another so that he was obliged to stagger back into the house with a wobbling column of cardboard secured under his chin.

"What's in these?" he said when he had piled the boxes on the kitchen table.

"No idea," Holly replied.

They managed to avoid the subject for the next two hours, talking instead about Gaddis's trip to Berlin—"A fantastic city. Wish I could have stayed longer."—and an audition Holly had done for a part in a new television series—"Another bloody medical drama. Why don't they just turn the BBC into a hospital?" Towards eleven o'clock, full of wine and conversation, they went to bed. To deny any eavesdropping spooks the dubious pleasure of listening to his pillow talk, Gaddis went into his office, loaded iTunes, and slid the volume control beyond halfway.

"Are you all right?" Holly asked as he came back into the bedroom. "Why are you putting music on?"

"Thin walls," Gaddis replied.

She looked at him. "You're being a bit weird tonight, Sam."

"Am I?"

"Very. Is everything okay?"

"Everything's fine."

He thought of Harold Wilson, of all people, a Prime Minister so convinced that MI5 were out to get him that he resorted to holding sensitive conversations in bathrooms with the taps running. If only he could tell Holly what was going on. If only he could come clean about Meisner, Somers, Charlotte, and Crane. Then again, perhaps she already knew all about them. Perhaps he was sleeping with a Russian asset.

"How did your mother die?"

"Wow. You really know how to sweet-talk a girl into bed."

"Seriously. You've never told me. I had the feeling the two of you weren't close."

Holly stopped undressing. She was standing barefoot in the middle of his bedroom with a strap of vintage dress halfway down her arm.

"We had our problems. Mothers and daughters, you know?"

ITunes shuffled to "It Ain't Me Babe." Gaddis thought about going into his office to change it, but wanted a reply to his question.

"She had cancer?" he asked.

"No. What makes you say that?"

"I just wondered how she died."

Holly's face jagged in irritation. "Why the sudden interest?"

She was losing patience. If he wasn't careful, she would grab her toothbrush from the bathroom, put on her platform shoes, and drink-drive back to Chelsea.

"Forget it," he said. "I don't know why I asked."

He did know why he had asked, of course. He wanted to know if the circumstances surrounding the death of Katya Levette had been in any way suspicious. He wanted to know if she had been murdered by the FSB. Was there something in the files that he had not yet discovered, a smoking gun in a shoe box? Had Katya unravelled the riddle of Dresden and paid the price with her life? The theory made no sense, of course: if the Russians had wanted to silence her, they would surely have destroyed her research as well. But Gaddis was in a mood of such persistent suspicion that he could not see the folly of his own thinking.

"She was an alcoholic."

Holly's declaration caught him off-guard. He had been switching off a light in the corridor and had come back into the room to find her sitting on the edge of the bed, unzipping her dress with a melancholy slowness.

"I didn't realize."

"Why would you?"

He walked across the room and knelt on the ground in front of her. He reached out his hand and stopped her in the act of undressing. "I'm so sorry."

"Not your fault," she said, smiling and ruffling his hair. He felt embarrassed and guilty. "If somebody wants to drink themselves to death, there isn't much anybody can do about it."

She continued to take off the dress. It was like an act of defiance against her mother, preventing her from ruining their evening. Gaddis saw the loveliness of her body and reached to touch her stomach. He knew that she had no intention of milking his sympathy, of playing the scene for emotional effect. It was one of the things that he most liked about her: she was an actress entirely incapable of melodrama.

"Come to bed," she said, unbuttoning his shirt. The sweet moisturized scent of her skin was a balm. She began to smile. "Just one thing."

"What's that?"

"Can we *please* turn off the Bob fucking Dylan?"

Three hours later, Gaddis was still awake. Being with Holly had done nothing to calm him. She was asleep in a peaceful curled ball beside him, but he was agitated in a way that he had not known since the worst periods of his divorce. He had barely slept since Berlin, yet the act of closing his eyes seemed to power up his imagination. He was haunted by images of Benedict Meisner, infuriated that he would have to shelve his work on Crane, determined to bring Charlotte's killers to justice.

At about quarter past two, abandoning any hope of sleep, he went downstairs, poured himself a glass of wine and—with nothing better to do—began to go through the files which Holly had brought over in the car.

It was the same old story: there was nothing of consequence in any of the boxes. Downing two ibuprofen, Gaddis turned his attention to the original files which he had examined only cursorily two months earlier. This time, he found the odd item which he had missed on first examination of the material: Anthony Blunt's death certificate, for example, and a copy of his will. There was the transcript of an interview with Sir Dick White, conducted by an unnamed journalist in 1982. Gaddis was briefly intrigued by this, but of course found no reference to ATTILA, nor any mention of Edward Crane. In another box, he found a photocopied obituary of Jack Hewit, the former MI5 officer who had been Guy Burgess's lover, as well as a newspaper review of Michael Straight's memoirs. There was also an entire folder dedicated to newspaper cuttings about Goronwy Rees and Vladimir Petrov. Katya had plainly intended to write a book about the relationship between British Intelligence and the KGB in the postwar era, but there was nothing—as far as he could tell—which was not already in the public domain.

Just after four o'clock he poured himself a third glass of wine and smoked a cigarette on the sofa. Holly's handbag was on the floor at his feet. It was open and some of the contents had spilled out onto the carpet, perhaps when she had retrieved her toothbrush. He was sure that she was asleep; if she woke up wondering what had happened to him, he would be able to hear her footfalls on the staircase. He just wanted to be certain that she was who she said she was. He just wanted to put his mind at rest.

So he reached for the bag.

In the main section he found a well-thumbed copy of *A Doll's House*, another of *The Time Traveller's Wife,* and an issue of the *NME*. He put all three on the sofa beside him and rummaged deeper. He was amazed by how much noise he was making. He found a broken seashell, an unopened packet of Kleenex, a tangle of headphones, a packet of the contraceptive pill—up-to-date, thank God—and the browned core of a half-eaten apple. He laid these out on the floor. He then found what were surely keepsakes: a small amethyst stone; a length of silk wrapped up into a tight bundle and tied with a piece of string; and a postcard from Katya Levette, addressed to Holly, postmarked 1999, showing a photograph of the Eiffel Tower.

What he wanted was her diary. He found it in a separate, zipped-up section of the bag and checked the entries for August and September, looking for anything unusual, for evidence of a double life. But there were just times of auditions, dates of parties, shorthand reminders to buy milk or to pay a bill. His own book launch was marked with the simple note: "Gaddis event / Daunt Holland Park" and their subsequent meetings were also touchingly mundane: "Dinner S 830"; "S movie Kensington?"; "Lunch S Café Anglais." On the morning of Charlotte's funeral, Holly had written, in block capitals: "SAM FUNERAL CALL HIM!" and he remembered that she had rung him at the house in Hampstead to make sure that he was all right. He felt wretched for not trusting her.

But still he was not done. Feeling around in the lint and the crumbs at the bottom of the handbag, he found Holly's wallet and proceeded to unload its contents, item by item, onto the sofa. The credit cards were all in her name. There were frayed photographs of giggling friends in passport booths, loyalty cards to Sainsbury and Tesco, a dry-cleaning receipt from a shop on King's Road and a mini statement from an ATM in Hammersmith. He did not know what he was expecting to find. A number for Sir John Brennan? A business card belonging to Tanya Acocella? On the basis of what he had seen, there was no suggestion that Holly was anything other than an out-of-work actress with an overdraft and an erratic social life.

Eventually, he gave up the search and replaced the wallet, more or less as he had found it, in the bag. In a second side pocket he found two sets of keys, a packet of Rizlas, a small tube of lip salve, and an electricity bill, in Holly's name, which was registered to the address in Tite Street. There was also an e-mail from a woman in Australia which Holly had printed onto A4 paper. It was a letter between friends, full of news and gossip, and Gaddis felt ashamed to have read it.

He lit a second cigarette. He replaced the bag on the floor and looked around for Holly's mobile. It was charging up on a plug beside the kettle. Without removing the power cord, he checked her incoming and outgoing calls, her text messages, even the cookies on her Internet browser, but there was nothing at all to arouse his suspicion, only a man called "Dan C" to whom Holly had sent a dismayingly flirtatious text message responding to an invitation to the theatre.

It's no more than I deserve, he thought. *At least Dan won't go through your stuff.*

He was at last beginning to feel tired. Time for bed. He put the phone back on the counter, emptied the ashtray, put his glass in the dishwasher, and re-corked the wine. Two of Katya's shoe boxes were still open on the table and he gathered up the loose pieces of paper in a halfhearted attempt to tidy up.

That was when he saw the letter. A single sheet of powder-blue, watermarked stationery with an address die-stamped at the top:

Robert Wilkinson
Drybread Road (RD2)
Omakau 9377
Central Otago
New Zealand

32

It was a love letter.

My darling Katya,

This is the last of the material I promised to send to you. If you look carefully, perhaps you will find something that catches the public's attention. Keep your eye on Platov. He is the prize. I cannot say any more than that.

Life on the property is much the same. I walk, I read, I feel a very long way from home. Mostly I do not mind that feeling. I see Rachel all the time, because she lives just a few hours away, and she has given me two wonderful grandchildren. I don't even seem to mind Rachel's husband as much as I once did—perhaps I am mellowing with age.

But I miss Catherine and I miss you, my darling. I think of you constantly. I am not a sentimental man. You know this about me. But sometimes I cannot stand to think that I will never hold you again, that you will never sleep in my arms, that we will be forever apart. I have made so many mistakes and now it feels almost too late.

I regret so much, not least choosing a career over the possibility of a greater happiness with you. But you have heard all this from me so many times before. What use are regrets? I only ask that you give some thought, one last time, to the possibility of coming here, to New Zealand, even if it is just for a week or two. I promise that you will like it.

Good luck with the book, Katty. I have tried to help you and only wish that I could have done more.

> With all my love, as always,
> Robert x

At the end of their first weekend together, Holly had mentioned to Gaddis that her mother had once had a boyfriend in MI6 who had leaked material to her about the KGB. This was surely him. Wilkinson was the source of the archive. The letter was dated 5 May 2000. But what had he meant by the lines in the first paragraph? *Keep your eye on Platov. He is the prize.*

It was almost half past four in the morning. Gaddis read the letter again, trying to work out the precise nature of the relationship between Wilkinson and Katya Levette. Had they been married? Christ, was he Holly's *father*? Only Holly would be able to provide the answers, but he could hardly wake her in the middle of the night. His questions would have to wait until morning.

"What are you doing?"

She was standing on the far side of the room with scrunched eyes and sleep-twisted hair, a section of it stuck to her face. He was startled by the sound of her voice and put the letter on the table, as if he had been caught reading Holly's private correspondence. She was wearing his dressing gown, the cord hanging loose at the side.

"Did I wake you?"

"No. I just needed a glass of water. You weren't there. I wondered what had happened to you." Her eyes were squinting against the light. "What are you doing up? What time is it?"

Gaddis looked beyond her, at the handbag on the floor, and felt a pang of remorse. "About half-four," he said. He was wide-awake again, the soporific effects of the wine and the ibuprofen long since worn off. "Who's Robert Wilkinson?"

"What?"

Her head had fallen to one side. She looked startled.

"So you know him?"

"Bob? Of course I know him. He was Mum's boyfriend. How did his name come up?"

"I found a letter." Gaddis held it up in his hand, inviting her to read it. But she was still half asleep and said: "Can't I see it in the morning?"

He shook his head. "No. It's important. Did he give your mum this stuff?"

He indicated the files on the table. It was surely too much of a coincidence that a letter from Robert Wilkinson should have been hiding all that time in a shoe box in the boot of her car. Why had she brought it over today, of all days? Holly was frowning, her half-open eyes still resisting the bright light of the kitchen.

"Sam, it's the middle of the fucking night. You've had this stuff for *weeks*."

"Not this." He tapped the letter with the print of his index finger. "This came today."

"Come back to bed," she said. "Bob was just in love with Mum. Obsessed by her. I'll tell you about him in the morning."

"What do you mean, 'obsessed'?"

She walked forward and grabbed his arm. "In the *morning*."

"No. Please." He had one hand on her waist, holding her. He caught the sudden sharp smell of her sex and thought of Tanya's betrayal. "I need to know. You have to tell me. You have to wake up. Can I make you some tea? Some coffee?"

"This is ridiculous." She allowed him to pull her into a chair. "If I tell you, will you promise to let me sleep?"

"I promise to let you sleep."

"Fine." She leaned her elbows on the kitchen table, eyes closed, head bowed, as if in the early stages of prayer. "Bob Wilkinson," she muttered to herself. She was plainly having difficulty remembering the details. "Mum's last boyfriend before Dad. Possibly first love. Can't remember."

"And you've met him?"

"Sure."

"What's he like?"

She looked up and stared at Gaddis in irritation, as if a character sketch was far beyond her remit at half past four in the morning.

He backed off. "Okay, fine. Then tell me when they were involved."

He had stood up as he asked the question and switched on a small digital radio in the corner of the kitchen. He didn't want the conversation to be overheard. Classical music began to pour into the room. Holly frowned, but she was too tired to question his bizarre behaviour. "Oh, I don't know, Sam. Early seventies, probably." She curled a strand of hair behind her ear. "Mum would have been about my age. They almost got engaged but Bob was sent abroad by the Foreign Office or something and they had to break up."

Gaddis didn't like that. "Foreign Office or something." It sounded as though she was overcompensating for a lie.

"He chose his career over your mother?"

"Well, that's one way of looking at it." She laughed. "Mum was actually *relieved*. She'd met my father, they got married soon after, they had me. And we all lived happily ever after." She began to play with the lid on one of the shoe boxes. "Only Bob never forgot about her. Got married, got divorced, always stayed in touch with Mum, then helped her a lot with her career after Dad died."

Gaddis saw that she was frowning.

"Why are you looking like that?"

Holly shook her head. "I think they may have had an affair, a rekindled thing, about ten years ago." She turned towards the radio. "Why the fuck have you turned on Classic FM?"

"It's Radio 3."

Holly stood up. She poured herself a glass of water from a bottle in the fridge, then turned down the volume on the radio. Gaddis wanted to object but understood the absurdity of his behaviour; he could not afford to alienate her with a paranoid rant about audio surveillance. Instead, he watched as she drank the water—the entire glass, like a cure for a hangover—before returning to her chair.

"Mum wrote about political issues, geopolitics, espionage." Holly dropped into a stage whisper, putting a finger to her lips. She was beginning to enjoy herself. "Bob was a *huge* spy. Iron Curtain. Cold War. Is that why you're worried about being bugged?" She looked as though she was about to burst out laughing. "Are you using Mum's stuff to write a book about MI6?"

He gestured at her to keep talking.

"Far as I know, Bob would feed Mum titbits of information all the time. Spy gossip, rumours from Washington and Westminster." She tapped the table with her knuckles. "He probably gave her fifty per cent of this stuff. It was his way of expressing his affection. Either that, or a way of assuaging his guilt for running off to Moscow. He said he wanted her to write a great book about Western intelligence, all the things Bob Wilkinson couldn't say because he was bound by the Official Secrets Act." She took Gaddis's hand in hers and her lively mood suddenly subsided. "But Mum never got round to it. She probably never even read the files. At the end of the day, Bob annoyed her. He was like a fly she couldn't brush off. And she was never well enough to do any work. I think Bob lives in New Zealand now. I haven't seen him for ages."

"Didn't he come to your mother's funeral?"

Holly shook her head. "Can't remember. I'd broken the world record for Valium consumption. Possibly. He may not even know that she's died."

Gaddis picked up the letter and passed it to her. A lorry tore past the sitting-room windows, hurtling over speed bumps in the dead of the night. He pointed to the line about Platov. "What do you think he meant by this?"

"Here?" Holly squinted, like an old woman in need of glasses. "Platov? I haven't got a clue."

Gaddis studied her face intently, still unsure whether he was being manipulated. "Your mother never mentioned that she was investigating anyone in the Kremlin?"

"Never, no." Holly leaned back in her chair with a scrutinizing frown. "I thought *you* were the expert on Platov. What's going on, Sam?"

"You tell me."

33

Inevitably, international directory enquiries had no listing in New Zealand for a Robert Wilkinson so Gaddis had to ask Holly for a favour. Did her mother keep an address book? Would it be possible to track down a number for Bob? Holly asked him why he was so keen to speak to Wilkinson, but Gaddis was deliberately vague about the details.

"He was in Berlin during an important phase of the Cold War. It's for the MI6 book. I want to try to set up a meeting."

The following evening, Holly had called from Tite Street with the details. There was no way of preventing her from reading out Wilkinson's number over an open line, so Gaddis had written it down and immediately walked outside to a phone box a quarter of a mile away on South Africa Road. If GCHQ had been eavesdropping on Holly's call, he reckoned it would still take them several hours to establish a bug on Wilkinson's phone in New Zealand.

It was eight o'clock in the evening in London, eight o'clock in the morning in New Zealand. He rolled four pound coins into the payphone and tapped in the number.

"Hello?"

"Is that Robert Wilkinson?"

"Speaking. Who is this?"

The line was very clear. Gaddis was surprised by the classlessness of Wilkinson's accent: he had grown up with the idea that all senior MI6 personnel sounded like members of the Royal Family.

"My name is Sam Gaddis. I'm a lecturer in Russian History at UCL. I've also just completed a biography of Sergei Platov. Does my name mean anything to you?"

"It means nothing to me whatsoever."

Silence. Gaddis could sense that he had another Thomas Neame on his hands.

"Is it a good time to talk?"

"As good as any."

"It's just that I wanted to speak to you about Katya Levette."

That got his attention. Gaddis heard a sharp, near-anxious intake of breath, the arrogance going out of him, then half a word—"Kat—"

"I understand that you were good friends."

"Yes. Who told you this?"

"Holly is a friend of mine."

"Good God. Holly. How is she?"

Wilkinson was opening up. Gaddis took out a pen and a scrap of paper and tried to pin them on the phone casing with his elbow. "She's very well. She wanted me to send you her love."

"How kind of her." There was a brief interruption on the line, perhaps a technical fault, perhaps the sound of Wilkinson finding a quieter and more comfortable place in his house from which to speak. "Who did you say you were again? Who am I speaking to?"

"My name is Sam Gaddis. I'm an academic, a writer. I'm calling you from London."

"Of course. And you're working with Katya on a story?"

He obviously didn't know about Katya. Wilkinson hadn't been told that Levette was dead. Gaddis was going to have to break it to him.

"You hadn't heard, sir?" He was surprised that he called him that, but had felt a sense of deference in the moment. "I'm so sorry. I didn't know that I would be the one to tell you. I just assumed that you already knew. Katya has died, Mr. Wilkinson. I'm very sorry. Six months ago."

"Dear me, that's terrible news." The reply was instant and stoic; Gaddis felt that he could picture the resilience in Wilkinson's face. He had just lost the great love of his life, but he was not going to display his grief to a stranger. "I'm sorry to hear that," he said. "How is Holly coping?"

"So, so," said Gaddis. "She's all right."

Wilkinson asked how Katya had died and Gaddis told him that she had suffered from liver failure, a euphemism which the older man immediately understood.

"Yes. I was afraid that would take her in the end. The bloody drink was a lifelong struggle for her. I'll write to Holly with my condolences. Is she still at the flat in Tite Street?"

"She is. And I'm sure she'd appreciate that."

"In fact, Catherine is getting married later this month. I might see if Holly can come along to the wedding. It would be wonderful to meet her again."

Gaddis knew, from conversations with Holly, that Catherine was Wilkinson's daughter, but he felt that he should feign ignorance.

"Catherine?"

"My youngest. Marrying an Austrian in Vienna. I'll be coming over for the wedding. We must try to entice Holly along."

"I'll certainly mention that."

Gaddis looked at the readout and saw that he was down to fifty pence of credit. He put four further pounds into the slot and coughed to conceal the noise of the coins chugging into the phone.

It did no good.

"Are you speaking to me from a phone box?" Wilkinson asked.

Even if Gaddis had wanted to lie, it would have been impossible to do so: a souped-up Volkswagen Golf had pulled up on the street beside him. The driver leaned on his horn repeatedly in an effort to gain the attention of someone in a nearby housing estate. It must have sounded to Wilkinson as though Gaddis was calling from the middle of the M4.

"The phone at my house is out of order," he said, accidentally knocking the pen and the scrap of paper onto the floor of the booth. As he bent down to retrieve them, stretching the receiver to his ear, he said: "I was just very keen to ring you as soon as possible."

"About what, Doctor Gaddis?"

"I've come into possession of some documents that I think you gave to Katya."

A pause. Wilkinson was weighing up his options. "I see."

"Holly gave them to me. A mutual friend thought that I might be interested in the material."

"And are you?"

Some of the obstructiveness which had characterized Wilkinson's tone in the early part of the conversation had returned.

"I haven't really had a proper chance to go through it all yet. I've been busy working on something else. I wondered if you knew what Katya was planning to do with the documents?"

"I'm afraid I really wouldn't know."

It sounded like a lie but Gaddis had not expected a straight answer. Wilkinson was guilty of passing potentially sensitive intelligence information to a journalist. He had no means of knowing whether Gaddis was a bona fide historian or an agent provocateur hired by SIS to elicit a confession.

"Perhaps we could meet in Vienna to discuss this?" Gaddis suggested, a wild idea which was out of his mouth before he had thought through its implications.

"Perhaps," Wilkinson replied, with a complete lack of conviction. Time was running out. If Gaddis wasn't careful, the conversation would soon be brought to an abrupt end.

"There was just one person in particular that I'm keen to talk to you about," he said.

"Yes? And who's that?"

"Sergei Platov."

Wilkinson produced a grunt of indifference. "But you told me that you've already written his biography. Why would you want to start all over again?"

"It's a different angle this time." Gaddis was wondering how best to play his trump card. "I'm interested in Platov's relationship with three former intelligence officers from the Soviet era."

"Intelligence officers—"

"Fyodor Tretiak was a high-ranking KGB resident in Dresden. Edward Crane was a British double agent for more than fifty years.

The man who ran him from Berlin in the mid-1980s used the pseudonym Dominic Ulvert."

Wilkinson's shock came down the long-distance line as a whispered expletive.

"You bloody idiot. Is this line secure?"

"I think so—"

"I will thank you not to contact me here again."

34

O n the transcript of the conversation shown to Sir John Brennan the following morning, the abrupt climax of the discussion between POLARBEAR and Robert Wilkinson was rendered with the simple phrase: "CALL TERMINATED."

Brennan, who had been led to believe that Gaddis had abandoned his interest in ATTILA, flew into a rage, calling a meeting with Tanya Acocella at which he admonished her for "failing to persuade this fucking academic" that "if he so much as goes near Edward Crane ever again, we will throw him to the wolves in Moscow. I didn't spend every waking hour of my fucking weekend on bended knee to the head of the BND asking him to turn a blind eye to Gaddis's handiwork in Berlin just so that he could immediately pick up the phone and start chatting to Bob bloody Wilkinson."

Tanya had attempted to interject, but Brennan wasn't finished.

"Does Gaddis have any fucking *concept* of what will happen to him if the Russians find out who he is? Does he know what's at stake? Didn't you make it plain to him after you landed at Gatwick? What did you *talk* about? House prices? Gastro pubs? Were you planning, Tanya, at any fucking stage, to do your job properly?"

She had been dismissed from Brennan's office with a parting shot which had enraged her.

"Here's what you'll do. Go back to CHESAPEAKE. Consider PO-LARBEAR closed for business. If you can't cope with a simple problem like Sam Gaddis, I'll have to take care of it myself."

With Acocella in the lift, Brennan had immediately contacted the British Embassy in Canberra and instructed Christopher Brooke, the thirty-five-year-old Head of Station in Australia, to catch the next flight to New Zealand where he was to have "a quiet word with one of our former employees." SIS activities out of Wellington had been wound down as part of a cost-cutting exercise, which meant that Brooke faced a seven-hour trip to Christchurch via Sydney, a further forty-five-minute flight from Christchurch to Dunedin, followed by a three-hour drive, in a rented Toyota Corolla, from Dunedin to Alexandra, which was in the heart of the South Island. Accounting for delays and transfers, the journey—from the moment he left his house in Canberra, to the moment he arrived in Alexandra—took just under fourteen hours and cost Brooke an explosive argument with his pregnant wife, who had been looking forward to a long-awaited five-day break on the Gold Coast. Brooke had fallen asleep more or less as soon as he had reached his hotel room, waking at dawn on Wednesday to discover that nobody had ever heard of Robert Wilkinson, nor of the property at Drybread.

"We know most of the people round here, luv," said the manageress of the Dunstan House. "Drybread used to be a gold mine. Nobody's lived out there for years."

"You sure you've got the right place, mate?" asked a petrol pump attendant at a garage on the edge of Alexandra.

Brooke drove all morning. He saw three people in three hours, none of whom were able to give him directions. He scanned road maps but could not access the Internet in order to download images from Google Earth which might have provided him with a route to Drybread. He was passing through some of the most dramatic scenery he had ever witnessed, yet for the most part his Hertz Toyota was filled with the sound of a worn-out, irritated British spook swearing at the injustice of being posted to the arse end of the intelligence world and blaspheming venomously at the prospect of spending three days searching for a retired Cold War spy who, if the locals were to be believed, had never set foot in New Zealand.

Finally, Brooke drove back to Alexandra, went to the public library, and found a reference to "Drybread" in a historical guide to Central Otago, dated 1947. Wilkinson's home had once been a gold-mining settlement and subsequently a farm. From the description in the guide, it was situated at the end of "Drybread Road" in a gully at the base of the Dunstan Range, forty-five kilometres northwest of Alexandra.

He set out from the library. He passed through a dry, barren landscape—identified on the map as the Maniototo Plain—stopping for petrol and some food in Omakau, a settlement which boasted little more than a pub and a local store. At about four o'clock, he turned from the S85 highway onto an unsealed, single-track road flanked by rivers and streams which turned a deep, sky-matching blue in the late afternoon sun. Every few hundred metres he was obliged to stop and to open farm gates, the road becoming more rugged with every passing kilometre. He was concerned that the Toyota would puncture at any moment, leaving him stranded in the centre of a vast, under-populated plain which would soon be cloaked in darkness. Just after six, however, approximately ten kilometres inland from the main road, he at last saw a battered sign for Drybread and turned onto a narrow, potholed trail which ran across a cultivated plain towards a screen of jagged hills. The property was a small, two-storey home-stead half a mile along the trail, nestled within a rectangle of willow trees. As he steered through the gate, Brooke spotted a figure in a prehistoric Barbour chopping wood on the eastern side of the prop-erty. It was beginning to spot with rain. He switched off the engine, stepped onto the drive, and was about to raise a hand in greeting when he saw Robert Wilkinson walking towards him brandishing a cold-eyed stare and a double-barrelled shotgun.

"Who the fuck are you?"

Brooke had his hands in the air within a split second.

"Friendly! Friendly!" he shouted, a hangover from three eventful years with the Service in Basra. "I'm with the Office. I've come from Canberra to talk to you."

"Who sent you?" Wilkinson was holding at a distance of fifty metres, shouldering the gun and keeping it levelled at Brooke's solar plexus.

"Sir John Brennan. It's about ATTILA. I have a message to convey to you."

Wilkinson lowered the gun, broke the chamber, and hooked it over his wrist.

"Convey it," he said.

Brooke looked around. He had been warned that Wilkinson had "turned a bit native," but had, at the very least, been expecting a cup of tea.

"Out here?"

"Out here," Wilkinson replied.

"All right then." He reached into the backseat of the Toyota, retrieved a North Face parka, zipped it up against the deteriorating weather, and closed the door. "Sir John is concerned that you may be establishing a relationship with a British academic named Sam Gaddis."

"Establishing a relationship? What the fuck does that mean?"

Wilkinson knew, instantly, that SIS had bugged Gaddis's call. Years of carefully cultivated anonymity had been obliterated in an instant by a reckless academic in a London phone box.

"Doctor Gaddis has discovered the truth about ATTILA. We believe that he knows you were running Edward Crane in East Germany in the 1980s. The Service is worried that you may be passing information to Gaddis of a sensitive nature, in breach of your commitment to the Official Secrets Act."

Wilkinson took a step forward. He was in his early sixties, stocky and imposing. His face, particularly in the fading light of a chill spring evening, had a quality of ruthlessness which had scared braver men than Christopher Brooke.

"What's your name, young man?"

"My name is Christopher. I'm Head of Station in Canberra."

"And you've come all the way from Australia to tell me this, have you, Chris?"

Brooke thought of his pregnant wife, of the Qantas cabin sprayed for insects, of freeze-dried in-flight meals, and the interminable roads of Central Otago. He said: "That is correct."

"And don't they teach you to keep civilized hours at Fort Monkton anymore? What do you mean by showing up here at dusk? You could have been *anybody*."

Brooke had been informed that Wilkinson was "paranoid up to the eyeballs about Russian assassins" and assumed that he would now regain some of his composure, safe in the knowledge that his surprise visitor had not been sent by the FSB.

"I apologize for startling you," he said, extending a hand. "Nobody in the local community had heard of you. I had great difficulty locating your address. It's only fractionally less remote round here than the Sea of Tranquility."

Wilkinson produced a grunt of indifference. "Is that your idea of a joke? Is that how you soften people up nowadays? A little galactic irony? A little lunar wit?"

Brooke could see that it was a lost cause. He put the extended hand back in the pocket of his parka and decided to abandon any pretence at camaraderie. He wanted nothing more than to be driving back to Dunedin, getting a good night's sleep, and catching a flight home to Canberra. He wanted to be away from this gun-wielding maniac. He wanted to be filing a report for Brennan, drinking a bottle of Pinot Noir, and eating Thai green curry with his wife. But he had a job to do.

"Here's the situation," he said. "Why don't I just get it off my chest, because it's fairly obvious that this isn't going to be a civilized conversation. I wasn't expecting a home-cooked meal, Mr. Wilkinson. I wasn't expecting a bed for the night. But if you want to do this out here, then we'll do it out here." Right on cue, a wind came gusting across the plain, rattling the leaves of the willow trees. "As I understand it, Gaddis is threatening to blow the lid off two of the most closely guarded secrets of the Cold War, secrets that my colleagues—yourself included—have done a very good job of covering up for the past sixty years. The Chief has asked me to remind you that there are—to use his word—*anomalies* in the final years of Mr. Crane's career which would have massive repercussions on our relationship with Moscow if they came to light. Now I don't happen to know what those anomalies are, but I am reliably informed that you do." He saw Wilkinson's face lift in the failing light and heard a short sniff, which he took to be a gesture of assent. "Sir John has always been deeply concerned that retired intelligence officers should not feel the need to sell their life stories to the highest bidder."

"I beg your pardon."

"I think you understand what I mean. The Service is aware that you disclosed sensitive information to a Mrs. Katya Levette at various stages of your career, as a means both of leaking politically damaging stories to the British press and as a channel for your own autobiographical recollections."

"You want to be careful with that smooth tongue of yours," Wilkinson said, shifting the gun into his right hand. "It could get you into trouble."

The rain was falling heavily now and Brooke pulled up the hood of his jacket.

"Is it not the case that you and Mrs. Levette discussed the possibility of ghosting your memoirs?"

Wilkinson had heard enough. He moved against the rain until he was face-to-face with Brooke, studying him rather as a crocodile might size up a snack for lunch.

"Let me tell you something. I woke up three days ago and made myself a cup of tea. The telephone rang and I answered it. This Doctor Gaddis was on the other end of the line. He was calling me from London, from a phone box, asking questions about Eddie Crane. I'd never heard of him. You see, I didn't realize that ATTILA was suddenly public knowledge. I also had no idea how an opportunistic British academic had managed to track me down. Let me assure you that I had absolutely no intention of discussing my career with him. I would assume that our private conversation was scooped up as a favour to the old country by local liaison. Is that the case?"

"I have no idea what role, if any, the GCSB has played in all this."

"No?" Wilkinson watched the rain sluicing down Brooke's face. "I bet you don't. You're only Head of Station in Canberra, after all."

He raised a hand when Brooke attempted to respond.

"Wait. I haven't finished." He was angry now, livid at the invasion of his privacy and infuriated that his relationship with Katya was once again being dragged through the mud. "Please tell Sir John—he was just 'John' when I knew him, but he was always keen on going places—tell *Sir* John that I will do whatever the hell I like in my retirement. If that includes talking to out-of-their-depth academics in London, so be it. You see, I remember how things ended. I remember a bomb under my car. I remember experiencing the distinct feeling that the Service would have preferred it if Bob Wilkinson had been blown up by Sergei Platov and thrown into the skies above Fulham." Brooke was wiping rainwater out of his eyes. "You look confused, Christopher."

"You've lost me," he replied. "I have absolutely no idea what you're talking about."

"No," said Wilkinson. "I expect you don't." Another gust of wind came buffeting across the plain. "But *Sir* John Brennan knows exactly what I'm talking about. Be sure to tell him that I understand the definition of loyalty. He never looked out for me, so why should I look out for him? If this Gaddis wants chapter and verse on ATTILA, perhaps I'll give it to him. It's time the whole story came out anyway. Christ, the British government would probably *benefit* if it did. Wouldn't you like to see the back of that maniac?"

"Which maniac?"

"Platov," Wilkinson replied witheringly, as if Brooke had laid out his ignorance for the world to see. "They really haven't put you in the picture at all, have they? You really have no idea what the hell is going on."

35

Late on Thursday afternoon, Sam Gaddis was squeezing through a pavement crush of students outside the School of Eastern European and Slavonic Studies when he spotted Tanya Acocella on the opposite side of Taviton Street. She was wearing a beige raincoat, leather boots, and a beret which brought out the stark white bones of her face. He thought that she looked tired, but felt the irritating pang of attraction nonetheless; he had to remind himself to look annoyed as he crossed the street to speak to her.

"I don't suppose this is a coincidence."

"No," she said. "Walk with me?"

She was taking a risk, being seen with him. Brennan could have eyes all over UCL. A simple surveillance photograph of the two of them together, fed back to Vauxhall Cross, would reveal that she had ignored the Chief's order to abandon contact with POLAR-BEAR.

"I wondered how you were getting along," she asked.

Gaddis took the question at face value and said that he had been "fine, absolutely fine" since the shootings in Berlin.

"We've managed to come to an arrangement with the German

authorities. They've put a squeeze on coverage of the incident in the media. The police won't be looking for a second gunman. The man who killed Meisner, the man you shot, was a Russian named Nicolai Doronin. MI5 had been observing him for several months. The Germans know that he has links to the FSB, but they're not expecting to pursue a complaint against Moscow. Doronin will make a full recovery and he'll be turfed out of Berlin. He'll know that if he tries to finger any of his colleagues in connection with the conspiracy, there'll be repercussions for his family in London."

"What a lovely story," said Gaddis, taking out a cigarette. Tanya asked for one and he lit it for her as a student came up behind them, asked Gaddis a question about an essay deadline, and then walked off towards Endsleigh Gardens.

"The Berlin solution is the best you're going to get," Tanya said, pointedly expecting some measure of thanks for the horse-trading SIS had done on Gaddis's behalf.

"I understand that," he said. "Believe me, I'm extremely grateful."

They walked in silence. She was wondering how best to say what she had come to say.

"You are being careful, aren't you, Sam?"

"Careful in what way?"

"You understand the terms of our arrangement? You can't go looking for Crane. You can't go seeking vengeance for what happened to Meisner and Charlotte."

She thought of Brennan lashing out at her in his office and wondered why she was being so considerate of Gaddis's feelings. A pigeon settled on the pavement ahead of them, hopped into the path of a taxi turning into the road, and flew off.

"If you leave the country, the minute your passport is presented anywhere in the EU, they'll know where to find you."

Gaddis stopped and turned. "What do you mean 'they'?"

"I've been removed from the operation. Pastures new. Brennan has a new team working on you."

He was confused. Did she want his sympathy?

"Why have they taken you off the case?"

"Long story." Gaddis felt that she might have been about to explain, but instead Tanya merely reiterated her earlier warning. "It doesn't matter who's running you now. The terms of the arrangement are the same. Don't go looking for Crane. Do you understand?"

Gaddis tried his best to convince her. "I have told you," he replied. "I *understand*, Tanya."

She didn't like to see him lying; it didn't suit him.

"It's just that Robert Wilkinson may not be in New Zealand forever," she said. "We wondered whether you might already know that. We wanted to be absolutely certain that you wouldn't make any attempt to see him if, for example, he came to Vienna."

Gaddis could only laugh, but it was a hollow sound, a breathless, near-silent surrender to the omnipotence of SIS. They had eyes and ears everywhere; they were listening to everything he said, even to a phone box on the edge of a housing estate in South Africa Road.

"Wilkinson doesn't want to have anything to do with me," he said. He dropped his half-smoked cigarette onto the ground and snuffed it out with his shoe. "Crane has disappeared. Even if I wanted to finish the book, I don't have any more leads. It's over."

"We both know that's not quite true." He marvelled at her ability to convince him that she was still on his side. Perhaps it was the outfit: she looked so elegant, so off-duty, every inch the beautiful, available, seductive Josephine Warner.

"You're right," he said. "I could go to Vienna. I could gatecrash Catherine's wedding. I could grab Bob Wilkinson over a smoked salmon canapé and ask him to tell me all about Dresden, just as a favour to an academic that he doesn't know and doesn't even particularly like. Do you really think that's what I'm planning to do?"

"I think you're capable of anything."

Gaddis reached out and held her.

"You need to trust me," he said. Her arms were gym-exercised, taut and wiry. "Check your surveillance records. I'm going to be in Barcelona for the rest of the month. I've arranged to spend a fortnight with Min."

"You have?"

Tanya was no longer privy to the POLARBEAR product; it was infuriating not to know even this simple piece of information.

"I have," he said. "So if Des feels like following me, tell him to pack his swimming trunks. My daughter and I will be spending a lot of time at the beach."

36

It was a half-truth, at best, but Gaddis reasoned that he owed Tanya Acocella a lie or two. Barcelona was just his way of getting even.

He had spent the morning out at Colindale, on the outskirts of northwest London, going through back issues of *The Times*. He could have searched for what he was looking for online, but what was the point of risking the Internet when there were hard copies going back as far as the eye could see? The issue he found was dated 6 January. Gaddis laid a private bet with himself that Catherine Wilkinson had accepted her fiancé's proposal on New Year's Eve, shortly before the corks had flown on the midnight champagne.

MR M. T. M. DRECHSEL AND MISS C. L. WILKINSON
The engagement is announced between Matthias, elder son of Mr. Rudolph Drechsel and Mrs. Elfriede Drechsel, of Vienna, Austria, and Catherine, younger daughter of Mr. Robert Wilkinson and of Mrs. Mary Edwards, of Edinburgh, Scotland.

That gave him the surname for the wedding party, which was the first step of his plan.

The second step was to ascertain the date of the wedding and to find the hotel in Vienna where the bulk of the guests would be staying. To that end, Gaddis printed out a list of all of the four- and five-star hotels in Vienna and called them, one by one, from two phone boxes at Colindale station, making the same request.

"Hello. I'd like to book a room for the weekend of the Drechsel–Wilkinson wedding. I've been advised that you are offering a special rate for guests of the couple."

The first fourteen hotels had "no record at all of a wedding booked under that name," but the fifteenth—the SAS Radisson on Schubertring—knew all about it and asked Gaddis for his surname.

"It's Peters," he said. "P-E-T-E-R-S. Peters."

"Yes, Mr. Peters. And when would you like to arrive?"

Gaddis now moved to the next phase of his strategy. He needed a precise date for the wedding, so he said: "Could you tell me if any of the other guests are arriving on the Thursday evening? Would that be too early, do you think?"

"Thursday the twenty-third, sir? Let me see."

Then it was just a question of whether the ceremony would take place on the afternoon of Friday the twenty-fourth or Saturday the twenty-fifth.

"Mr. Peters?"

"Yes."

"It is difficult to say, sir. We have a number of guests arriving on Thursday evening, but the majority appear to be checking in on Friday."

So, the reception would be on Saturday the twenty-fifth. "I see," he said.

Gaddis had played along for a few moments more, requesting a double room for the Friday and Saturday nights, but when it came to divulging his full name and address, he had pretended that he had "an important call coming through on another line" and promised the receptionist that he would complete the booking online.

"Of course, Mr. Peters. Of course. We very much look forward to seeing you in Vienna."

37

wo days later, Gaddis left London for Spain, catching an evening flight from Heathrow to Barcelona. He experienced no difficulties at passport control but assumed that SIS would have Natasha's apartment under tight surveillance. His plan was straightforward: to spend a few days in Spain with Min and then to go to Austria by train. Under the terms of the Schengen Agreement, it was possible to travel all the way to Vienna without displaying a passport; Gaddis assumed that this would make the task of tracking him considerably more complicated. He planned to arrive at the Radisson on the evening of Friday the twenty-fourth, in time to mingle with the other guests. He would pretend to be a friend of the Drechsel family, discover the location of the wedding reception, and perhaps accompany some of his new-found friends to the service the following day. That would bring him into direct contact with Robert Wilkinson.

As it transpired, SIS were short on manpower and had to task the observation of POLARBEAR in Barcelona to two local officials based at the British Consulate-General on Avenida Diagonal. Their surveillance reports, sent directly to Sir John Brennan in London, recorded a staggeringly mundane series of visits to local playgrounds, branches of VIPS restaurant, shivering swims in the October waters of Icaria Beach, and father-and-daughter strolls along the Ramblas. Brennan was shown photographs of Min piggybacking on her father's shoulders, emerging from a cinema carrying an ice cream, and laughing as Gaddis told her a story on the Metro. There was evidence that POLARBEAR had been involved in a heated exchange with his ex-wife over tapas at a restaurant named Celler de la Ribera, but this was put down to the commonplace anxiety of a messy divorce. In every respect, POLARBEAR appeared to have abandoned any interest in pursuing Crane and Wilkinson.

Gaddis, of course, had done his bit to convince the boys and girls at GCHQ that he was a reformed character. He sent a Facebook message to Charolotte's husband, Paul, for example, telling him that he had "not been able to make any headway at all" with Charlotte's book and had therefore decided to "set it to one side, at least for the time being." He made deliberate decoy appointments by e-mail, arranging to see a Ph.D. student at UCL on the morning of Friday the twenty-fourth. Using his regular mobile phone, he had also called Holly in London, telling her how much he missed her and inviting her to dinner at Quo Vadis on the night of Saturday the twenty-fifth.

Brennan knew there was a possibility that POLARBEAR was laying an elaborate trap which would be sprung in Vienna, but he was more immediately concerned by the report Christopher Brooke had filed describing his encounter with Robert Wilkinson. Two passages, in particular, had alarmed him to the point of fury:

EYES ONLY / ALERT C / AUS6HAW
... Wilkinson referred to the incident which, in his view, necessitated his exile to New Zealand. Plainly he still holds the Office responsible for the attempt on his life and suggested—without corroborating evidence—that SIS either arranged the assassination attempt or, at best, could have done more to protect him in its aftermath. I must record that Mr. Wilkinson was behaving throughout in a manner which I can only describe as aggressive and paranoid.

... Wilkinson brought our brief exchange to an end by threatening to pass Doctor Gaddis what he described as "chapter and verse on ATTILA." Digital recording of the conversation states: "It's time the whole story came out anyway. Christ, the British government would probably benefit [emphasis] if it did. Wouldn't you like to see the back of that maniac [Platov]?"

Brennan felt that he had no choice; he had surely exhausted every other available option. Picking up the phone, he instructed his secretary to put him through to Maxim Kepitsa, Second Secretary at the Embassy of the Russian Federation and one of three declared FSB officers operating in London.

The call went through to Kepitsa's private line.

"Maxim? It's John Brennan."

"Sir John! How delightful to hear from you."

"I wondered if you fancied joining me for a quiet lunch? Wanted to have a word with you about a man your government has been looking for since '92. One of ours, in fact. Fellow by the name of Ulvert . . ."

38

It took Gaddis almost two days to travel from Barcelona to Vienna. The first leg of the journey involved catching an overnight sleeper to Fribourg in Switzerland. He then made a short commuter connection to Zurich before catching a third, nine-hour train across the north face of the Alps. On the first night, in a bunk which he could ill afford, he had slept as deeply as he had done for many weeks; on the final leg of the journey, he had read *Archangel* from cover to cover, surviving on processed cheese sandwiches from the dining car and cups of increasingly vile black coffee. Every hour or so, he would move position on the train in an effort to ascertain whether or not he was being followed; on the rare occasions that the train stopped, he would shoulder his overnight bag, step down onto the platform, make his way towards the ticket inspectors, then climb back on board at the last minute.

As far as he was aware, his departure from Spain had gone unnoticed. He had taken three hours to get to the Estacio Sants in Barcelona, leaving Natasha's apartment at dusk and taking a series of taxis, trains, and buses in eccentric loops in the hope of shaking off any watchers. At the same time, he had left his regular mobile, fully charged and set to "Silent," hidden underneath a filing cabinet in the sitting room of Natasha's flat. He hoped that the signal given off by the phone would give the impression to GCHQ that he was still in Barcelona. He had then bought a new mobile at a Corte Inglés department store and placed the Tottenham Court Road SIM into the slot at the back.

If he was honest with himself, there had been something tawdry in all this, a sense of betraying Min by visiting her in Spain and then involving her, however indirectly, in the grisly business of deception. She was five now, still captivatingly innocent, yet when he had played with her on the swings near Natasha's apartment or held her tiny hand in the flickering gloom of a deserted matinée cinema, he had felt the awful conflicting stain of his ambition, a sense that his determination to avenge Charlotte and to solve the riddle of Dresden was more powerful even than the security and well-being of his own child. Was that the case? Was he so stubborn, so desperate to succeed, that he would rob Min of her own father? That was the reality: he was putting his life at risk by pursuing Wilkinson. There was no other way of spinning it. And yet, he was surely too far in to stop now. Sooner or later, the Russians would work out his links to ATTILA. He would almost certainly be killed for what he already knew. On that basis, there was no point in obeying Tanya's instructions.

Of course, he still had his doubts. There had been a moment on the sands at Icaria, for example, when Min had emerged from the freezing sea and Gaddis had held her thin, shaking body in a giant beach towel, thinking that there was nothing more important in the world than his precious, growing, giggling daughter. The times they would spend together in the future, however infrequent, would be infinitely more rewarding than any book about Edward Crane. But money intruded on everything. That same night, he had argued with Natasha over dinner at Celler de la Ribera, insisting that he was down to "thin air" financially, only to hear her accuse him of "making false promises about Min's future" and "abandoning your daughter to the prospect of a third-rate Catalan education."

So it was money, in the short term, which had convinced him to continue. Without funds to support Min, he was failing in his duty as a father. When he hid the mobile phone under the filing cabinet, for example, Gaddis had rationalized the act as a necessary subterfuge; he simply couldn't write the book with SIS on his tail. Just a few minutes earlier, he had tucked Min up in bed and kissed her good-bye. He had then gone into the kitchen, shaken the feckless Nick by the hand, kissed a dry cheek proffered by Natasha, and gone outside to hail a taxi.

There was an irony in the timing. If he had stayed just fifteen minutes longer, Gaddis might have seen the incoming call from "Josephine Warner" in London. As it was, Tanya left a message on his voicemail:

> Sam, it's me. I'm worried about something. I don't know if you're still in Barcelona or if you've come home, in which case I'm calling unnecessarily. But according to a colleague who's been keeping me in the loop, there's been a lot of chatter from our Russian sources. A lot of talk about Dominic Ulvert.
>
> There's something else, too. The FSB know that there was a third gunman in Berlin. They've spoken to Doronin. He has almost certainly given them your description. As you know, I've been taken off the case but this has come from a reliable source. So just be careful. Don't go to Vienna. Come home.

It was a touching message, as candid as it was risky to her career. Yet there was a further piece of information of which even Tanya Acocella was not aware.

That afternoon, disembarking from a BA flight out of Heathrow, a high-ranking Russian diplomat with suspected links to the FSB had calmly strolled through Vienna International Airport in the company of a Mr. Karl Stieleke, who, according to MI5, was a known associate of Nicolai Doronin. The diplomat's name had flashed up as soon as he had presented his credentials to the authorities. Alexander Grek was in Austria.

39

addis's train pulled into Vienna's Westbahnhof a little after eight o'clock on the evening of Friday the twenty-fourth, so it was nine by the time he had checked into the Goldene Spinne Hotel on Linke Bahngasse, a two-star in the centre of the city manned by a jovial receptionist in late middle age who appeared to be the only member of staff on the premises. Gaddis registered under his own name and was obliged to hand over his passport, but it was with a sense of relief that he saw the manager making a record of his personal details by hand, rather than storing them on a computer.

He had chosen the hotel because it was functional, cheap, and anonymous. His spartan room on the top floor resembled a daytime cabin on a cross-Channel ferry: crisp white sheets were pulled taut across a narrow, hard-mattressed bed; there was a small tiled bathroom with a sink and shower; a kettle with sachets of tea and instant coffee; a view of a cobwebbed airshaft.

He was travelling light but had a linen suit rolled up in his overnight bag and a pair of leather shoes for the wedding. He took out the suit, requested an iron from reception, then hung it on a coat hanger behind the door. He showered and shaved, a blessed release after the cramp and sweat of his long journey, changed into a fresh cotton shirt, and found a restaurant two blocks away where he wolfed a pepperoni pizza and half a carafe of red wine. It had gone eleven by the time he had paid the bill and set out for the Radisson.

Gaddis knew how overseas weddings worked. The guests usually knocked off work in the UK at around lunchtime on Friday, caught a budget flight to the host country in the late afternoon, inevitably bumped into some of their old school and university friends at one of the restaurants recommended by the happy couple in the literature posted out with the wedding invitation, sampled a couple of local dives, then headed back to their hotel to drink into the small hours at the residents' bar. As Gaddis walked through the automatic doors of the Radisson, beneath the EU flags and the wrought-iron lampposts on Schubertring, he could hear the confident bellows of British laughter emanating from a room adjacent to the lobby. Somebody was shouting out: "Gus! Gus! Do you want ice with that?" and there was a piano tinkling in the distance.

The bar was smaller than Gaddis had expected. He counted perhaps twenty guests seated at half a dozen wooden tables dotted around the room and a further twenty standing in the spaces between them, armed with schooners of lager, glasses of wine, and tumblers of Scotch and brandy. There were photographs on the walls of famous guests who had stayed at the hotel: Gaddis picked out signed shots of Bonnie Tyler, Silvio Berlusconi, and the African-American actor from *Miami Vice* who was either Crockett or Tubbs; he could never remember. At the bar, a thirtysomething Brit wielding his room key in lieu of payment recognized Gaddis as a fellow traveller and struck up a conversation.

"You one of us?" he said. "The wedding?"

"I'm one of you," Gaddis replied. "Just checked in."

"Phil," said the Brit, proffering a damp, though iron-strong handshake. "Friend of Catherine's?"

"Of Matthias. Have you seen him around tonight?"

It was the one major flaw in his strategy; if either Catherine or Matthias showed up, Gaddis would have to head back to the Goldene Spinne and find another way of gaining access to the wedding. Thankfully, Phil put his mind at ease.

"Nah. Big family dinner over at the Sacher. Doubt we'll see him. His lot are all staying over there."

"Catherine's family as well?" He was trying to ascertain whether or not there was a chance of bumping into Wilkinson.

"Far as I know. What are you drinking, mate?"

Moments later, Gaddis had an eighteen-euro balloon of cognac in his hand and was being led to a table near the door which was occupied by Phil's wife, Annie; his "oldest mate," Dan; two women on a narrow, upholstered sofa whose names he didn't quite catch; and a pink furry elephant with its trunk lodged inside a table lamp.

"The wife won it at the Prater!" Phil exclaimed. "Know it? Massive amusement park."

Gaddis knew the Prater. "Congratulations," he said, smiling. Annie looked as though she had escaped from three small children for the first time in five years; there was a disconnectedness about her and shadows of sleepless nights around her eyes. "Coconut shy?" he asked her. "Tombola?"

"Shooting." She shouldered an imaginary gun, aimed it at Phil, and Gaddis knew that he had lucked on the right crowd; this lot were drunk and easygoing. They would tell him where the wedding was being held, what time the service began, probably how many sugars Catherine Wilkinson took in her tea.

"Sam's an old friend of Matthias," Phil announced, placing a hand on the small of Gaddis's back and gesturing him into a nonexistent space beside the two women.

"You are?" said one of them, budging along the sofa. "Tell us more. What's he like? None of us has ever met him."

"I've met him," said Annie quietly. "He's lovely."

Thanks to the magic of Google, Gaddis had done his research on Matthias Drechsel. Catherine's fiancé was thirty-six, worked in shipping (specifically "the chartering of gas carriers") and, according to his online company profile, had taken a graduate diploma in business administration from the International University in Vienna.

"To be honest, I haven't seen him for years," he began. "I was quite surprised to be invited."

"How do you know him?" Dan asked. It didn't look as though he was particularly interested in the answer.

Gaddis embarked on the lie. "I taught very briefly at the International University here. Matthias was a student of mine before he switched to business administration."

"Conscientious, was he?" asked the second woman. She was flushed with alcohol and wearing a scarlet skirt which had risen up above the knee.

"Extremely," Gaddis told her, grinning.

After that, it was plain sailing. He laughed at Phil's jokes, told a couple of his own, asked interested questions about Catherine's past, and bought several rounds of drinks. By one o'clock, he was firm friends with all of them, not least the lady in the scarlet skirt who had taken what his late mother would have described as "a bit of a fancy" to him.

"I hope we're sitting next to each other tomorrow," she said, just as Gaddis was trying to bring an end to the conversation they were having about her brother's "nightmare" girlfriend. "You're really lovely to talk to. You really know how to listen, Sam."

"Kath!" Annie exclaimed. "You have to forgive her, Sam. She doesn't know how to behave herself when she gets a few drinks inside her."

"I don't even know where the reception is," Gaddis replied, seizing an opportunity to discover the last piece of information he needed before heading back to his hotel. "I left all my bumph back in London."

"Next door," said Phil, who was in the habit of overhearing other people's conversations. He pointed behind him, in the vague direction of Schubertring. "Big building across the street. 'Kursalon' or something. In the Stadtpark."

"And the service is at, what, two o'clock?"

"Three, mate. Three."

40

Sure enough, at around half past two the following afternoon, wedding guests began drifting into the Stadtpark in all their finery. Gaddis had been seated at a bench beneath a gold-plated statue of Johann Strauss, reading a copy of the *Herald Tribune* and smoking a succession of Winston Light cigarettes. He was wearing his linen suit and carrying a notebook and pen in the inside pocket of his jacket. He had spent the morning wandering around Vienna, dutifully eating Sacher torte at Café Pruckel and confirming to himself a long-held suspicion that the city, though undoubtedly beautiful, was as lifeless and as irredeemably bourgeois as a Swiss museum.

It was a bride's idea of a perfect wedding day. Sunshine poured through the windows of the Kursalon, a neoclassical pavilion on the western perimeter of the Stadtpark, and the sky was obligingly blue for the series of photographs which a moustachioed Austrian began to take as the guests filed inside for the ceremony. Gaddis remained outdoors until, at five to three, he spotted Phil and Annie coming towards him with Kath in tow, each of them wearing a pair of thick-rimmed hangover sunglasses.

"I was waiting for you," he said, kissing Annie and then Kath on the cheek. "What time did you get to bed?"

"Don't ask," Annie mumbled.

They sat together in a row, on cushioned, hard-backed chairs at the centre of a gilt-ceilinged reception hall in the heart of the Kursalon. There were perhaps two hundred guests in attendance. Gaddis could only wonder how many of them were former colleagues of Wilkinson's from SIS, or surveillance officers with orders to prevent Gaddis making contact with ATTILA'S final handler. At exactly five past three, a string quartet struck up the opening bars of "Gabriel's Oboe" and Matthias Drechsel, a short man with a lumbering, agricultural gait, turned to acknowledge the arrival of his bride with an unexpected look of terror in his eyes. Catherine Wilkinson had appeared at the back of the aisle on the arm of her father, Robert. Gaddis craned to get a better look. As a sigh of appreciation rippled through the congregation, he was perhaps the only person in the room whose gaze was not fixed on the beaming bride. Wilkinson was as physically robust as his future son-in-law, but considerably more visually arresting; in his steady, humourless eyes, Gaddis sensed the unyielding determination of a career spy who would suffer no fools. He recalled the quick rage with which Wilkinson had dismissed him on the telephone—*You bloody idiot. I will thank you not to contact me here again*—and knew that it would take all of his charm and persuasiveness to convince him to talk.

The ceremony lasted three-quarters of an hour, more than enough time for Gaddis to consider how best to make his approach. He knew, from a brief conversation with Annie, that dinner was planned for five o'clock. He had no seat at table, of course, which meant that there was, at best, only an hour left to him before Wilkinson would disappear indoors for at least five hours of speeches, Wiener schnitzel, and disco dancing. Therefore, just after four o'clock, he made his way outside into the crisp sunshine of the park. Kath was at his side, resplendent in canary yellow, talking about "how spiritual the service was, even though, you know, they hadn't gone for anything religious." Meanwhile, the newly minted Mr. and Mrs. Matthias Drechsel were being photographed on the steps of the Kursalon, their occasional demonstrations of public affection met with whoops and cheers from the gaggle of family and friends gathered around them.

"Oh, that's nice," said Kath, capturing a kiss on the camera of her mobile phone. "They look so in love, Sam. Don't you think? Doesn't Cath look *beautiful*?"

Robert Wilkinson was standing a few paces from the bride, studiously avoiding eye contact with a woman whom Gaddis took to be his ex-wife. Beside him, an emaciated geriatric of at least eighty, her face puffed with collagen and smothered in makeup, was attempting to engage him in conversation. Wilkinson looked bored. Kath took several more pictures, waved at somebody in the distance, then offered Gaddis a cigarette as she lit up under the shade of a chestnut tree.

"Not for me," he said. "I'm just going inside for a moment. See you in a bit."

He had decided that there was only one failsafe option open to him. He could not approach Wilkinson directly, at least not in person in the broad daylight of an October afternoon with his daughter getting married and the Secret Intelligence Service watching him from every orifice of the Stadtpark. Besides, there was every possibility that Wilkinson would simply call security and have Gaddis escorted from the premises. No, he would have to rely on a third party. He would have to get a message to him before the guests sat down for dinner.

To that end, he found a bathroom on the first floor of the Kursalon, locked himself inside a cubicle, and took out the notebook and pen. He began to write.

Dear Mr. Wilkinson
 I was the man who telephoned you at your home in New Zealand ten days ago. I apologize both for my tactlessness on that occasion and for contacting you on this, of all days, but it is vital that I speak to you about Katya Levette. I believe that she was murdered by agents of the Russian FSB.

It was a wild claim, almost entirely without basis in fact, but Gaddis needed some way of grabbing Wilkinson's attention. He continued, composing the words carefully:

Since then, three individuals with links to Edward Crane have been murdered: a journalist named Charlotte Berg; a nurse, Calvin Somers; and a German doctor, Benedict Meisner. Somers and Meisner were present at St. Mary's Hospital, Paddington, in 1992, when Sir John Brennan (using the alias Douglas Henderson) faked Crane's death and set him up with a new identity—Thomas Neame. I was given your name by Ludmilla Tretiak. As you know, her husband, Fyodor, was also murdered by the FSB because of his association with Crane.

I have had detailed conversations with Edward himself and, with his blessing, plan to reveal the truth about ATTILA. I know, from speaking to Holly, that you had made a similar arrangement with Katya regarding your own memoirs, which she was unable to fulfil. All of the files that you gave to Mrs. Levette are now in my possession.

I will be at Kleines Café in Franziskanerplatz this evening from 10 P.M. and again tomorrow morning from 10 A.M. You may also reach me at the Goldene Spinne Hotel on Linke Bahngasse. I am registered under my own name. Again, I apologize for intruding on this important day for your family, and for failing to present myself in person, but you can understand that I am wary of who may or may not be watching. There was no other opportunity nor method of contacting you.

Sincerely,
Dr. Samuel Gaddis

He read the letter back three times, but was reluctant to cross anything out or to make changes to the text for fear of conveying the impression of an undisciplined mind. Instead, having added the telephone number of his hotel, he folded the note in half and, after brief consideration, wrote "Mr. Dominic Ulvert" on the front. Emerging from the bathroom, Gaddis saw one of the members of the string quartet coming out of the reception hall and decided that he would make as good a messenger as any.

"Excuse me?"

"*Ja?*"

"Do you speak English?"

The musician was in his early twenties and carrying a violin in a black case. He was smothered in acne. In a thick Austrian accent he said that he spoke "some" English and waited for Gaddis to respond, his head bobbing from side to side.

"I wondered if you could do me a favour?"

"Of course, sir. What, sir? Yes."

"Would you come with me?"

He took him to a window offering a view out onto the bridal party. The photographer was now arranging the guests into a family group. Wilkinson, still looking bored and out of place, was seated two chairs to the right of Matthias Drechsel.

"Do you see the man with the pale cream waistcoat and the dark blue tie? He has grey hair, sitting in the front row on the left-hand side."

It took a few moments to explain the phrase "pale cream" and to ensure that the musician had correctly identified Wilkinson.

"He is the father of the bride, *ja?*"

"Yes. That's right." Gaddis produced a smile of entreaty. "When they have finished the photographs, would you be kind enough to pass him this note? I have to rush off and I don't want to disturb him. We haven't seen one another for a long time and—"

The young man saved Gaddis the effort of amplifying his lie. "No problem," he replied, as if he performed similar tasks every day. "I do this for you."

"You're very kind."

Moments later, the musician was trotting down the steps of the Kursalon, violin case in hand, as the family photographs were drawing to an end. He approached Wilkinson immediately and engaged him briefly in conversation. Gaddis, who had followed him outside, returned to the chestnut tree, where he found Kath talking to Dan.

"Hello there, stranger," she said. "I thought we'd lost you."

He turned to see the musician handing Wilkinson the note. Their encounter did not seem in any way unusual: he might even have been presenting an invoice to the father of the bride for the string quartet's services. The musician then said something to Wilkinson and pointed up at the window of the Kursalon where Gaddis had been standing only moments earlier. Wilkinson, who had now seen the name on the front of the note, swept his gaze, in a barely disguised state of alarm, through three hundred and sixty degrees, searching for whoever had employed the musician as an errand boy. Gaddis turned around so that his back was facing him.

"I can't find your name on the table plan," Kath was saying.

"That's why I went inside," he replied. It was the last lie he would have to tell. "Truth is, I'm not feeling all that good. I just pulled out." He felt a sudden rush of anxiety, as if he could sense Wilkinson coming towards him. "I've asked them to take my name off the list. I'm going to head back to my hotel."

"You are?" Kath looked crestfallen.

"Afraid so. I might pop back later. Make sure you save me a dance."

Gaddis turned and walked away into the park. In doing so he bumped into a tourist carrying a 35mm camera around his neck. Gaddis's arm knocked against the telephoto lens and he felt obliged to apologize.

"Excuse me," he said, then, in German: "*Entschuldigen*."

Karl Stieleke did not respond.

41

Gaddis had chosen the Kleines Café from a photograph in a Phaidon guidebook to Vienna which had been left by a guest in the dining area of the Goldene Spinne. The photograph suggested that the café was the sort of low-key, inconspicuous place that Gaddis was looking for, and so it proved. Visiting Franziskanerplatz early on Saturday morning, he had discovered a small, pedestrianized square, about half a mile west of the Radisson, with a fountain at its centre, birds hopping in and out of the water and local residents reading newspapers over cups of coffee in the sunshine. The Kleines Café occupied the corner of the ground floor of a recently renovated building just a few metres from the fountain. There were two entrances: one leading into the square itself, where half a dozen tables were set out in neat rows; and a side exit, in the lower section of the café, which led out onto a cobbled street running downhill into Singerstrasse.

Just inside this back entrance was a single, mirrored booth. It was here that Gaddis established himself at nine o'clock on Saturday evening. He felt that it would be the perfect place to talk to Wilkinson: there were no other seats or tables close by, only some cardboard boxes and empty kegs of beer. In a rerun of his convoluted journey to the Estacio Sants in Barcelona, he had taken a circuitous route to the café, trying to shake off any potential surveillance by using three different modes of transportation—foot, taxi, train—in a journey which had lasted almost an hour. He was certain that he was not being followed.

He ordered a beer from the manager and waited. He had a new Yeltsin biography to read, cigarettes to smoke, and felt quietly confident that Wilkinson would appear as soon as he was no longer required at the wedding. But Gaddis had not counted on the sheer volume of customers who began pouring through the back door at around half past nine. It turned out that the Kleines Café was one of the most popular bars in Vienna: by ten, it was impossible to see the exit from Gaddis's seat at the booth, despite the fact that he was only a few feet from the street. He counted at least thirty people crushed into the tiny lower section around him and assumed that there were at least twice as many in the main body of the café. If Wilkinson walked in, there was a real possibility that he would fail to spot Gaddis.

He need not have worried. At twenty past ten, Gaddis looked up to see Wilkinson peering over the head of a plump Viennese banker who was wearing wire-rimmed glasses. He nodded at him, to establish his identity, and Wilkinson pushed his way through the shoulder-to-shoulder crowd before settling on the opposite side of the booth in a seat which Gaddis had been jealously guarding since nine o'clock.

"Let me guess," he said, his weight jogging the small circular table as he sat down. "You didn't think I would come."

"I'm certainly glad to see you," Gaddis replied.

It was hard to read Wilkinson's mood. His normally impassive face was touched by an odd sense of mischief. Wilkinson had changed out of his morning suit into a pair of brown corduroy trousers, a shirt, and a dark, V-neck jumper. He removed the same tattered Barbour that had witnessed the unsolicited visit of Christopher Brooke and set it on the bench beside him.

"You have quite a nerve, Doctor Gaddis. I was warned about you."

"You were?"

"Certain people are reluctant for us to speak. Certain people are concerned that we might cause trouble. How do you get a whisky around here?"

He wondered if Wilkinson was a little drunk from the festivities. He had been expecting criticism for making the phone call to his home in New Zealand, but the veteran spy seemed to be in a relaxed, forgiving mood. Had he taken any precautions in coming to the café? Had he paid any attention to the surveillance threat?

"I'll go to the bar," Gaddis told him. "How do you take it?"

It took ten long minutes to make his way through the crowds, to order two Jamesons on ice, and to return to the table. He found Wilkinson flicking through the Yeltsin book.

"Any good?"

"Not particularly." Gaddis sat down and put the whisky in front of him. "Cuttings job."

There was music playing, lounge jazz, but set at a volume which made conversation relatively straightforward. They would not need to raise their voices above the music and the babble of the crowd. After a brief exchange about the wedding, Wilkinson asked Gaddis for what he called "some background" on his relationship with Katya. His manner was still unexpectedly amiable and cooperative, and Gaddis interpreted the question as a broader request to lay out everything he knew concerning ATTILA. To that end, he set about telling the entire story of his involvement with Crane, including Charlotte's initial research and sudden death, the murders of Calvin Somers and Benedict Meisner, as well as the revelation that Tanya Acocella was an MI6 officer who had masqueraded as an archivist at Kew. Throughout this long process, Wilkinson interjected only rarely, either to clarify a detail or to ask for a phrase to be repeated on account of a sudden noise in the bar. He did not appear to be unduly surprised by anything Gaddis was telling him and remained, for the most part, inscrutable in his reactions. When, for example, Gaddis related what had happened at Meisner's apartment in Berlin, he merely nodded sagely and muttered, "I see," while staring at the ice in his glass. It was increasingly apparent to Gaddis that he was being sized up, rather in the way that a father takes his time to consider the strengths and weaknesses of a prospective son-in-law. Clearly Wilkinson had yet to decide whether or not to divulge the wealth of information he possessed to a writer he did not know or trust. As a consequence, he had about him the slightly overbearing self-confidence of a man who knows that he can walk out on a situation at any moment, at no personal cost.

"So you subsequently discovered that Neame and Crane were the same man?"

Wilkinson's question had no obvious tone of condescension, but the implication was clear: Gaddis, a supposedly bright, intelligent academic, had been hoodwinked by an old-age pensioner.

"What can I tell you?" he replied, holding his hands up in a gesture of mock surrender. He had decided that the most sensible strategy was to be as candid and as honest as possible. There was no point in trying to finesse a man of Wilkinson's experience. "I was duped by a master liar. My only consolation is that I probably wasn't the first person to fall for Crane's silver tongue."

"No," Wilkinson replied steadily. "You certainly weren't. Nor, I imagine, will you be the last." He took a sip of his drink and appeared to catch the eye of a blond American woman who was standing close to their table. "But it makes absolute sense that Eddie would have wanted to get his story out in that way. After all, he's spent his life being two people."

It was strangely exhilarating to hear Wilkinson speak of Crane so intimately, but any hope Gaddis held that the conversation would now turn to his recollections of ATTILA were quickly snuffed out.

"You said in your note that you think Katya was murdered." Wilkinson was a physically imposing man and when he stared directly into Gaddis's eyes, Gaddis had to remind himself not to look away. "What is your evidence for this?"

"A pattern of behaviour," he replied uncertainly. It was the first unconvincing thing that he had said all night.

"I have to say that I disagree with you." There was a finality to Wilkinson's reply which brooked no argument. "If the FSB had been on to Katya, they would have followed my files to your house and you'd be dead by now as well."

"Possibly," Gaddis said, though he knew that Wilkinson's assessment was completely correct.

"Where *are* the files, by the way?"

"At my house."

"Your *house?*" Wilkinson's sangfroid briefly deserted him. "Under lock and key, I hope? In some sort of safe?"

It was the first hint of his willingness to cooperate. There was clearly something hidden in the files, something of value to him.

"No safe would be big enough," Gaddis replied, trying to calm things down. "The boxes are just piled up in my sitting room."

Wilkinson appeared to bury a rebuke. Instead, in a more controlled voice, he said: "Well, it's unlikely that they'll be there for very much longer."

"Why do you say that? I've had them for weeks. If SIS wanted to get hold of them, they'd have broken into my house long ago."

Wilkinson shook his head. "The Office aren't the ones you should be worrying about. Platov is the one who will want the files."

"Platov?" Gaddis leaned forward. "With the greatest respect, there's very little in the files that would be of any interest to anyone, even in academia. I found nothing about ATTILA, certainly nothing about Sergei Platov."

"That's because you don't know what you're looking for."

Gaddis felt a wave of excitement. Wilkinson looked as though he had finally made the decision to divulge what he knew.

"So what *am* I looking for?"

Wilkinson paused. He stared again at the ice in his empty glass. Gaddis took it as a hint that he wanted another drink.

"More whisky?"

"Sure."

This time it took just five minutes of battling through the crowd before he could return to the booth. The clutch of customers, including the American woman, who had been standing beside their table, were now pressed in even closer. They were using the near-side of Gaddis's table as a place to rest their glasses and bottles of beer. Wilkinson appeared completely oblivious to their presence; he might as well have been sitting alone in a box at the opera.

"You're right," he said, passing the Yeltsin biography back across the table. "Cuttings job."

Gaddis smiled. He set the drinks down and tried to restart the conversation.

"You were saying . . ."

"Saying what?"

"That I wasn't looking at the files in the right way. That I didn't know what I was looking for."

Wilkinson tipped his head back. "Oh, yes." He seemed almost surprised by the topic of conversation. He tapped the photograph of Yeltsin, rapping it with the back of his hand. "You've written a biography of Platov, haven't you?"

Gaddis drank. "It was more of a comparative study of Platov and Peter the Great, but—"

Wilkinson didn't let him finish. "Tell me what you know about Platov's career in the KGB."

Was this another test? Gaddis would have to be careful. Wilkinson, the Head of Station in Berlin in the warmest years of the Cold War, would know far more about Platov's brief engagement with the secret world than any historian at UCL.

"I know that he was ambitious," he began. "I know that those ambitions were frustrated. Platov had a far higher estimation of his own abilities than his masters at the Lubyanka."

"That's certainly true."

"He felt that he deserved one of the plum jobs in the West. Washington. Paris. London. Instead, he got Dresden, a backwater in East Germany. Which, I imagine, is where you first bumped into him."

Wilkinson looked up. His heavy, pale face was still.

"What makes you think I knew him?"

"Oh, you knew him," Gaddis replied.

It was a risk, but it paid off. Wilkinson took a long hard look at the crowd, grinned, and turned to Gaddis. There were secrets coming.

"Platov's only trump card in East Germany was ATTILA," he began, "a moribund, seventy-year-old British spy sitting on the board of a bank in Berlin. He took a long, hard look at his life. He took a long, hard look at his career. He knew that the Soviet system was on its last legs and that Mother Russia had lost the Cold War."

"That's not the official version."

"Of course it's not." Wilkinson lowered his voice. Even with the noise of the bar, he was concerned that he might be overheard. "As far as all you journalists and academics are concerned, young Sergei was an unwavering patriot."

"So what's the truth? What did he do out there? What happened to Platov that he would be prepared to murder countless innocent men and women in order to cover it up?"

"You want to know?" Wilkinson breathed in very deeply. His eyes were suddenly black in the darkness of the booth. "You want to know the reason why your friend was killed, the nurse, the doctor, Tretiak? You want to know why Eddie Crane had to become Thomas Neame, why Platov's cronies planted a bomb under my car? Well, I'll tell you." He was smiling now, because he was going to enjoy the look on Gaddis's face when he told him. "The president of Russia, a man with eighty per cent approval ratings from his countrymen, a patriot credited with restoring Russia's economic might and sense of national pride, tried to defect to the West in 1988."

42

He what?"

Gaddis was dumbfounded. Of all the things he had been expecting to hear from Wilkinson, this was not it.

"February of '88. What we call a walk-in." Wilkinson was looking up at the blond American. He obviously had an eye for a pretty girl. "Sergei Platov wanted to live in a nice big house in Surrey and he was prepared to give us whatever we wanted in order to get it."

"Christ. If that came out, he'd be finished. His political career would be in tatters."

"Precisely." It wasn't as though Wilkinson was unaware of the implications. "The saviour of modern Russia—your latter-day Peter the Great—exposed as a hypocrite who sold out his country in her hour of need and tried to flee to the West with a suitcase full of Russian secrets."

"And he came to you? You were the man he approached?"

Wilkinson nodded. It was plainly a source of considerable personal pride. The group of Americans who had been pressed up against the table had finished the last of their drinks and now began to file out of the café, the blonde going with them. Gaddis overheard one of them saying something about "finding a club that goes all night."

"I was in Berlin," Wilkinson continued. "A freezing bloody winter. Platov followed me into a cinema on Kantstrasse. There was a film playing to a half-empty house. *The Searchers,* if memory serves. I used to like going there in the evenings. My marriage had broken up. I was spending rather a lot of time on my own, you know?" Gaddis nodded. He knew. He was at last able to reconcile the image of Wilkinson as a sensitive, romantic soul—the man revealed in the letter to Katya—with the brusque spook in front of him. "Suddenly, taking a seat right next to me, is a little man, taut and tough as a rat. Later, of course, we discovered that Comrade Platov was something of an expert in judo. I'd never seen him before. Too far down the food chain. But he hands me a piece of paper letting me know that he's an officer in the KGB and wishes to defect to the West. I read it while he was sitting there, then looked straight at him and told him to fuck off."

"You what?"

"I thought it was a bluff. One of their boring little games. But Sergei was insistent. 'You must believe me, sir,' he says. 'You must trust me.' 'All right,' I said. 'If you're serious, meet me here again in twenty-four hours.' That gave me time to have him checked out, to get a car ready, a safe house wired for sight and sound."

"And did he show?"

"Of course he showed." Wilkinson looked bewildered by Gaddis's naïveté.

"And you interviewed him?"

"Yes."

"In the presence of John Brennan?"

A nod of appreciation. "Very good. In the presence of John Brennan, yes. Now see if you can riddle me this one. When asked to demonstrate that he was serious, guess whose name Platov gave us to prove his bona fides?"

"ATTILA," Gaddis said, with a rush of exhilaration. The last piece of the puzzle had clicked into place.

"Precisely. He betrayed Eddie to the Brits, blissfully unaware that

ATTILA had been one of ours all along." Wilkinson leaned back in his chair. "That's when I made my one and only mistake. I brought the interview to an end, implying that we needed more time to process the implications of Crane's betrayal. I left Platov with the impression that we would be in touch—same time, same place, the cinema on Kantstrasse—and immediately arranged to have dinner with Eddie. Told him over a bowl of onion soup that some greedy KGB thug who fancied an easy life in the West had been prepared to give him up."

"And how did Eddie take that?"

It was the first time that Gaddis could remember referring to Crane as "Eddie." He felt faintly ridiculous, like a schoolboy trying to be cool in front one of the senior boys.

"Not well," Wilkinson replied. He was shaking his head slowly, regretfully. "Eddie Crane was a complex animal who didn't take too kindly to acts of betrayal. His entire life had been a delicate balancing act between East and West, a process of convincing highly intelligent people that he was somebody other than the person that he really was. I suppose, when you look at it, he had lived in fear of exposure for most of his life. Exposure during the war, exposure in the wake of Burgess and Maclean, and of course, exposure in the last, great phase of his career."

Wilkinson stopped in mid-flow, perhaps to organize his thoughts. He soon picked up where he had left off.

"Eddie, against his better judgement, decided to exact his revenge. Before we'd had a chance to properly evaluate Platov, to decide whether or not we wanted him to come across, Eddie went to see his KGB controller—"

Gaddis interrupted. "Fyodor Tretiak."

"Exactly."

"And told him that Platov was attempting to defect?"

Wilkinson nodded. It was as though they were now streaming the same information.

"Tretiak, of course, was very low budget and *deserved* to have been posted to a backwater like Dresden. Rather than go to Moscow with this alarming piece of information, he confronted Platov in person and young Sergei managed to convince Tretiak that the whole thing had been a setup. 'I had no intention of defecting, Comrade Fyodor. This was a high-level influence operation on a British officer organized by Moscow Centre.' The whole thing was then forgotten. Tretiak didn't report the matter to his superiors and Platov vanished. London, of course, was furious that Eddie had prevented us getting our hands on a KGB asset, but let him off on the grounds that he was a star. We weren't to know that the whole Communist system was going to go tits up in less than two years anyway."

Gaddis reached inside his jacket for a cigarette. Wilkinson saw the packet and winced.

"Do you mind if you don't? I know nobody in continental Europe obeys the bloody smoking ban except the law-abiding Brits, but if you feel like killing yourself, please feel free to do it out on the street."

"I'm fine," Gaddis said, replacing the packet. "Dozens of people in MI6 must know about this. How come it's never leaked out?"

"Not dozens." Wilkinson was scanning the review quotes on the back of the Yeltsin biography. "We're not a country club. What you might call the 'circle of trust' was actually very small. Apart from myself, Eddie, and Brennan, the only other name in the loop was Colin McGougan, who was 'C' until 1994. He's dead now. Far as I know, nobody else had an inkling about Platov. He was small potatoes. The file was sealed and we went off in new directions."

"But you could finish Platov's career at any point."

Wilkinson reached across the table and held Gaddis's forearm. It was like the passing of a secret from one generation to the next. "What do you think I'm doing now?"

"You want *me* to destroy it?"

"Precisely. I know how you feel about him. I've read your book."

Gaddis knew that he was being flattered. "Fine. But I would also be avenging *you*."

Wilkinson allowed himself a brief moment of reflection. "All right, yes. Platov tried to kill me, I demand some measure of vengeance. Is that childish? I handed Katya the scoop of her life and she drank it into the grave. Now I'm passing it to you."

Gaddis had known for some time that the offer was coming. And now he had it. He had what he had been waiting for. He was the perfect conduit for the story, just as Charlotte had been the perfect vessel for Crane. And yet he felt cornered.

"Look"—Wilkinson picked his words carefully—"of course it's not all about revenge. I believe that Platov is dangerous. I think he's bad for Russia, I think he's bad for Britain. The world, as they say, would be a very much better place without that monster in the Kremlin. So I'm asking you to tell the truth about the so-called saviour of modern Russia. I'm asking you to reveal that by 1992 Sergei Platov had been spotted by our good friend Mr. Yeltsin"—Wilkinson tapped the biography—"and had developed some serious political ambitions. He went full bore into politics and was fast-tracked to the very top. So, the last thing he needed was men such as Fyodor Tretiak, myself, and Eddie Crane roaming the quiet countryside telling anybody who would listen that the risen star of Russian politics, the man anointed by Yeltsin, had tried to defect to the West during the death spasms of the Cold War."

"How does Brennan fit into all this?" Gaddis asked.

"Oh, well, that's a lovely subplot." Gaddis almost laughed. "Platov hired some of his pals in organized crime to bump me off. I'd developed some fairly unsavoury contacts in St. Petersburg over the years, and those same cronies were able to make it look as though I'd been on the take. It was ingenious, simple and effective. I give him credit for that. But Brennan, rather than listening to my pleas of innocence, believed the rumours and cut me loose. Unlike Eddie Crane, who got a brand-new identity and a slot in a nursing home, I was offered no protection, no assistance whatsoever from SIS. As far as the Office was concerned, I was a traitor to the cause."

"Hence New Zealand," said Gaddis.

Wilkinson nodded. "Hence the reason I live at the side of a hill, surrounded by sheep, looking over my shoulder, wondering when one of Sergei's henchmen is going to come round the corner."

"And why has Brennan never been touched?"

Wilkinson shrugged. "Must have come to some sort of an arrangement with Platov."

"What kind of arrangement?"

"Search me." Wilkinson looked genuinely baffled. "John was always very good at looking after his own interests."

Gaddis shifted the direction of the conversation. "Do you have evidence of the meeting in the safe house? A recording of Platov attempting to defect? Is that the smoking gun, or did Brennan destroy everything?"

"Not quite everything." Wilkinson was clearly pleased that Gaddis had arrived at the heart of the matter. "You said earlier that you had found nothing in the files."

"That's right. Nothing. Nothing at all."

Wilkinson looked at his hands. "What's the lovely Eric Morecambe line? 'You're playing the right notes, but not necessarily in the right order'?"

"Something like that." Gaddis wondered what he was implying.

"What's your poison?" Wilkinson asked abruptly. "High time I bought us a round of drinks."

"Can you wait two minutes while I go to the bathroom?" Gaddis didn't want to lose the table if Wilkinson went to the bar. "When I get back, you can put them in the right order."

43

There were two men inside the cramped bathroom, one washing his hands in a chipped sink, the other coming out of a narrow cubicle, adjusting his fly. Gaddis squeezed between the two of them, no eye contact, went into the cubicle, and locked the door. There was an odd, crisp smell of mint on the air, as if his predecessor had sprayed breath freshener into the room out of consideration for his fellow man. Gaddis immediately pulled out the pen and notebook on which he had written the letter at the wedding and began to write quickly. He could not afford to forget any detail of what Wilkinson had told him and did not trust his fortysomething brain to reproduce a completely accurate account of their conversation in the morning.

The door of the bathroom opened and the two men left. Gaddis could hear the dull thump of what was now rock music in the café, muffled conversations beyond the door. He had no shorthand, but wrote at speed in an abbreviated script perfected over years of attending lectures: there were words, parts of words, and coded abbreviations on the pages of his notebooks which made sense only to him.

The bathroom door opened again. Two men were talking to each other in German as they came in. Gaddis knew that he had only two or three minutes left in which to write his notes; after that, Wilkinson might lose patience and start to wonder why he was taking so long. He set down the details of Platov's approach to Crane, closed the notebook, and stood up.

At that moment, Karl Stieleke walked through the side entrance of the Kleines Café, removed a Beretta Px4 Storm and, in a single fluid movement, fired a silenced double-tap shot into the head of Robert Wilkinson, driving a fist of brain into the wall behind him. Stieleke, who was no more than four feet from the door of the café, did not pause to verify that Wilkinson was dead; he knew as much. Instead, he turned and pushed his way through the stunned crowd before anyone had time to react. He then sprinted northeast to a waiting vehicle and, within twenty seconds, was in the passenger seat of a Saab SUV, sitting alongside Alexander Grek and accelerating to seventy kilometres per hour along Singerstrasse.

Gaddis was putting the pen back in the inside pocket of his jacket when he sensed the commotion outside. At first, it sounded as if the music system had failed, the irritation of a song skipping repeatedly on a scratched CD, but then he heard a woman shouting *"Hilfe!"* in a way that unnerved him. He opened the door and walked out of the bathroom into a scene of total panic; it was as if the café had tilted into another dimension. The music had stopped completely and crowds of drinkers were surging up out of the lower bar, pushing and tripping over themselves as they bottlenecked towards the main entrance on Franziskanerplatz. People were shouting, swearing. At first, Gaddis wondered if a fight had broken out, but this part of Vienna was surely too civilized, too orderly and conservative, for a couple of drunks to have begun trading blows. He tried to move against the tide of people and to get back to Wilkinson, but was caught in the energy of the panicking crowd and almost lifted off his feet as it carried him up a short, narrow flight of stairs towards the entrance. It was only then, in the first dim seconds of adjusting to the chaos around him, that Gaddis began to fear for Wilkinson. He said, in English, to a woman who was partly supporting herself on his shoulders: "What's going on?" but she ignored him, seemingly too shocked by what she had witnessed to explain why fifty or sixty people were suddenly hurrying out of Kleines Café into a deserted Viennese square at two o'clock in the morning.

Outside, almost immediately, Gaddis heard the word "gun." It was spoken, very clearly and in English, by an American man whose face he could not see. He picked up further cubist snatches of conversation, phrases in both English and German which gradually assembled into the horrifying picture of what had happened. A man had been shot at point-blank range. An elderly man. Nobody had seen the gunman. Nobody had heard the gun.

Gaddis turned and tried to reach the booth, weaving through the dazed crowds. He was determined to get to Wilkinson. He was convinced that he was still alive. But there were too many people jammed into the narrow doorway and no means of getting past them. He recognized a woman who had been drinking near their table in the lower bar. She was holding a cigarette in her hand but seemed too dazed to remember to smoke it.

"What happened?" he asked her. There was no response. He said: "*Problem?*" in German, and this time she reacted.

"Somebody has been shot," she said, in English. "That is all I know." She reached for his arm, as if they were old friends and she needed Gaddis to steady her.

"A customer?" he asked.

"Yes."

It could only have been Wilkinson. Gaddis felt a dull charge of fear. His sense of dislocation was sudden and overwhelming. He was experiencing the same sense of bewildered shock that he had known in the apartment in Berlin and tried to void his mind of panic. Was he safe himself? He looked around the square and felt that at any moment he might be felled by a bullet. Simply by standing outside the café he was inviting a second shot. And what if he was recognized as the man who had been sitting with the victim? It was only a matter of time before somebody in the crowd pointed Gaddis out to the police.

In some obscure, still-functioning recess of his mind, he began to act decisively. A survival instinct kicked in. He noticed that people were running away from the bar, jogging into side streets, dragging their friends with them against a background of distant sirens. Gaddis followed, realizing that to get away from the scene of the attack was his best option. He turned southeast out of the square, moving swiftly downhill as part of a group of perhaps ten or twelve people. He passed between a shop selling English-language books and, on the opposite side of the street, what looked like a brothel or lap-dancing club. Ahead, Gaddis could see the traffic on Schubertring and the low trees of the Stadtpark. The street was no more than a few hundred metres from the Radisson and, for a moment, he toyed with the idea of going inside. But it was surely crazy to think that he could talk his way past a night porter who might later turn him over to the police.

He took out his mobile. He dialled Tanya's number because there was nowhere else to turn. She picked up almost immediately, her voice groggy and disorientated.

"Hello?"

He was convinced that she had betrayed him, yet there was a strange kind of reassurance in hearing her voice.

"Why did you do it, Tanya?"

"Sam?"

"Bob Wilkinson has been shot."

"*Shot?* What?" She sounded genuinely appalled, repeating what Gaddis had told her as if to absorb the full implications of what he was saying. "Where are you?"

A siren blasted in the near distance, matched instantly by a second vehicle, tearing towards the Kleines Café.

"Why did you do it?" he asked her again. "Company orders?"

"I don't know why you think I had anything to do with this. Where are you? Tell me what's going on."

He could almost believe in her innocence. He wanted to believe in it. But there was no trust left between them. He said: "How am I supposed to know? I went to the bathroom, I left Wilkinson sitting at a table, next thing I know he's been killed. You tell me what happened. You're probably in fucking Vienna. You tell me how the hell they found out where he was."

"Sam. Listen to me." Tanya had composed herself. She was suddenly preternaturally calm. "This is what I was worried about. I thought you were still in Spain. What is this number you're calling from? Is it a new mobile?"

"Yes," he said.

"Hang up. Switch it off and take out the battery. Get at least a mile away from where you are, find a public phone, and call me back. Do that."

"What?"

But she had already broken the connection. Gaddis spoke against the dead line, but Tanya was gone. He concealed himself in the recess of an apartment block entrance and stared at the screen. She was obviously worried that the Russians had a fix on his mobile. But was she genuinely trying to protect him, or just buying time in which to call John Brennan? Either way, he knew that he had no option other than to do as Tanya had instructed. He turned off the phone, his nail digging hard into the power switch, slid back the casing and removed the battery. He then placed the battery in his pocket, jogged down onto Schubertring, and hailed a cab.

He fell into the backseat, unbalanced as a drunk, the driver staring at him in the rearview mirror, waiting to be told where to go. Gaddis realized that he knew of no address, no destination in Vienna beyond the Goldene Spinne Hotel and the Ferris wheel at the Prater. It was surely madness to go to the hotel, and the Prater would be closed at this time of night. On an instinct, he blurted out "Hotel Sacher" because it was the only other landmark in Vienna that he could think of. The driver made a noise at the base of his throat which was at once irritated and amused and within two short minutes Gaddis understood why: the Sacher was three blocks away. He could have walked there in under five minutes.

"My mistake," he said. "I'm sorry," though there was no indication that the driver spoke any English. "I didn't mean the Sacher. Can you take me to Sud Bahnhof?"

The driver now turned in his seat, a middle-aged man at the end of a long shift who didn't much feel like being messed around by a drunk British tourist. "Sud Bahnhof?" he said, as if Gaddis had asked him to drive to the moon. "No trains now."

"I'm meeting somebody," Gaddis replied and within an instant the driver had sighed and engaged first gear and swung out into the street, zipping through green lights towards the southern section of the city. They did not speak again. After a few minutes, Gaddis spotted a phone booth at the side of the road and instructed him to pull over.

"Halt, bitte."

"This not station," the driver muttered.

"I don't care. Pull over."

He paid him, a ten-euro note thrust through the window and no time to wait for the change. The pavement was covered in a puddle of thin mud which splashed against his shoes as he walked towards the payphone. There were no people in sight. The phone was covered in stickers, the box scratched by coins and knives. He dialled Tanya's mobile.

"Sam?"

"I'm in a phone booth."

"Listen to me very carefully. We don't have long. If your number was compromised, mine is too. It's not safe for you out there. We're going to get you out of Austria. Exfiltration. If they came for Wilkinson, they will come for you."

Gaddis, stunned, did not respond. Tanya mistook his silence for scepticism.

"Think about it. The police will almost certainly get a good description of whoever was sitting with Wilkinson tonight. They'll be looking for you. You can't go back to your hotel. That would be suicide. You can't rent a car. You can't go to a train station or out to the airport. The last thing we need is Sam Gaddis being taken into the custody of the Austrian police."

He wondered why Tanya had started to refer to him in the third person. Is that how spooks operated? They turned you into a concept, an "asset," anything to convince themselves that they weren't dealing with a human being.

"Believe me," he said, "the last thing Sam Gaddis wants right now is to be taken into the custody of the Austrian police."

"Good. Then listen. Do you still have your regular mobile phone?"

"No. I left it in Barcelona. Everything else is back at my hotel."

"Don't, whatever you do, go back there." He could see the logic in that request, but a stubborn part of his nature was still convinced that he had time to go back to the hotel, to pack his belongings and to leave Vienna. "It's the first place they'll wait," she said. "Do you have your passport?"

"Tanya, everything is in my room. I came out tonight with a notebook, a pen, a packet of cigarettes. No, I don't have my passport, I don't even have my wallet. I've got about eighty euros in cash and a Tube pass. That's it."

A frustrated silence. "Doesn't matter," she replied eventually. "I need to clear this line. We need to stop talking. Get away from wherever you are and try to go somewhere safe. Find a basement. Find a bar or a nightclub. Go somewhere where you can disappear until five o'clock."

"What happens at five o'clock?"

"What happens is that you'll turn on your mobile for as long as it takes me to send you the instructions for your exfiltration. You have to trust me, Sam. Don't go back to your hotel. We can arrange to have your stuff picked up. Go to another part of the city. Lie low for three hours. At five o'clock, I will send the instructions. As soon as you've received them, switch off your phone and do everything that I have told you. Understood?"

He was at once perplexed and yet humbled by her willingness to help him.

"Understood."

44

addis replaced the receiver. It was almost two o'clock in the morning. He was standing on a deserted street in a city that he did not know, wanted by the Austrian police, pursued by the Russian secret service, at the mercy of a British spy who had consistently lied to him about her identity. This was what his life had come to. He felt as if he had been on the run for months. He tried to remember what he had been doing at the exact same time the previous year and realized that he had been in Spain, in a seaside village about an hour north of Barcelona, trying to teach Min how to swim. He managed to smile briefly at the comparison but the memory did little to calm his frazzled nerves.

What to do now? Walking away from the phone booth, cutting down a side street, Gaddis tried to will within himself a determination not to fail. There was no time to feel sorry for himself, no time to panic. This was now a game of survival, a challenge which he had to face. Arriving at this conclusion did not feel like a particularly courageous act; it was simply that he had no choice.

It began to rain. A cab hissed by and Gaddis hailed it, instructing the driver to take him to the International Centre on the north side of the Danube. It was the address he should have given on his first journey, a landmark building in Vienna which was home to both the United Nations and to the International Atomic Energy Agency. The journey would take at least fifteen minutes and give him time to assess his options in the back of a car, away from prying eyes. He knew that the Russians had pinpointed either himself or Wilkinson to the Kleines Café. He also knew that Wilkinson's death had been premeditated. But why had the assassin spared his life? Had he waited for Gaddis to go to the bathroom, or intended to kill both men, only to find Wilkinson sitting alone at the table? There was no way of knowing.

The rain was falling harder now. The driver slowed on approach to a bridge, stopping briefly at a set of traffic lights before crossing the Danube at speed. To the east, in the near distance, Gaddis could see moored river boats and, beyond those, the dimmed lights of the Prater amusement park. He wondered what Tanya would do with the information he had given her. Tell Brennan, who would surely instruct her to abandon Gaddis to his fate, or keep her word and find some way of getting him out of Vienna? He remembered the word she had used on the phone. *Exfiltration*. It was as if he was some Cold War political renegade, a dissident or *agent provocateur* who needed to be spirited across the border. How had it come to this? For a moment he wondered if Tanya was overreacting and thought of instructing the driver to turn around and take him back to the Goldene Spinne. Why couldn't he just pick up his passport, pack his bags, and take the first flight out of Vienna? But, of course, that was crazy. Every move he now made, every decision he took, was fraught with risk.

The cab raced southeast along a two-lane highway and, within minutes, had pulled up outside the UN building, a sci-fi compound of fountains and concrete walkways, drenched in rain. Now the obvious question arose. What the hell was he going to do for the next couple of hours? Get out and walk around?

"Is there a bar near here?" he asked the driver. "A nightclub?"

It was the option which made the most sense: to disappear into a crowded after-hours club, to find a secluded corner and to bide his time until 5 A.M. But the driver merely grunted and shrugged his shoulders. It wasn't clear whether he had failed to understand the question or simply knew of nowhere suitable to suggest. Gaddis looked out of the window at the pouring rain, at the security guards in their strip-lit booths. He noticed a police car parked on the opposite side of the street, apparently unoccupied.

"*Sprechen Sie Englisch?*" he said, but again the driver merely grunted and shrugged. There was an odd kind of childishness in his behaviour. Gaddis tried again. "*Ich bin ein club finden*," he said, fudging the language and adding to his sense of embarrassment by miming a dance in the backseat. "Club? Dancing? *Ist ein bar?*"

"*Hier? Nein*," the driver muttered, tapping the wheel. Gaddis felt foolish. The radio was on and he wondered if reports of Wilkinson's murder would soon filter through to the local news. As Tanya had said, it was possible that the police had already assembled a vague description of the middle-aged man who was seen drinking with the victim, a tourist with dark brown hair, around six feet tall, and wearing a dark jacket. Gaddis would be regarded as a suspect or, at best, an accomplice. He had vanished moments after the killing and conveniently abandoned the table just as the killer was approaching. He said: "Bar," again to the driver, this time with more urgency in his voice, and the vehicle pulled away from the kerb.

"*Danke*," Gaddis told him.

The cab turned through one hundred and eighty degrees, passing within a few metres of the police car. Suddenly, behind the rain-obscured windscreen, Gaddis saw a shadow move in the front seat. There was somebody inside the car. The headlights switched on and the police vehicle moved out into the road behind them. Gaddis felt a wretched sense of bad luck, sure in the knowledge that he would now be pulled over and questioned. How was he going to explain what he was doing at the UN at two forty-five in the morning? It was one of the most sensitive buildings in Western Europe, watched round the clock by police and security. It was stupid to have told the driver to come here, sloppy thinking. Why hadn't he just gone straight to a bar? Now a random Austrian cop, some preadolescent cadet twiddling his thumbs on the night shift, held it in his power to bring the entire Crane investigation to a halt.

"You want nightclub?" the driver asked, but Gaddis was too distracted by the police car to absorb what he had been asked.

"What's that?"

"I say, you want nightclub?"

He was startled to hear broken English. *"Ja, ja,"* he replied, feeling that they were suddenly allies lined up against the might of the Austrian police force. The cab rejoined the two-lane highway running perpendicular to the Danube, the policeman trailing them at a distance of no more than twenty metres. *"Nightclub güt,"* Gaddis said. He looked through the back window, the wipers on the police vehicle slicing against the rain.

"Problem?" the driver asked.

Gaddis turned back to face him. "No, no problem. *Kein problem.*"

Now the cop was alongside them, running parallel with the taxi. Gaddis could hear the fizz of tyres on the wet road. The driver's face was obscured in the darkness, yet Gaddis was sure that he saw him turn briefly and look across into the cab. It was surely only a matter of time before a siren was switched on and the taxi gestured onto the hard shoulder.

But, to Gaddis's intense relief, the police car suddenly pulled off into the distance, accelerating to top speed in the darkness. Within moments his own driver had made a turn back onto the bridge and the cab was soon depositing him outside a nightclub in the centre of Vienna. Gaddis had no idea what district he was in, nor what sort of club he had been taken to, but paid the driver forty euros nonetheless and thanked him for his trouble.

It turned out to be the perfect place to lie low. For the next two hours, he was able to sit at an anonymous corner table in a dimly lit basement bar which thudded with the sort of music he heard all the time at UCL and which he could never successfully identify. A waitress kept up a constant supply of nuts and Polish beer and he smoked with impunity because the ban was being flouted seemingly by every customer in the place. There were pretty girls on the dance floor and clean-cut men wearing chinos and ironed blue shirts trying their best to seduce them. They looked like the future CEOs of Saatchis and the World Bank. At one point, Gaddis was sure that he spotted two of the guests from the wedding, but they did not appear to recognize him and left soon after four o'clock.

Just after four thirty, as the last of the customers were being thrown out, Gaddis attached himself to a group of students stumbling drunk into the morning. At the top of the stairs, he turned away from them and decided to walk for a few blocks in search of a secluded spot where he could wait until five. The rain had stopped and he began to look around for a cash machine, only to realize that any transaction he made would instantly give away his position to any interested party with a track on his credit cards. Some of the paranoia and anxiousness he had felt before entering the club now began to return. The sun had come up, bringing a low blue light to deserted streets still damp from the early morning rain. Three times Gaddis looked at his watch, only to find the time creeping towards five o'clock with a maddening slowness. He felt that his body language, his entire demeanour as he walked, was a living clue to his guilt. Any passerby would surely notice this strange foreigner, walking the streets to no discernible purpose, turning around too frequently, looking nervously down every alleyway and street. Gaddis was conscious of moving his hands incessantly in and out of his pockets, of touching his face and hair. He was finding it impossible to relax.

Eventually, pulling out the last of his cigarettes, he turned into a straggly park populated by dogs and restless pigeons and settled on a bench to smoke. He would get through the cigarette, then switch on the phone, waiting for Tanya's instructions. He had no passport, no change of clothes, no means of contacting his friends or colleagues, other than by using a mobile phone which, when switched on, would give away his position like a fire lit suddenly in the darkness of a valley. The isolation was total.

He stubbed out the cigarette. The park was overlooked by a concrete flak tower smothered in incomprehensible graffiti. A relic of the Second World War. Gaddis took out the phone and switched it on. The simple act of pressing the power button felt like an admission of defeat, as if he was deliberately surrendering to the inevitability of his own capture. He listened to the innocent pings and melodies of the phone as it booted up and felt sure that, within moments, an army of jackbooted militia would come tearing down the street to arrest him. He stared at the phone's tiny screen. He was at the mercy of a piece of technology smaller than his own hand. The system appeared to have locked on to a signal, with five full bars of reception.

But nothing was happening. No text from Tanya. No missed call. Nothing.

A minute passed, two. Gaddis looked at his watch repeatedly. It was already almost five past five. How long could he afford to keep the phone switched on? He wondered if he had misunderstood Tanya's instructions and booted up either an hour too early or an hour too late. Had she meant five o'clock Austrian time, or five o'clock in London? Across the park, a woman was stretching her back beside a set of children's swings. Two hundred metres to her left, half obscured by a screen of trees, two men appeared to be eating breakfast in the front seat of a car. Everybody now was a potential surveillance operative or paid assassin. Gaddis wondered if he would ever again be free of this constant paranoia.

The phone beeped. Gaddis plunged to it with a manic relief.

CUCKOO CLOCK. DIZZY MOUSE.

He spoke aloud to himself: "What?" and looked again at the screen. It made no sense. Cuckoo clock? Dizzy mouse? What did Tanya mean? He had been expecting detailed instructions, the address of a safe house in Vienna, at the very least the timetable of trains leaving for Prague or Zurich. Not this. Not four apparently meaningless words in the small hours of the morning.

Cuckoo clock. His mind went to work. It was plainly a code. Tanya was trying to conceal her instructions from third parties who might be looking in. She could not afford to risk anybody knowing where MI6 were intending to meet him. That meant that she was speaking directly to Gaddis, using what she knew about him to create a private language which only he would understand. Dizzy Mouse. What did *that* mean? Was there more to come? He waited another thirty seconds for any further messages, but the mobile remained frustratingly inert. He knew that he had to switch it off and did so as he stood up off the bench, walking quickly out of the park.

Cuckoo clock. It was a reference to Switzerland. Was he supposed to head west, for the Alps? Or was the Cuckoo Clock a bar or café in Vienna? But Tanya wouldn't be so literal. If such a bar existed, it would be the first place that anybody would think to wait for him.

Finally the answer came to him, as simple as taking a breath. She was referencing *The Third Man*. They had even talked about the film at dinner in London. Orson Welles at the Prater, delivering his famous speech to Joseph Cotten:

> In Italy, for thirty years under the Borgias, they had warfare, terror, murder, and bloodshed, but they produced Michelangelo, Leonardo da Vinci, and the Renaissance. In Switzerland, they had brotherly love, they had five hundred years of democracy and peace—and what did that produce? The cuckoo clock.

Gaddis grinned, admiring her conceit. She was paying homage to the most famous Viennese film of them all. She was telling Gaddis to go to the Ferris wheel.

45

B ut why Dizzy Mouse?

Gaddis rode the U1 subway, clean and plastic, northeast to Praterstern station. The last half of Tanya's message made no sense to him. He tried blending the words and reworking them as an anagram, attempted to think of nicknames or word associations with "Dizzy" and "Mouse," but nothing materialized. He could only conclude that it was a phrase or code word he would have to use at some point later in the morning.

It was a quarter to six by the time the train pulled into the platform. Gaddis took an escalator up into a low-roofed indoor shopping mall, deserted in the air-conditioned chill of a Sunday morning. He passed a shuttered newsagent, a café serving a single customer, his every move tracked by banks of surveillance cameras. Walking outside through a set of automatic doors, he emerged into a wide pedestrianized square. Three hundred metres to the northeast was the Ferris wheel, her red booths stilled above a line of chestnut trees, ancient radiating spokes almost invisible against the pale morning sky. He quickened his pace and crossed a main road which ran alongside the square, joining a path towards the wheel. To his right was a broad, well-maintained park, dotted with picnic tables; to his left, a Shell garage surrounded by parked cars. A group of migrants were crouched at the base of a tree and they stared at Gaddis as he walked by. He passed a line of ice-cream booths and was soon walking beneath a low bridge which led into a deserted square lined with mock-Regency buildings. This was plainly the entrance of the amusement park, a mini-Disneyland overlooked by distant roller coasters, death slides, and dodgem circuits. Gaddis had only a few vagrants and cleaners for company as he walked towards the base of the Ferris wheel, wondering if he had even come to the right place.

He saw immediately that he had, because no more than thirty metres away was a cutout of a huge cartoon cat with bared teeth beneath a pair of gleaming yellow eyes. A child-size roller coaster track was disappearing into its open mouth. Above the cat was a technicolor sign: DIZZY MOUSE.

"Sam?"

Gaddis turned quickly to find a stocky, matronly woman in blue jeans and a cream sweater emerging from the shadows beneath the Ferris wheel. Her hair was dyed black, her face pale and round. She extended a gloved hand which he shook, coming to terms with his surprise.

"I'm Sam, yes." He was amazed that Tanya had worked so quickly, amazed that anybody should have found him in such a place.

"I was sent by your friend. You knew her as Josephine Warner. This is something that she told me she regrets. Her real name is Tanya Acocella. Does that reassure you about my identity?"

"Yes it does, yes it does." Gaddis looked up at the wheel, half expecting to see a crowd of smiling onlookers observing their conversation.

"My name is Eva."

"Sam," Gaddis replied, pointlessly. He acknowledged his mistake with a smile. "Are you with the Embassy?"

She ignored the question. "I understand that I am to take you to Hungary."

"*Hungary?*" Here, if he needed it, was final validation of the seriousness of his predicament.

"I have a car nearby," she added, noting his surprise. Eva's voice was clipped but heavily accented. Gaddis noticed her gaze shifting to various corners of the park. It was clear that she was concerned about surveillance and wanted to leave as quickly as possible. "Won't you come with me, please? The message that Tanya sent to you was not secure. It was not as complex as we would have preferred. Many of us have seen *The Third Man,* Doctor Gaddis."

"Of course."

So he followed Eva, a half-step behind, feeling like a child in the company of a stranger whose decency he has no reason to doubt. They walked back beneath the low bridge and headed for the forecourt of the Shell garage. The migrants were still sitting under their tree, but did not look up this time as Gaddis passed them. Entering a small area for parked cars, he heard the double sonics of an infrared lock and looked up to see the rear lights on a grey Volkswagen sedan blinking briefly. Eva opened the passenger door, walked around to the driver's side, and switched on the engine. The car smelled of Deep Heat and Gaddis turned to see a muddied football boot, a pair of shorts, and some shin pads lying on the backseat. He assumed that they belonged to Eva's son, but their appearance was as incongruous to him as it was surprising. Was she a soccer mum with a parallel life? Were people like Eva the footsoldiers of the secret world, ordinary men and women with families and jobs who just happened to moonlight as spies? He was fastening his seat belt when she began to ask him a series of questions about his life in London. *Do you have children? What work do you do? Is London very expensive?* It was plainly a prearranged tactic designed to put him at ease. No mention was made of the Wilkinson killing, nor of the reasons for Gaddis's flight from Vienna. Eva kept things very light, very ordered. They were already fifteen minutes outside the city before he was able to turn the conversation around and to get some answers.

"So, you never told me. Do you work for the British Embassy?"

She smiled, in the way that one might smile at an impertinent stranger. She had been driving, he noticed, at precisely five kilometres beneath the Austrian speed limit. The last thing she needed was a traffic cop pulling them over.

"Oh no. I am a schoolteacher." She turned and saw that Gaddis looked confused. "But I help your friends when the telephone call comes through. It is a good arrangement."

It was one of the strangest remarks he had ever heard. How did such an "arrangement" come about in the first place?

"So you know what happened to me last night?" he asked. "You know about the shooting?"

This time Eva did not smile. "The details of your situation are not my direct concern, Doctor Gaddis. My only job is to make sure that I deliver you safely to your destination. If, on the way, I can help to allay any concerns you might have, or to answer any questions, I am also happy to do this."

Gaddis looked out of the window. The pale, flat countryside was sliding past like a dream. He craved a cigarette but remembered that he had finished his packet in the park.

"So where are we going?" he asked. The ashtray in the car was clean and there was no sign of any cigarettes. "What's the plan?"

Eva took a satisfied intake of breath. The conversation was developing along lines that she had predicted.

"It's very simple." She overtook a lorry travelling slowly in the lane ahead of them. "I am taking you into Hungary where we will stop at Hegyeshalom station. There you will board the train to Budapest. I will return to Austria."

"You're not coming with me?"

He felt embarrassed to have asked the question, to have sounded alarmed. It was as if he had revealed some evidence of cowardice.

"I am afraid not."

"You don't normally take people all the way?"

Eva raised a matronly eyebrow. "Every case is different." The response had a tone of censure. "Because of a prior arrangement, I need to be back in Vienna before lunchtime. These arrangements were made only in the last few hours. If I had been given more warning, I might have been able to accompany you to the Budapest airport. But it is often the way."

"So I just get on a train? How do I get home? Has Tanya planned that far ahead?"

He realized that he sounded rude, but he was tired and fractious. He should have been more grateful to this woman who, after all, had left her home in response to an emergency call in the small hours of the morning. She was putting her life at risk by helping him. But the shock of the night's events was still vivid to him; he was allowing basic courtesies to slip.

"Tanya has planned everything," Eva said. "You simply stay on the train until it terminates in Budapest Keleti. On the platform, you will walk and find a man sitting on a bench wearing a green jacket. He is the next link in your chain. His name is Miklós. He has a beard and will be drinking from a bottle of Vittel water. He has seen your photograph so he will recognize you, even if you do not recognize him. Miklós will then take you to the airport and see that you are flown safely back to London."

"That's extraordinary." Gaddis marvelled at the speed at which Tanya had worked, the favours she had called in, the networks she had activated. "And if I'm stopped at any point? If the Russians are on to me?"

"It is a good question." Eva conveyed how seriously she was taking it by slowing down slightly and rubbing the back of her neck. "I have to tell you that there is very little possibility you will be stopped or asked questions at any point in your journey. Austria is not a police state, Doctor Gaddis. Hungary is not a police state. I have been following the news reports of the incident at Kleines Café and no mention has been made of a man fitting your description. Nevertheless, it is possible that the police are buying time and that they have a closed-circuit image of you from the bar. Is this possible?"

"I don't know." Gaddis was suddenly concerned. It was the one angle that he hadn't considered. He thought of the Goth at Meisner's apartment and tried to remember if he had seen a camera bolted to the wall of the café. Surely the blanket surveillance of CCTV cameras in public spaces was a uniquely British disease? "I don't think so."

"But a member of staff or a customer may have spoken to the police. Again, we cannot be sure. Now, there is no formal customs at the border because of Schengen. If, however, we are stopped by a guard for some reason, you are to say that you are my friend from England and that we are going to Budapest for a few days. You have been staying at my apartment in Vienna since Thursday." There was a slight pause. "If necessary, we will give the impression that my husband and your wife would rather not know about this."

It was Eva who blushed, not Gaddis, and he was relieved to see this calm, resourceful woman succumbing to a momentary embarrassment. It brought them closer together.

"Do I stick to my own name?"

"At this stage, yes. A new identity has been prepared for you by Miklós. You will leave Hungary using a false passport."

Gaddis felt so reassured by the arrangements that he allowed himself to close his eyes and to relax briefly as the car sped towards the border. He thought that he saw an army of wind turbines stretching from horizon to horizon but could not be sure if he had been dreaming. The next thing he knew, Eva was pulling into a Soviet-era railway station on the Hungarian side, having crossed the border without need of disturbing him. They were in Hegyeshalom.

"Wait here, please," she said when she saw that he had woken up. By the clock on the dashboard of the car, it was just before nine o'clock in the morning.

"What's happening?"

"I buy ticket."

He was alone in the deserted car park. A starved cat was scratching around in a small pile of rubbish. Some blue plastic tarpaulins had been piled up next to an old truck which looked as though it hadn't been driven since the Cold War. Gaddis felt that he had woken up in Russia: a world of crumbling, Communist-era apartment blocks, of railway carriages abandoned on weed-thick sidings, of tangles of loose wire in overhead cables. Everything less neat, everything less manicured. He caught the smell of his own breath and craved some water. Falling asleep had been a mistake. The brief respite had left him feeling more, not less tired.

Eva returned five minutes later armed with a cheese sandwich, a half-litre bottle of water, and a ticket to Budapest.

"You got a return," Gaddis pointed out, devouring the sandwich and drinking the water until it was almost finished.

"You are coming back tomorrow," she replied, with a knowing smile. "A one-way journey always looks more suspicious. Which reminds me . . ."

She stepped out of the car and opened the boot, returning with a faded leather bag which contained some toiletries, a couple of paperback books, and a T-shirt.

"This is for your journey." She closed the door of the car. "A foreigner who gets onto a train without a bag may look suspicious. Try to find a seat next to a young person, if you do not wish to be disturbed. They are less likely to bother you with conversation. Within an hour you will be in Budapest. There is absolutely nothing to worry about. I am just sorry that I cannot come with you."

"It's fine," Gaddis replied.

"Could I have your mobile phone, please?" He was not surprised that she had asked. "I will take it back to Austria and switch it on in a park near my house. It may distract the people who are following you. They may believe that you are still in Vienna. On the other hand, they may assume that it is a trick. Either way, it is not safe for you to be carrying it. Do you have any further questions?"

There were hundreds more, of course, but Gaddis could not think of them. Probably better that way. There was no need to complicate things further. After all, how hard could it be? All he had to do was get on a train and meet a man called Miklós. He looked up to see the Budapest train sliding into the station. Eva had timed things perfectly. He stepped out of the car.

"Thank you," he said. "You've been very kind. I don't suppose we'll get the chance to meet again."

"I don't suppose," Eva replied. Gaddis gave her the phone and the battery. "You will be fine, Doctor Gaddis, you will be fine. I wish you the very best of luck."

46

The train hummed and sighed on the tracks. Gaddis walked into a carriage halfway down the platform and saw that only a handful of empty seats remained. He looked for somebody young, as Eva had advised, spotting a crew-cut Hungarian with tattooed biceps seated at a table opposite a bottle-blond woman in her early twenties who was staring moodily out of the window. Their legs were entwined beneath the table. There was a spare seat beside the girl. Gaddis nodded at it and the Hungarian indicated that it was free with a flick of his eyes, nothing more. Gaddis thanked him with a nod, swung his bag up onto the rack, and sat down.

The train began to pull away from the station. An old woman stared at Gaddis as he settled into his seat, but when he caught her eye she looked away. Across the aisle, a young teenager was listening to an MP3 player on headphones which were covered in pink and yellow stickers. Beside her was a middle-aged businessman in a brown suit who was fast asleep, his mouth hung open, a blob of spittle pooling on his chin. It didn't look as though anybody was going to start making polite conversation. People appeared to be minding their own business.

On the table in front of him was an open can of Coca-Cola and a crumpled copy of a Hungarian daily newspaper. Gaddis wanted to get a look at the front page, even though he knew that there was no chance of Wilkinson's murder having made it into the early morning editions. A female passenger across the aisle was reading an Austrian gossip magazine with a picture of Katarina Witt on the cover, skating in a red dress. Gaddis was feeling fidgety and needed something to do with his hands. He remembered the paperback books in his bag, yet did not want to draw attention to himself by reaching up onto the rack so early in the journey. So he stared out of the window. He absorbed the roads and the fields and the woods of the quiet Hungarian countryside, conscious of every tic and movement in his facial expression. It was impossible to relax. How many times in his life had he sat on trains, staring out of windows, his mind successfully and unself-consciously blank? Thousands. Yet today he was aware even of his own breathing.

Fifteen minutes passed. A ticket inspector appeared at the rear of the carriage and began making his way down the aisle, checking passengers who had joined at Hegyeshalom. It took the inspector what felt like an age to reach the block of seats around Gaddis, to request his ticket and to return it with a brisk nod. Gaddis watched with relief as he moved on. Buoyed by this first successful brush with authority, he stood up, nodded at his tattooed companion, and walked in the direction of the dining car.

It was deserted. There were rows of tables, set for four, laid out with red tablecloths and leather-bound menus advertising goulash and five ways with chicken. Gaddis could not recall whether or not Eva had advised him to move around the train, yet he had felt so static in his seat, so trapped, that the walk had seemed essential to his well-being.

He went to the bar. A young man in an ill-fitting jacket was serving a customer with a few precious strands of greasy hair combed neatly across his scalp. Gaddis bought a cup of white-hot coffee and a sticky pastry filled with glutinous yellow custard. It would do his gut no good, but he was still hungry and felt that the caffeine might sharpen his wits. He sat on a stool beneath the logo of a NO SMOKING sign, chewing on the pastry and slowly sipping his coffee. Everything about the train was clean and smooth but debilitatingly slow. It felt as though they were travelling at walking pace, stopping every half mile; even the air-conditioning was sluggish. When he had finished eating, Gaddis walked back to his table, passing through carriages where the seating was divided into compartments accessed by sliding doors. The curtains were closed on certain booths; others were occupied by weary businessmen and old-aged pensioners who, lacking something better to do, stared at Gaddis as he walked by.

He returned to his seat. The crew-cut Hungarian was slumped asleep against the window, his girlfriend checking her makeup in a compact. She looked up at him, then slid her gaze back to the smudged mirror. Across the aisle, the teenage girl was still listening to her MP3 player and Gaddis thought that he could hear the melody of a Beatles song coming through the headphones. The businessman beside her had now woken up, wiped his chin, and was busily inputting data into a laptop. Gaddis sat down and returned the smile of a woman whom he had not noticed before; a red-haired executive in a black pin-striped jacket who must have boarded at the last station. There was nothing to occupy him. He grew bored and wanted something to read. It would be interesting to see what books Eva had found for him.

Gaddis stood up. He was about to reach for the bag when the train came to a sudden halt. He would have thought nothing of it, but from his standing position in the carriage he could see through a window towards the front of the train. They had stopped at a level crossing. Two police cars were parked on a deserted country road, blue lights revolving noiselessly. Gaddis felt a caving sense of dread as the mute sirens pulsed against the late morning sky; he had a sure sense that the train had been stopped by the Hungarian police, in cooperation with their Austrian colleagues, as part of a coordinated search for the murderer of Robert Wilkinson.

He sat down without a book. This in itself seemed a reckless act. Why stand, only to sit down again without unzipping his bag? He felt a dozen eyes upon him, as if his guilt was as plain to his fellow passengers as some mark on his body. He was being blamed him for what was happening, for the delay to the journey. The tattooed man, his girlfriend, the teenager with the MP3, the red-haired executive with the smile and the pinstriped suit—all of them knew that he was on the run from Vienna.

Then the engine of the train shut off, like a definitive signal of the hopelessness of his predicament. There was a moan of frustration throughout the carriage as the suspension shuddered and then fell silent, all power stripped from the train. There were shared looks of annoyance at the seats around him; Gaddis tried to join in by frowning and shaking his head. *I'm one of you,* he was saying. *None of this has anything to do with the Kleines Café.* The red-haired executive caught his eye and he produced what he hoped was a look of friendly camaraderie; instead, she frowned, as if Gaddis had in some way offended her. She looked past him at the far end of the carriage. Somebody was coming through the door.

Gaddis turned. There were two uniformed policemen ten metres from his seat. Was it his imagination, or did the taller of them immediately double-take, as if he had recognized him? Gaddis looked across the aisle at the teenage girl, who was bobbing her head to "Eleanor Rigby." He felt a rush of panic involuntarily turn his face scarlet. He began to imagine a scenario whereby he would be arrested not by the police, but by the executive, who was again staring at him, and whom he was now certain was a plainclothes Austrian law enforcement official positioned close by in order to facilitate his capture.

Calm down, he told himself. *Take it easy.* The train could have stopped for any number of reasons. There could be illegal immigrants on board, a smuggler taking drugs or cigarettes into Budapest. Behind him, Gaddis could hear the policemen working their way through the carriage, as slow as the ticket inspector, as thorough and as sinister as jackbooted thugs in the Waffen SS.

"Tickets, please."

The taller of the two policemen, the one who appeared to have recognized him at the door, was standing above the table. Gaddis fumbled in his jacket for the ticket Eva had handed to him at Hegyeshalom. He could not remember any of the advice that she had given him. Why had she not joined him on the train? Had he been set up? Why had Tanya not arranged for a second MI6 agent to accompany him to Budapest?

"Thank you," said the policeman, as Gaddis passed him the ticket.

He made a deliberate point of looking the policeman in the eye, trying to seem bored, trying to seem indifferent. For a wild moment, he was convinced that he was the same man who had tailed his cab from the UN.

"You are English?"

Gaddis had not spoken. How had the policemen managed to establish his nationality? The game was up. They knew who he was, where he was from, what he was doing. For a split second he considered responding to the question in Russian, but if the police had seen his face on CCTV at the Kleines Café, any attempt at subterfuge would simply convince them of his guilt.

"Yes. From London. How did you know?"

Though he had asked his question in English, the policemen did not appear to understand the reply. Gaddis looked behind him, at the second officer, who was busily checking tickets on the opposite side of the carriage. This, in itself, gave him a glimmer of hope: why would they carry on with their search if they knew that they had found Wilkinson's companion? The girl with the pink-and-yellow headphones was reaching into the pocket of her jeans; she had not even bothered to take off the headphones. Gaddis was staggered by her sense of calm. But what was she looking for? A ticket or an identity card? If the police asked Gaddis to produce a passport, he was finished. Across the table, the crew-cut Hungarian had woken up. One of the tattoos on his arm was a caricature of Elvis.

"So you are going to Budapest?"

"Just for the night, yes." Gaddis remembered what Eva had told him. *You are coming back tomorrow. A one-way journey always looks more suspicious.* He cursed her for not providing him with a passport, a driving licence, some kind of photo ID with which to bluff his way through. What kind of tourist crossed an international border without a passport? What kind of intelligence agency left a man to fend for himself on a train crawling with cops?

"Enjoy yourself," said the policeman.

Gaddis wasn't sure that he had heard correctly. Was he imagining it? But the officer had turned his attention to the Hungarian and his girlfriend, both of whom flashed tickets at him with complete indifference to his authority. Perhaps these kind of searches were commonplace. Just then, a radio crackled on the jacket of the second officer. He responded instantly to the message, walking directly out of the carriage and down onto the track.

"What happened?" Gaddis asked.

"They find him," said the Hungarian.

Both men stood in their seats and craned to look at the police cars parked at the level crossing. Through the cluster of passengers trying to see the same thing, Gaddis made out a young man who was being bundled into the backseat of the furthest car. A policewoman pushed his head downwards with the flat of her hand, and there were handcuffs on his wrists, secured behind his back.

"Any idea what that was?" Gaddis asked.

The Hungarian shook his head. "No. I do not," he said, and leaned over to kiss his girlfriend.

47

An hour later, the train was pulling through the ghost-town suburbs of Budapest, past abandoned freight cars on sidings, clusters of wild poppies and weeds. Gaddis saw the entrance to Keleti station opening up ahead in a delta of gleaming tracks. It felt like a cause for celebration. It was now surely just a question of meeting Eva's contact and of being driven out to the airport.

He stepped down onto the platform and was immediately surrounded by a gaggle of local men and women offering him a room for the night, a taxi into town, a meal at a local restaurant.

"Car?" they said as he shook his head. "Where you like go, sir?"

He ignored them and stuck to Eva's instructions, walking towards the great glassed roof of the station in search of Miklós. There was a bench fifty metres along the platform, positioned just a few feet from the ticket inspectors. Sitting on it, exactly as she had described, was a man with a beard wearing a green jacket. Gaddis could see a bottle of Vittel in the man's left hand. At that moment, Miklós looked up and caught Gaddis's eye, smiling broadly. Gaddis knew immediately that he would like him: the Hungarian, who was about fifty, had quick, lively eyes, mischief in his face, and the aura of a man who was lucky and self-assured.

"Mr. Sam?" he said, reaching to shake his hand.

Gaddis took it. Miklós was wearing brown leather gloves. The palm was sticky and cold against his own.

"Will you forgive me if I ask who sent you here?" Gaddis asked.

"Of course I will forgive you." Miklós was still smiling, still pumping his hand. "It is important to be certain about these things, no? My name is Miklós. I was sent to meet you by our mutual friend, Eva, in Vienna, who was in turn acting for the woman you once knew as Josephine Warner."

Gaddis felt a wave of relief. Miklós took his bag, against Gaddis's protestations, and walked past the ticket inspectors without a glance. They went outside to a four-door Seat parked just a block from the station.

"We go to my apartment first," Miklós explained. Gaddis thought that there was nothing unusual about this. "Your aeroplane, it does not leave for a few hours."

He had opened the rear door of the car, as if entering a taxi, but realized his mistake and moved to the passenger seat. Outside, Budapest felt a world away from Vienna, churning and chaotic and still touched by the faded grandeur of Communism. Gaddis was reminded of the grey, dirty light in Moscow; there was that same blanket smell of bitumen and diesel on the air and he felt the kinship of a world with which he was far more familiar. Miklós drove quickly, swerving and leaning on the horn, down film noir boulevards that, to Gaddis's romantic eye, were full of all the bustle and wonder and threat that had been scoured clean from modern Vienna. For a blessed instant he felt free. Then he thought of Wilkinson and the screaming crowds in the Kleines Café and knew that he was far from safe.

"So I am to understand that you have been through a very difficult trauma," Miklós said.

The word "trauma" sounded excessive, even melodramatic, but Gaddis found himself replying: "Yes."

"Well, do not worry. It is all right now. You are in good hands. I take you to my apartment quickly. My wife, she fix you the soup. I will hand you your new passport, also some money. By sunset you are back in London."

"You're very kind." He wanted to ask the same questions that he had tried to put to Eva. *How did you come to be working for MI6? How often do you do this kind of thing?* But he knew now that it was best to allow these angels of the secret world the privilege of their anonymity.

"Are you from Budapest?" he asked instead. It was an unimaginative question, but a little conversation seemed important.

"I am," Miklós replied. "I give you the language lesson, okay? Quick guide to Hungarian."

"All right."

They were turning down a narrow street, heavy brownstone buildings weighing down on all sides. Gaddis was amazed to see a small branch of Tesco on one corner.

"You order cheeseburger, you say 'Shiteburger.'" Miklós was laughing. It occurred to Gaddis that he must have used the same line on every foreigner who crossed his path. "Is funny, no?"

"It's funny."

"And the nipple we call the 'mellbimbo.' Male bimbo. Crazy language, Hungarian. You like it? Crazy."

Soon they had parked on a wide avenue beside a pile of neatly chopped wood, around which had been thrown a makeshift fence of orange plastic. Miklós retrieved Gaddis's bag from the boot and led him down a passageway which ran between an electrical shop and a small restaurant. They emerged into the large internal courtyard of a nineteenth-century apartment building. A creaking lift carried them to the third floor.

"I live just down here," Miklós said, steering Gaddis down a corridor which was open to the courtyard on the eastern side. He took out a set of keys and opened the door of his flat.

Inside, there was a large, modern kitchen with a staircase at one end, unprotected by banisters. A woman was standing at the stove, chopping mushrooms.

"Let me introduce you to my wife," said Miklós. "Viki."

Viki was an attractive woman, at least fifteen years younger than her husband, with long, dark hair and a slim figure partly concealed by a navy blue apron. Gaddis raised a hand in greeting but did not approach her; she had indicated that her hands were dirty from cooking and it did not seem appropriate to kiss her on the cheek. He felt as though he had popped round to a neighbour's house for lunch; there was no sense of anxiety in the room, no undercurrent of alarm. Was Viki in on the situation? Was she another Hungarian on the MI6 payroll? Miklós spoke to her briefly in their native tongue, then offered Gaddis a stool at a breakfast bar in the centre of the room.

"You have a beautiful place," he said, setting his bag on the floor.

"Thank you. The building is very typical, but we make some adjustments. You will take a coffee? A shower?"

"At the same time?"

Viki laughed, turning to catch her husband's eye. There were expensive pots and pans on butcher's hooks above the stove, black-and-white prints in frames, an iPod hooked up to some Bose speakers on a shelf adorned with paperback novels. A dog wandered into the kitchen, glided past Viki's legs, and settled beneath a deep ceramic sink.

"Bazarov," said Miklós. "Our best friend."

"After Turgenev?"

His face lit up. "You know *Fathers and Sons*? You are an educated man, Mr. Sam."

Gaddis explained that he was a lecturer in Russian History and, before long, he had a cup of coffee in front of him and was knee-deep in a conversation about nineteenth-century Russian literature. Viki produced some bread and a bowl of soup and they sat together, at the breakfast bar, pinging opinions about Tolstoy back and forth while Gaddis wondered why he felt so relaxed.

An hour after he had first sat down, he was offered "a good hot shower and a nice change of clothes." He duly went upstairs, armed with a fresh white towel which smelled of chemical pine, and stood under the torrent of a steaming shower, cleaning away all the sweat and the worry and the rage of his long night in Vienna. Miklós had laid out a shirt and a jumper in a small bedroom nearby, as well as a pair of blue jeans which appeared never to have been worn. All three items fitted him perfectly; it occurred to Gaddis that MI6 even knew his sizes. He shaved and changed in front of a faded poster of Steven Gerrard brandishing the European Cup. The bedroom presumably belonged to Miklós and Viki's son.

By half past twelve Gaddis had made his way downstairs. Viki complimented him on his appearance and helped to pack his dirty clothes in the bag given to him by Eva. Miklós advised him to change his jacket—"in case a witness from the Kleines Café has described it to the police"—and in its place provided a long black overcoat which was slightly tight at the shoulders. Gaddis found a tweed cap in the pocket, but did not want to put it on, arguing that it would draw unnecessary attention to him at the airport.

"You are probably correct," Miklós replied, rolling the first jacket into a ball and stuffing it into the bag. "You look good anyway, Mr. Sam. You look normal."

They went into a sitting room cluttered with books and lamps. Viki did not follow them. There was a chessboard on a low coffee table in the centre of the room, the black king toppled over. Beside the board, resting on a copy of *The Economist,* was a battered British passport and 40,000 Hungarian florints, the equivalent of about £200. Miklós handed them to Gaddis.

The passport seemed a perfect fake. There were stamps from Hong Kong, a stamp from JFK, even an exact copy of the photograph which appeared in Gaddis's regular passport, taken eight years earlier. How had Tanya acted so quickly? Where the hell had the passport been printed? The British Embassy in Budapest must have been involved. He flicked through the watermarked pages and looked up at Miklós.

"Astonishing," he said.

"I have seen better."

The Hungarian now produced a mobile phone from his pocket and handed it across the chessboard. A number by which he could reach Miklós was listed under the name "Mike." Gaddis knew now that the hard part was to come. The long journey home was ahead of him.

"So." Miklós had also sensed the change in mood. "You now have what you need. I suggest we make our way downstairs to the car."

Viki appeared in the doorway of the sitting room and came towards Gaddis, kissing him on both cheeks. He assumed that she had been listening all the time.

"Good luck," she whispered, the smell of her skin like a strange memory of Holly. "Miklós will take good care of you."

"Thank you for all your kindness," he told her, and they stepped outside into the corridor.

Miklós's car was still parked outside the entrance to the apartment building, close to the pile of wood. A tram chimed past, almost knocking over a stooped, elderly lady pulling a shopping basket across the street. Gaddis tried to catch Miklós's eye but saw that his attitude was now altogether more serious. They placed his bag in the boot, stepped into the car, and fastened the seat belts.

It was a measure of the extent to which Gaddis trusted the Hungarian that he had not checked the contents of his bag before zipping it up. Had he done so, he would have discovered that Viki had placed a small package inside it, wedged between his jacket and dirty clothes.

It had been decided that Dr. Sam Gaddis was going to act as a courier.

48

"listen carefully." Miklós had started the engine and was pulling out into traffic. "We drive to the airport. You are booked on the 15:30 easyJet to London Gatwick. According to the computer in my house, the plane is on time. We can check this for certain when we arrive at Ferihegy. If there is a problem, we just sit together in a café and make a conversation. Okay? You have your passport in the coat?"

Gaddis reached into the inside pocket of the overcoat. He found the passport and held it out.

"As you can see from the back page, your name is not Samuel Gaddis today. For the purpose of this journey, you are Samuel Tait. You have the same forenames, you have the same birthday. You can see that, for the purposes of realism, we have also given a name and address for persons to contact in the case of emergency." Gaddis looked at the inside back page. Somebody had written an address and telephone number for "Josephine Warner" in blue ink. "If you need to contact Tanya in London, use the number for 'Jo' in the mobile. It will go through a switchboard."

"What's my job?" Gaddis asked. He knew that it was incumbent upon him to seem alert and professional, to ask the right kind of questions, though in truth his mind was scrambled by doubts.

"Good thinking." Miklós made a left turn onto a single-lane high-way and sounded his horn as a man riding a moped cut them up on the inside lane. "You have the same job. You teach history at the University College in London. This has not changed. Nothing has changed except your address, your surname, and your passport number. We always try to keep things simple."

Always try. Gaddis looked out of the window at an ordinary day in Budapest. Who else had been through this process? What kind of people and under what circumstances? How different would things have been, say, thirty years earlier, with informants in every apartment block and the secret police on every corner? The car was held at a set of traffic lights and, for the first time, Gaddis experienced a burst of panic, as if he were about to be surrounded by gunmen or pulled over to the side of the road. But the moment passed. He put it down to nerves and sleeplessness and reminded himself to buy cigarettes at the airport. The traffic lights turned green and Miklós pulled away, past a secondhand car dealership and faded billboards advertising Samsung televisions, whisky, brands of Hungarian lingerie.

The airport appeared sooner than he had anticipated, a brand-new building finished in the style favoured by architects looking to save time and money: the departures terminal resembled an aircraft hanger shaped from moulded plastic. Gaddis had been expecting something akin to the chaos of Sheremetyevo, but the interior reminded him of a branch of IKEA. It was spotless and gleaming, with hard plastic seats the colour of terra-cotta and white walls which amplified the harsh artificial light in the terminal. Miklós chatted amiably as they strolled towards the Departures board, saying, "Very good, excellent," when he saw that the easyJet was on time. After queuing only briefly, Gaddis checked his bag into the hold, received a boarding pass, and then sat with Miklós at a branch of Caffé Ritazza, drinking espressos and occasionally scoping the building for any sign that he had been recognized. It was an utterly mundane environment, seemingly entirely without threat. Miklós, continuing to put Gaddis at ease, revived their earlier conversation about Russian literature and encouraged him to talk at length on the subject of Tolstoy's childhood. By the time they had drunk a second round of coffee and picked their way through a brace of tasteless muffins, it was time to catch the plane.

The two men walked towards the security area. There were no cops at the entrance, no sniffer dogs, no heavyset Russians lingering in the shadows brandishing black-and-white surveillance photographs of Dr. Samuel Gaddis. It was just a regular afternoon at a regular budget-flight airport. Gaddis could not imagine that any problem was going to befall him.

"So," Miklós placed a hand on his back, "we are old friends, okay? You have been to stay with me for a few days. We have done nothing but get drunk."

Gaddis suddenly felt alarmed. He realized why Miklós had left it this late to furnish him with the final details of his cover. He had obviously been concerned that he would forget them.

"We met on a stag weekend in Budapest five years ago." Miklós grinned and rubbed his beard, as if recalling the sordid details. "So now you must go, Mr. Tait. Now you must have a safe journey."

Gaddis managed to smile, though his gut was churning with nerves.

"Thank you for everything," he said, and reached to shake the Hungarian's hand. But Miklós had other ideas, seizing him in a bear hug which punched the wind out of his stomach.

"We are friends, remember?" he said, growling into Gaddis's ear. He pulled away, still holding him by the arms. His grip was very strong. "If you have a serious problem, you call the British Embassy. By law, Sam, you are entitled to seek representation from your government. An official will come to you, an official who is aware of your situation. Does that make sense?"

"It makes sense." He brushed away what felt like a bead of sweat above his temple and tried to arrange his face so that he would look more courageous. "You've been extraordinarily kind to me. I wish there was some way that I could thank you."

"There is nothing to thank me for," Miklós replied quickly, and Gaddis saw the sparkle in his eyes, the mischief he had noticed at Keleti. "It has been an interesting day to spend with you. Such interesting conversations. I wish you a very happy and safe journey home."

There was a slight pause as Miklós set himself up for a cruel joke. "If they ask you if anybody could have interfered with your bags, you know what to say."

Gaddis laughed and walked towards the security check. He felt as though he was in a room in which all the pictures had been tilted to one side. What if the passport was recognized as a fake? What happened then? Would Miklós wait for him, come forward and help? Would he ensure that he made it through to Departures, or was the Englishman now on his own?

He was held in a queue behind a young Polish couple and a man carrying what looked like a guitar in a brown leather case. He turned to aim one final wave at Miklós.

But he was gone.

49

It was like Berlin all over again, only this time Gaddis was alone. This time there was no Tanya for company.

He made it through the X-ray and metal detectors, removing his shoes, removing his belt. Miklós had bought him a *Guardian Weekly* and a copy of Malcolm Gladwell's *The Tipping Point*. Gaddis had put them in a plastic bag along with a packet of cigarettes and a slab of Toblerone. He put his shoes back on, threaded the belt through his jeans, and took the plastic bag from the container in which it had passed through the scanner. It was soon time to queue again. Passport control was just a stone's throw from security.

He picked the closest of two queues and found himself standing behind an elderly British couple and a young man with dreadlocked hair who was shouldering a canvas satchel which had been attacked by a plague of moths. He was in the shortest line, but as he looked ahead at the border guard, felt that he had chosen badly. There was a woman operating the adjacent desk who looked easygoing; his own guard had the stern, officious look of a dyed-in-the-wool bureaucrat. Just the sort of person who might get a kick out of making a British tourist sweat.

Gaddis was summoned forward with a flick of the wrist. He had the counterfeit passport ready and passed it underneath a thick glass screen. The guard did not take it but instead let him rest it on the shelf, as if checking to see if his hand was shaking. Gaddis could feel the guard's gaze tracking upwards towards his face and made a point of looking at him directly and of making eye contact. The guard's expression was utterly cold. He snapped open the passport with what Gaddis took to be an almost contemptuous sense of suspicion and said: "What is your name, please?"

"Tait," said Gaddis, trying out the pseudonym for the first time. "Sam Tait."

The guard had already flicked to the back of the passport and was studying the photograph. It was almost as if he knew that it had been secured there by an MI6 forger just a few hours earlier.

"Why were you in Budapest, please?"

Gaddis experienced a system-debilitating fear. He was sure that he was on the point of being arrested. Was this the final double-cross of Tanya Acocella? Had Miklós deliberately tipped him into the arms of the Hungarian police?

"I'm sorry?"

"I asked you, what was the purpose of your visit to Budapest?"

"Oh. I'm sorry, I didn't hear you properly." Somehow, Gaddis remembered how to lie. "I was visiting a friend. Pleasure, not business."

The guard seemed momentarily satisfied by the speed and concision of this reply but soon returned his gaze to the photograph. He looked up at Gaddis's face. He looked back down at the photograph. He looked up again, obliging Gaddis to stand slightly straighter at the desk. Then, to Gaddis's horror, he took out a magnifying glass and began studying the photograph, like a diamond dealer examining a stone for flaws. His right eye was pressed up against the passport, roaming across the page, checking every watermark, every cross-hatch, every pixel of the forgery. Gaddis switched the plastic bag from his left hand to his right and looked beyond the desk at the safety of the departures area, trying to appear calm. It was like an oasis that he would never reach. At any moment he was expecting to be asked to step aside and to accompany the guard into an interrogation room.

"Thank you, Mr. Tait. Enjoy your flight."

Gaddis managed not to snatch back the passport in wild relief.

Moments later he was standing in an area reserved for smokers, drawing deeply on a cigarette and silently giving thanks for the brilliance of Tanya Acocella. He felt now that, unless he was profoundly unlucky, there was no threat to him, either from the airport police or from Russian surveillance.

Within two hours, the easyJet had landed at Gatwick. Gaddis had managed to close his eyes for twenty minutes during the flight, snatching some much-needed sleep at a window seat. Yet he felt no sense of joy as the plane landed in a drizzly England, no welcome glow of homecoming. If anything, it felt as though he was walking back into a trap from which he had just escaped. It was as though he knew that his problems had not come to an end; they were only now beginning.

Everything was fine until he was ready to pass through customs. He had collected his bag from the carousel, been effusively thanked by an elderly couple whom he had helped with their suitcases, and carried his own luggage towards the green channel at the far end of the hall. He was no more than ten feet from freedom when a customs officer stepped across his path, pointed at the leather case, and indicated to Gaddis that he should move to one side.

"Could I just take a look at that, please, sir?"

Gaddis felt a wretched sense of disappointment. As he moved towards a row of low, steel tables at the side of the hall, he was convinced he was the victim of a setup. In years gone by, he had passed through customs a dozen times with more than his fair share of Camels and Glenlivet; now his luck was up. He knew, in the way that you know of a sickness coming, that somebody had tampered with his bag. It was the only probable outcome. Ahead of him was a greyed-out mirror, smudged and scratched, on the other side of which he could imagine a lineup of grinning MI6 officers, Tanya among them, observing his final moments. Had she betrayed him, or did he look so strung out that the officer had no choice but to question him? Gaddis put the leather case and the plastic bag on the counter. The customs officer was in his midforties and slightly overweight, with pale, indoor skin and a short-sleeved shirt which fitted him too loosely. He peered into the plastic bag, inspected the bar of Toblerone, picked up the copies of *The Tipping Point* and the *Guardian Weekly*, then replaced them. It was as though he was deliberately killing time until he went for the case.

"Could you just open this up for me, please, sir?"

It was the politeness of the request that grated on Gaddis, the sense of procedure being followed, of sticking to the letter of the law. *They make you open the bag yourself so that you can't later accuse them of planting evidence. They make you open the bag yourself so that they can watch your hand shaking as it pulls on the zip.* He felt a great rush of heat pulling up through his body and suspected that the customs guard was merely toying with him. Perhaps he should just come clean? Perhaps he should just tell him the whole story? *Look, I'm being exfiltrated by MI6. There was a murder last night. I'm travelling on a fake passport.* But there was still the small chance that it was all just a mistake. In a couple of minutes he could be sent on his way. Gaddis told himself that he fitted a profile; he was a dishevelled-looking middle-aged man, travelling alone, returning from Eastern Europe. Customs were *obliged* to stop him.

He unzipped the case. Inside, he could see his so-called possessions: the paperback books given to him by Eva in Hegyeshalom, the can of Austrian shaving foam, the tube of Colgate toothpaste. His dirty clothes—the clothes he had worn at the Kleines Café—had been placed alongside the jacket that he had bought in Great Marlborough Street. Viki had rolled it up into a ball.

The officer pulled at the jacket. As he lifted it free, Gaddis saw to his horror that something had fallen loose inside the case. A package of some kind. A small parcel.

The guard immediately picked it up and showed it to him.

"What is this, sir?"

The heat again. The electric fear of capture. Gaddis stared at the package. It was about the size of two paperback books, wrapped in brown paper and secured in a thick skin of Scotch tape. There were no markings on it, no address, no stamps. He was about to deny ever having seen it before, but a stubborn refusal to kowtow in the face of authority convinced him to lie. Before Gaddis knew what he was saying, the words were coming out of his mouth:

"It's just a present for somebody."

"A present?"

"Yes."

It was a ridiculous thing to have said. The package could have contained narcotics planted by Miklós or Viki. Gaddis had that feeling again of a second man inhabiting his body and speaking on his behalf. He could sense a constant flow of passengers passing behind him, staring at his back and condemning him with their eyes. He even heard a child say: "What's that man done, Mummy?" and wanted to turn around to proclaim his innocence.

"What sort of present, sir?"

The officer's question was put in a way that sounded almost disengaged, but Gaddis saw that he was studying his reaction carefully.

"I'm not precisely sure, to be honest," he said. "A friend wrapped it up. A friend put it in there for me."

"You've never seen this package before?"

Eye contact now. Gaddis's gaze flicked involuntarily to one side. He pulled it back and smiled, as if to assure the officer of his good character.

"No. I've seen it. But I left Budapest in a bit of a hurry. A friend packed my bag."

"Somebody else has interfered with your luggage?"

Gaddis felt that his words were being twisted, that his lies were being unravelled even before he had uttered them. Why hadn't he simply told the officer the truth? Then he remembered Miklós's final words to him, the joke they had shared. *If they ask you if anybody could have interfered with your bags, you know what to say.* He felt sick to have been so easily duped.

"Not interfered," he replied, hardly remembering what had been said. "We were just in a bit of a hurry."

The officer had heard enough. He placed the package on the counter, searched through the rest of the case, then reached for a box cutter in the pocket of his trousers.

"Let's open it up, shall we?"

He immediately began slicing through the loops of Scotch tape. *It's drugs,* Gaddis thought, *it can only be coke or pills.* The officer was removing the brown wrapping paper. *A sniffer dog picked up the scent and they waited to see who collected my bag.*

"So here we go," said the officer. Gaddis was staring at a small dark plastic box which the officer was holding in his hand. "Let's have a look inside."

He had stubby fingers, the nails cut short and clean. The lid of the box clicked open on a hinge. Inside, concealed in a nest of tissue paper, was not a wrap of cocaine, not a block of hashish, nor a vial of pills, but a wristwatch with a worn metal strap. The officer took it out.

"A present," he said.

If anything, he seemed more surprised than Gaddis. The two men looked at each other. Gaddis could only assume that the package had been in the leather bag all along and that Miklós and Viki had failed to notice it. Why else would they plant a watch in his luggage?

"It must be Dan's," he said, conjuring another lie.

"Dan?"

"A friend who was staying in Budapest last week. He must have left it there."

"Where?"

"In the apartment where I was staying."

"Ah."

Gaddis had no sense of where the lies were coming from, only that they appeared to be having the desired effect. The officer was beginning to look bored. He had plainly been expecting a greater haul.

"I see. Well, sorry to take up your time."

"Not a problem."

If there had been a sofa in the customs hall, Gaddis would gladly have collapsed into it and lit a triumphant cigarette. Instead, he picked up his bags and walked towards a set of automatic doors. Tanya was waiting for him on the other side. She was standing beside a pillar in the same beige raincoat she had been wearing when he last saw her outside UCL. She looked tired and he realized that she had most probably been awake since his first, panicked phone call from Vienna. All those plans, all those contingencies, orchestrated from Vauxhall Cross within the last few hours.

"I don't know how to thank you," he said, though he was still mystified by the watch. They did not embrace, nor did they shake hands. It was like meeting a lover many months after an affair has ended: the atmosphere between them was charged, the mood civilized.

"Don't mention it," she said.

"I had some trouble at customs."

She looked at him quickly, concern in her eyes. "Trouble?"

"There was something in my bag. A package. Your friends may have put it there without telling me." Gaddis looked back in the direction of the customs hall. "A guard pulled me over and went through my case. Do you know what that's about?"

Tanya swore under her breath, steering Gaddis away from the arrivals area. "Fucking Miklós."

"What about him?"

"I told him not to complicate things. I told him to find another way of sending the watch."

"So you know about it?"

Tanya nodded. "Sure." She looked as irritated as he had ever seen her. "I'm sorry he got you involved."

Gaddis looked around, half expecting to see Des coming out of a branch of WH Smith with some Murray Mints and a copy of the *News of the World*. "We seem to be making a habit of spending quality time together at Gatwick Airport," he said, trying to ease the tension. "I have no idea how you did what you did, but I feel as though I've been carried here, watched all the way."

"Sounds like you were," Tanya replied. Her irritation with Miklós was still palpable. He had plainly crossed a professional boundary. Gaddis wondered what was so precious about the watch and why Miklós hadn't simply told him to wear it on his wrist.

"There's information inside it," Tanya said, as if she had heard the question.

"In the back of the watch? In the mechanism?"

"There is no mechanism. It's a false casing. The less you know, the better."

"Very James Bond."

"Very."

They walked the short distance to the car park. Tanya's muddy Renault was parked on the upper level of a clogged multi-storey. Gaddis recognised it from Kew.

"Talking of presents," she said, "I've got something for you."

Gaddis was standing behind her as she popped the catch on the boot. He could hardly believe his eyes. Somehow, Tanya had managed to retrieve his overnight bag from the Goldene Spinne.

"How the hell did you get *that* back?" he asked. He opened it to find his suit, his clothes, his house keys, and wallet all packed inside.

"Eva got them," she replied. "DHL to Gatwick did the rest."

He surprised himself by reaching out and kissing her on the cheek. Tanya did not seem to object. "You're a miracle worker."

"We do our best, Doctor. I used up a few favours. I'm just glad you're back in one piece."

It was only when they were inside the car, heading north towards the M25, that she asked what had happened in Vienna. Gaddis described the scene at the Kleines Café, his long night in the city, the journey with Eva, and his time with Miklós and Viki in Budapest.

"I owe you an apology," he said. "I shouldn't have gone to Vienna. I didn't think the Russians were following me."

"They most probably weren't."

He was surprised by this.

"How can you be sure?"

"I can't. But only a handful of people knew that Wilkinson was going to be in Austria. Who alerted the Russians? Who tipped them off? He's lived peacefully on the South Island of New Zealand for more than a decade. Why do they suddenly come looking for him now?"

"Maybe they wanted me."

Tanya produced a brief, one-note laugh. "Believe me, Sam, if the Russians wanted to kill you, they would have done it already. Vienna was a specific hit on Wilkinson. It was just lucky you were in the bathroom."

He concluded that this was the moment to tell her what Wilkinson had revealed.

"Look," he said. "There's something you should know."

"Go on."

"Bob told me something before he was killed. Something that explains everything that has happened."

He realized that he trusted her completely now. It was a total reversal. He did not even think twice about the consequences of what he was going to say.

Tanya looked across at him. "Tell me, Sam."

"Sergei Platov tried to defect in 1988."

She almost swerved onto the hard shoulder. *"What?"*

"He went to MI6. He gave Wilkinson ATTILA's identity as proof that he was serious. He was disenchanted with life in the KGB and wanted to make something of himself. Didn't think he was valued highly enough by his superiors."

"So he tried to *come over*? Jesus." Tanya was nodding to herself. "That explains the killings," she said. "Everybody who knows about this has been assassinated."

"Except for Brennan." Gaddis had been chain-smoking since the airport. He slotted a third cigarette butt through a small gap in the window and watched it whistle past the door. "Your boss must have something on Platov. They must have come to some kind of arrangement. Tretiak and Wilkinson were both killed. Crane knew about Dresden as well, which explains why Brennan had him sent to St. Mary's in '92. You've never heard this?"

"Of course I've never heard it." Tanya was such an accomplished liar that he could not tell whether or not her reaction was genuine. "Do you have any idea what it would do to Platov's career if this became public knowledge?"

"No shit." Gaddis went for another cigarette and was about to press the lighter when Tanya said: "Is there any chance you could *not* smoke? Just for five minutes? I feel like I'm driving an ashtray." He replaced the cigarette. "So why has MI6 kept it a secret? Surely once Platov rose through the ranks, his file was opened up and his defection became common knowledge? Surely Brennan or one of his predecessors must have reported what happened?"

Tanya shook her head. "It doesn't work like that."

"How does it work?"

"Number one, exposing Platov would have exposed ATTILA, and the Office has never wanted anybody knowing that we had another Cambridge spy on the books. It took thirty years to get our reputation back. We're not about to throw it away again."

"But Eddie was a bloody *hero*. He was the greatest double agent in the history of Anglo-Russian espionage. Isn't that a triumph to be *celebrated*?"

"Maybe." Tanya was a member of the new generation of twenty-first-century spies: post–Cold War, post-9/11, post-ideological. Her attachment to the old ways was by no means an article of faith. "But where's the proof of Platov's defection? It would just be our word against his. The Russians would write it off as crude propaganda, an influence operation."

Gaddis was silenced. "Influence operation." The secret language of the secret world. He closed the window and found himself thinking about Min. He had wondered, in the depths of the Viennese night, whether he would ever see his daughter again.

"Wilkinson told me that he interviewed Platov in a safe house in Berlin in the presence of John Brennan."

"So?"

"He said the safe house was 'wired up.' Does that mean he would have recorded the interview? Videotaped it?"

"Recorded certainly." Tanya was clearly intrigued. "I don't know about video. If it was the late eighties, perhaps. The technology would certainly have existed to use a concealed camera in low light."

"What would have happened to those tapes after the interview? Would they be kept in a vault at Vauxhall Cross?"

"Doubtful. If the tape ever made it to London in a diplomatic bag, it would have been destroyed by Brennan."

Gaddis twisted in his seat. He was on to something.

"There are tapes in the boxes Holly gave me, tapes in Katya's files." His voice had quickened. "What if the interview is on one of them?"

"Keep talking."

"Before I went to the bathroom, Wilkinson quoted Morecambe and Wise at me. 'You're playing the right notes, but not necessarily in the right order.' I thought it was just a joke at first, but he said that I wasn't looking at the files in the right way. What if Katya's material isn't a paper trail? What if it's something else? What if the smoking gun is a *tape*?"

Tanya braked suddenly as a van swerved out in front of her. Gaddis swore, because his nerves were still on edge. The car beside them sounded its horn and he looked across, lip-reading the driver shouting out in anger.

"I'm not sure I follow you," she said.

"What if Wilkinson made a copy of the tape and sent it to Katya along with the other documents, hoping that she would make use of it?"

"That's a big 'if.' "

"But just say she did."

"Then the Russians have probably stolen it. Or it's lost. Or they've lobbed a Molotov cocktail through your sitting room window and burned down your house."

Gaddis ignored the joke. "Let's go there now," he said. "Let's go to my house and go through the boxes."

"Not going to happen."

"Why?"

"Come on, Sam. It would be suicidal. Doronin gave your description to the FSB. They're probably sitting outside your house as we speak. The minute you show your face in Shepherd's Bush, they'll come for you."

"Then why are we on the M25 heading back into London?"

"Because I'm taking you to a safe house."

Gaddis felt an odd mixture of relief and despair: relief that Tanya was guaranteeing him some measure of safety; despair that he was being forced out of his home.

"How dangerous can it be?" he said. "Let's just poke our heads round the door. I need a change of clothes anyway. All my papers are there, my stuff for work. It would take five minutes."

"No," Tanya replied.

"So that's it?" He felt a sudden anger, confronted by the stark limits which would now be imposed on his life. "I can't go home? That's the directive from MI6?"

"It's not coming from MI6."

"Then who's it coming from?"

"Me."

He had been on the point of extracting a cigarette, on instinct, but again returned the packet to his coat.

"You?"

"Brennan wants you out of the picture." Tanya almost spat the words, as if she could not believe what she was saying. "You're a thorn in his side." Gaddis could see the conflict in her, the doubt. "I'm going to take care of you for a few days. I'm worried that it might have been Brennan who tipped the Russians off about Wilkinson. And I didn't apply for this job so that my boss could betray his own people to the Kremlin and put innocent lives at risk."

There was a moment in which he thought that she was playing him again. Her words sounded heartfelt, but the stark admission was so out of character that he wondered if the whole thing was rehearsed. It was a habit Gaddis had developed, a safety valve to avoid being manipulated. But when he took her hand in his, he knew that Tanya was utterly serious. He could sense it by the way she glanced at him quickly and then looked away. She squeezed his hand back, then released it, the reassurance of a friend. Was her theory possible? It was an astonishing accusation, yet Brennan had every motive to betray Wilkinson. Gaddis turned around and looked behind his chair. Dry cleaning was folded on the backseat of the Renault, a tin of Roses chocolates spilled open on the floor. This was her vehicle, her operation. He thought of Eva, of football boots and children.

"Let's go to my house," he said, as if they were starting the conversation all over again.

"You're not listening to me. It's pointless going after the tape. Your story will never come out. It will never be *allowed* to come out. The government will slap a D-Notice on the Crane book before you've typed the opening paragraph."

Gaddis seized on this.

"I don't believe that. I think that's just a line you're feeding yourself to get out of what you know we have to do. Take a look at Platov, Tanya. Isn't it time for a change of scene in Moscow, a change of personnel?" She shook her head, but it was the reflex of a bureaucrat. "Look at his record. Platov has taken Russia to within a few years of outright totalitarianism. Innocent civilians are being killed to justify illegal wars overseas. Exiles are murdered in foreign cities to silence dissent. Newspaper editors with the nerve to challenge the orthodoxy are left to die in hospital. *Fuck* the D-Notice. If we can get hold of that tape and get it broadcast, even if it's just on the Internet, we have the power to put that scumbag out of office."

Tanya was gliding past a convertible MG.

"Five minutes," she said. "That's it. That's all I'm giving you. Five minutes."

50

They parked three hundred metres from Gaddis's front door, at the northern end of the street.

"This isn't my house," he said.

"I'm aware of that. What number are you?"

"I thought you knew everything about me, Josephine. You must be getting sloppy."

Tanya explained that she would walk down the street and check for surveillance around Gaddis's house. If there were Russian or British watchers positioned outside—in vehicles, in a first- or second-floor stakeout, dressed as street cleaners or parking attendants—she would be able to identify them.

"Give me ten minutes," she said, and stepped out of the car.

Gaddis smoked a cigarette while he waited. He saw one of his neighbours coming towards him, a widow walking her poodle, and ducked down in his seat, scrabbling around on the floor of the Renault until she had passed. Tanya came back just as he was dropping the cigarette butt into a storm drain.

"Everything seems clear," she said, starting the engine. "I walked up to Uxbridge Road, came back down the other side, had a look around.

But they may have a trigger on your front door. If you go in, it will tell them you're back and they'll send somebody round faster than the time it's taking me to tell you about it. So you don't have long. Get the tape, get your papers, get your toothbrush and your razor, then get out of there."

She drove up to the house. Gaddis was obliged to negotiate a hop-scotch of pavement gob and dog turds en route to his front door, deposited by boxer dogs and uncastrated Dobermans whose owners used the street as a rat run between White City and the pubs and betting shops on Uxbridge Road. He put the larger of his two house keys into the Chubb lock and turned it, as he had turned it a thousand times before. He inserted the Yale and lifted the latch. His frayed nerves half expected the obliteration of an explosion, the scream of an alarm, but the door opened and he found himself in the hall of his house, home again.

There was a small package on the doormat, addressed to Dr. Sam Gaddis "BY HAND,' next to a bank statement and some junk mail. He went into the sitting room and walked straight towards the files in the corner of the kitchen. *They may have a trigger on your front door.* He turned each of the boxes upside down so that their contents sprayed across the floor. It was like watching stones sliding on ice. Everywhere he looked there was paper. Gaddis could not remember which of the boxes contained the tapes and looked around in increasing desperation for signs of a package or cassette.

Wilkinson's letter to Katya was still on the kitchen table, which he took as a sign that no one had broken into the house during his absence. There were two other boxes in the corner of the room, jammed up against the door which led out into the garden. Gaddis pulled open the cardboard flaps, inverted the boxes, and again allowed the contents to pour out onto the floor.

Straightaway he heard the clatter of a VHS cassette, saw it and picked it up. It was not labelled, but looked unscathed. He set it to one side and reached for the second box. He could feel how light it was in comparison with the others. He looked inside. There were just three pieces of A4 paper and—hidden beneath these—a blank BASF music cassette with "Prokofiev" written down one side in faded blue ink.

He was sure that this was it: an audio recording of the interview with Platov. The VHS was also promising. Though relatively un-marked, it could have been a copy of the original film shot in the safe house in Berlin. He grabbed a plastic bag from a stash under the sink, put the tapes inside it, and headed for the front door.

He stopped just as he was reaching for the latch. Gaddis turned and looked back at the house. Min had crawled up those stairs. The books in the hall were the books he had bought and shared with Na-tasha. In that sitting room, he had eaten dinner with friends, watched England win the Ashes. It was a place of memories. And now he would have to give it up. If what Tanya was saying was true—and he had no reason to doubt her now—the house would have to be put up for sale. That was the price of consorting with Edward Crane. That was the price of a blood feud with the FSB.

He picked up his post, put the package in the plastic bag alongside the tapes, opened the door, and walked back out to the car.

51

id you find anything?"

"Two tapes," he said, and took them out of the plastic bag. Tanya pulled away towards Uxbridge Road.

"What's on them?"

"One of them is a tape with 'Prokofiev' written down the side. The other is a blank VHS. Is there a video machine at the safe house?"

"Probably."

They headed west, through the gridlock of the Shepherd's Bush roundabout, then south in the direction of Kensington High Street. The pavements were crowded with families heading home at the tail end of the long afternoon, mothers and fathers doing their Sunday thing. On Earl's Court Road, Tanya turned left into Lexham Gardens.

"Where are we going?" Gaddis asked.

"Patience."

She drove into a narrow mews and parked beside a black four-by-four with tinted windows. An elderly couple wearing bottle-green Huskies were coming out of a house three doors down. They looked up and spotted Tanya.

"Hello, dear," said the woman, raising an emaciated hand. Her husband, who was using a walking stick and looked even older than Edward Crane, struggled to lift his head as he greeted her.

"You know those people?" Gaddis whispered. He wondered how secure the safe house could be if members of the Secret Intelligence Service were on nodding terms with its neighbours.

"Friends of mine," she said.

Her reply made sense as soon as they walked into the house. Gaddis saw a photograph on a side table and reacted in disbelief; it was a picture of Tanya with her arms around another man. This wasn't a safe house. This was her home. The man in the photograph was her fiancé.

"You live here?"

"I live here."

"Is that a good idea?"

"You don't like Kensington?"

"I meant, is it a good idea to be inviting me back to your house?"

"It's fine for the time being." She closed the door behind them. She hooked up the security chain and slid a bolt across the top of the door. It was a first, symbolic indication of Gaddis's confinement. "We can work something else out tomorrow."

He did not know whether to be alarmed by the fact that Tanya had no access to a safe house or grateful to her that she was prepared to risk her well-being in order to provide him with sanctuary. He looked again at the photograph, fascinated by the man who had won her heart.

"What's his name?" he asked, tapping the glass.

"Jeremy."

Jeremy looked exactly as Gaddis had imagined he would when he had first had dinner with Josephine Warner: well financed, reliable, sporty. He felt a pulse of envy.

"Do you live together?"

"A lot of questions, Sam."

"Forgive me. I don't mean to intrude."

Tanya threw the car keys on the side table. "Yes you do," she said, and offered him a forgiving glance. "We normally live together, but he's abroad this week. Works for an NGO in Zimbabwe. We're getting married next year."

She gestured Gaddis into the living room, a compact area with a large window on the street side, a staircase in the centre, and a door at the back leading into what appeared to be a small kitchen. The sitting room was lined with hardback books and hung with various portraits and landscapes by artists Gaddis did not recognize. There was a varnished wooden dining table parallel to the window and two sofas arranged in an L-shape around a large flat-screen television. It wasn't a house that felt particularly cosy or hospitable and for a moment he entertained the thought that Tanya had tricked him yet again. The photograph could have been posed with an SIS colleague; the pictures of Tanya dotted around the room, taken at various stages of her life, might easily have been transferred from her real home. But he could see no sense in that particular conspiracy. Why would she do it? What would be the point in continuing to fool him?

"Tea?" she asked.

"Sure."

The kitchen was as slick and contemporary as a mock-up in IKEA, but at least it felt lived in. There were messages and newspaper clippings attached to the fridge by magnets, well-worn recipe books on a shelf in the corner, a burned wok hanging from a hook near the garden window. *So this is how spies live,* Gaddis thought. *Just like the rest of us.* He told Tanya that he liked his tea black with two sugars and she made a remark about taking it "in the Russian style." To watch her move around the room—removing spoons from a drawer, pouring milk from the fridge—was as strange to him as the sight of the wristwatch at Gatwick. It was something that he had thought he would never see, something that he had never imagined.

"What are you smiling at?" she asked.

He decided to be honest. "It's just interesting to see where you live," he said. "You don't think of spies having toasters and microwave ovens. I was expecting a gun cabinet, an E-Type Jag."

"Oh, I sold those."

He wondered how much time she had spent in the house, how often she and Jeremy were together. Was "NGO" a cover for SIS? Almost certainly. They had probably met and fallen in love at work. Their jobs took them to all the corners of the Earth; they were probably lucky to meet for dinner three or four times a year.

"The video," Tanya said.

Gaddis went back into the sitting room and retrieved the tape from the plastic bag. He turned to find her walking up the stairs.

"I think Jeremy has an old machine in his office."

Moments later, she was back, bearing a dusty video recorder and a tangle of cords.

"Success."

They knelt in front of the television. He could smell her perfume and wondered if she had applied more in the bedroom upstairs. The television was state-of-the-art, a screen the size of a small deckchair, and Gaddis was concerned that the technology in the video would be out of date.

"There's a SCART plug," Tanya said hopefully, and slotted it into the back.

His next concern was the tape itself.

"We need to take it easy," Gaddis said. "These things can chew."

He pushed the power button. The television was already on and automatically switched to an AV channel which appeared to support the video.

"Give it a try," Tanya told him.

Gaddis slid the tape into the mouth of the VHS, felt it pull away from his fingers and clunk down onto the heads of the recorder. He heard the noise of the tape beginning to spool.

"Don't chew, you bastard," he muttered. "Don't fucking chew."

Tanya laughed. Her knee was touching his and he was aware that she did not seem interested in moving it. Suddenly, the television flared into life. But there was no sign of Sergei Platov. Instead, they were confronted by the credit sequence of the Parkinson show.

"Can you turn the sound on?" Gaddis asked.

Tanya pushed a button on a remote control and the theme tune jumped out at them. "Hang on," she said, and turned down the volume.

It appeared to be a relatively recent episode. The identity of the first guest—Jamie Oliver—confirmed that the show had been recorded within the last ten years.

"Can we get past this?" Tanya asked.

Gaddis held down the fast-forward button and they watched the programme spinning past in a blur of close-ups. Joan Rivers. Cliff Richard. Parky. For five minutes they were hunched on the ground, their eyes fixed on the screen, growing dizzy for any sign of a break in the transmission. But it never came. There was no film of Sergei Platov secluded in a Berlin safe house; instead, there was an episode of *Cheers*, followed by over an hour of blank, unrecorded fizz and static. As the tape came to an end, ejecting from the machine, Gaddis felt a dead weight of disappointment and voiced the thought that perhaps he had been too optimistic.

"There's always the other one," Tanya said, nodding at the plastic bag. As she stood up, the joints in her knees creaked.

Gaddis retrieved the BASF cassette. Tanya had opened a cupboard near the table containing a small Denon hi-fi. A tape deck was stacked halfway down. He handed her the cassette and sat in a hard wooden dining chair. She pressed Play. There was a three-second silence as the tape began, then the opening bars of Prokofiev's *Romeo and Juliet*. Gaddis met her eyes.

"Patience," she said. "Patience."

For more than an hour they listened to the ballet, wandering around the room, drinking second cups of tea, making scrambled eggs on toast. Halfway through the second side, Tanya gave up and opened a bottle of wine, convinced that no recording of Platov existed. Gaddis dutifully heard the tape to the end, then took his plate through to the kitchen.

"Back to square one," he said.

"Back to square one."

She was sitting on a stool in the corner of the kitchen. He began to wash up the pan in which Tanya had made the eggs, a guest earning his keep. It was past ten o'clock, the long, strange day drawing to an end.

"You must be exhausted," she said.

"Holly can't have given me all the boxes." He rinsed the pan in a stream of hot water. "Her house is a tip. Most of the files were in a storeroom in the basement of her building. It's possible there are more of them in Tite Street."

"You can't call Holly," Tanya said.

The finality of the instruction annoyed him. "What?"

"We don't know if her phone is compromised, if her house is being watched." Tanya's tone was businesslike and matter-of-fact, as if she was deliberately killing off the intimacy which had built up between them since the airport. "You ring her and it could draw the Russians right to you."

Gaddis was silent as he dried their plates. He wondered why Tanya's mood had changed at the very mention of Holly's name. Was she jealous? As the evening had drawn on, they had been as relaxed in each other's company as lovers. Now she had offered him a stark, blunt reminder of his circumstances. He began to resent the power that she held over him.

"How am I supposed to reach her, then?"

"Let me work it out," she replied, though it sounded as though she was running short of ideas. "I have to go to the Office first thing in the morning. Brennan knows about Wilkinson. There have been reports on the news. He probably won't know that I got you out of Vienna. He certainly doesn't know that you're staying here. I'll have a lot of explaining to do. But there's a possibility that we can still find a way of protecting you and resolve everything with the Russians."

It sounded like hot air. Gaddis looped the tea towel over the back of a chair. "You're not listening to me," he said. "I don't want to be wrapped in cotton wool. I don't need protecting. There's a chance that Holly has the Platov tape gathering dust in the basement of her house. All I'm asking is that you give me the chance to call her to see if she'll look for it. It's that simple."

"Patience," Tanya replied, for what seemed like the tenth time in as many hours, and Gaddis's anger boiled over.

"Is there any chance you could stop saying that? It's like you're talking to a four-year-old. I'm grateful for everything you're doing, Tanya. Seriously. But I'm not going to sit on my arse for the next few days and hope that John Brennan suddenly changes his mind about me. What did you think I can *achieve* here? Watch some daytime TV? Do the crossword?"

Tanya, to his astonishment, took him at face value. "I'm afraid so. Until we can find somewhere safe for you to go, you'll have to stay here. That means you can't make phone calls. It means you can't even go outside."

He looked at her in astonishment. He had a glass of wine on the kitchen table and drained it as he absorbed what she had said. He was amazed by how quickly their flirtatious rapport had evaporated; there had been several moments during the course of the evening when he had even entertained the possibility that they might spend the night together. Now Tanya seemed to be taunting him with the stark fact of his imprisonment.

"Fine," he said.

"What do you mean 'fine'?"

He recalled their conversation on the street outside UCL. *Don't go looking for Crane. Don't go looking for Wilkinson.* He had made promises to Tanya Acocella before. He could do so again.

"I mean that I'll do as you say. I'll stay here while you go to work. I'll watch *Countdown* and go through your knicker drawer. Forget about Holly. Forget about the tape."

Tanya knew that he was lying.

"That simple?" She produced a look which suggested Gaddis was making her job even more difficult than it already was. "That's not a Sam Gaddis I-swear-I-won't-go-to-Austria type of promise, is it? The last time you said something like that, a few days later you were in a bar in Vienna."

"It's not that type of promise."

Tanya shook her head. She knew that Gaddis would stop at nothing to avenge Charlotte and to retrieve the tape. What choice did he have? She could hardly keep him under house arrest indefinitely. If he walked out of the mews, there was nothing she could do about it.

"Fine," she said eventually, walking into the sitting room. She began to puff the cushions on the sofa, like a physical demonstration of her desire to bring the conversation to an end. "Why don't we get some sleep? It's been a long day. You must feel like a bath or something."

"In the morning, Mummy." Gaddis was surprised that she had let him off the hook so easily and seized the opportunity to lighten the mood with a joke. But Tanya did not laugh. Instead, she said: "I've laid out one of Jeremy's T-shirts for you," which made Gaddis feel like an unwanted suitor who has outstayed his welcome.

"Terrific."

"There's a towel as well, whisky in the kitchen if you want it." She yawned in a way that was stagey and self-conscious and Gaddis began to resent her again. "You're in the room at the end of the corridor. Jeremy uses it as a study."

"Is he likely to come back and climb into bed with me?"

She allowed herself a smile, the glow in her eyes like a break in bad weather. "No," she said softly, and Gaddis reflected that she was probably just tired and worried.

"Thank you," he said, because it was right to acknowledge the huge sacrifice she had made. "I don't know what I would have done without you. I'm sorry for all the trouble I've made."

"All in a good cause." She surprised him by kissing him gently on the cheek. "Most of it, anyway." She turned and walked up the stairs. "Sleep well. Will you turn off the lights before you come to bed?"

"Of course. I'll be five minutes."

Gaddis found the whisky in the kitchen and poured himself four fingers. Switching on the television, he surfed briefly for a twenty-four-hour news channel which might be covering developments in the Wilkinson shooting. But CNN was fixed on an American political story, Sky News broadcasting a business programme. He turned the television off, checked the bolt on the front door, and made his way upstairs.

He could hear a shower running when he reached the landing. There was a line of light under Tanya's bedroom door. He thought of the pleasure, the blessed release of spending the night with her, but walked resignedly in the other direction, down the corridor towards Jeremy's study. Sure enough, Tanya had laid out the towel and the T-shirt, as well as a packet of aspirin, a bottle of mineral water, and an alarm clock to put beside his bed. Gaddis showered and changed into the T-shirt, briefly flicked through a copy of *The Spectator* and was asleep before midnight.

He woke at eight to find that Tanya had already left for work. There was a note on the kitchen table reiterating her demand that Gaddis remain in the house. "If you have to smoke," she said, "keep doing it in the garden." He scrunched the note into a ball and threw it into a bin, noticing a spare set of house keys hanging on a nearby hook. He pocketed them, fixed some cereal and a percolator of coffee, read the second half of *The Spectator,* and smoked a cigarette through an open window. At about nine o'clock he had another shower, changed into a shirt which Tanya had hung for him on the landing—"another one of Jeremy's" the note had said—and wondered how he was going to kill the next ten hours under effective house arrest. He was not nosey by nature and had no interest in going through Tanya's private possessions; his own encounter with a permanent blanket of MI6 surveillance had made him more, not less respectful of other people's privacy. He flicked through a couple of photo albums, which were lying on a table in the sitting room, but learned only that Tanya and Jeremy had been on holiday together in Paris and Egypt and that Jeremy wore Speedos—without apparent irony—whenever he came within striking distance of a body of water.

By ten o'clock, Gaddis was bored out of his mind. He washed his clothes using the machine in the kitchen and hung them up on a line in the garden. By eleven he had resorted to watching daytime TV, settling on an old black-and-white thriller starring Jimmy Cagney. Was this his future? Whenever he stopped to think about what Brennan and Tanya were cooking up for him, he could only conclude that he would soon be sucked into the same witness protection programme which had claimed Edward Crane. It was no kind of life. It was too depressing even to contemplate. Such an existence would shut him off irreversibly from Min, from his work at UCL, from the entire structure of his life. He *had* to contact Holly. Finding the tape was his only route to freedom.

At half past two, he found a Tesco spaghetti bolognese and some salad in the fridge. It was only as he was mopping up the sauce with a slice of stale brown bread that he remembered the package which had been posted through his door in Shepherd's Bush. He retrieved the carrier bag from the sitting room and sat on the sofa with a kitchen knife, slicing through the seals on the envelope.

He did not recognize the handwriting on the front of the package. He assumed it was a book of some kind, a document sent by a colleague.

But it was not.

There were photographs inside. Seven of them. Gaddis pulled them out, along with a note which had been typed, unsigned, on a folded sheet of A4 paper.

THE SUM OF ONE HUNDRED THOUSAND POUNDS WILL BE PAID INTO YOUR BANK ACCOUNT. THIS BUYS MORE THAN YOUR SILENCE.

He turned the photographs over and felt his soul twist like a corkscrew.

There were seven pictures of Min.

Min at the beach. Min with a friend. Min with Natasha. Min outside her school.

Gaddis stood up and ran to the door.

52

addis found a phone box fifty metres from the Cromwell Road, the roar of six lanes of traffic funnelling into the booth as he picked up the receiver. He scrabbled in his pockets for change and had to turn the contents out into his hands as he searched for a twenty-pence piece. He had only pound coins, pushing one of them into the slot and accidentally dropping three others onto the floor of the booth as he did so.

The money clunked through but did not register on the readout. Gaddis swore and tried a second time, losing another pound in the same way. He dialled 155 for the international operator and was put through to a woman with a thick Liverpudlian accent.

"I need to make a reverse charge call to Spain."

"Certainly, sir. What number, please?"

He knew Natasha's landline by heart and, within a few seconds, could hear the phone ringing out in Barcelona. *Be at home,* he whispered. *Be at home.*

"*Hola?*"

It was Nick, the boyfriend. The operator explained that a man was calling "collect" from London and would Nick accept the charge?

"Sure." They were connected. "Sam?"

"Yes. Is Min there?"

"What?"

"I said is Min there?"

Nick wasn't taking too kindly to Gaddis's tone. He had accepted the charges, after all. He deserved a bit of respect for his generosity, some appreciation, a little small talk. "You want to talk to Min?"

"Yes, Min. My daughter. Is she there?"

"She's at school, Sam. You sound flustered. Is everything all right, mate?"

Gaddis didn't want to be called "mate" by anybody at a time like this, least of all by Natasha's feckless, underfunded boyfriend.

"No, nothing is all right. Where's Natasha?"

"I think she's at work."

"What do you mean, you 'think'?"

"Tell you what, mate. Why don't you call her there? Sounds like this is a conversation you should be having in private."

"I don't have her num—"

To Gaddis's disbelief, Nick hung up. He swore at the phone so loudly that two passersby on the street turned and looked at him with a look of fear in their eyes. Slamming down the receiver, Gaddis gathered up the loose change from the floor and realized that he could not remember the name of the company that Natasha worked for in Barcelona. All of his numbers were stored on a mobile phone still lying, battery-dead, under a filing cabinet in her apartment. He could not even recall the name of Min's school. It was a Catalan word, some regional anomaly that he had always found impossible to remember. How was he going to find out if she was okay?

He stopped. He tried to regain his composure. *No news is good news,* he told himself. If Min had been harmed, Nick would know about it. Besides, the note had been a warning. All he had to do was drop the Crane story, forget about Platov and Dresden, and all his problems would be over.

He opened the door of the phone booth. Cars were being held at lights on the Cromwell Road. It was cold and Gaddis zipped up his coat against the wind. He lit a cigarette and smoked it while pacing the street, back and forth, like a prisoner in a yard. He could conclude only one thing: that he would never be free of the FSB. The note was meaningless in this context, the hundred grand just a lure. As long as he was alive, he posed a threat to Sergei Platov. If he agreed to the blackmail, it would only postpone his demise—in a car crash, from a gas leak, from a little polonium-210 in his California roll. He walked back to the phone. The only way of securing Min's future was to get his hands on the tape. That would at least give him some leverage, something priceless with which he could negotiate her safety.

This time the phone accepted the pound coins. He dialled Holly's number. Her voice as she picked up was like his last chance of salvation.

"It's me," he said.

"Sam? Where have you been?" She was more perplexed than irritated. "I've been trying your mobile for days. Where are you?"

"I had to stay in Barcelona longer than I thought. My mobile got stolen." What choice did he have but to lie to her? "Just got back to London. I haven't got round to replacing it."

"We were meant to go for dinner."

Christ. Quo Vadis on Saturday night. He had completely forgotten making the plan; it had just been a smokescreen for Tanya and GCHQ. He apologized and waited for Holly to say something, but she remained silent. Did she know that he was lying to her? Did she know what had happened to Wilkinson?

"I need you to do me a favour," he said.

It was far from the best approach. He owed Holly an explanation for his behaviour. Now, without bothering to ask how she had been, without even being honest about Wilkinson, he was expecting her to do his bidding in an emergency, the details of which he could not reveal to her. He was thinking only of Min's security. Whatever it would take to keep her safe, Gaddis would do it, even if that meant manipulating Holly.

"You want me to do *you* a favour?"

"I know it's a lot to ask."

"You haven't even asked it yet."

He was grateful that he had found her in a reasonable mood. "It's about your mum's files. Are you sure you gave me everything? The other day you said there might be other boxes in the basement."

"There are," she replied plainly. It sounded as though she was being distracted by something in the room from which she was talking.

"Are you at the flat now?"

"No. An audition."

"Could you go down there as soon as it's finished? Would you be able to do that?"

"Probably." Again, Holly sounded distracted. Gaddis experienced a strange desire for her to succeed at the audition, to be given a part that she could sink her teeth into, something that would take her away from him. She didn't deserve to have been dragged into all this. He wanted her to be safe and yet, at the same time, he needed her to save Min. "Why don't you come over and we can both do it?" she said.

It was as though she was testing him. "I can't get away." Gaddis looked out at the Cromwell Road and knew that he was no more than ten minutes by cab from Tite Street. But if he went there, it would surely draw FSB surveillance towards the tape. "I'm right in the middle of this MI6 thing. The book."

"About Bob?"

"About Bob, yes." The lies were paper thin. "If you could just go down there and have one more look, particularly for any tapes or cassettes that your mum might have mislaid."

"Tapes or cassettes?"

A woman in a raincoat appeared outside the phone box, waiting to make a call. Gaddis opened the door ajar and said: "I'm going to be a long time, I'm sorry," in a low voice. Holly was saying: "Sam?"

"Yes?"

"Are you all right? I'm worried about you."

His body was bound in sweat. He had realized, even as he was talking, that he would never be able to publish the Crane biography, that there was now no hope of Platov's defection becoming public knowledge. The president would remain in power and there would be dozens more Charlotte Bergs, dozens more Katarina Tikhonovs, who would lose their lives simply to prop him up in power. "I'm fine," he said. "There's just a deadline on the manuscript. I can't get away. I can't come to meet you."

"What if I find the tape?"

"Then you must bring it to me."

"Where? In Shepherd's Bush?"

"No." That wasn't safe. Holly would be observed and the tape stolen. He had to think of an alternative location. UCL was undoubtedly being watched. "Take it to the Donmar Warehouse and leave it with Piers."

"With *Piers*? Why?"

How could he explain that one? It made no sense. Gaddis cobbled together another shabby lie.

"I'm working around the corner in a UCL building."

"Then why don't I just bring it to you there?"

"Security's a pain in the arse. They'll either lose it or tell you they've never heard of me." He was amazed by the speed of his lies. "The Donmar is less than a quarter of a mile away. I go there for coffee all the time. You can leave it at the ticket desk. Just call me at this number if you think you've found anything."

He gave the landline number of Tanya's house, wondering if even that was a safe means of communicating with her.

"What number is that?"

"UCL."

Gaddis was sick of deceiving her, sick of the effort of accumulating excuses. He tried to change the subject.

"What's the audition for?"

"A play."

But he did not listen to the answer. Instead, focused only on the tape, he said, "Will you have a chance to look for it today?" and finally Holly's patience ran out.

"Sam, I've told you: I'll look for the fucking tape. But it might help your cause a bit if you stopped acting like a paranoid schizophrenic and explained to me what the fuck is going on. Try asking a girl out for dinner. Try asking how I've been. It's not difficult. Last time I checked, we were having a pretty good time together. Now every time I speak to you I feel like your fucking secretary."

"I'm so sorry." He wanted nothing more than to be alone with her, back in his old life, Min safe in Spain, students coming to his office at UCL. But it had all been ripped away from him.

"It's okay. I just hope you're being honest with me." She paused before adding: "If there's somebody else—"

Gaddis looked out at the passing traffic and shook his head. "I promise you it's not that. It's about my daught—" He almost choked on the word, lost in the wretchedness of his situation.

"Sam?"

"Please don't worry. Just find the tape, okay? Just try to find it. You have no idea how important it could be."

53

Gaddis went back to the mews house and locked the door. There was a laptop in Jeremy's room and he found the name of Min's school on Google. He called the number, using Tanya's landline. To his relief, the headmistress reassured him, in broken English, that Min was "completely fine" and would be going home "as usual, in a few minutes." Gaddis hung up, lit a cigarette, and went out into the garden. The small, enclosed space was overlooked by more than a dozen windows in five or six separate buildings, but he was certain that here, at least, he was safe from FSB eyes.

He took the crumpled note out of his pocket and looked at it again.

THE SUM OF ONE HUNDRED THOUSAND POUNDS WILL BE PAID INTO YOUR BANK ACCOUNT. THIS BUYS MORE THAN YOUR SILENCE.

Something about it didn't ring true. If the Russians knew his home address, they would have killed him. Why bother with a crude blackmail? The FSB wanted anybody with any connection to Dresden out of the picture—Platov wasn't interested in buying Gaddis's silence.

His political career, his reputation, his hold on power, was worth far more to him than £100,000. Besides, Tanya had insisted that the FSB knew nothing about Gaddis's search for Edward Crane. So how come they knew about Barcelona? How come they could identify Natasha and Min? Only SIS had access to that information. The note could have come only from Brennan.

Back inside, he stared at the phone, willing Holly to ring, but knew that he would have to wait. Her audition would continue until five or six, she might then have dinner with friends and would not get home until late. It wasn't even certain that she would bother looking for the tape once she did.

Gaddis knew that he had panicked in the aftermath of seeing the photographs. He realized that he had been a coward. He was entrusting his fate, and that of his daughter, to Holly, who could lose her life if she was caught in possession of the Platov evidence. He had to go to Tite Street himself. He would have to talk his way into Holly's building and then somehow break into the basement.

He found a toolbox under the sink in Tanya's kitchen. Inside it, there was a small steel saw, some screwdrivers, and a hammer. He took them and put them in a plastic bag with no clear idea in his mind what he intended to do with them. He tried to compose himself, wondering if he was even making the right decision by leaving the safe house. But surely, in final analysis, he had no choice? He locked the house, went out onto Earls Court Road, and waved down a cab.

In the taxi, he formed the basis of a plan. The storage cupboard was located in the basement of Holly's building behind a door which was secured by padlock. Gaddis would use the metal saw to cut through the bolt. The basement could be accessed via an exterior staircase leading down from the street. Gaddis would need only to walk down this short flight of steps, to break the glass on the door, and then to open it from the inside.

But he had never broken into a building in his life. He had seen private eyes picking locks on a thousand television shows, watched crime prevention advertisements in which hooded thieves entered properties via conveniently flimsy windows, but there was no reason to believe that he would be able to break in simply by smashing some glass and reaching for a door handle. After all, this was a basement in the heart of Chelsea—burglar country. At the very least, Holly's residents' association would have put steel bars on every door and window in the building.

Gaddis told the driver to pull up on Royal Hospital Road, fifty metres from the corner of Tite Street. He had concluded that his best tactic would be to behave as naturally as possible. From the point of view of a surveillance officer, there was nothing at all unusual in a man visiting his girlfriend at her flat.

A light was on in the first-floor window of Holly's building. By a quick calculation, Gaddis worked out that the flat number was either 5 or 6; Holly was one storey higher in 7, with 8 on the opposite landing. He walked up the steps and pushed the buzzer for Flat 6.

No answer. He waited fifteen seconds, then pressed it again. Nothing. He tried the buzzer for 5. This time the owner answered almost immediately.

"Yes?"

It was an elderly woman. Gaddis hoped that she knew Holly.

"Delivery. Flowers for a Miss Levette."

"Holly? You want number seven," came the reply. "Nobody's sent me flowers for years."

"There's no answer on seven, I'm afraid, luv." Gaddis had switched his accent to delivery Cockney. "Any chance you could let me in?"

"Well, I don't—"

The door clicked open. He could not hear what the old lady had said. Had she triggered the lock or had somebody in Flat 6 eventually come to the intercom and buzzed him inside?

He called out, "Thanks," and stepped into the foyer. There was a staircase ahead of him and he immediately walked down towards the basement. There were two flats at the bottom of the stairs, on either side of a small landing. To reach the storage area, Gaddis had to go through a fire door, walk a few metres along a short corridor, and then turn right into a narrow passage. He pushed a timer light and saw ten storage cupboards, one for each flat, on either side of the passage. There was a heavy padlock on "7" and he took out the saw.

It was utterly quiet: no sound of a television or radio, no muffled conversations, no child crying out or laughing. He began to cut the bolt. The noise of this was so obtrusive that Gaddis was certain he would be overheard. The saw slipped on the metal; he wasn't able to angle the blade so that it could grip on the bolt. He tried sawing with his left hand but that was also hopeless. He turned around and lifted the padlock as far from the door as it would allow, almost slicing through his index finger as he attacked it from the opposite side. He moved the blade more slowly this time, but still it slipped. He swore and then the timer light gave out. Gaddis released the padlock, walked back down the passage, and pushed the switch. He reckoned he had no more than a minute before it would black out again. This time, though, the saw made a narrow incision in the bolt; the blade warped repeatedly, but at least it was cutting.

He began to saw, steadily and methodically. The noise was still embarrassingly loud: anybody who overheard what he was doing would surely immediately conclude that he was cutting through a lock. The light gave out a second time. Gaddis switched it on again and, within a few seconds of returning, finally cut through the bolt. He opened the storage cupboard door, found a light switch, and cast his eyes over the piles of boxes, books, bin liners, and hangers of dry cleaning left by Katya Levette. He would have to go through each box, one by one, until he found what he was looking for. He was convinced that he would find the tape, but it was the conviction of a man who has nothing left in which to believe.

He started at the back first, on the basis that most of the files Holly had given to him had come from the front section of the cupboard. He made a small space for himself and ducked down to floor level, reaching for the boxes. It occurred to him, in the sweat of the cramped space, that Holly could come home at any moment, walk down to the basement, and find him busily going through her mother's private possessions with a sawn-off padlock at his feet. How was he going to explain that one?

A small box tucked in the far corner caught his eye. It had the name of a New Zealand winemaker printed along the side. Gaddis opened up the flaps and saw a stack of hardback books and manila envelopes stashed inside. He pulled out the books and held them open to the ground so that anything concealed inside them would drop out. Nothing did so, except a bookmark from a shop in Dunedin. He went for the envelopes instead. Gaddis had the vivid sensation that if he did not find the tape in the next thirty seconds, he would never find it at all.

A clear plastic folder. A DVD. Not a tape, not a cassette, but a DVD. Written in marker pen on the front of the disk were the words P INTERVIEW 88 I. Gaddis felt a rush of excitement, almost as if his skin were humming, but it was checked by the realization that this was not the master tape. Wilkinson must have made a copy onto DVD and kept the original in New Zealand. Or did MI6 have the master tape in a vault at Vauxhall Cross? At the same time, he experienced a profound fear that he was about to be disturbed. Had he come so close to his prize only to have it snatched away at the last minute? He had heard no sound in the basement, no voices on the stairs, only the noise of the occasional car or pedestrian passing on Tite Street. But he knew that he would have to move fast. He put the DVD into the inside pocket of his coat, switched off the storeroom light, closed the door, and looped the broken padlock over the handle to give an impression of security. Then he turned, walked back down the passage, and opened the fire door leading back towards the stairs.

Holly was coming towards him, carrying a set of keys and a bag from Marks & Spencer.

"*Sam?* What are you doing here?"

"No time to explain," he said, grabbing her arm and spinning her back up the stairs. "You have a DVD player in your flat, don't you? We need to sit down and watch some TV."

54

Fifteen minutes earlier, Alexander Grek had pulled his blue C-Class Mercedes into a vacant parking space on the corner of Tite Street and Royal Hospital Road and made a call on his mobile phone. Karl Stieleke had picked up and informed Grek that he was less than a quarter of a mile away, walking down King's Road half a block behind Holly Levette. She was on her way back from an audition and had just gone into Marks & Spencer. Stieleke anticipated that she would be home within ten or fifteen minutes.

Three days earlier, the two men had broken into Holly's apartment and conducted a two-hour search for any trace of the documents that had purportedly been sent to her late mother, Katya, by Robert Wilkinson. Grek had been acting on instructions from Maxim Kepitsa, who had himself been tipped off about the relationship between Wilkinson and Levette by Sir John Brennan. Grek and Stieleke had looked on every shelf, in every drawer, under every carpet, and inside every cupboard of the apartment, but had found no sign of any material relating to Sergei Platov or the KGB. They had subsequently put a tap on Holly's T-Mobile account and overheard a fraught telephone call from "Sam," logged that afternoon at 15:21 hours and traced to a phone box near Cromwell Road. "Sam" had made reference to a "tape or cassette" apparently stored in the basement of Holly's building. It was the one place that Grek had not thought to look. He would now wait for Holly to search the basement and to obtain the tape, then follow her to the Donmar Warehouse. This would lead him to "Sam," who was the final link in the chain. Grek suspected that Sam would turn out to be the same man who had shot Nicolai Doronin in Berlin. An eyewitness in Vienna had provided a description of "an Englishman in his early forties" who had been sitting with Robert Wilkinson at the Kleines Café. Grek suspected that this was also "Sam." Once he had been eliminated, Grek assumed that Kepitsa would consider the ATTILA case closed. He was not aware that Gaddis had entered Holly's building less than an hour earlier.

Looking up, he saw Holly coming down Tite Street carrying a shopping bag full of M & S groceries. Stieleke was on the opposite side of the road, following her at a distance of about forty metres. Grek watched as Holly took out a set of house keys and walked into the lobby of the building. Stieleke moved past her, walked up to the Mercedes, opened the passenger door, and stepped inside.

"Will she get the tape?" he asked.

"She will get the tape."

55

"Any chance of explaining to me what's going on?"

Holly was trailing Gaddis as they walked up the stairs to her apartment. Two steps below the third-floor landing he suddenly pulled her towards him and moved his head against hers so that he could whisper into her ear without risk of being overheard.

"Listen to me," he said. She was trying to wrestle free of him but he held her body tight against his own. "Don't say anything. Don't talk when we get into the flat. Go across the room, draw all the curtains like it's a normal evening, and switch on the radio. Put it on as loudly as possible without pissing off your neighbours. The disk I found in your basement is a recording of Sergei Platov attempting to defect to the West in 1988. It was filmed by Bob Wilkinson. Bob is dead. He was assassinated in Vienna. Your apartment may be under observation by MI6 and the Russian FSB. I am so sorry. Do not say *anything* when I let go of you."

She pushed away from him, her eyes flooded by tears. "Bob?" she mouthed and he suddenly saw an older woman's face in Holly's, the face of her mother, the face of Katya Levette. He pressed a finger against his mouth, shaking his head, imploring her not to speak. He looked across the landing at the door of her flat. He nodded to her, encouraging her to take out her keys and to open the door. Holly did so and crossed the room, switching on the radio as Gaddis had asked and drawing the curtains. Gaddis double-locked the door behind them, went to the television, and saw the DVD player on the ground. There was a newspaper discarded on the sofa. He took a pen out of his jacket pocket and wrote on a corner of the front page: *Do you have any blank DVDs?*

Holly's head was tilted to one side, as if evaluating Gaddis anew. He realized, sooner or later, that they would have to speak, so he whispered to her, not knowing who was listening or what, if anything, they could hear.

"The disks you use to make your demo reels," he said. "I need to make copies of this disk."

She nodded. "Sure. I have loads."

Her eyes were heavy and he said: "Don't worry," reaching out and holding her hand. "Everything's going to be fine."

"I'm not worried," Holly said, and pulled her arm away.

Gaddis took the disk out of the plastic folder and inserted it into the DVD player. Within a few seconds, he saw what he had dreamed of seeing. Sitting on a wooden chair in a well-lit German suburban living room was the young Sergei Platov. It was unmistakably the same man: Gaddis had seen dozens of photographs of the Russian president in his youth while researching *Tsars*. Platov was wearing a white shirt, a striped tie, and his full lips glowed under the unforgiving glare of a bright overhead light. His carefully combed hair was parted on the left-hand side and he appeared calm and relaxed. There was a small glass of water in front of him. Gaddis heard a voice on the tape.

"So, let's start talking. Could you identify yourself, please?"

It was Wilkinson. The accent was unmistakable. As if to confirm this, Holly, who was looking over Gaddis's shoulder at the screen, said: "That's Bob's voice," and put her hand on the nape of Gaddis's neck.

Platov began speaking in Russian. "My name is Sergei Spiridonovich Platov. I am a major in the Komitet Gosudarstvennoy Bezopasnosti. I live at Radeberger Strasse with my wife and daughter. I am one of eight KGB officers based in Dresden under the control of Colonel Anatoly Lubkov. I work on political intelligence and counterintelligence."

"What is your official cover?" Wilkinson asked. He had not appeared on camera and Gaddis suspected that he would not do so. Platov took a sip of water.

"I am Deputy Director of the Society of German–Soviet Friendship. My work entails forging links between the KGB and the East German Stasi."

"Could you confirm the name of this operation?"

"LOOCH," Platov replied, without hesitation.

Gaddis briefly looked away from the screen as he tried to recall the details of the plan. *Looch* meant "beam of light" in Russian. The operation had entailed the KGB building a network of informers in East Germany who would continue to provide information to Moscow Centre in the event of the Communist regime collapsing. MI6 had learned about LOOCH in 1986; Wilkinson was clearly evaluating Platov's willingness to give up state secrets.

The interview continued for what Gaddis estimated was at least another two hours: he forwarded the disk several times and saw no change either in the setup of the camera or in Platov's preternaturally calm demeanour. But there was no time to watch it. He ejected the disk and turned to Holly.

"Can you burn this onto your laptop, make copies of the film?"

"Rip, not burn," she said, and smiled. He saw that she had already retrieved the laptop from her bedroom and booted it up.

"I'd need three DVDs, minimum."

She shrugged, as if this was the easiest thing in the world, and Gaddis felt a surge of gratitude towards her. "Might take an hour to do that many copies," she whispered. "Depends how long the film is."

They worked out that the Platov interview lasted just under two hours. It took almost exactly as long as Holly had predicted to rip the three copies onto blank DVDs. They spent the intervening period talking in the bathroom about what had happened in Berlin and Vienna. Gaddis had switched on the taps and put the radio on the floor to give the impression that Holly was having a bath. He told her about the threat to Min. He also revealed everything about Edward Crane. Throughout, she reacted as a true friend: her only thought, seemingly, was for Gaddis's safety and well-being.

"I need you to do something for me," he said, as the last of the disks was finishing.

"So what else is new?"

"The woman who lives downstairs in flat five—"

"Mrs. Connelly."

"How well do you know her?"

"Quite well. I shop for her every now and again. Why?"

"I want you to go down there and to stay with her until I come back. It's not safe for you to go outside anymore and it's not safe for you to stay here when I'm gone."

He saw fear flicker in her eyes again, the same look that she had given him when he had told her about Wilkinson.

"Tell her you have a power cut. Fuse box. Ask if you can sit with her until your boyfriend gets back at nine. Thank her for the flowers, too."

"What flowers?"

"It's a long story. I pretended to be delivering a bunch of flowers so that I could get into your building. She buzzed me inside. Give me your mobile as well."

"Why?"

"Just give it to me."

She passed it to him from the back pocket of her jeans. Gaddis was thinking of Tanya, of microphones and triangulation signals, as he pulled off the casing and removed the battery.

"Better this way," he said.

The last of the three disks was complete. He retrieved it from the laptop and gave it to Holly. The other two, as well as Wilkinson's original, were in the inside pocket of his coat.

"Why have you given me this?"

"Hide it in Mrs. Connelly's flat. Hide it somewhere that nobody would think to look. And tell nobody that you've been to see her. If something happens to me, but *only* if something happens to me, get the disk to the BBC, to ITN, to Sky. Get it out on YouTube. Do you understand?"

"I understand." She reached out and touched his face. "I'm worried about you."

"Don't be. I'm sorry I dragged you into this."

"You didn't," she said. "Bob should never have sent Mum the disk without telling her what was on it."

Gaddis hesitated. "Perhaps."

"Where are you going now?"

He took two envelopes, a pen, and a book of stamps from her desk. "I need these. I have to talk to Tanya. I need her to get a message to Brennan and the FSB. But please don't worry. You're safe now. Just make sure you go to Mrs. Connelly. If she's not there, try any of your neighbours, even if you've never spoken to them. But don't leave the building unless you have to. I'll come back here as soon as it's done."

56

es," the veteran of Tanya Acocella's Berlin surveillance operation against POLARBEAR, had been watching Holly Levette's
apartment—at Tanya's request—for almost six hours. As luck
would have it, he was parked no more than fifty metres from Alexander Grek's blue C-Class Mercedes, which had pulled up on the corner
of Tite Street and Royal Hospital Road a little after half past four.
About twenty minutes later, a Slav in his late twenties had opened
the passenger door of the Mercedes and stepped inside. Des had noticed that the Slav had followed Holly down Tite Street, so he was
keeping a close eye on the vehicle as the sun set over Chelsea. The two
men seemed unusually preoccupied by activities in the third-floor
window of Miss Levette's apartment.

Des had started his shift before midday, so he had also noticed
Dr. Samuel Gaddis getting out of a taxi at about four o'clock. Recog-
nizing his old mark from Berlin, he had immediately telephoned
Tanya.

"Strange thing just happened," he said. "You remember POLAR-
BEAR?"

"I remember POLARBEAR."

"Well, he just walked into Tite Street. I thought you said you had him under lock and key in a safe house?"

Tanya, who was in the middle of a four-hour meeting with Sir John Brennan at Vauxhall Cross, had sworn silently into the telephone and reassured Des that she would "cut off Sam's balls" when she saw him.

"That might hurt," he replied. An hour later, he rang back with an update.

"POLARBEAR's been in there for a long time. Curtains are closed now, radio on, doubtless he's making sweet love to sweet Holly Levette."

"Holly's there as well?"

"Yeah. Showed up about quarter of an hour ago."

Des wondered if Tanya had developed feelings for the redoubtable POLARBEAR. Did he detect an undertow of jealousy in her voice? "One other thing . . . ," he said.

"Tell me."

"Holly was being followed down Tite Street. Foot surveillance. Caucasian male, late twenties, winner of the Dolph Lundgren lookalike contest. We've also got a Mercedes parked across the street with a view of Holly's sitting room. Dolph and another man sitting inside."

"FSB?" said Tanya.

"FSB," said Des. "I ran the number plate. Vehicle is registered to the Russian Embassy."

57

Tanya had been led to believe that her meeting with Brennan would be a private affair. When Des rang the first time, she had just finished informing her boss that she was shielding Gaddis at her house in Earls Court "until we can work out how to protect him." Brennan had reacted calmly to the news, just as he had seemed almost indifferent to the revelation that Acocella had activated two separate networks in Austria and Budapest in order to finesse Gaddis's exfiltration from Vienna.

But the appearance of Maxim Kepitsa, shortly after Des had telephoned a second time, had taken Tanya by surprise. Up until that point, she had been prepared to give Brennan the benefit of the doubt. After all, Wilkinson's assassination at the Kleines Café could have been a coincidence; she had no evidence that her boss had tipped off the FSB about Wilkinson's movements. But Kepitsa's demeanour, and his seedy bear hug with Brennan shortly after he strode into the room, stank of a stitch-up.

"Mr. Kepitsa has come here today to help us try to piece together what may have happened in Vienna," Brennan began.

"Is that right?"

Tanya remembered what she had said to Gaddis on the way back from Gatwick. *I didn't apply for this job so that my boss could toady up to the Kremlin and put innocent lives at risk.* It was straightforward, really. She didn't want to be answerable to a man who was prepared to overlook the cold-blooded murder of at least two British citizens in order to preserve the status quo of Westminster's relationship with Moscow.

"Here's where we are on this thing," Brennan continued. "Our government has civilian and state contracts with Russia worth many billions of roubles. These would be severely compromised by any change of leadership in the Kremlin."

"You think?" It was one of the least credible theories Tanya had heard during her entire career at Vauxhall Cross.

"You know, Tanya, as well as I do, that the man most likely to succeed Sergei Platov in the event of any Russian election is in every way antagonistic towards Great Britain, the United States, and to the entire European project. It would hardly be in our best interests to encourage such a man into power."

That was the second least credible theory that Tanya had heard during her career at Vauxhall Cross. Nevertheless, Kepitsa was nodding vigorously in agreement. Tanya suddenly became aware of what Brennan was up to. It was obvious. Why hadn't she realized it before? Platov *knew* that Brennan had the master tape of his defection. SIS had been using it as leverage against him for years. Whenever Moscow became too heavy-handed, Brennan would simply apply the thumbscrews of 1988. Stay away from our natural gas. Have a quiet word with the Iranians. Why get rid of a Russian president over whom SIS exercised such immense control?

"What we propose to offer Doctor Gaddis is the sum of one hundred thousand pounds, which is more or less what he requires to extract himself from a mountain of personal debt." Brennan was pacing the room now, occasionally touching the spine of a volume by Sir Winston Churchill. "In return for this, he will agree to cease all enquiries into, and academic publications on, Edward Crane and the agent known as ATTILA. He will also choose to forget, of course, that

Mr. Platov, in a moment of youthful indiscretion, offered his talents to SIS during what was, after all, a very difficult time in the history of his country." Kepitsa coughed. Brennan caught his eye and offered the Second Secretary a reassuring smile. "Maxim, for his part, will ensure that rogue elements within the Russian state apparatus, who may have believed, however misguidedly, that they were operating on the wishes of Mr. Platov, will be brought under the formal control of the FSB. In short, they will be ordered to cease all activities against Doctor Gaddis, who is, after all, a British citizen and an academic of not inconsiderable reputation. What we want, after all this hoo-hah, is a little peace and quiet."

Tanya looked across at Kepitsa. He was a small thug of a man, not unlike Platov, she concluded. He was wearing an expensively tailored suit which still managed to make him look shifty and cheap.

"So Mr. Kepitsa knows about the tape?" she asked.

"What tape?" Brennan was looking worried.

"Platov's interview with MI6 in Dresden. It was recorded. It was filmed by Wilkinson. He sent a copy to Katya Levette. Gaddis is in Tite Street as we speak trying to retrieve it from Holly's basement."

"I don't understand," said Kepitsa, touching a spot on his chin.

"Oh, it's quite simple." Tanya suddenly felt liberated, a puppet severing her strings. "You see, Gaddis knows that you'll try to kill him unless he has an insurance policy. You murdered his friend, you murdered Calvin Somers, you murdered Benedict Meisner, and you murdered Robert Wilkinson. You can walk out of this room and reassure us that peace will reign and that the FSB bears no grudge against Gaddis, but, let's face it, the evidence is against you. Your organization has a historical tendency to shut people up when they know too much or say the wrong thing. And Gaddis knows too much. He knows, for example, that the so-called saviour of modern Russia is just a power-hungry thug who was prepared to betray his country at its most desperate hour."

Kepitsa looked imploringly at Brennan, as if it was beneath his dignity to be insulted quite so brazenly, particularly by a woman. Brennan was on the point of obliging him when Tanya cut both men a look that would have frozen the Neva.

"The insurance policy is the tape," she said. "I assume that Doctor Gaddis has already made plans to have the film shown on every news channel and on every Web site in the civilized world should anything happen to him. If, on the other hand, you leave him in peace, he will go back to work at UCL and forget that he ever met any of us."

Brennan spoke first. "What about Crane?"

"Gone. Forgotten. It's too late for that. Crane will remain a myth."

Kepitsa stirred once again. He appeared irritated that Brennan had not leaped more robustly to his defence. Opting to fight his own battle, he rose to his feet and directed his attention towards Tanya. It was to his considerable disadvantage that she was at least five inches taller than he was.

"Let me be clear about something, young lady. I would ask you formally to withdraw the accusation that my government would be in any way responsible should anything happen to Doctor Gaddis. As far as the FSB is concerned, British journalists and academics may write what they like about Russia and its politicians. We would not consider Doctor Gaddis an enemy of the state simply because he has written a book—"

Even Brennan looked uncomfortable at the effrontery of the lie. Tanya was grateful for the opportunity to skewer Kepitsa on his hypocrisy.

"So it's okay for *British* academics, is it? But as soon as you have a Russian academic, a Ukrainian journalist—say, a Katarina Tikhonov—then it's a different story. You murder people like that, don't you, Mr. Kepitsa? You poison them. You send thugs to gun them down in their homes. You allow them to rot in prisons and deny them basic medical care. Isn't that the case?"

The Russian was already reaching for his briefcase. Tanya expected him to say: "I have heard enough of this," but instead he opted for the more tried and tested: "I have never been so insulted in my life."

"Oh, I expect you have," she said. "Just before you go, Max, do tell Sir John why you have two surveillance operatives sitting in a Mercedes, registered to the Russian Embassy, looking up at Holly Levette's apartment as we speak? Tell him that. I'd like to hear your reasoning. I thought Doctor Gaddis was just a harmless British academic? If that's the case, why are you taking such an unusual interest in his private life? Is it the tape? Are you trying to get to it before he does?"

"Is this true, Maxim?" Brennan asked.

Kepitsa turned for the door.

"This meeting is concluded," he said, shooting Brennan the look of a deceived man already plotting his revenge. "The next time I come to visit you, John, I expect to be treated with a good deal more respect."

58

It was dark when Gaddis came out of Holly's building and stood momentarily on Tite Street, looking up at a pale orange sky. He now had two disks concealed beneath his coat. In his left hand he was carrying an envelope addressed to a colleague in the United States which contained a DVD.

He needed a cigarette. He took out the packet, struck a match, and brought the flame to his lips. It was his only mistake. The face of Dr. Samuel Gaddis was momentarily lit up for the world to see.

"I know that man," said Karl Stieleke.

"Who?" said Grek. "The guy who just came out?"

"On Saturday. In Vienna. He was at the wedding. I saw him after the ceremony in the Stadtpark."

"You're sure?"

"I am certain. He bumped into me."

Grek watched as Gaddis turned south and came directly towards them. For an instant, he thought that he was going to approach the car. Instead, he crossed Royal Hospital Road and walked towards a red letter box just a few feet from the Mercedes. He posted the envelope through the slot, then continued south, heading in the direction of the river. Grek, who had been close enough to touch Gaddis as he passed the Mercedes, realized that he, too, had seen the man before. Several weeks earlier. He was the unidentified male who had left Charlotte Berg's residence on the night that he had broken into her office. Approximately six feet tall, about eighty kilos, wearing a corduroy jacket with a leather satchel slung over the shoulder.

"That is Sam," said Grek. "He posted the tape. Call Kepitsa and tell him to send somebody to break into the box. I will follow him."

Stieleke nodded.

"Stay here, Karl. Stay with the vehicle and keep an eye on the girl. When I call you, when I tell you that Sam has been brought under control, you go in to Holly and you finish the job. Understood?"

"Understood."

Des was watching them. He, too, had seen POLARBEAR coming out of the building and had privately admonished him for lighting a cigarette with a "fucking Swan Vesta" so that "Dolph can get a really good look at your face." Then he wondered why POLARBEAR was posting a package into the neat red letter box on the south side of Royal Hospital Road.

"I hope that's not what I think it is," he muttered to himself, pulling out his mobile phone. "They'll just nick it, you twat, they'll just nick it."

He dialled Tanya's number but she wasn't answering. Des left a message.

"POLARBEAR has left the building. He's also just posted a package on Royal Hospital Road. Think it might be your tape. Give me a call, will you? I reckon things are about to get busy round here."

Sure enough, a moment after Des had hung up, he saw Alexander Grek stepping out of the Mercedes and buttoning up his overcoat. Des redialled Tanya's number, but she was still not answering. He left a second message.

"Like I said, things have just got busy round here. Foot surveillance. One of the FSB boys just went south after our man. POLARBEAR is heading for the river."

Gaddis was leaning on a stone balustrade, looking out across the Thames at the distant outline of the Japanese Peace Pagoda in Battersea Park, when he heard a voice behind him.

"Excuse me, sir."

It was a deep, languid voice, with a certain music in it, a certain charm.

"Yes?"

He turned to find that a well-dressed man of about thirty-five had crossed the road from the south end of Tite Street. He was wearing a light brown overcoat and a pair of expensive leather brogues. Oligarch chic, Charlotte would have called it, but Gaddis didn't feel like laughing.

"It is Sam, yes?"

"Do we know each other?"

Gaddis had been waiting for this. He had known that they would come.

"We do, we do," said Grek, extending a hand which Gaddis reluctantly shook. "My name is Alexander Grek. We met at the Russian Embassy in July, no? You came to our fund-raiser for small businesses."

The lie had the odd effect of emboldening Gaddis. He was almost insulted by it.

"Is that the best you can do?"

"Excuse me?"

"A fund-raiser? A party at the Russian Embassy? With all that you know, after everything you've seen, you think I'm going to fall for that?"

Grek's pale brown eyes, so soft and conciliating, suddenly lost their innocence; it was merely a question of narrowing them, like a man sighting a target on a shooting range. Moments earlier, Gaddis had thrown the butt of his cigarette into the churning waters of the Thames. Grek now took out a cigarette of his own from a pristine silver case and lit it with a Zippo lighter.

"I see that you are direct, Sam. A straight talker." He closed the Zippo. Click. "Fine. If that is how you like to do business, then let's be frank with one another. Let's do business. You have something that I want. Something that my government will pay a lot of money for. Would you be so kind as to pass it over?"

Des had watched Grek disappear towards the Embankment. He wondered if he should have followed him. But that was against Tanya's instructions. She had told him to keep an eye on Holly's apartment.

His phone rang. He saw Tanya's number flash up on the screen.

"Des? Where are you?"

"I'm still in the car."

"You're still in the *what*?" He heard her swear against the sound of traffic. It wasn't clear whether she was walking along a busy street or speaking from inside a vehicle. "Go after them. Follow the Russian. Something could happen to Sam. Did you see where they've gone?"

Des told her that POLARBEAR had been heading towards the river.

"I'm in a cab," she said. "Half a mile away. I'll be there in less than five minutes."

Grek inhaled deeply on the cigarette and gazed at the passing traffic on the Embankment as if the noise of it was an encumbrance to his enjoyment of what was an otherwise pleasant London evening.

"Do you have it in your possession?" he said. "Do you have the tape?"

Gaddis held his nerve. He had two of the disks in his coat pocket. The other two, he knew, were safe. "You say it's your government who are willing to pay for the tape?" He did not dare smoke another cigarette of his own in case his hand shook as he lit it. "So you accept that you have been operating under the orders of Sergei Platov? You admit that Charlotte Berg, Calvin Somers, Benedict Meisner, and Robert Wilkinson were killed with the approval, tacit or otherwise, of the Kremlin?"

A pretty girl jogged past them wearing a Comic Relief T-shirt and tracksuit trousers set off by a pair of bright pink leg warmers. She was oblivious to the city beneath the rhythm of an iPod. Grek stared after her and nodded in appreciation.

"I am sorry," he said, turning back to Gaddis as though already bored by the direction that their conversation was taking. "I have no idea what it is that you are referring to. If these people, as you say, are dead, you have my condolences. It has nothing to do with my organization."

"How do you do that?" Gaddis surprised himself by moving towards Grek.

"How do I do what, please?"

"How do you justify it to yourself?" Grek still looked bored, though Gaddis was now only a few inches from his face. "Did you *know* anything about Charlotte? I knew her very well. She was my closest friend. She was a sister to Amy. She was a wife to Paul. Her husband hasn't been able to work, to sleep, to do anything very much these past few weeks except to grieve for the one person who ever meant anything to him. You did that. You took away his only happiness."

There was a tiny flicker of irritation, not remorse, at the edge of Grek's pale brown eyes.

"Did you know anything about Benedict Meisner?" Gaddis was on a roll now, a distilled enmity boiling inside him. He watched the comet of Grek's cigarette as he flicked it into the Thames. "Did you know that he had two teenage daughters, one of them anorexic? Did you *know* that? Did you know that he was an only child? His mother had moved to Berlin to be close to him. She was a widow. Her husband had been killed in a car accident. It was in the German papers. She was unable to identify her son's body because of the gunshot wounds. You took away his face. You did that to a mother, to a woman of seventy-five. You forced her to see that and you shattered that family. Was it worth it?"

Grek raised his face to the sky and sniffed at the chill evening air as though he had no intention of responding.

"What was it *for*?" Gaddis wanted to grab Grek by the arms and to shake an answer out of him. "I just don't see how you rationalize it, how you square it with your conscience." He took a step backwards and found that he was almost smiling. "I don't believe that people have no conscience. I *can't* believe that. Otherwise such people are just animals, no better than a vulture or a snake, no? They say that everybody has their reasons, but it's a mystery to me why you would destroy lives as freely as you do. There are so many other choices available to you. Is it just the thrill of it, the sense of power? Or are you so loyal to your country, are you such a patriot, that it short-circuits your decency? Perhaps it's about status. Enlighten me. I'd really like to know."

"You are an interesting man," Grek replied, because he was too self-assured ever to be drawn into such a game. "Tell me about yourself. How did you become involved in these things?"

Only then did Gaddis realize that Tanya had been right all along. The Russians really did know very little about him. He said: "You know exactly who I am," but only because he was so surprised by what he had heard.

"Really, I don't," said Grek. "You are a mystery to us."

"And yet you want to buy a tape from me, a tape that is worth a lot of money." Gaddis finally caved to his desire for a cigarette and extracted one from the pocket of his coat. Grek immediately rolled the Zippo lighter across his hip and held out the flame. Gaddis snubbed it and struck a match of his own, cupping it steadily against the easterly wind.

"We would like to buy that tape," Grek said.

"Yes? What do you think it's worth?" Gaddis had taken himself beyond any further attempt to appeal to the Russian's conscience; it was pointless. Better to conclude their "business" as quickly as possible and to get back to Holly.

"One hundred thousand pounds."

Gaddis winced, remembering the typed note, the photographs of Min and Natasha, and he realized that Tanya had been right about Brennan as well: the FSB and MI6 had joined forces against him. For a strange and terrifying moment, like a waking dream, he imagined that Grek was about to produce yet more pictures of his daughter, only this time in the nightmare of some terrible captivity. He knew in his bones that the Russian would stoop to such a thing as easily as he could hail a passing cab.

"How did you arrive at that price?" he asked.

"We can arrive at any price you like."

"*Any* price?"

Another jogger grunted by, a man in late middle age with a glowing face and a potbelly. Grek ignored him.

"Does your British conscience tell you that you cannot accept money of this kind from the Russian government?"

Gaddis was grateful for the chance to strike back. "Why would my conscience tell me that? I would happily take as much money from the Russian government as I possibly can."

Grek detected no irony. "So the sum offered to you for the protection of your child is not enough?"

If Gaddis had possessed any doubts about the wisdom of his plan, they were extinguished by this casual threat to Min. "No, it is not enough," he said, and spoke in Russian so that no idiosyncrasy of his reply would be lost in translation. "I want half a million pounds. A hundred thousand each to the families of Benedict Meisner, Robert Wilkinson, and Calvin Somers. One hundred thousand pounds for Paul Berg. And one hundred thousand pounds for myself. You will also guarantee that no harm comes to my daughter, to Holly Levette, to Tanya Acocella, or to my ex-wife. Do I make myself clear?"

"These things can be very easily guaranteed."

"Don't forget about my wedding."

Tanya's voice took both men by surprise. She had appeared from within the shadows of a tree, the sound of her approach obscured by the noise of the rush-hour traffic.

"Excuse me?" Grek looked as though he was having trouble bringing Tanya into focus.

"Just a private joke between myself and Doctor Gaddis," she said, moving towards them. She was also speaking in fluent Russian and, for a wrenching moment, Gaddis thought that they were working in tandem. "I'm getting married," she said. "Could do with the extra cash if you're doling it out. Sam, would you introduce us?"

Startled, he began to say: "This is Alexander Grek—" but Tanya interrupted him.

"I know who he is." She reverted to English. "And I know his friend in the Mercedes parked just over there." Tanya gestured in the direction of Tite Street. "In fact, a colleague of mine is currently asking to see the friend's identification." It was a lie, but Grek's impassive demeanour finally cracked.

"What is going on here?"

"What is going on here is that you are going to do exactly what Doctor Gaddis asks. You are going to give him five hundred thousand pounds. In return for this, Doctor Gaddis will guarantee that the copy of the tape in his possession will never be shown or distributed during his lifetime. Is that the case?"

Gaddis felt as though a vest, as heavy as lead, had been lifted from his body. "That is the case."

Grek adjusted his stance, his hips shifting forward in a way that looked awkward. He was struggling to maintain his equanimity, a climber slipping on a wall.

"We will need that tape," he said.

"Fine." Gaddis found the courage to be almost dismissive with the tone of his reply. "But it won't be any good to you. I made several copies. Each of them will be kept in a secure location. Should anything happen to me, the people charged with looking after them will release the Platov footage to the media."

Grek looked hard into Gaddis's eyes, because he sensed that he was lying.

"You had time to make several copies?" It was an opportunity to claw back some lost pride. "I doubt that very much. I imagine that the only copy of the tape is currently at the bottom of a letter box not five hundred metres from where we are standing. I think you are bluffing."

"Try me," Gaddis replied.

A teenage girl with what looked like a cold sore on her lip walked past them on the arm of her boyfriend. Gaddis saw that it was a lip piercing and smiled to himself.

"Something funny?" Grek said.

At that moment, his mobile phone pulsed in the inside pocket of his coat. The Russian reached for it and both Gaddis and Tanya flinched, assuming that he was going for a gun. But he reassured her by unbuttoning the coat slowly and retrieving the phone with the tips of his fingers.

"Relax. You assume that I would shoot you? What do you think of me?"

He looked down at the screen. It was a message from Kepitsa. Gaddis used the moment to glance across at Tanya, who reassured him with a nod. Grek looked up and spoke.

"It would appear that you are right, Doctor Gaddis." In Russian, he added: "My instructions are to leave you in possession of the tape. I have your word that our business is concluded?"

"You have my word," he replied.

Grek replaced the phone and turned in the direction of Chelsea Bridge, so that his back was facing them. He seemed to consider the possibility of a parting remark but thought better of it and walked away. Within moments he had disappeared into the glare of the London night. Almost immediately, Des materialized beside Tanya and said "Hi" to Gaddis as though they were still in Berlin.

"Get to the Mercedes," Tanya told him. "Go back and keep an eye on Holly. And find someone to take a look at that postbox."

"Don't bother," Gaddis told her. "It's a decoy. It's a DVD of Holly's demo reel. I gave one of the real copies to a cleaning lady in the lobby. She told me she was going to post it to Princeton on her way home."

Des acknowledged the trick with an admiring bob of the head and then crossed the Embankment, walking north up Tite Street. Gaddis leaned once more on the stone balustrade and saw an old wooden toy abandoned in the sands of the river, as if trapped by time.

"What about Brennan?" he said. "Does he know about the deal?"

"Yes." Tanya was beside him, their arms almost touching. "The master tape is at Vauxhall Cross. I didn't know that. It was the last of the many secrets he kept from me. Let's just say that Brennan uses it for leverage whenever Platov gets ideas above his station."

"Realpolitik," Gaddis replied, and watched a double-decker bus crossing the hump of the Albert Bridge. "What about Grek?"

Tanya took his hand with a barely disguised look of triumph on her face.

"This will be his last night in our fair capital. Grek and Doronin will be called back to Moscow, their pal in the Mercedes as well. Brennan is also going to ask that Kepitsa be replaced."

Gaddis wanted to congratulate her, but something was bothering him.

"It doesn't work, you know," he said, arriving at the words slowly.

"What doesn't work?"

A pleasure boat, packed with partygoers, was sliding on the current. "The Platov deal. What happens when he's eventually turfed out of the Kremlin? What happens when he loses power? That's when they'll come for me."

"I doubt it." He was glad that there was conviction in her voice. "Platov is a tsar. You should know that. He'll reign for as long as his health holds up. Why else did he change the constitution? Twenty years? Thirty? There'll be no change in Moscow during that time. And afterwards, he'll have his reputation to think about. He'll know that the tape still has the potential to obliterate his political legacy. He wouldn't be dumb enough to come after you."

It was a comforting thesis and Gaddis was too worn out to argue against it. He reached into his coat and took out one of the disks. It was a final demonstration of his faith in Tanya Acocella.

"I want you to keep one of these," he said. "Keep it safe."

"I will." She put the disk in her pocket but did not thank him for his act of trust. Instead, she produced a document of her own, a clipping from a daily newspaper. It was folded twice and slightly torn in one corner.

"Did you see *The Times?*"

Gaddis shook his head. "Been a bit busy with one thing and another. House arrest until three o'clock this afternoon, then I had to run some errands."

She smiled. "Take a look."

Gaddis took the clipping and opened it up. It was a page from Saturday's *Times*. There was a circle of red ink halfway down.

BIRTHS, MARRIAGES, AND DEATHS
NEAME, Thomas Brian, died peacefully on 26 October aged 91 after a short illness. Private funeral service at Magdalen Hill Cemetery, Alresford Rd. Family flowers only. Any donations to Marie Curie Nurses.

He passed it back to her.

"Where have I seen that before?"

"You don't believe it?"

"I don't believe it."

There was no more left to be said. It was time to go back to Holly. He wanted to telephone Natasha in Spain. He longed to speak to Min.

"We'll call you into the Office in a couple of days," Tanya said. "There's the money to sort out."

"Ah yes, the money."

He went towards her and they embraced. Tanya squeezed his chest, as if reluctant to let go.

"Thank you," he said, kissing her on the cheek. Her skin was soft and cold. "For everything. Without you—"

"Don't mention it," she said, already turning to leave. "I'll see you in a few days."

59

On the orders of Sir John Brennan, Thomas Neame had been moved from the Meredith nursing home on the outskirts of Winchester to a retirement village in the suburbs of Stoke-on-Trent. His name had been changed to Douglas Garside. He was denied Internet access and a mobile phone. He was largely confined to a two-bedroom house which he was obliged to share with a fifty-eight-year-old Scottish spinster named Kirsty who cooked his meals, washed his clothes, and occasionally drove him to the local multiplex to watch whatever costume drama or arthouse hit had managed to force its way north from London.

Kirsty was ex-MI5. She had been told all about Peter, all about the trouble in Winchester, and had given Edward Crane so little wriggle room that, on at least two occasions, he had thrown her "filthy bloody food" across the kitchen in a blizzard of crockery and threatened to "burn her in her bed" if she didn't stop "watching him like a hawk twenty-five hours a day." Three times, he had rung Brennan direct (from a phone box near the local fish-and-chip shop) to complain that he was being treated "worse than a member of the ANC on Robben Island." Crane entertained frequent dreams of making a break for Hull by taxi, where he knew that he could catch an overnight ferry to Rotterdam. It would have been a glorious homage to his old pal Guy Burgess, but SIS had left him with no passport, no money, and with no contact details for any of the agents—many of them long since dead—whom ATTILA had known during the Cold War.

"You just cause too much trouble, Eddie," Brennan had explained. "We can't afford to take the risk."

It was a BBC documentary about the Taliban that had caught Crane's eye. The modern fanatic, he learned, had resorted to Moscow Rules. Your average Islamist freedom fighter didn't use a mobile phone, didn't communicate by e-mail. They were too easy to trace. Instead, he had adopted more old-fashioned means: the letter, the dead drop, the go-between. All of which gave Edward Crane an idea.

He had read several articles in the broadsheet press by a stalwart of Radio 4's evening schedules whose views on everything from Sergei Platov to Salman Rushdie were taken as gospel by a spellbound and grateful British public. The broadcaster in question had written books, appeared on talk shows, even lectured at the Smithsonian.

Edward Crane decided to write him a letter.

Sir,

As an undergraduate at Trinity College, Cambridge, in the 1930s, I studied alongside a man named Edward Crane who was a close friend of Guy Burgess and who later worked at Bletchley Park with John Cairncross.

For reasons which are perhaps obvious, I can say very little more at this stage. Only that Edward Crane became a close personal friend throughout my life, to the extent that he gave me a copy of his memoirs shortly before his death. These memoirs reveal that Crane was a Soviet asset every bit as successful as his more celebrated comrades in the so-called "Ring of Five."

I would like to find a publisher for Crane's memoirs. A broadcaster and historian of your standing, prepared both to validate the book's authenticity and to make its existence known to a wider public, would be of incalculable value. I do hope you will consider visiting me in Stoke, where alas I am confined to barracks in a retirement village, battling on at the age of 92.

Should you wish to contact me, please send a message to the PO Box listed above. Since this letter is personal to you, I would be grateful if you would respect its confidentiality.

Yours sincerely,
Douglas Garside

Crane sealed the envelope, found a stamp in the kitchen, walked out into a damp Staffordshire morning, and dropped the letter into a postbox less than a hundred metres from his front door.

Kirsty didn't see a thing.

ACKNOWLEDGEMENTS

My deepest thanks to Melissa, to my mother and father, and to Stanley and Iris. To Julia Wisdom, Rachel Rayner, Anne O'Brien, and all the team at HarperCollins. To Keith Kahla, Monica Katz, Kathleen Conn, Sally Richardson, Dori Weintraub, and everybody at St. Martin's Press. To Tif Loehnis, Luke Janklow, Will Francis, Rebecca Folland, Kirsty Gordon, Claire Dippel, and their colleagues at Janklow and Nesbit. To Emily Hayward and Tanya Tillett at the Rod Hall Agency. And to all the staff at *The Week*.

I am also very grateful to Melinda Hughes; Sam Loewenberg; Craig Arthur; Matthew Beaumont; Maxim Chernavin; Rory Carleton Paget; Annabel Byng; Tom Miller; James Owen; Guy Walters; Rupert Allason; James Holland; Alanna O'Connell; Giles Waterfield; Josie Jackson; Jonathan, Anna, and Carolyn Hanbury; William and Mary Seymour; Grant Murray; Cal Flyn; Tom Cain; Sue and Stephen Lennane; Christian Spurrier; Annette Nielebock; Boris Starling; Ali Karim; Nick Stone; Michael Stotter; Nick, Bard, Chev, and Viki Wilkinson.

The following books were very useful: *Their Trade Is Treachery* by Chapman Pincher (New English Library, 1982); *The Defence of the Realm: The Authorized History of MI5* by Professor Christopher Andrew

(Allen Lane, 2009); *My Five Cambridge Friends* by Yuri Modin (Headline, 1995); *The Crown Jewels: The British Secrets at the Heart of the KGB's Archives* by Nigel West and Oleg Tsarev (HarperCollins, 1999); *Anthony Blunt: His Lives* by Miranda Carter (Pan, 2002). During his talk at Daunt Books, Sam Gaddis ought to have acknowledged the debt he owes to the scholarship of Peter Truscott.

—C.C.
London 2010